VITAL SPARK

VITAL SPARK

A POST-MODERN PYRATE YARN

The Chesapeake Tugboat Murders

by Leah Devlin

www.Penmorepress.com

ISBN-13: 978-1-942756-62-0(Paperback)
ISBN -978-1-942756-63-7 (e-book)

BISAC Subject Headings:
FIC008000 Fiction / General
FIC031010 Fiction/ Thrillers / Crime

Edited by Terri Carter

Cover Illustration by Christine Horner

Address all correspondence to:

Penmore Press LLC
920 N Javelina Pl
Tucson AZ 85748

Dedication

For Jere and Hugh,
who instilled in their daughter a love of wondrous stories

Vital spark of heavnly flame!
Quit, O quit this mortal frame:
Trembling, hoping, ling ring, flying,
O the pain, the bliss of dying!

-Alexander Pope

Chapter 1

Day 1

The Upper Chesapeake
June 2017

"Once upon a time there was a tugboat ..." started every story her grandfather ever told her. "... named ... "

She had gazed expectantly into his eyes overhung with bushy eyebrows. Gull's nests, he called them.

"... named ..." he'd tease again.

"What, Papa?"

"... the *Old Gray Mare*." On another day "... *the Crabby Crab*" or "... *the Gimpy Gull*."

But more often than not Papa's story started with "Once upon a time there was a tugboat named the *Vital Spark*."

That revealed, she had settled into the sofa that had long given up and bowed into the floorboards. Then there unwound a tale of perilous adventures on the waters of the Chesapeake, starring the courageous Papa Randy—never was a person more aptly named—and his equally courageous granddaughter Alex, master and mate of the intrepid tugboat, the *Vital Spark*.

Alex was no longer a dreamy child, nor courageous. Nor was her current mode of transportation intrepid. Anything but. Her car with almost two hundred thousand miles on the engine just needed to deliver her a few more miles up the road before it was permitted to die. North of Chestertown, Maryland, she pulled into a gas station, stepped out of her car and removed her polyester suit jacket. It was ridiculous to have bought a suit to interview for a job in which she'd be wearing a wetsuit, a bathing suit, or a pair of waders. But the suit had paid off, and so had the haircut, cut just to her shoulders. A shorter haircut would make her look "mature and professional," Richard had told her at the start of the job hunt. At the interview, an honest "yes" could be answered to all of the employer's questions. Yes about operating boats, scuba diving certifications, statistical analysis, the writing of technical reports for funding agencies, conducting water monitoring tests ... all of the predictable questions. Yes, yes, yes. And yes, she knew every thing about every species of invertebrate, fish, and bird in the Delmarva region. She'd grown up on the Chesapeake, after all.

Alex pressed Papa's number on her smartphone and listened to it ring. No answer; no surprise. He had an aversion to technology of any sort.

"Papa," she said to his voicemail, "I'll be there very soon, before dinner. I have a surprise."

Over a dinner of crab cakes at the Dockside Café, she'd tell him her wonderful news. Old Ben would certainly join them, as she'd sent him a text with orders not to tell Papa of her surprise. She and Ben were co-conspirators in all sorts of surprises for her grandfather. Alice and Harry Hoffman, who owned the café, would be there. So would Luna the palm reader. And hopefully Alan and Jacob. All the usual suspects.

She'd landed the job and would be moving back to River Glen!

No more sporadic contract work. No more part-time teaching at the community college. Finally a full-time job with benefits! So what if, according to Mr. Ward in the Human Resources office, the marine station was very isolated, just a desk and a computer that sometimes worked, a rickety dock, and salt water tanks. It was pretty much a one-man operation, Mr. Ward had said. It all sounded fine to her. Things had ended with Richard without as much as a whimper, since there wasn't much passion there in the first place, so no strings tied her to Washington DC. Best yet, the marine station was just a few miles from her grandfather's house where she'd grown up. Her gas tank full, she climbed back into her car and headed up 213 North.

Papa would be easy to find as his world was circumscribed within a quarter mile circle surrounding his house and dock. Either he'd be listening to CDs on the porch with Old Ben, pulling crab traps from the mouth of river, or awaiting some bleached blonde divorcée from the marina to drop onto the bar stool next to his.

Some time, many years ago, Alex had stopped keeping a tally of her grandfather's women. His first wife, her biological grandmother, had departed long before she was born. The woman's presence in the village had been as transient as a wind sweeping across the bay. Wife Number Two was a music teacher at the elementary school. Alex had liked Number Two because she came with a piano. Number Three worked in the public affairs office for the Baltimore Ravens, so for the year and a half she lived with them, Alex got free NFL apparel. Papa's tastes then shifted toward the exotic: the Romanian gypsy, the Somali painter, and the Australian wanna-be-rock star. By the time Alex was in junior high, she'd come to regard the assorted wives as temporary lodgers. Six wives were apparently Papa's limit;

after that it was easier and less costly to date the women in Harlow's Pub. Besides, the younger ones could be instantly accessed by the marvel of texting, his sole reason for purchasing a smartphone. By the time she'd left for college, she'd simply lost count of Papa's assorted flames and flings.

Alex's wristwatch, a birthday gift from Richard, vibrated on her wrist. "As a favor, I entered in all your important appointments," he'd said. "Since you're late for everything."

Okay, she'd concede she had punctuality issues. But Papa was partially to blame for that. There were no clocks in his house where she grew up.

"You can keep time by watching the tides, sweetheart."

That method worked fine when one was at the water's edge but proved problematic inland. And Papa caused her to miss an entire year of elementary school because on the spur of the moment he'd decided to home school her. When school officials finally appeared, asking of her whereabouts, they found that she'd missed an entire year of math and social studies, but was the only third grader in the state of Maryland to have read *Moby Dick*. No more home schooling, the officials insisted; and they made her repeat third grade. She was late to school so many times in eighth grade (it was so much more fun pulling crab traps in the morning with Papa and Ben than waiting for the school bus) that she had to repeat that year as well. When she finally entered the ninth grade, two years older, inches taller and more curvaceous than the other girls, the boys were relentlessly annoying. Worse, they'd assumed that she was like her notoriously amorous grandfather. That whole year was just plain awkward.

According to her buzzing smartwatch, she was supposed to meet Richard at the gym in thirty minutes for Hot Yoga for

Couples. Eventually the complicated settings would have to be changed, but figuring which part of the screen to tap or swipe was too daunting a task. Even though they'd broken up a month before, the watch still reminded her ... many times a day ... where she was to be were she still the girlfriend of Richard Wells. He'd programmed in her appointments six months out. The good news about the all-controlling watch was that it had gotten her to her interview on time. She finally had a job!

She turned off the AC and unrolled the window. A blast of heat and humidity and the smells of Chesapeake country, steamy grass and brackish water, enveloped her. She started down the hill toward the river, passing the bed & breakfast owned by the Dennisons, the seafood restaurant and gay bar run by Alan and Jacob, and the marina owned forever by the Smyth family. She rattled over the bridge and turned down the river road, passing the Hoffmans' Dockside Café, Harlow's Pub, Luna's Tarot Cards, and a boatyard. Through the trees were the houses of the two inseparable friends, Ben Hancock and her grandfather. She passed Ben's cottage and slowed at Papa's house. Her eyes were drawn to the shimmering river. Tied to cleats at the end of his dock was the intrepid tugboat, the *Vital Spark*.

She parked next to Papa's pickup truck and climbed out of her car. She pulled her shirttails from the constricting suit pants and rolled up her sleeves. Water Boy bounded off the porch and pinned her against the car door. The puppy was a gift from Papa's last girlfriend, the dog groomer. Water Boy jumped and nipped at her hands.

"Ouch, shit, down!" There was no collar with which to restrain him. "Sit, Water Boy! Sit!" He leapt up, snapping once again. Dog obedience was a foreign concept to Papa. Maybe if she ignored the dog, he'd calm down. She pulled her duffel bag from the backseat while he lifted his leg and peed on her tire. He accosted her once again and clamped onto to the cuff of her pants. "No, no, Water Boy! No bite!" He refused to release her cuff so she dragged him across the driveway. By the time they reached the porch, he had shredded the hem and coated her pants with drool. But no matter. After today she'd never have to wear a stifling suit again. She had a job with benefits! All was perfect in the life of Alexandra Allaway.

"Papa!" She pushed through the door and dropped her bag on the U-shaped sofa. An Allman Brothers CD played in the kitchen. Odd—she'd never heard Papa listen to the Allman Brothers. His passion was for the British Invasion bands, the Who, the Stones and the Animals. Another strange thing ... usually when she'd pull in, he'd stride out the door—followed always by a rambunctious dog—lift her off her feet and spin her around, all culminating with a scotch-scented kiss on her cheek.

The house was unnervingly still.

She glimpsed Papa's head over the back of his recliner. He was probably napping. During her last visit, when she'd brought Richard to meet him, a disastrous weekend all in all, he had appeared wan and tired. Richard had that effect on people. She tiptoed around his chair and put her hand on his shoulder.

"Papa?"

Alex's knees gave way. Thrust through Papa's faded Pink Floyd t-shirt, into his heart, was a bloody carving knife.

Alex had no idea how long ... seconds? ... minutes? ... she was crumpled into a shaking ball on the living room floor.

She glanced up at the blood-soaked body once again. Then it dawned on her ... the murderer might still be about!

She scrambled to her feet and dashed over to Old Ben's cottage. Ben was calm and rational; he'd protect her, help her think through this. She pounded on his crab knocker. No answer. She rounded the side of his cottage. His hammock was still. Nor was he was out back in the herb garden. She gazed at the dock. Ben's sailboat, *Star Gazer*, was gone. He could be anywhere ... Annapolis, St. Michael's. He had a girlfriend in Norfolk. Maybe he was in Virginia? It was unlike him not to return her text of the previous evening.

What to do? She spun frantically about. Hopefully the murderer was long gone. What next? Call the police!

Water Boy nipped at her ankle. "Jerk! That hurt!" She snatched up a stick and shook it furiously. "You bite me again and I'll ..." He cowered and backed away.

Now what? Call the police! Call 911! Where was her cell phone? Where? Where? In the glove compartment ... yes, she was sure of it. She'd stuffed it there before leaving Washington to avoid Richard, who still texted her many times a day. She hurried to her car and was about to press 911 when she remembered ...

The weed stash!

She ran through Papa's backyard and into the woods, finally stopping at a vine-covered greenhouse and shed. Water Boy had pursued and stared hungrily at her ankles. She shook the stick. "If you come near me ..." He dropped sullenly into the leaves.

What to do with Papa and Ben's marijuana harvest? The police would be combing every inch of the property within minutes. Why did this even matter? Were they going to arrest a dead man for possession? She'd simply explain to them that she hadn't lived there for years; she never knew the plants were there. She pushed open the greenhouse door and halted.

Baffling. The tables were covered with potted plants: begonias, coleus, small hostas, marigolds, African daisies and more. There were trowels, potting soil, and plant vitamins. This had been a grow house for as long as she could remember. Her high school friends loved hanging out at her house and adored Papa. Everyone adored him, except Richard and some other sick bastard ... who'd plunged a knife through his chest.

She pulled the phone from her pocket and called 911. "S-someone k-killed my gr-grandfather."

She staggered back to the house. No way could she stay there now. She pushed through the screen door to retrieve her duffel bag. She'd stay on the *Vital Spark*. It had a small berth, head, and galley. A macabre impulse drew her eyes to Papa.

What was that? An envelope with ALEX written in prominent letters sat on the coffee table next to his recliner, but it was not Papa's handwriting. The killer knew she was coming? The killer had left her a message?

It read: *ALEX ... open my hand.*

The killer had a sick sense of humor, writing as if it was Papa's request. She stared at her grandfather's wrinkled hands and wiped sweat from her forehead. One of Papa's hands was on his knee, but his other was clenched in a fist. Had the killer positioned Papa's hands like this? She inched forward and pried open his stiff fingers. Metal fell from his hand and clinked onto the wood floor. The afternoon sun hit it at once, and it glimmered gold. She shuddered, recognizing it at once. She and Papa had read every pyrate story ever written. It was Spanish gold, a piece of eight.

Alex grabbed the slice of gold and envelope, slung her duffel bag over her shoulder and fled the house. She hurried along the dock and climbed aboard the tugboat. She stuffed the envelope in her duffel bag and tossed it on the berth. She stepped on to the deck. The windows of Papa's house were dark and lifeless. Sorrow struck like an avalanche. Her last relative, beloved Papa, was gone. She collapsed amongst the crab traps and sobbed.

Police cruisers screamed across the River Glen bridge and down the river road. Time had no dimension. Noise cluttered the late afternoon: sirens, voices, door slams, a dog's yelp. Uniformed officers and the CSI team scoured Papa's yard and house for evidence. Footsteps creaked down the planks of the dock, so Alex struggled to her feet. It was a plain-clothes officer in a white dress shirt, tie, and grey pants. His hair was pure white like snow, but his face was surprisingly youthful and tan, making it impossible to guess his age. He'd tied a rope from Old Ben's canoe around Water Boy's neck and dragged the whimpering puppy down the dock.

"Can you watch your dog? He's really irritating."

She sniffled. "He's not my dog."

He tied Water Boy to a boat cleat and pulled out his I.D.

"Detective Braden, Homicide."

The word 'homicide' and all its horrible implications caused another eruption of tears. He waited while she fumbled with her tissues.

"You're the granddaughter who made the 911 call."

"Yes."

"Your name?"

"Alex Allaway."

"My condolences about your grandfather. I knew him, but only casually."

"From where?"

"From around the village."

The words on the envelope—*ALEX … open my hand*—still distracted her. Why was the message written in the first person? "This couldn't be a suicide, could it?" she asked Braden. Admittedly, it was an absurd question. A suicide just wasn't possible; it wasn't in Papa's zest-for-life nature.

"No. Why do you ask?"

"I don't know. I don't know anything right now." She honked into a tissue.

"Are you aware of anyone that Randy didn't get along with? Any incidents, disputes?"

Heavy footsteps thumped along the dock and she craned her head around Detective Braden. Oh no! No, no way! Could this day get any worse? Will Wilkins was the most obnoxious guy in her high school. Worse, the crew-cutted pinhead had turned up at her same school, the University of Maryland, where he'd played football. Then he'd had some injury, she'd heard through the River Glen grapevine, and had disappeared.

"This is my partner," Braden said, "Detective Wilkins."

A detective required some basic level of intelligence. Detective Wilkins … impossible! Pretend you don't recognize him. His was clearly the same tactic, as he shook her hand, avoiding her eyes completely.

"Did Randy have any enemies?" Braden asked again.

"Doubtful, but I haven't been around for years."

"And you live where?"

"Washington DC. Actually, nowhere right now. I was planning on staying with my grandfather until I found an apartment nearby."

Will's eyes widened. "You're moving back here?"

"What about it?" Her voice sounded vaguely snappish.

"Why are you moving back?" Braden said.

"I'm starting a new job at the marine station. I'm a fisheries biologist."

The two cops glanced at one another.

"What?" she asked.

Braden shrugged.

"What about that? You just gave each other a dubious look. What?"

"When do you start?" Braden asked.

"Tomorrow. Mr. Braden, there's something you're not telling me!"

"The person who hired you didn't tell you?" Will interjected.

"Tell me what?"

"Your predecessor at the marine station, Frank Whitby, is a missing person," Braden said.

Alex's throat tightened. "How—how long has he been missing?"

"A few weeks now," Braden said. "He left for work one morning and was never seen again. We've been all over his house and the marine station. But there was no evidence of foul play. When did you arrive in River Glen?"

"This afternoon."

Braden balled his hands in his pockets and gazed upriver.

She turned also. What was so goddamn interesting about the promontory at a time like this? "What?"

Braden said nothing. The silence felt heavy.

"Sir?" Will said quietly.

"Hm." Braden frowned. "Ms. Allaway, is there anything you can tell us about Randy that you think might be pertinent? Anything at all?"

"No. Who could do this to him?" She dropped onto a crab trap and pressed a tissue to her eyes.

"If anything comes to you, will you please call us?" Braden said.

"Yes, of course." She blew her nose again.

"We'll be back in the morning, when things settle down a bit. I'm going to put a patrol car at the house tonight. Here's my card with my number. It would give me peace of mind if you'd plug my number into your cell phone."

"Yes, okay," she sniffed.

Braden and Will stepped off the *Vital Spark*.

"Wait," she called. "Do either of you want this dog? He's a full-bred lab."

"No thanks," Will said. "My apartment doesn't allow pets."

"My wife's allergic," Braden said.

The two cops departed, murmuring to one another. They completely bypassed the house and headed straight for the grow house in the woods. Papa's side business was well known amongst the villagers.

The second the police cars cleared out, Alex's neighbors scurried down the dock. The Dennisons, who owned the B&B across the river, plied her for the ghoulish details. Alan and Jacob brought her fish cakes and squash fries from Nauticus, their restaurant. They bantered back and forth about her shorter haircut. In the end, they agreed that longer hair was a better look on her. Alice and Harry Hoffman offered Alex their daughter's bedroom, as the daughter was grown and hadn't lived at home for decades. Luna grabbed Alex's hand and insisted that she was in no danger; in fact she had an astonishingly long lifeline. "More good news," Luna said. "The bowl of blackberries in the hatchway is guaranteed to ward off evil spirits." The hospitable offers, incantations, and lurid speculations dizzied Alex. She mumbled through the neighborly chitchat while two facts remained. One: Papa was in a body bag in a morgue. Two: He'd been murdered. The conversation dwindled; Alex passed on the offers of accommodation and opted for the solitude of the *Vital Spark*. As Braden had promised, a patrol car cruised by the house in regular intervals. The neighbors departed, and she looked despairingly at Water Boy. Not one of them was willing to adopt the impossible dog.

"Come, monster." Alex held out a stick to Water Boy. He chomped on it while she dragged him toward the water's edge. One revelation in this horrid day was finding that the dog preferred sticks to her ankle. She threw the stick out to the water, and he splashed and frolicked through the water after it. Her watch vibrated. Ballroom dancing was in thirty minutes. She had two left feet; the whole experience had been humiliating beyond words. She supposed that she should notify Richard. He'd drop everything, rush across the Bay Bridge, and be more irksome than the dog. No, no Richard. That's the last thing she needed. She tossed the stick into the water until her shoulder ached and the dog was exhausted.

By the time darkness fell Water Boy had learned the drill. She presented the stick, he chomped on it, and she dragged him back to the tugboat. She stacked crab traps on the deck to create a dog pen. She had to give him something to eat, but the dog food was in the house. Papa's body had been removed and so had the blood-soaked recliner, but the crime scene shouldn't be disturbed. She spotted the Stryofoam container from Alan and Jacob. Her appetite was gone, so she placed the fish cakes and squash fries and a bowl of water in Water Boy's crab trap pen.

She entered the cabin of the tugboat, locked the door behind her, and climbed into the berth. Nothing made sense. The envelope to her said *ALEX ... open my hand*, as if Papa had left it for her. But it couldn't be suicide. Besides, who would stab a kitchen knife through his own chest? There were less violent ways to kill one's self. And a man couldn't stab himself and then position one hand on his knee and clench his fist. Could he? Braden had said a definite 'no' to suicide. Why hadn't the killer taken the piece of eight? Hadn't he noticed what was in Papa's hand when he stabbed him? And it was real gold! It was exactly the same hue as the gold earrings that Richard had given her last Christmas. The piece of eight had to be worth a fortune. The killer hadn't placed the gold in Papa's hand. Where had Papa come upon Spanish gold?

Was it a revenge killing? Had Papa messed with a married woman? No, impossible. He only dated single women or divorcées. It wasn't his way to interfere in a relationship.

A business deal gone bad? Everyone knew of Papa and Old Ben's side business. The whole village was stoned during RiverFest, the River Glen Arts Festival, and Giles Blood-hand Day. For a time he and Ben had tried to make moonshine, but it was horrible; no one bought it. That was a short-lived enterprise.

Stranger yet were the contents of the envelope. Just an old highway map with three numbered dots: *1. Bohemia River, 2. Sassafras River, and 3. Mutter Island.*

"Tell no one Alex. No one! JAllaway might come," was written along the edge of the map.

Tell no one what? And who was JAllaway? She'd never heard Papa speak of another Allaway, except his brother, Jason, who'd been killed in Vietnam in the mid-sixties.

She blew into the tissue, huddled in the corner of the berth, and pulled a blanket over herself. Beyond the porthole the river flowed through the black night. She was too exhausted to change from the dress shirt and suit pants, or to rummage through her duffel bag for her toothbrush ... just too, too exhausted. Her eyelids dropped. Papa's voice wound through her slowing thoughts.

"Once upon a time there was a tugboat named the *Vital Spark.* On it lived a pyrate named Giles Blood-hand, the scourge of the seven seas ..."

"No, Papa. Pyrates prefer sloops or schooners," she, then a ten-year-old, had interrupted. "Because of their speed."

His gull-nest eyebrows had risen in surprise. "Are you too old for my stories, darling?"

"Never. But you must tell the story correctly," she had scolded.

"Yes, okay. On a fleet schooner lived Giles Blood-hand. He was a most ruthless pyrate, an escaped convict from Scotland. Giles was very clever and very lucky. One day the winds of fortune blew his ship into the pathway of a Spanish galleon, her holds bursting with Incan gold from the Andes ..."

During the night Water Boy's barking woke her. She sprang from the berth and checked the lock on the hatch door. It was locked securely. She peered nervously out a porthole. The dog yapped and jumped up on the gunwale. A slender woman leaned over the rail, whispering to him. Her white night gown shimmered in the moonlight. She was dripping wet. She looked at Alex with black remote eyes, executed a perfect dive off the dock and swam away into the night.

Chapter 2

Day 2

River Glen

Alex checked the time on her cellphone. No way ... impossible ... it couldn't be that late! She scrambled from the berth. There was no time for a shower. Besides, the *Vital Spark* didn't have one. She whipped off her clothes from yesterday's interview, peed in the head, sponged herself off at the galley sink, brushed her teeth and threw on shorts and a t-shirt. She grabbed her backpack, sunglasses and ball cap, and stepped into the morning glare. Water Boy attacked her ankle. "Ouch! Shithead!" She yanked his rope collar and shoved him down the dock. "Go pee!"

During the night the dog had eaten part of the Styrofoam food container and shredded the rest. She'd deal with the mess later. Her first priority was to locate the stick to protect her ankles from the savage beast. She hopped down the dock while pulling on her sneakers. The police had already returned to the house. Jay Braden and Will Wilkins were supervising the packing boxes of Papa's papers. It was best that she go to the marine station even though she'd be too agitated to work; she'd be under foot all day if she remained at home. If nothing else, she'd be able to organize her workspace, see where the supplies were, and start the experiments by the end of the week. If she could calm herself down ...

Water Boy splashed through the water, jumped and nipped at the policemen loading evidence boxes into the van, then bounced through the water once again. As the dog dashed by Braden, he grabbed him by the scruff of the neck. Yelp! From his pocket, he pulled a collar and leash and fixed them to the subdued dog.

Braden handed Alex the leash. "Here."

"Can I go inside for a sec? I need to get the dog some food," she said.

"Yeah, yeah, but be quick about it, and don't touch anything," he grumbled. "I'll hold him."

"I'll be super quick because I'm late for work." She sprinted up the porch steps, wove through the police officers, found a box of dried dog food in the kitchen and returned to the detective.

"You're taking this dog with you today, right?" Braden said.

"Ur, yes. Unless someone wants him. He really is a great dog." She turned toward the house. "I forgot his bowl. Oh, no matter." She opened the back door of her car and sprinkled dog food across the backseat. "Up." Water Boy hopped in and she closed the door behind him.

"We'll come by the marine station a little later to talk," he said.

"Okay." She climbed into the front seat.

"And we need to look around the tugboat."

"Yes, fine. It's open. That's nothing of value in there. The navigation system is antiquated."

Will approached and handed her a coffee and a brown bag. "I thought you might be hungry. Donuts. I didn't know if you liked coffee, and cream and sugar, so I got you everything."

"Thank you," she said. Some time since high school Will had evolved from *Homo neanderthalensis* to *Homo sapien*.

"Keep your wits about you, Alex," Braden said sternly.

She nodded and drove down the river road toward the highway. Yesterday morning at this time she'd just started the interview at the Human Resources office in Annapolis. Actually it had been a second interview with Mr. Ward; she'd been almost certain that she'd be offered the job. They'd already conducted a background check on her. Her only run-in with the police had been the night Gillian White, Linda Morgan and she had jumped off the bridge after that wild party at Alan and Jacob's place on Giles Blood-hand Day. The old police officer who'd caught them had simply told them to put their clothes back on and go home. She'd never been cited for it.

By the end of the interview Mr. Ward had given her a set of keys to the marine station and asked her when she could start.

"Immediately," she'd said eagerly. "Will the person I'm replacing have left me any notes on where he was with the surveys and experiments?"

"Doubtful. Frank Whitby left suddenly, without giving notice. He was a bit of a womanizer. He likely ran off with some girlfriend. " Mr. Ward had shook her hand and sent her out the door.

No matter. She'd figure it out, she'd thought at the time. She'd blared rock all the way along Route 301/50 East, across the Bay Bridge and up 213, imagining her new life out of the chaos of DC, the perfect evenings with Papa, his woman du jour, Old Ben, Alan and Jacob, and Luna all after a perfect day at the marine station.

But instead Papa was dead. Frank Whitby was missing. And a meaningless road map was tucked into her backpack.

Tell no one Alex. No one! JAllaway might come. Written in whose handwriting? Tell no one what? Why did she need to be so secretive about a map of the northern Chesapeake with three random dots? And who was the mysterious JAllaway? Was his coming good news or a warning? And what about the ghostly woman on the dock, who swam gracefully into the night? That was not a dream. Whoever she was, Water Boy had been thrilled to see her.

At the sign to the River Glen Marine Station, Alex turned off the highway onto a dirt road. "Cut that shit out!" Water Boy had decided to feast on her earlobe. She swatted over her shoulder and the car swerved into the underbrush. After wrestling the car onto the road, she spotted the marsh and the weathered marine station. She'd only seen the building from the water, never from land. She parked near a maintenance shed and opened the back door.

"Yuck. You slobbered all over me." She dried off her neck with her shirt.

Water Boy jumped from the car and bounded after an Eastern cottontail. He disappeared into the marsh. "And never return!" she called. She appraised the damage to the passenger side of the car. The paint was scratched down the entire side. She sighed. It was a worthless car anyway.

The laboratory building sat at the edge of the marsh. At a dock floated a rowboat and a work skiff with an outboard engine. Buckets, nets and clam rakes sat next to an outdoor sink and shower. She dropped onto the edge of the dock with her coffee and donuts. The water shimmered green. Birds chirped, insects fiddled their songs from amidst the marsh grass, and water lapped against the pilings. Papa was no longer around to share glorious Chesapeake mornings with her. She bent her face into her shirt and wept.

A Duck Blind

"Interesting, very interesting." Clyde Whitby stuffed a wad of chewing tobacco into his cheek and pressed his camo binoculars against the slats of the duck blind. It was the first sign of activity at the marine station in weeks. He'd spied the two useless detectives, Jay Braden and Will Wilkins, wandering mindlessly around the building weeks before ... uncovering nothing! They were a study in police incompetence. All they found was Frank's car, filled with the usual empty beer cans and fishing gear. Frank's wife, Donna, had no knowledge of his whereabouts.

"He left for work one morning and I never saw him again. Good riddance," Donna had told Braden and Wilkins. "I'm finally free of that asshole."

Asshole? Frank was the best of men. He was a highly trained ecologist, a member of the Rotary Club and the local School Board.

Now some black-haired chick and hyperactive black lab occupied Frank's dock. What the fuck did she have to cry about? He was the one with the missing brother. He lifted his high-powered hunting rifle onto his shoulder and put her in his sights.

"Bang," he snarled.

River Glen

Vital Spark

A rapping sound caused Will Wilkins to turn from Randy Allaway's porch. Harry Hoffman from the Dockside Café, a white apron tied around his stout waist, knocked on Ben Hancock's cottage door. No answer. Harry peered through the window. Will wandered over. "Old Ben"—everyone in the village had always called him that. Even as a boy, Will remembered the crabber being referred to as Old Ben. The man was all bones and knobs, loose and shaky like a scarecrow in the wind. Nice guy, polite, timid, content to let Randy to do all the talking.

Will moved next to Harry at the window. The smell of Old Bay seasoning wafted off the cook. Harry's crab cakes were the best in Maryland because the cook knew the secret: never dilute the taste and texture of crab with breading.

"Will, Ben didn't show up for our bridge game the other night." Harry's doughy face was twisted with concern. "He said he was going sailing but would be back for bridge."

Will glanced toward Randy's dock where Ben tethered *Star Gazer*, a West Wight Potter 19. The only boat at the dock was the *Vital Spark*. Randy and Ben had sold their workboat years before, when they'd retired.

"Let me try the door. " Will reached for the knob. "Hey, it's unlocked."

Despite being neighbors in the same village for over two decades, this was the first time Will had stepped into Ben's cottage. The single-story place consisted of a narrow kitchen, a bedroom with a single bed, a living room and a back porch with a hammock. Nothing more. The only remarkable thing was a worktable in the living room, covered with model paints, paintbrushes, razor blades and clamps. Boxes of plastic model kits were stacked on the table. On the bookshelves were countless plastic boat and ship models, constructed and painted by Old Ben's expert hand. He seemed to have no historical preference, as the boats were from all eras, Phoenician and Viking ships, the ships from the Voyages of Discovery, Darwin's *Beagle*, pyrate ships, everything, all the way to the present, including the US Navy's current destroyers and aircraft carriers.

Will searched Ben's desk. Ben led a relatively spartan existence. All of the drawers were empty except for one with pencils, pens and a calculator. Next to a laptop and printer was a neat stack of papers. Ben had printed out an itinerary for a Caribbean cruise leaving from Norfolk next week. He had booked passage for two, himself and a woman named Dott Garski.

"Harry, did Ben ever mentioned a Dott Garski?"

"Yes, he's been dating Dott for years. They met on a senior citizens' cruise. She's the widow of a Navy captain. Ben can't get her to leave Norfolk, so he sails down to see her."

Will continued to leaf through the papers. Receipts for new eye glasses and a hearing aid. On the bottom was a large manila envelope. It read "Benjamin Hancock's Will". He tentatively opened the envelope. It was a standard will, very simple, handled by James Collins, the estate attorney in the village. It had been dated just weeks before. His bank account, 401K, and a life insurance policy were to go to a sister in Oklahoma, and the cottage and all its contents—the boat models—were left to Alexandra Allaway. That was no surprise. Ben had had an equal hand in raising Alex. Among Will's many memories of her were her hauling crab pots out on the bay with Randy and Ben.

In the manila envelope with the will was a small white envelope. The writing on it read: "*Whoever finds this must deliver this message to Alexandra Allaway immediately. URGENT. Please deliver immediately.*"

Will held the envelope up to the light, but all that was discernible was an odd series of numbers and letters. A code?

A Marine Station

Water Boy rounded the corner of the marine station and jumped on Alex's back. He paddled circles around the boats and sniffed horseshoe crab carapaces on the shore before running back to the dock. He pressed his snout into Alex's cheek and panted in her face.

She moaned and averted her face. "Your breath smells like dead fish." She rose from the edge of the dock and filled a bucket at the outdoor sink. "Come, Maniac. Water. Drink." His coat, collar and leash were covered with mud and burrs. "You're so not coming inside." She frowned. A tick was attached to his ear. She searched his entire coat, removed three more ticks and washed them down the sink. She tied him to a bollard on the dock and pulled the lab keys from her pocket. Mr. Ward in Annapolis had meticulously labeled the keys for her. She opened the back door and stepped inside.

The lab was trashed. It was clear the police had searched the place, as the drawers at Frank Whitby's desk and a filing cabinet were open and papers were strewn randomly about. The computer on the desk was an ancient model with floppy disc drives. "Like this dinosaur's going to work." She pushed the *on* button. Nothing.

The watch vibrated on her wrist.

Richard again. "How's the new job?"

"Great," she typed. That much of the high-tech watch she'd mastered.

She stuffed Whitby's papers back into the desk—she'd deal with them later—and set up her laptop. Her cell phone could be used as a hot spot. While her computer booted, she opened the windows. A salty breeze moved through the musty room.

The analytical balance, aquaria and glassware on the lab bench were dusty. Had they ever been used? What the hell had Whitby been doing? Clearly not conducting experiments or testing samples. Water Boy yipped, prompting her to rush to the window. An unmarked police sedan pulled up next to her car. Braden and Will climbed out. Internally, she dithered whether to tell them about the cryptic map.

Tell no one Alex. No one!

Did that include the police? Would it help them find Papa's killer? Would the police know a person named JAllaway? She unlocked the front door.

"How's it going so far?" Braden scanned the room.

"It's odd. It looks like nothing's been done here for a while. There's dust and cobwebs everywhere."

"We'd like to ask you some more questions."

She nodded.

"I'm going to ask you this again. Can you think of anyone who'd want to harm your grandfather?"

"No. Everyone loved him."

"The medical examiner has determined that he was killed the evening before you arrived. Probably by someone he knew. There were no defensive wounds. No signs of a struggle. There was no forced entry into his house."

"He never locked his door," she said. "He and Old Ben wandered back and forth between their two houses all day."

"I searched Ben's cottage," Will said. "Ben appears to be taking his girlfriend, Dott, on a cruise soon."

"He visits her all the time," she said.

"I couldn't reach Ben's cell, but I spoke with Dott this morning," Will said. "She confirmed that Ben was on his way, and that they're going to the Bahamas next week."

"Did you tell her what happened to my grandfather?" she asked. "Ben will be devastated."

"Yes," Will said.

"I guess I'll have the funeral when Ben returns." She pulled a paper towel from the dispenser at the sink and blew her nose. She turned to find Will smiling at her. "What's so goddamn funny? Nothing's funny right now!"

"Sorry. Your back. It's covered with paw prints."

"Did Randy have a drug problem, or a problem with alcohol?" Braden asked.

"No! Ridiculous! He loved his scotch but he was never impaired. I never ever saw him impaired in any way. Why are you asking that?"

"He had massive amounts of alcohol and narcotics in his bloodstream when he died."

Alex shook her head vigorously. "That's impossible. Okay, sometimes he smoked weed. And he grew it. But it wasn't for distribution. It was just for friends, for parties."

"Yeah, yeah, we know about that," Braden said. 'The tox report didn't find metabolites for THC, only alcohol and narcotics. Did he have any other business partners besides Old Ben?"

She shook her head again. "No. It's just not possible that he was using narcotics."

"We need you to swing by the station today to give us your fingerprints and make a statement. We're trying to identify all of the prints in Randy's house," Braden explained.

"Okay."

Will pulled the white envelope from his folder. "This was in Ben's papers. It's for you."

She opened it. It read:

Alex ... 1OGM 2CC 3GG Love you honey, Old Ben.

She felt herself heat up. It was the same handwriting as on the envelope on Randy's coffee table and the edge of the map. No wonder the familiarity. *Open my hand!* Ben had written that for Randy. But why didn't Randy write it himself? Had the murderer, in his haste, not noticed Randy's clenched fist or the envelope on the coffee table next to the recliner?

"Alex, what's 10 GM? What's any of this mean?" Will asked.

Braden tilted his head. "I think it's a 1 and an OGM. What is this?"

She was completely bewildered. "I have no idea."

Braden gave her a hard gaze. "Are you sure?" His cell phone rang. "Braden here ... Okay." He rang off. "Forensics is done at your place. You can go back into the house now."

"The house gives me the willies. I'll stay on the *Vital Spark* for a while."

"Be around in case we have more questions," Braden said.

"Alex, are you going to the Giles Blood-hand festival this weekend?" Will asked.

"No. I'm too depressed to do anything."

"If anything occurs to you, you call us. " Braden headed toward the door.

"I will." She suddenly remembered. "There was one weird thing. I have no idea if it relates to my grandfather's murder, but there was this woman on my dock …"

"When?" Braden cut in.

"Last night. In the middle of the night. She was swimming in her nightgown."

Will went rigid.

"Okay, we'll check on it." Braden strode hotly out the door.

Headquarters

Randy Allaway's papers were typical of an elderly man and war veteran, Will Wilkins discovered. Allaway's medical records from the Veteran's Administration and literature from the AARP now cluttered Will's desk at the River Glen police station. Randy had apparently been shot in the leg in Vietnam, an injury that had troubled him throughout his life. Randy had saved the childhood artwork and report cards from his son, Colin, and granddaughter, Alex. Will felt vaguely voyeuristic scanning materials belonging to Alex. He sifted through a shoebox of curled photographs that chronicled brief moments from Randy's adult life: his platoon in Vietnam, assorted women (all remarkably attractive) he'd married or dated, his boy Colin, and many of Alex as a little girl. Often Old Ben, Alan and Jacob, Luna, and Alice and Harry Hoffman were present. The one of a teenaged Alex in a string bikini by the tugboat's water cannon caused a flurry of unwelcome thoughts. Don't go there. Will tossed the photos in the box.

Sergeant Lisa Paco turned from the desk next to his. "Is everything okay, Will?"

"Yes, fine."

The whole thing—investigating a case involving Alex Allaway—was just plain uncomfortable. Ditzy Alex who'd dashed down the hallway to make the morning bell, zipping and buttoning as she ran. The object of every schoolboy's fantasies, yet she was completely oblivious. She'd certainly remembered him. When he'd walked down the dock yesterday, her expression had been one of overt dread.

Focus on the case ... focus on the important clues, like the beer cans.

Randy had had a well-stocked liquor cabinet in his kitchen containing bottles of Scotch whiskey. There was no beer in either his or Old Ben's refrigerator, yet crushed cans of Bud Lite were in his kitchen trash, as well as a Styrofoam coffee cup. Forensics had dusted the cans and cup and found them covered with unknown fingerprints, belonging neither to Randy nor Old Ben. Forensics was testing the cans and cup to obtain the DNA from the saliva. Had Randy been drinking with his killer? Did things get out of hand? Had the visitor stabbed him? With the amount of alcohol in Randy's blood, he must have been sloshed, maybe irrational and out of control. The murder weapon was a carving knife from a wooden block in Randy's own kitchen.

Randy's living room had a shelf with rock music CDs, mainly from the 60s and 70s, and mostly British bands. There was no southern rock. Yet when they'd entered the house yesterday after Alex's call, an Allman Brothers CD had been playing from the kitchen, on a cycling mode. It must have been playing continuously since the previous evening when Randy and the killer had met. The same fingerprints from the beer cans were all over the plastic CD case, but not the CD player. Presumably the killer had brought the beer and Allman Brothers music to Randy's house, but Randy had put the CD into the CD player.

Will heard a commotion down the hall and leaned from his chair. He jumped to his feet.

"Sit! I said sit! I thought that if I brought him in with me he wouldn't chew through my backseat." Alex was talking to Jay Braden at the front entrance. Jay had just returned from his personal errand. His face was exhausted and aggravated, the way it looked all the time these days.

Jay snatched a bag of Cheetos off the desk of a clerk. "Here's how you train that goddamn dog! Sit!" He shoved Water Boy's butt down and fed him a Cheeto. "Stay." He fed him another Cheeto. "Reinforce the good behaviors with treats."

"With Cheetos?" Alex said.

Jay huffed in exasperation. "No! Go to a pet store and get him proper treats. Keep them in your pockets all the time and train this stupid animal!" He pointed Alex down the hall. "Second door on the left! Get your prints done there. Give a statement to the officer about your whereabouts for the past few days."

"Okay, okay!" She departed, her watch vibrating on her wrist.

Jay approached the desks and glared at Will. "What are you looking at? You sit! We have work to do. You do this box." He slammed a box onto Will's desk. "Paco, that one's yours. I'll do this one."

Will dropped obediently into his chair and got to work. His box was from Randy's filing cabinet. He read through it, his cheeks and ears still warm with embarrassment. It was more old medical records, tax returns, Alex's immunizations and birth certificate. Her father was a man named Colin

Trevor Allaway, her mother, Carole Jane Lowe. Alex had been born in Philadelphia, two years before him.

"I wonder what happened to her parents?" Will thought aloud. "Why was she raised by her grandfather?"

"Stay on task," Jay grumbled.

Lisa Paco rolled her eyes at Will and continued through her box. The three of them worked in tense silence.

"Do you scuba dive, Will?" Jay asked after a while.

"No sir. But I snorkel."

Jay's eyes were fixed on a paper. "Where's your gear?"

"In my trunk. With all my sports equipment."

"A bathing suit too?"

"Yes."

"Good. You and I are going for a swim."

Cooper's Creek

Will felt like Charlie Allnut dragging *The African Queen* through leech-infested waters. Parts of Cooper's Creek were similarly dense and impassable, so he was left with the grim chore of dragging Jay's Boston Whaler through the lily pads while his feet were sucked into inches of slime and muck. If the boat had to be pulled in, then it would also have to be pulled back out. When he'd climbed into the boat on Jay's dock earlier that afternoon, he'd realized that, wherever they were going, he would be doing the swimming because Jay had remained in his khakis and dress shirt.

"I've been reduced to a pack animal." Will climbed back into the boat.

Jay restarted the outboard. "You still have a functioning back."

Will smacked at a mosquito. "There better be something back here. I've donated half my blood supply to these little vampires."

Jay motored forward and studied the paper once again—a hand-drawn map found amidst Randy's papers. "It should be here somewhere. Just up here, where the creek widens."

Will squinted into the sunlight sifting through the trees. "Seems like we can't go any farther than that pool."

Jay cut the engine and lowered the anchor. "It's weird that Randy's "X" was in the middle of the creek and not on the shore."

Will peered into the brackish, brown water. "So I really have to go down there?"

"Yes. Really."

"Sir, can't we get police divers ..."

"They're too expensive. Go."

Will pulled on his dive mask and slipped down the ladder.

"Watch out for the copperheads and water moccasins," Jay called.

Will whipped off the mask. "What!"

Jay gave him a wry smile. It was the first levity Will had seen in days. Jay had problems, big problems. So big that he'd left the Baltimore Police Department and transferred to a quiet rural police force in Kent County.

Will took a giant breath and swam downward. There were only a few feet of visibility around him; he kicked minimally so as not to stir up any more particles. Suddenly his hands grazed slimy metal. He resurfaced.

"Sir, the camera. I think it's a car. I only felt the roof."

Jay handed an underwater camera over the gunwale; Will filled his lungs and disappeared once again. This time he slid his hands over the roof and down the windshield to the wiper blades. The paint on the hood was dark green or brown, impossible to tell in the murk. He followed the hood to the grill and bumper. He groped around. The front right headlight was shards of glass, and the surrounding metal was dented. No license plate. Will's lungs burned, so he resurfaced.

"No license plate on the front," he panted.

"What type of car?"

"Hard to tell. Let me check."

He dove down again and swam across the roof, this time moving to the rear of the car. No license plate there either. He crawled across the back hood and pressed his mask against the back window. He took a photo of the car's logo. His lungs screamed for air. One more photo ... of a community college parking registration sticker on the rear window, dated from almost three decades ago. He burst through the water and gasped for air. He handed the camera up to Jay and climbed aboard.

"I owe you a beer," Jay said.

Will lifted a towel. "Why am I drying off? Now I have to pull the boat out of here. Two beers?"

"Deal." Jay swiped through the photos. "Why was Randy Allaway so interested in a Saturn car from a student at the community college twenty-six years ago?"

Chapter 3

Day 3

Giles Blood-hand Day
June, 2017

After a second night of sleeping on the *Vital Spark*, Alex Allaway awoke, fed the dog and rummaged through Papa's back shed. She found the tattered cardboard signs. Painted in bright red letters was

PARKING YE SCALLYWAGS
$10/land ship

There were pros and cons to the village's annual pyrate festival. The cons first. The entire population of Washington DC, Baltimore, and Philadelphia, clad as pyrates and wenches, crowded into the village for a weekend bacchanal. Lawyers, lobbyists, life coaches and other suburbanites shed their skins of middle-class respectability and trashed the village. Papa had likened the event to a swashbuckler tailgating party. The river was clogged with watercraft, making it impossible to get one's boat out to the bay. The roads into and out of village were blocked by orange traffic cones, so it was impossible to leave, even if one wanted to. But the single pro outweighed all the cons. Vast amounts of money flowed into the River Glen economy. There'd be face-painting, Moon bounces, and pony rides for the children. The restaurants, gift shops and bars would be packed. Bands would be playing; there'd be dancing on the town pier, and craft beers and wine from local vineyards would be drunk by truckloads.

And Alex's own personal economy would be stimulated. In keeping with Papa and Old Ben's age-old tradition, she'd open up the front yard and driveway for tourist parking. Even though Ben was sailing the Chesapeake, he wouldn't mind if she allowed the throngs to park on his property as well. She'd give him his share of the booty when he returned. By the end of the day she'd have hundreds of dollars, all in ten-dollar bills. The cash would defray the cost of the leashes, leads, and chew toys bought the previous night at the pet store. She wandered the river road, placing the parking signs where Papa had always put them, in highly visible areas.

Banners of Giles Blood-hand hung from the lampposts in the village. Pyrate flags flapped from every post, pole, and lanyard. Countless generations ago, some entrepreneurial town father or mother had started the rumor that the legendary Giles had sailed up the Chesapeake and buried his cache of Spanish gold in River Glen. An equally clever commercial artist who'd designed the banner decided to make Giles dashingly handsome, with jet-black hair and incandescent green eyes.

The signs placed, she walked listlessly toward home. On Papa's porch where she'd tied him, Water Boy yapped and jumped for her to return. Never again would a Giles Blood-hand Day be spent merry-making on the porch with Papa and Ben and dancing with them at the village pier. The windows of Ben's cottage remained ominously dark. She ached to talk to him. Suddenly the rope snapped and Water Boy hurled himself off the porch. He raced toward her like a black torpedo and knocked her into Ben's maple tree. Instead of festivities on the pier, her dismal day would be spent attempting to manage an unmanageable dog.

It was a chaotic morning for Will Wilkins. Before picking up his daughter, Carly, for the pyrate festival, he stopped by headquarters.

"You've got to be kidding me," he said to Lisa Paco. His mousy partner was dressed as usual in an immaculately pressed uniform. He furiously scratched his arms. "We could have driven to Cooper's Creek? I was up all night itching from the bug bites."

"Yes," Lisa laughed. "They just cut through the underbrush and found a dirt road that leads right to the creek. They pulled the car out this morning."

"At least I'm getting beer out of the deal."

"From the algal growth and rust, forensics said that it had been submerged for about twenty-five years. There were no plates or anything inside. The car was completely cleaned out. The VIN had been etched away. Someone definitely didn't want that car identified."

"Because it was clearly in an accident. The front headlamp was smashed to bits."

"I checked with the Motor Vehicles Administration. Allaway always drove a Ford pickup truck. He never owned a Saturn. But guess who did?"

"Who?"

"Frank Whitby."

Unfortunately Will didn't have time to discuss it further. He rushed to pick up Carly in Middletown, Delaware, then changed them both into their pyrate costumes at his parents' house on Main Street.

The pyrate festival was a highlight of his daughter's year, as important to her as her birthday, Halloween, or Christmas. At the moment the face-painter was putting the finishing touches on the pink and purple butterflies on his five-year-old's delighted face.

"You look beautiful, sweetheart," he said.

She beamed back at him. How could such an adorable child be the offspring of such a conniving witch? How could one man be so stupid! He didn't mind paying child support if he could be sure the money was going to Carly, but every time he picked up Carly for his weekend, her mother, Penny Bannister, had a new hair color, haircut, and glamorous fingernails. If Penny never had any money, as she claimed, how did she afford a Girls' Week in Cancun? And when was she going to find a job, instead of spending her days at Massage Envy and Pilates ... that he was no doubt financing! Carly was in all-day kindergarten now. It was time for the woman to find a full-time job.

Devious cheerleaders. Dingy fraternities. How had he had been so stupid? Penny had slid onto the barstool next to his after the Michigan game.

"Tell me about that amazing play in the third quarter. You'll certainly be invited to the Combine and the NFL Draft, won't you? Every NFL team needs a good tight end." She'd bounced her knee against his thigh and slid him another shot of vodka.

One remembrance of that night stood out like no other ... he'd not drunk enough to blackout. Months later, he was ordered by the court to supply a DNA sample. Most certainly Penny had slipped a date rape drug into his drink when he was in the men's room, but what court of law would believe that a two hundred and forty pound football player had been taken advantage of? And then came the knee injury in the South Florida game. But from that messy year, he'd gained a daughter ... a precious daughter ... the only thing in his life that mattered.

Carly glanced at the village green. "Daddy, can I ride a pony?"

"Sure."

She skipped along the edge of the dock, scattering the seagulls that were eating spilt popcorn.

"Be careful, Carly. Don't go too near the edge."

Will's cell phone vibrated from the pocket of his pyrate vest. It was Lisa. She was still at headquarters on a Saturday afternoon. She hated fieldwork of any kind, but was happy to unravel cases from behind her laptop. Take a vacation or personal day? Never.

"I just found another interesting thing," Lisa said. "Frank Whitby attended the community college during the same period as the year on the parking registration sticker. And guess who was his classmate?"

"Randy Allaway?"

"No, Benjamin Hancock. I checked their transcripts. They were in the same freshman math course, in the same semester."

"Randy clearly knew where Whitby had dumped his car," he said. "If Whitby knew that Randy's knew that, it might be a motive for killing him. We'll need to see if Whitby's prints match those on the beer cans, coffee cup, or CD case."

"Yikes!" Lisa said. "So Whitby might not be a missing person after all, but might be in hiding or in flight!"

"We've got to get in touch with Ben ASAP. If Whitby murdered Randy, then he might go after Ben next!"

"You're wearing the pyrate dress." Gillian White rummaged through Alex's bedroom closet. "No more discussion. You're wearing it."

Alex slumped on the edge of the bed. "Papa's dead. I'm in no mood for any of this."

"He wouldn't want you sitting here, feeling sorry for yourself. You've filled your entire lawn with cars." Clothes hangers jingled as Gillian continued her search. "You have a pocket full of cash. He'd want you to go to the village and celebrate. Besides, we might run into old friends."

Water Boy gnawed at the leg of the dresser. Alex tossed a bedroom slipper at him. "Cut that shit out. Sit. I hate this dog, Gill. He's deranged, demented, or something."

"He's adorable. Here it is." Gillian displayed the dress. "Put it on. You know the tradition. We always dress as pyrate wenches." She tossed the dress onto Alex's lap. "Does Randy have any weed left?"

"Doubtful. The police have been all over the place."

"Come, you," Gillian called to Water Boy. She departed down the stairs, the dog trotting after her.

Alex tugged off her shirt and shorts, slid the dress over her head, and tightened the red velvet corset. Any other year the annual ritual would have thrilled her ... primping in front of the mirror, curling her hair with a curling iron, applying rouge and black eyeliner, culminating with garishly bright lipstick. But this year she'd forego the make-up, eye patch, fishnet stockings, and black boots. She frowned at the mirror. She was a pyrate frump instead of a pyrate badass. The whole thing was ridiculous; she was in no mood for this.

She slipped her feet into sandals and dragged herself downstairs. The watch vibrated on her wrist. In half an hour she was to be on a tour of the National Gallery with Richard and his docent friend to look at works by Gustav Klimt and other Viennese painters.

"Can't we go to the aquarium or zoo instead?" she'd asked while he'd plugged that event into her watch.

"No, Alexandra, you really should know more about the Vienna Secession movement."

Whatever...

Alex found Gillian inspecting Papa's liquor cabinet. Gillian shook her head in obvious disappointment at her feeble attempt at dressing for the festival. Gillian, on the other hand, had perfected the pyrate look ... eye-patch, the green parrot, Blind Pew, on her shoulder, and a low-cut peasant blouse. She took a long guzzle from a bottle of rum.

"Here." Gillian handed her a shot glass of rum.

"But I haven't eaten anything today."

"All the better. You'll get a better buzz."

Alex tossed down the rum and moaned at the burning sensation in her throat. Water Boy paced at the front door. Gillian had tied her skull and cross bone bandana around his neck and put on his leash.

"No way, Gill, he's not going. He's retarded."

"Retarded is not PC."

"Fucked up?"

"Much better. He just needs socializing."

"If he bites anyone that's all I need. To be sued when I haven't even earned my first paycheck." Alex turned to the space where Randy's bloody recliner had been. That terrible memory and the rum made her light-headed. "Let's get the hell out of here."

It was less than a five-minute walk down the river road to the festivities. The village already swelled with visitors. Long queues had formed outside Luna's Tarot Reading shack, the Hoffmans' Dockside Café, and Alan and Jacob's Nauticus. Harlow's Pub was also packed. The Smyth's marina was clogged with boater buccaneers. Pyrate flags snapped in the breeze, while a band on the pier sang "... Wasted away again in Margaritaville ...."

Gillian pointed up to the village green and the ponies. "There's Will and Carly."

"Who's Carly?"

"His daughter." Gillian nudged Alex. "From his one-night stand. Yum, yum, Will's looking good." She smiled devilishly. "Do you remember that double date we went on when I dated him? You were dating my cousin Eddie."

"I don't remember."

"You do too, you bull-shitter! What a crazy night that was!" Gillian grinned again. "Let's go to the wine tasting. I'm always up for free wine." She pulled Alex by the hand toward the booths sponsored by local vineyards.

Suddenly Water Boy sprang forward. His leash ripped from Alex's hand. He zigzagged through the dancers. Alex dashed after him. His target was a lone woman at the end of pier. Her back was to the crowd and she gazed out to the bay. She was dressed in an ornate purple and black velvet gown. Fluttering from her black hat was an ostentatious orange feather. Water Dog yipped gleefully and she turned. He dropped submissively at her feet and rolled on his back. She knelt and tickled his belly. Her face was shadowed by the black brim. Finally she stood and stared at Alex. The woman was about fifty; her skin was deathly white, her eyes wide, dark, and inscrutable. Then she spun and executed a perfect dive off the edge of the pier.

Gillian burst from the stunned crowd. "That's Laura Braden," she whispered to Alex. "The cop's wife. She's as mad as a hatter."

Headquarters

Lisa Paco blew a giant pink bubble and let it pop loudly. Weekends and holidays are the best! This weekend most everyone was at the pyrate festival, where the inhabitants of the mid-Atlantic region rejected their banal identities to assume the more interesting personas of buccaneers. No fantasy life was necessary for her.

#pacoislivingthedream #acopbetteryet

Better still, a detective working on a gruesome homicide. She looked stealthily around the empty office. The state trooper, Denny, and the new recruit from the police academy were out back having a smoke. She unbuttoned her uniform sleeve and rolled it up. It was only the zillionth time she'd inspected the new tattoo. Her priggish captain would freak if he noticed it! In his estimation anyone with a tat was a social deviant. Anyway, what business was it of his? All her tats were carefully etched in her skin below the collar line or above her shirtsleeve cuff. She grinned smugly. The artist at Sublime Ink had really outdone himself with this one. It had taken numerous appointments in the evenings after work, but it was finally done. The ink was still fresh and bright, her skin still tender and tingly. They'd taken complete poetic license with this one. From her left wrist, above the cuff line of course, to her shoulder, shades of gray, blue and purple ink depicted Sherlock Holmes and Dr. Watson chasing the silhouette of Jack the Ripper through a narrow Whitechapel alley. Everyone knew that the investigating officers on that case were Reid, Moore, Andrews, McWilliam and Swanson, but had Holmes and Watson been more than fictional, the Ripper case would surely have been solved. The background detail was amazing: the cobblestone street, the crumbling brick archway, the prostitute with ennui in a doorway, the bony dog by a trash heap. There was still some un-inked skin left on her right leg. What to go there? Some humorous murder scene from *Midsomer Murders*? Or something lugubrious from *George Gently*, *Inspector Morse*, or an Adam Dalgliesh mystery? Maybe she was overdoing it with British murders. Maybe something American, like from *NCIS*? Yes, definitely. Yes, a tat of that hot computer specialist, Timothy McGee. The back door opened and Denny and new trooper entered, so she quickly buttoned her sleeve. She spit her spent bubble gum into a metal trashcan and stuffed two new pieces into her mouth.

Chewing energetically, she returned to the Randall Allaway murder investigation. Allaway, upon returning from Vietnam, had not sought a college education but had instead worked as a crabber. He later used his GI Bill to fund the education of his granddaughter, Alexandra. He had married numerous times. None of the ex-wives lived anywhere near Maryland. Four lived abroad and two were deceased. #exwivesoffthehook

Benjamin Hancock and Randall Allaway were both infantry in Vietnam. Hancock was released for a head injury and psychological reasons at approximately the same time as Allaway's leg injury. Two decades after his return from

Vietnam, Hancock had attended the local community college in the evenings to obtain a degree in mathematics.

According to Hancock's college transcript, he was in his mid-forties when he took his first college math course, College Algebra. In the same Tuesday evening class, was the twenty-five-year-old biology major, Franklin Whitby.

There are no coincidences where murders are involved, Lisa had heard over the countless years of watching murder mysteries with her mother. There are no coincidences. She reviewed the two men's transcripts from that fall semester. Hancock, a part-time student, received an A in his math course. Whitby had taken a full course load: College Algebra, General Biology, Inorganic Chemistry, Introduction to Social Issues, and Art History I. In all of the courses, he'd earned Cs and Ds.

There was no evidence, so far, that the paths of Randall Allaway and Franklin Whitby had ever crossed. Yet Benjamin Hancock and Franklin Whitby had sat in the same classroom every Tuesday for an entire semester. Had something happened that fall semester that led to a carving knife in Randall Allaway's heart twenty-six years later?

Giles Blood-hand Day

Will lifted Carly off the back of a worn-out pony and slung her onto his shoulders. It would be an impossible wait to get into one of the restaurants. Besides, Carly was always fidgety in lines, so a lunch of pizza or hot dogs at a concession stand would have to do. They strode from the village green, across the bridge to the pier. In the distance was Randy Allaway's house.

It was a daunting task to identify all of the different fingerprints in his house. The house had been River Glen Party Central for decades. The villagers, most of whom he'd known since boyhood, had willingly offered up their fingerprints. Alan and Jacob's fingerprints were there. Currently there was a long line outside their seafood restaurant and bar. On the night of Randy's murder they had been catering a retirement party in Delaware. The Hoffman's Dockside Café was also hopping. Alice and Harry's fingerprints were all over the place as well, but on the night of the murder they had been hosting a bridge tournament at their home. The fingerprints of Gary Smyth from Smyth's Marina were all over the *Vital Spark*, because he'd been tuning up the engine, but they were not found in the house. Both Marv and Sue Denniston's prints were in the house, but on the night of the murder they'd been busy with a rowdy hen party that had rented out the rooms in their B&B. Luna's prints were there also. On the night of the murder, she was hosting a séance for the mayor and his family.

A security camera on the bridge had revealed none of those villagers crossing the bridge, either by foot or by car, or heading down the river road on the night of Randy's murder. Still, all of them had boats, and so could have cruised down the river to Randy's dock. But they were all life-long friends. Motive? None—that whole line of thinking was absurd.

The following afternoon, around three pm, the footage had showed Alex Allaway inching across the bridge to avoid the workers affixing Giles banners and pyrate flags to the lampposts. Her car windows were down, her hand tapping on the side mirror to some unheard music.

And then there were the unknown fingerprints. Only on the beer cans, CD and CD case, and empty coffee cup. Not on the doorknobs, counters, refrigerator—nowhere else. The knife that struck the single fatal blow had been wiped clean of fingerprints. The alcohol and the narcotics, two depressants, would have certainly made Randy groggy. There was no evidence that he'd attempted to defend himself. And in his haste, had the killer forgotten to take his CD? Beer cans? Coffee cup? Was the killer Frank Whitby and, as Lisa had inferred, in flight? Now, on top of everything else, they'd need to check with Border Control to see if Whitby had left the country.

If the police could just get in touch with Ben Hancock ... the old man certainly could provide an accurate timeline of Randy's movements in the past few days. Old Ben's absence was unnerving. Why wasn't he answering his cell phone? Dott Garski had confirmed that Ben was en route to see her. Will could only hope that that was the case. Randy and Old Ben were inseparable friends. If Randy knew about Whitby's dumped car, then Ben knew about it too.

Suddenly it dawned on him. Security cameras! Bridges! He whipped his phone from his vest pocket. Lisa always answered immediately. "Lisa," he whispered, "I have a really bad feeling about Ben not answering his phone. Can you get the footage from the Bay Bridge? Check to see when Ben's sailboat passed under the bridge? Look for a West Wight Potter sailboat named *Star Gazer*. It's all white with a single mast. Ben spoke with Harry Hoffman on the day of the murder. Ben said he was going sailing. If we can locate his boat, we'll at least know that Ben's okay, that Whitby hasn't found him."

"On it!" Lisa rang off.

Carly tugged on his pyrate sash. "Can I have a chili dog and cotton candy?"

"Sure, honey."

They purchased food at a concession stand and wandered toward the dancers. The band was playing "Brown Eyed Girl." That song never appealed much to him because his weakness had always been for green-eyed girls. Alex Allaway and Gillian White were on the edge of the dock, beyond the bandstand.

"Let's go meet some high school friends of mine."

"Okay," Carly said.

Gillian waved to him. She was still a looker. Her job as a personal trainer at the River Glen fitness center kept her trim and fit. She was always good for a few laughs. He could use a laugh right now, since his thoughts were mired in the murder investigation. Could Frank Whitby be a double murderer and have killed both Randy and Old Ben?

"What a sweet little wench!" Gillian said to Carly.

"Wench, Daddy?" .

"I'll explain when you're fifteen," he said.

Carly giggled and pointed toward the harbor. "Look at that funny lady, swimming in her costume!"

Will's mood plummeted. Laura Braden was doing the breaststroke between the boats. Jay pushed through the crowd to intercept her at the bridge.

"And look at that!" Carly said. "That pyrate is Giles' sister!"

Will's eyes shot up to the banner flapping in the breeze. The resemblance was startling. The same jet black hair and incandescent green eyes. The pyrate Carly pointed to was Alex Allaway.

"Too many fucking pyrates." Clyde Whitby scowled at the packed pub. "Had to close the shops for the weekend. None of my men wanted to come to work this weekend. Instead they wanted to play dress-up like a bunch of fairies."

"I have no gripes about the festival," said Miles Harlow, the bartender. "This weekend alone puts me in the black every year. So what made you brave the crowds today?"

"The wife. Thinks she's going to make her fortune selling homemade jewelry." Clyde squinted out the window to his wife's craft table. No fucking way was he going to leave his wife in the presence of rich lawyers from Washington and Annapolis. His first two wives had run off with not so much as a good-bye. No fucking way was he losing a third. He pointed toward to the edge of the pier. "Is that John Wilkins' boy?"

Miles craned his head around the beer taps. "Yeah, it's Will. Shame about that knee. He was a shoe-in for the NFL. I was hoping he'd play for the Ravens. They could use a tight-end that can block."

"Who are the gals with him?"

"The child is Will's daughter, Carly. I don't know the one with the green parrot, but she's a pretty thing, ain't she?"

"Yup. And the one with the black dog?"

Miles's face saddened. "My heart bleeds for that girl. It's Alex Allaway."

"Allaway? Any relation to the Allaway that was murdered?"

"His granddaughter. There are a lot of broken-hearted women in this town right now. That old Randy was a charmer. I gotta get clean mugs." Miles departed for the kitchen.

"Interesting, very fucking interesting," Clyde muttered to himself. He positioned his hand into a pistol and blew on his finger, the gun barrel. "How very fucking convenient that

Frank mysteriously disappears and a fucking Allaway steals his job."

Jay Braden readjusted his sunglasses to avoid the afternoon glare. He prayed that none of the boaters would be drunk or stupid enough to turn on their engines. Please God, just let her swim between the boats, without getting carved up by some goddamn outboard engine! She continued to swim gracefully through the harbor. With any luck, she'd hear him, swim to the river's edge and he could walk her safely home.

Of course he'd be a spectacle when he called down to her, the tipsy tourists in their boats no doubt howling with laughter at him, the man with the wife who dove off the pier in her pyrate gown. But the villagers of River Glen, watching in embarrassed silence, knew better. He was the cop with the crazy wife. The cop whose wife had been arrested when she'd stripped and swam in the Union Square fountain in Baltimore, who'd screamed out in panic that there were terrorists on the plane during their thirtieth anniversary trip to Paris, who in New York had tried to climb on stage and join the chorus line of *A Chorus Line* ... who'd tried to slit her wrists. The idea was that the quiet house on the promontory in River Glen, outside the chaos of Baltimore, with the slow river in which she could swim, would have healing, restorative powers. Now he was sure of nothing.

He waited for Laura's approach. Thankfully she'd maneuvered through the clutter of boats unscathed. How beautiful she was when she swam! There was no fear of her drowning. In college she was a state champion in both the breaststroke and freestyle.

The day nurse, Mrs. Pulacki, was a godsend who vigilantly watched Laura during the day. Since hiring the cantankerous old woman, there'd been no mishaps. Laura liked the nurse and her Eastern European cooking, but his latest concern was that Laura was slipping out of the house at night. On his watch, or while he slept, she'd wandered outside. And more than once—he was sure of it.

He scanned the festival once again. By the band on the pier, Will was dancing with an athletic woman with a green parrot on her shoulder. Carly was holding the front paws of Alex Allaway's manic dog and dancing with him. Alex was seated alone at a nearby table, looking as if she was going to burst into tears at any minute. His attention returned to Laura. She was now within earshot under the bridge.

"Laura!" He waved. "Up here."

She turned and floated on her back. She smiled her enchanting smile, and waved back. His heart leapt. There was momentary clarity in her eyes.

"Time me, coach. I bet I can make it back to the house in less than three minutes," she said.

"You're dragging twenty pounds of wet velvet," he reminded her. "Please come out of the water and we'll walk home."

"Time me, spoil sport."

"One, two, three ... go!"

"You're not even looking at your watch. I'm serious, time me."

"Okay, when the small hand gets to the twelve." He studied his watch. "Now ... go!"

She turned quickly and swam through the water, freestyle. He walked briskly off the bridge. He'd have to follow the shoreline across a number of waterfront properties, but no one in River Glen would mind. He cut across the lawn of the Dennistons' B&B. There was clarity in his wife's eyes and voice. Maybe they might have a barbecue on the deck, sit in the hot tub, watch the sun set over the Chesapeake, listen to their favorite jazz CDs, make love for the first time since ... who could remember the last time she wasn't delusional.

His listlessness, the malaise of the past few weeks, seemed to lift. Perhaps, finally, his beloved Laura was healing. Maybe the new medication from her psychiatrist, Dr. Richmond, was finally working. Maybe he could finally concentrate on his work, the Allaway case, and mentor Wilkins and Paco, the young detectives assigned to his charge. There was a renewed vigor in his step. He checked the time and looked out to the river. The weight of the fabric slowed her down, but still she persisted. How wonderful to have his old Laura return to him—his beautiful, vibrant Laura!

He crossed the yards of the Culps, Larsens, and Wynskis and walked along the shore path out to the promontory. She'd be exhausted after such a swim. Maybe she'd want her favorite dinner, steak and cheddar cheese mashed potatoes. She'd become frighteningly thin.

He waited on his dock as she paddled toward shore. Somewhere down the river, the black hat with the orange feather had disappeared. She struggled into the shallows, black and purple velvet in her wake. She bent over, her hands on her knees.

"What was my time?" she gasped.

He reached down and pulled her up the grassy slope. He glanced at his watch. Seven minutes and forty seconds. "Two minutes and fifty nine seconds, a new world's record. Congratulations!"

"Really?" Her delighted squeal sounded like a schoolgirl. "Was I really that fast, Coach Browner?"

He paused. Coach Browner was Laura's swim coach in college. He looked to see if she was kidding, but there was no jest in her face.

Instead Laura gazed at their house, completely befuddled. "Coach, can you tell me the way to the women's locker room? I don't remember."

This day's a complete disaster, Alex thought. It had started with the shot of rum in Papa's kitchen and the wine tasting with Gillian. Next, Jim Pitcher from the Pitcher Family Vineyard brought her a mammoth glass of merlot while expressing his condolences about Papa. To absorb the alcohol, she tried to eat a Philly pretzel, but she was so tense that salivation was impossible. The warm wine, hot sun, and body heat from the crowd made her woozy. She didn't trust herself. It was best to sit quietly by herself.

Will had asked to her dance. Why was that so distracting? Of course, she'd said no. How would it look to be dancing only days after Papa's murder? But she'd wanted to say "Yes, yes, yes!" She'd wanted to dance ... dance wildly, spinning, leaping, holding nothing back. Unrestrained and orgiastic, primal dancing, fueled by rum and wine on an empty stomach.

Thankfully, Gillian had saved the day. "I would love to dance. Especially since my days of dancing with beautiful men are nearing their end." She'd grabbed Will and Carly's hands and pulled them to the bandstand. Gillian was getting married next month to another personal trainer from the gym.

Though Alex wasn't sure why—it was the wine, definitely the wine—she watched Will amidst the twirling tourists. His costume was a red bandana and skull and crossbones eye patch, and a shiny red and black vest, with no shirt underneath. It was a great costume, though the orange and blue running shoes detracted from the brigand look. He had sculptured arms, nice pecs and abs. The pinhead had grown out of the lanky gawkiness that characterizes most teenage boys to Hot. But that was just the booze talking.

Why had Gillian brought up that double date? Alex hadn't thought of that night in ages; now it was the only thing on her mind. Don't think about it. She turned toward Harlow's Pub. Were Papa here, he'd be buying drinks for the tourist women at the bar, while taciturn Old Ben would be fixed on the Orioles game. If she could only talk to Old Ben ...

A shadow loomed over Alex.

"Is that your dog?" The voice shrilled from a strawberry blonde hair with black roots.

Alex leapt to her feet. "No, ur—"

"Get it the fuck off my dog!"

Tourists at the adjacent tables tittered. Water Boy was humping a white, poofy something. Alex yanked him off.

"The dog's tied to your chair! Whose is it?" Black Roots ranted.

"My grandfather's."

"I want to talk to him immediately! My Betsy is a Pekingnese with champion bloodlines! If your fucking mutt knocks up my Betsy ..."

"Mutt? He's a full-bred lab!"

"Does he have papers from the Kennel Club? Is he neutered?"

"How the hell do I know? He's not my dog!"

Black Roots stamped her foot. "I want to talk to your grandfather right now!"

"My grandfather's dead!"

"Then I want your cell number!" She puffed beer breath into Alex's face. "If he knocks up Betsy, the litter's showing up on your doorstep!"

"No way I'm giving my number to a lunatic!"

"You fucking better!"

"Betsy's an ugly slut!" Alex glared down at Water Boy. "And you have no taste!"

Black Roots' eyes bulged. "W-w-what did you just say?"

Alex's fists clenched. "Ugly! Slut!"

"You are so fucking dead!" She grabbed Alex's dress.

Will stepped from the crowd of dancers. "Get your hands off her."

"Get lost, freak!" Black Roots barked. "This isn't your business!"

He pulled his badge from his pocket. "Police. Please get your hands off her."

The crowd fell quiet. Suddenly a rich laugh filled the silence. All eyes turned. Seated alone at a table near a bollard was an older woman. She tipped back in her chair and clapped. "Bravo! Absolutely brilliant!"

Headquarters

Lisa Paco stared at a Google image of a West Wight Potter 19 sailboat to commit it to memory. She had an encyclopedic memory, like Sherlock. The cook, Harry Hoffman, had told Will that Ben was going sailing but would be back for a bridge tournament that same night. Why had Ben told Harry that when his real intent was to sail to Norfolk and take Dott Garski on a cruise to the Bahamas? #unsettlinginconsistency

The Maryland Transportation Authority had security cameras along the Chesapeake Bay Bridge and Lisa downloaded the footage. Since she had no idea when the conversation between Ben and Harry had taken place, she started watching the footage from early Thursday morning, the day of Randall Allaway's murder.

It was a tedious exercise, staring at an expanse of grey-blue bay with an occasional whitecap when the wind picked up. She played a few games of Candy Crush on her smartphone while a few cargo vessels and tugboats headed north toward Baltimore. While she checked Facebook, two fishing boats anchored under the bridge. While a speedboat pulled a water-skier under the bridge, she read the synopsis on the BBC's website about the next episode of *Endeavor*. Ridiculous ... too easy ... the murderer was clearly the Vice Chancellor at Oxford University. The writer gave far too much away. She posted a selfie on Instagram of her amazingly cool uniform. She focused back on the footage; still nothing resembling a West Wight Potter.

How long did it take—to sail from the Glen River to the Bay Bridge? A few hours? A day? Nothing about boats and the water was remotely interesting. She'd barely passed the swimming test at the Police Academy. But one simple thing she did know. It took longer to sail into the wind.

She spit her gum into the metal trashcan, opened two new pieces, and checked the NOAA weather report for the Thursday of the murder. The prevailing winds were from the south-east, which would have slowed Ben's progress. She checked into the Murder Room Chat Room, but no one with half a sleuthing brain was online. She fast-forwarded through the footage, chewing intently. Even at night, the bridge and water were well illuminated. For several hours, she played and replayed the footage, observing every single commercial and personal watercraft from the Thursday morning of the murder to that Saturday afternoon. By day's end, Lisa was sure of it. Benjamin Hancock's West Wight Potter had never passed under the Chesapeake Bay Bridge en route to Norfolk, Virginia.

Giles Blood-hand Day

I knew it ... just knew it! Alex told herself. It was a bad, no, horrible mistake to go the pyrate festival in her current state of mind. She'd completely lost her marbles, and most publicly on the dock in front of the entire world. It would probably be on the evening news and on all forms of social media. But thank God for Will Wilkins, who'd threatened to arrest that bitch who owned the bitch for a drunk and disorderly if she persisted in shrieking about mixed breed puppies.

"Alex, go home. I'll handle this." Thank you, Will! She and Water Boy had dashed from the crowd and crossed the bridge to the river road. How does one thank a cop? With a thank-you card to his office? She should let Richard know of her ordeal. No, terrible idea. That would only make things worse. She picked up a stick from the roadside and presented it to Water Boy to chew on instead of her heel. "And you, you horny little bastard, are no help."

The cars were beginning to clear from Ben and Papa's property. She and the dog headed toward the dock, all the while facts dangled, disconnected from one another like objects on a mobile. A slain grandfather, a piece of eight, mysterious code from Old Ben and then the weird observation by Carly. Were any of these things connected? There was a resemblance between her and Giles Blood-hand, but that was purely coincidence. The pyrate was merely a cleverly concocted legend to attract money to the region. There were Allaways and Whitbys all over the town cemetery, but no one with the name Giles Blood-hand, or Giles Anything Else.

The rocking tugboat and a cup of tea would calm her. She entered the *Vital Spark* and booted up her laptop. She typed Giles Blood-hand into the search box and was directed to Wikipedia. Giles' image was the same as on the banners all over town. She half-expected to read about a savvy advertising campaign by the River Glen town council to attract money to the village, but instead she read:

"Giles Ian Hale (1663-1702) aka Giles Blood-hand, a minor pyrate during the Golden Age of Pyracy."

Incredible ... Giles was a historical person! Papa had said that he was real, but she'd presumed it to be another one of his fantastical stories.

She scrolled to the references at the bottom of the webpage, and clicked on a history dissertation, "The Pyrates of the Chesapeake: The Pre-Secessionist Years," written by one Levon Bakanian, currently an assistant professor of history at the University of Virginia. There were a few paragraphs written about Giles Hale.

Born in Aberdeen, Scotland, illegitimate son of a servant girl, Molly Brodie, and Sir Edmund Hale. Giles was convicted of murder and incarcerated at Old Tolbooth until the jailbreak of December 1684. He escaped with four others: James Lancer,

Charles Allaway, and two brothers, Neville and Conall Whitby.

Allaway? Whitby? She shifted in her seat.

The five companions resurfaced two years later in Tortuga and joined the pyrate captain Bartholomew "the Hangman" Dodd and the crew of the *Raven*. On May 1688 the *Raven* intercepted the Spanish galleon, *Espíritu de la Virgen*, near current Tampa, Florida. Reputedly, a month later, Hale, Allaway, and the Whitbys instigated a mutiny and commandeered the *Raven*. James Lancer was not alive during the uprising because he'd died of gangrene after a knife fight in Jamaica the year before. Bart "the Hangman" was fed to sharks off the Florida Keys. Then the *Raven* fled ...

Water Boy barked. Alex leaned back in her chair to see the deck. He was furiously leaping up on the gunwale. "What now?" she sighed. Was Detective Braden's crazy wife back on her dock?

The dock was empty and the cars had cleared from the river road and her property. Water Boy continued to yip. He'd spotted a woman pulling a rolling suitcase behind her. It was probably a tourist walking to the Point where there were picnic tables, a gazebo, and a scenic view of the bay.

Wait a minute—it was that older woman from near the bollard, whose arms had been splayed across the back of the adjacent chairs ... who'd guffawed at her plight on the village dock. "Bravo! Absolutely brilliant!" she'd said in her Scottish brogue.

Leah Devlin

On the water

The *Star Gazer* bounced over the waves of the Atlantic. Old Ben tucked the tiller under his arm as he poured coffee from a thermos. He could barely hold the metal cup still. His hands had been shaky for weeks through all the preparations. Shaky like they were when he returned from Vietnam. Then he'd been all jitters and stammers. The slightest sound had made him leap from his skin.

Ben's platoon had been mired in some godforsaken jungle near La Drang when he first met Randy Allaway. For months, maybe a year, he'd muddled about in a mist of depression. Which was worse—it was a toss up—his brutal father or his CO? Whether in Oklahoma or Nam, his was a living hell of violent men. Were he a college boy, or the son of a Senator, he wouldn't be stuck in a shithole of mud, excrement, and blood. There wasn't a warmongering bone in his body; the weaponry, explosions, everything, were terrifying. His smothering tent of nine others was momentarily empty. Thank you, God, a few minutes to himself, a few minutes of quiet and peace!

His solitude ended when Randy Allaway bent between the flaps of the tent. Ben had been reassigned to this tent a few days earlier, when all of Tent Eight, except him and Luis Garcia from New Mexico, had been killed in an ambush. It had taken Ben only seconds to realize that Allaway was a chancer. His strategy was to avoid the Marylander at all costs, so he had pretended to be asleep. As Allaway fumbled in his duffle bag, Ben watched from under his pillow. Allaway's nose was covered in a bandage. He'd broken it in a fight with the private from Montana, while "defending the honor of the red-headed nurse from Kentucky." Right, yeah.

He was trying to get into her pants, like all of them. If anyone would succeed, it would be Allaway. No doubt the broken nose would require many visits to the nurses' tent to insure that it was healing properly.

Allaway sifted marijuana into a ragged piece of paper. Ben expected him to slide the joint along the tip of this tongue, but instead he pulled a flask from underneath his pillow. He pushed his finger into the flask, and slid it along the joint, sealing it with alcohol.

"Hancock, you awake?" Allaway nudged his cot with his muddy boot.

Ben was taller than the Marylander and the other men by nearly six inches, so no one messed with him. "I am now, asshole," he groaned.

Allaway grinned, undeterred. "Hawaiian. The best I've ever had." He lit the joint and inhaled. "Here's the secret. Always seal the joint with scotch. McClellands from Islay, when I can get it." He handed it across the narrow space that separated their cots. "You'll notice a taste of peat, seaweed, and sea salt."

Ben lifted himself onto his elbow. "Anything to stop the ringing in my ears. A mortar went off right by ... I think it shattered my ear drum." He inhaled deeply and held the smoke in until his lungs burned. He passed the joint back to Allaway.

Allaway inhaled and blew smoke into a clothesline of moldy socks strung above them. "You know, Hancock, the finest thing in life is a stack of crabs in Old Bay spices, and ice cold beer, all culminating with a glass of Scotch whiskey. Neat. With the sun dropping over the glistening Chesapeake." He smiled again. Allaway had a rare quality: an unburdened, reckless affability.

All of the soldiers had different coping mechanisms. Allaway's was simple. He dreamt of home and women. At his words, Ben was struck by an overwhelming sadness. Never had he experienced a moment ... or a place ... of pure pleasure and beauty. After Nam, if he survived, he'd travel to far and exotic places, places of mystery, wonderment, and inexpressible beauty. He'd never tasted a crab, never seen the Chesapeake, and scotch, forget it. With what his skinflint father paid him, he could barely scrounge change for a beer at the tavern.

Upon discharge months later, Randy had said, "Come home with me, Ben. River Glen's a quiet place. You can crab with me, while you settle down. Then you can decide what you want to do."

At the time he was too scrambled to think on his own. He knew only one thing. There was no going back to Oklahoma.

"My family's lived there for ... who knows ... maybe centuries. All of them pyrates!" Randy had jested.

At the time Ben had grave doubts about fixing his star to his tent-mate's, as he was always mixed up in some mischief. And the idea of working on a boat was ludicrous. The only time he'd seen salt water was when he'd shipped from San Diego to Nam. His entire world was cornfields, farm equipment, and a town consisting of a parched main street. But with no other plan in mind, he followed Randy to River Glen. He surprised himself, as he took to the water with the instincts of a hatchling turtle. The water had a healing effect on his PTSD.

Those early years in River Glen were now blurred; crabbing during the days, catching a buzz on Randy's porch in the evenings. The shakes and jitters disappeared and bits of confidence emerged. Then all that changed during the week of the Arts Festival, some fifty years before. The production at the village playhouse was *Othello*. Desdemona unfurled on the stage and Randy's eyes fixed on her like a hunting dog's. So did his own. The actress was breathtaking: a raven-haired, green-eyed stunner. Randy fumbled through the playbill, searching for her name.

"Look, Ben!" Randy had whispered. "Hale. That's a Scottish name like Allaway!"

The actress' Scottish lilt sealed the deal; her words danced and skipped like a butterfly through the air of the small playhouse. Randy had rushed backstage to introduce himself, and hosted the entourage for a week of parties, very stoned parties. It was 1967, after all. When the theatrical group packed up and moved on its way, the actress, Julia, promised she would return. "When I've finished the tour." Ben had his doubts. She was too gorgeous and talented to settle down in a fishing village on the Chesapeake. But some months later, he and Randy were motoring their crab boat up the river, and there it was. At Randy's dock floated a red and blue tugboat with Julia aboard, waving with great drama and fanfare. She was also quite pregnant. A year after the birth of her and Randy's son, she disappeared once again. Urgent matters to attend to back in Aberdeen, she'd said. That was the last they'd seen of Julia Hale. Randy and he were suddenly two young men raising a small boy. Father and son, Colin, were polar opposites: Randy, gregarious and free-spirited, Colin introspective and silent, content to sit on the porch with a book. Those years blurred. Colin had grown up, studied architecture at Penn, and remained in Philadelphia. He married a civil rights lawyer named Carole Lowe, and they had a daughter.

Ben swallowed down the rest of his coffee and secured the tiller. The breeze was brisk. He was making good time. He walked to the navigation station, stepping over the axe and buzz saw and studied the GPS. At the current speed, he'd make the rendezvous point with Dott as scheduled.

One singular event, one singular day, twenty-six years ago had led him to this place off the coast of New Jersey. It was the day before Thanksgiving. That day he recalled with crystal clarity. The infant Alexandra was napping in the spare bedroom. He and Randy were in the kitchen preparing dishes for the feast and listening to Randy's favorite, *Dark Side of the Moon.*

Colin had said to his father, "Carole and I are going to run to the grocery store to get more gravy. And pick up some wine. I can't drink your home-made stuff."

"Ben and I'll watch the baby." Never were more portentous words spoken.

Two grim-faced policemen arrived less than an hour later. "There's been an accident up the road ..."

Giles Blood-hand Day

Jay Braden looked longingly at his Boston Whaler floating on the Glen River. If he could find a quiet inlet upriver, drop his fishing pole into a silent pool of water ... that's all he'd need, a secluded place to hide for a few hours. It was an increasing challenge to settle Laura after such episodes. Hopefully she'd be asleep by now, in the spare room that she now preferred. And it was taking longer to settle himself. His nightly gin and tonics were now drunk out of beer mugs. He opened the sliding glass door and lifted the damp heap of black and purple velvet from the deck. Laura had decided to strip out of her gown outside, insisting on "undressing in the women's locker with the girls." His urging to go inside proved futile. Thank God for the relative privacy of the promontory. He turned his gaze toward the village where the crowds were finally dissipating. And thank God for the quirky little town of River Glen where almost anything goes, a village of artists, artisans, crabbers, fishermen and random oddballs, more accepting than most to a woman spiraling into madness. His mood darkened. And one of them was a murderer. Randall Allaway had most definitely known his killer; he'd let him in, played his CD, possibly drunk and drugged with him. Or her?

And he, Detective Jay Braden, could barely focus on the case! At the festival, Will had briefly mentioned his and Lisa's new leads, and the information had gone in one ear and out the other. His soul, his spirit, Jay feared, was withering and turning to dust.

He passed through the slider into the family room. Laura had decided to rearrange the books on the shelves according to color. Now each shelf was a color spectrum, going from warm to cool colors, and always from left to right. And something was vexing her about lampshades. Every lampshade in the house had been removed, as they were "blocking cosmic energy particles." At every turn his bloodshot eyes were assaulted by the glare of bare light bulbs. And there was the living room furniture in the dining room, and the dining room set in the living room. And forget about watching the new large screen TV. The clickers were now at the bottom of the hot tub. This was his new normal.

He lumbered down the basement stairs to the laundry area and lifted the lid of the washing machine. He stuffed the gown inside and poured in the laundry detergent. Something didn't look right. The black rubber tube that drained the soapy water from the washing machine into the sink was missing. He looked inside the dryer and into the crack between the washer and dryer. No rubber tube. He scanned his workbench. Nothing there either. He got down on his hands and knees and pressed his head between the machines and the cinderblock wall. A piece of clothing was lodged behind the dryer. He reached to retrieve it. The fabric was dry and stiff. It had been there for some time. He lifted himself off the floor, shook out the material and held it up for inspection. It was a long white night shirt with red sleeves. Definitely not Laura's, nor her style, but that of a young woman, a college student. *Maryland Terrapins* was written across the chest. Then he noticed. His eyes jumped back and forth in panic between two singular features, maroon stripes of blood near the shoulders, and a name written in black pen at the neckline. A. Allaway.

"Wait. Wait!" Alex ran down the dock.

The woman hefted her rolling suitcase onto Papa's front porch.

"Please wait!" It was probably one of Papa's countless girlfriends from Harlow's needing a place to stay. *This is all I need right now*, Alex sighed.

The woman strode back and forth across the porch, like a queen surveying her kingdom. Hands on hips, she leaned back, stretching out her back. "Well, don't just stand there, lass. Take my bag up to my room."

"Excuse me?"

"I know you're not deaf. You could hear just fine on that pier. You have quite the mouth, love. I've heard dogs called a lot of things, but never ugly slut. Truly priceless. Well … don't just stand there like an imbecile. Get my bag upstairs. My back's weary from all the walking today."

Alex remained at the bottom step. Definitely a lost old woman, a very bossy one. "I think you're looking for the Dennistons' B&B. I'm happy to show you where it is."

"Don't treat me like a doddering old fool. Fine." The woman slung her suitcase through the screen door.

"Whoa! Stop! You can't just go into someone's house." Alex rushed up the stairs.

"My house, love," the woman said over her shoulder. "I bought this house with my last husband." Her luggage thudded onto the floor. She moved—no, it was an arrogant strut—to the spot where Papa's recliner had been. She gazed with ghoulish fascination. "So it was here. Yes, most certainly here."

"I'm sorry, ma'am, but you're going to have to leave." Alex held the door open.

Exasperated, the woman pulled off her sunglasses. "Now, Alexandra ..."

Alex stared into her own face, fifty years in the future. "You're the JAllaway that Old Ben said would come."

"Ben, lovely Ben." The woman's eyes narrowed to crafty green slits. "You, darling, have something that's mine."

Alex tilted her chair to the porthole. Julia Allaway was still on the porch, vigilant and sly-eyed, watching her and the *Vital Spark*. Incidentally, Julia said the tugboat was also hers, but Alex would be permitted to live on it for a while ... well, thank you very much. Julia was smoking a slender cigar from a black cigarette holder, drinking Papa's scotch and throwing sticks to the dog. Perfect ... now to go along with the crazy dog was a crazy old lady, allegedly her grandmother.

"I've been around the world many times, Alexandra, darling. I've known sultans, sorcerers, wizards, and kings," Julia had boasted in her musical lilt. She did have a great voice and she knew it, which was why she loved to talk. About herself.

"Yeah, yeah, and I know the man-in-the-moon," she had quipped.

"Hackneyed response, Alexandra, but that's to be expected from a product of the American educational system."

By now Alex was quite sure she couldn't stand the woman. "You deserted Papa and your son, Colin, if you even remember his name, when he was one year old."

"That's harsh. And that's water over the bridge."

"Water *under* the bridge, or *over* the dam."

"So now we're the clever the one!" Julia had laughed condescendingly.

Alex knocked another aspirin out of the bottle and swallowed it down with chamomile tea. If she could just forget the entire conversation, the entire day, she could refocus her attention on Bakanian's dissertation in her laptop. She'd left off at the part where Bart the Hangman was fed to sharks off the Florida Keys. Then the *Raven* had fled up the eastern seaboard, robbing coastal villages before heading into the Chesapeake. The pyrates settled in the upper Chesapeake in the area now known as River Glen. And that was it. The next section of Bakanian's dissertation was on the Spanish pyrate, Juan Carlos del Castillo, who operated briefly at the mouth of the James River in the southern Chesapeake.

Alex inched toward the porthole again. Julia waved and smiled with that obnoxious grin. Julia Hale-Allaway. Alex's knees had nearly collapsed when Julia said that her maiden name was Hale. Alex typed the words "Hale Clan Scotland" into the search engine. Information on the family history immediately appeared. Julia Hale. Giles Hale. Randy Allaway. Charles Allaway. Frank Whitby. Neville and Conall Whitby.

This nebulous family history was the reason that Julia Hale-Allaway had returned to River Glen after fifty years, Alex was sure of it. And something was encrypted in the two papers from Papa and Old Ben that she'd denied any knowledge of. She'd dismissed Julia with an innocent shrug ... "What papers?" Julia had glared back, annoyed and distrusting.

Alex stepped onto the deck and whistled for Water Boy. He trotted down the dock. She tossed a dog treat behind the crab traps and barricaded him in for the night. Puffy rain clouds were moving up the bay. She slid aside a crab trap and he dashed out of the enclosure. "Inside, but you're not sleeping in my bed."

"Better dogs than men, darling!" Julia shouted with a boisterous laugh. She flung a goodnight kiss skyward, her hand like a leaf on the wind. She disappeared into Papa's house.

That treacherous old bat made Alex want to hide under the covers, but there was one more chore before bed. She went onto the website for the History Department at UVA and located the webpage for Levon Bakanian, Ph.D., and typed an email:

> Dear Dr. Bakanian,
> I'm a resident of River Glen, Maryland, and the granddaughter of an Allaway and a Hale, and am

researching my family genealogy. I read a part of your dissertation that was online, and am wondering if you might have any information about what happened to Charles Allaway and Giles Hale once they settled in River Glen, circa 1690. Any information is greatly appreciated.

Sincerely, Alex Allaway

SEND.

Chapter 4

Day 4

River Glen

Alex jerked her head toward the wall. "Your breath's atrocious." Water Boy pressed his nose into her cheek and licked her neck. "Down. Down. Off the bed." There was splashing in the river. She rose from the berth and peered through the porthole. Julia was skinny-dipping off Papa's beach. "You have my permission to bite her." She let the dog off the boat out to pee, while she prepared herself breakfast and turned on her laptop. An email from Dr. Bakanian was waiting. No surprise there; most academics are online and working 24-7.

> Dear Ms. Allaway,
>
> Pretty amazing to be a descendent of both an Allaway and a Hale! I made a research trip to the National Library in Edinburgh recently and found some interesting documents, but it's too lengthy for an email. Feel free to call me. I'm in my office all day today. My cell's below.
>
> Regards, Levon

Alex glanced out the porthole again. Julia was inspecting Papa's tiger lilies. Alex reached for her cell phone. It was almost nine o'clock. She'd chance it. She pressed Bakanian's number into her phone. It was answered immediately.

"Hello," said a pleasant voice.

"Hi. I'm Alex, who sent you the email last night. Thanks for getting back to me so soon."

"I thought it might be you. I don't get many calls on a Sunday morning. So tell me, how are you both a Hale and an Allaway?"

"I was raised here in River Glen by my grandfather, Randy Allaway. My father was Colin Allaway. Then yesterday, this woman appears out of nowhere, claiming to be my long lost grandmother from Aberdeen, Scotland. Her last name is Hale."

"It's possible," the professor said. "The Hales are originally from England; however, a number of them are in Scotland. Giles Hale was from the Scottish lineage."

"There have always been Allaways and Whitbys around River Glen, but no Hales that I know of."

"There's a reason for that," he said ominously.

'That doesn't sound good."

"Giles Hale, Charles Allaway, and the Whitby brothers were a vicious bunch. They were convicts who cast their lot together at Old Tolbooth Prison in Edinburgh, a truly dismal place. They then fled to the Caribbean. After they killed Bart Dodd and took over the *Raven*, they pillaged up the coast of the Carolinas. In Virginia they razed a farm and freed the indentured female servants, most of them convicts from the slums of London and Dublin. So you can imagine the atmosphere in colonial River Glen, where the pyrates and their new brides set up camp. They disassembled the *Raven* to build shelters and survived by fishing and hunting. Children were born, and the secluded community grew. Then there was a dispute in the village ..."

"Over what?"

"The documents didn't say, but things turned violent. Charles Allaway was killed by Neville Whitby, then Giles Hale slaughtered Whitby and his entire family. That's the reason he's called Blood-hand."

"What happened to the alleged Incan gold from the Spanish galleon?"

"Who knows? They were pyrates. I'm guessing that they drank and whored it away long before they reached the Chesapeake."

"What a fascinating account! Thanks for your time."

"The pleasure's mine. I love talking about pyrates to anyone who'll listen. By the way, there are other genealogists in River Glen who are interested in local pyrate history. I was contacted recently by Clyde Whitby. Do you know him?"

"No. When was that?"

"A few weeks ago. And another man from River Glen, but it was a while back. Years ago. Umm, Ben something?"

"Hancock?"

"That's the one. You might compare notes with them."

Headquarters

This was the time Lisa dreaded ... when the tattoo started to peel. Good-bye bright, vibrant ink. Hello infuriating itches. She unbuttoned her sleeve under her desk and scratched very slowly so that Denny and the new recruit on the weekend shift wouldn't notice. Should they ask what she was doing under her desk she might say that she had an irritating sunburn, except that she hated the outdoors and any location away from her laptop. Sun and surf ... yeah, right. Maybe she could say that she had hives? Or an allergy to ... what blooms in June? How about some highly infectious skin disease? Yes, definitely! That would keep them far away from her desk and computer. The recruit smiled at her from across the room. No, pal. She put on her headphones, turned up her music, and stared directly at the screen, as if she were thinking intently. That would be the game plan for the rest of the morning.

She opened up the database for motor vehicle violations and incidents from twenty-six years ago. In January there had been two DWIs, on the morning after New Year's Eve, though the cars involved were a Honda Civic and a Chevy pickup truck. In March, a delirious old man had driven his Caddy into a cornfield and had to be towed out of the spring mud. In June, after the prom at the River Glen High School, some graduating seniors had driven to Cooper's Beach and forgotten to engage the emergency brake. The minivan had to be pulled from the river. Some more DWIs over the summer, especially around the Fourth of July; in October a housewife arguing with her teenage son had driven her SUV into a tree, but they were unharmed.

With morbid fascination, Lisa leaned toward the computer screen. "Gotcha," she whispered. Will's questions sprang to mind: "I wonder what happened to her parents? Why was she raised by her grandfather?"

She lifted her phone, took a photo of the screen, and sent the image to Will and Jay. On Wednesday, November 24th, 1991, a Philadelphia couple had been killed on the coastal road in a car accident.

Vital Spark

River Glen

Alex put the keys to the *Vital Spark* in the ignition. The engine, she was sure, would turn over immediately because Gary Smyth from the marina tuned up the engine every spring at the start of boating season. Besides, she'd turned on the engine the day before, to check. She peered nervously through the porthole. So far, so good. There was no sign of the alleged grandmother. With any luck the old bat was in the shower after her swim and wouldn't hear Alex start the boat. Then the mooring lines could quickly be cast off and she could motor down the river and out to the bay, unnoticed. For an entire wonderful day she could cruise the Chesapeake on her own.

Water Boy barked.

"Shhh! Shut-up, Water Boy!"

She looked out the porthole again. An unfamiliar compact car pulled into Papa's driveway. Will got out, walked around the car, and removed Carly from her car seat. Carly skipped down the dock ahead of him. All hopes for a discreet escape to the bay vanished. She stepped through the hatch.

"I just wanted to see if you were alright," Will's voice boomed in greeting. Shit ... no way Julia didn't hear that. With any luck, Julia hated boats and would be content to smoke cigarettes from her pretentious cigarette holder on the Adirondack chair-turned-empress's throne, while she motored away.

"Only a headache from all the stress, and too much wine on an empty stomach. Thank you for yesterday."

"Sure. No problem."

He and Carly stepped onto the boat.

"No biting, Water Boy," Alex said. "You bite and you go to the SPCA today."

"Have you heard anything from Old Ben?" he asked.

"No. I've called him a few times, but there's been no answer. Maybe's there no satellite reception in the middle of the bay?"

"Things don't add up. Ben tells Harry Hoffman that he'll play bridge and he never shows up. He tells Dott Garski that he's sailing down to Norfolk and never sails under the Bay Bridge. There's no way he'd go the Atlantic route when it's quicker and smoother sailing down the bay." He turned his gaze toward Old Ben's cottage. "I'm going to pick up Ben's laptop."

The screen door on Papa's porch slammed.

"This person appeared yesterday," she whispered. "Supposedly my grandmother."

Will's eyebrows rose. "The woman on the pier yesterday."

She nodded. "She must have followed me. She says she's from Scotland."

"Interesting how long lost relatives always appear when there's a death. And a possible will."

"I know you're busy, but can you check to see how long she's been in the country? She says her name's Julia Hale. She says the house and boat are hers. She was skinny-dipping on the beach this morning. Can't you lock her up for indecent exposure ... for a few months or years, if possible?"

He grinned. "I'll do that."

Julia swept down the dock, her colorful skirt and blouse billowing in the breeze. Her long, black-grey hair was dripping wet, making her blouse somewhat see-through.

"Who do we have here?" Julia asked coyly. She filled the air with perfume.

Alex tightened. Great ... on top of everything else ... the confidante of sultans, kings, and wizards was a cougar.

"Will Wilkins." He looked at his daughter, petting the dog. "And my daughter, Carly."

Julia extended your hand. "Julia Hale, of the Royal Shakespeare Company."

Alex rolled her eyes. "And I'm a Nobel Laureate."

Julia smiled and let the sarcasm pass. "So, you're a police officer ..."

"Yes, I'm investigating Randall Allaway's death."

"My husband, you know," she said, without a shred of sadness.

"Ex-husband," Alex said.

"No, darling. We never divorced," Julia said.

"He had five wives after you!" Alex said.

"Did he now?" Julia chuckled. "Too late to arrest him for polygamy. Right, Will?"

"That's not funny," Alex said.

"Will, I'm afraid that Alexandra didn't inherit my or Randy's splendid sense of humor." Julia's eyes crawled all over him.

He was unfazed, used to gawkers from his days as a football prodigy. "I've got to get Carly home, and get Ben's computer to forensics. Let's go, sweetheart." He pulled a business card from his shorts pocket. "Alex, will you call me later today at this number?"

Julia snatched the card away. "She'll call you after our boat ride," she said coolly. "There's work to do now. A pleasure to meet you, Will, and you too, Carly. Now off with the two of you." She shooed them off the boat.

"Call me, Alex. Please!" he called from the dock.

"Untie those lines, Alexandra." Julia sauntered to the helm and turned the key. The engine started right up. "Call me, Alex. Please," she said, mimicking Will. "Now who's the bitch in heat?"

The Morgue

You're lower than pond scum, Jay told himself. First, he'd called Mrs. Pulacki on a weekend. She was happy to get the overtime, she'd said, instead of spending money at antique shops with her sister. The pair were fascinated by clocks from the colonial period. Worse, he'd lied to Laura. "A sudden breakthrough in the case." He'd hurried to his car the moment Mrs. Pulacki pulled into the driveway. A. Allaway's blood-streaked nightshirt was in a plastic bag in his brief case.

Dr. Zera Lim, the medical examiner, had agreed to meet him on the weekend. He'd driven like an insane man—after all, he was one—down the highway to her office. His words spilled out incoherently to her "... behind my dryer ... somehow Laura ... swims at night ... Will and Lisa can't know ... not yet ... analyze the blood stains."

The Asian doctor listened as she always did. Her glistening black eyes probing his, her head tilted slightly toward her shoulder. "It might be nothing, Jay," she said consolingly. "Laura might have picked it up anywhere."

He lifted his head from his hands, embarrassed by the outburst, the confession.

"Really, Jay. It's probably nothing," Zera repeated. "I'll check on it. No one needs to know anything about it."

He nodded. His eyes drifted from her face to her neck to breasts. He'd never seen her out of her light blue scrubs or a business suit. At the moment she wore a faded Princeton Tigers t-shirt, black workout pants, and flip-flops. She was about his age. His view moved to her immaculately organized desk with her laptop and photographs of two adult children and one grandchild. No wedding ring; no photos of a husband or significant other. If only Laura ... then he and Zera might ... Stop!

Zera must have read his mind and returned it to business. "I was going to call you tomorrow, but since you're here—" She turned on her laptop. "The completed tests from toxicology and cytology. First, the tox results. Randall Allaway had a very large quantity of a narcotic in his system, as I informed you before. We now know the specifics. It was OxyContin."

"Are you telling me that he died of a drug overdose?"

"No, not necessarily. It would depend on his level of tolerance. But the amounts were at lethal limits. And it wasn't street heroin. It was definitely OxyContin. Pills. There was no sign of inhalation or needle use."

"But no OxyContin pills were found in his house. Only over-the-counter medications. Aspirin, cough syrup and the like. There were no prescriptions of any kind. Some of Allaway's paperwork showed that he went to a VA hospital to rehab a leg after he took a bullet during Vietnam, but that was decades back. He probably self-medicated with his marijuana plants. There were no recent visits to a doctor as far as I know."

"He should have gone," she said firmly. "Because his abdomen was riddled with late stage cancer. His stomach, small intestine, pancreas, all over. I checked with the local hospital. There was no indication of him going in for any treatments, no chemo, radiation, no nothing."

"Yet someone plunged a knife into his chest."

"There's no denying that."

"Which killed him? The drug or the knife?"

"Hard to tell. Possibly simultaneous."

Silence lingered in the room while both of them mentally recreated the scene in Allaway's living room. Finally Zera stood. "I've got to go. I have some plans later."

What plans did a beautiful pathologist have on a Sunday afternoon? was his impulse to ask. He refrained.

"One last thing," She locked her office door behind them. "What's Laura's blood type?"

"B."

"And yours?"

"O."

"Okay. I'll call when I know something."

He watched Zera climb into a Porsche Boxster convertible and head off toward the highway. As he drove home, fantasizing about an afternoon in the bed of his colleague the medical examiner, he prepared to tell Laura Lie Number Two. He was pond scum, after all.

On the bay

"'If we are together nothing is impossible. If we are divided all will fall.' Who said that, Alexandra?" Julia quizzed her from the wheel of the *Vital Spark*.

"How the hell would I know?" Alex said from her slump on a crab trap.

"How do you not know that?" Julia said incredulously. "It was Winston Churchill. The greatest statesman of the twentieth century."

"That was my first guess," she muttered.

"Americans have such a terrible sense of history. They're all about making money."

"The Americans bailed Britain's sorry ass out of two World Wars. There's a reason you're still drinking beer in pubs and not in *einen Biergarten*. That much history I do know."

That silenced Julia; but more quotes, likely Shakespearean, would be forthcoming, Alex was certain of it. Julia Hale, her grandmother. The uncanny resemblance was disconcerting. It was irksome to know exactly what one would look like at seventy. It took the mystery out of growing old. The whole business of having a grandmother at all felt unnatural. There had never been a gaping, nagging hole in her psyche due to the absence of a mother or grandmother. Her mother had died when she was only months old. Her female role models were schoolteachers and Gillian White's high octane mother, a state representative. And there had been Randy's wives (after Julia). Mrs. Hoffman and she had sold Girl Scout cookies in front of the café every year and made cookies for school bake sales. On her sixteenth birthday Luna had shown her how to make hash brownies with walnuts, an important rite of passage. Instead of an elderly female explaining to her "the facts of life," she'd learned about sex from the Internet, TV, and from tumbling around on beaches and backseats, like every other teenager on the planet. Alan and Jacob had taken her clothes shopping at the mall every fall, and delighted in helping her pick out prom dresses. Gary Smyth had shown her how to tune up outboard engines. She'd been raised by a loving community and two kindly potheads. Hers was an ideal childhood.

She pushed the crab traps aside and spread out her towel. Since she was hostage on this ridiculous cruise to find whatever with some crazy old coot, she might as well make the best of it. Work on her tan. She pulled off her shirt and shorts, and stretched across a towel in her bikini. If she hadn't been so stupid as to leave her headphones and iPod in the car, she could have blotted out the chatterbox completely. Her phone vibrated on her wrist. She lifted her sunglasses to see the screen. Cooking class was in thirty minutes. Even baking French pastries with Richard would be preferable to this.

"Alexandra, darling, we don't have time for lounging. Ben and Randy left you—us—some information in the two papers, profoundly important information."

All morning she had denied having any knowledge of the "two papers." How did Julia know of the mysterious messages? That, too, was disconcerting.

"Ben said to start at the Bohemia River. Please work with me. 'Our individual responses will be all the stronger for working together and sharing the load.' That was Queen Elizabeth, by the way, the Second, not the First."

"Blah, blah, blah." Still, Julia's last comment caught her attention. Ben had never said to start at the Bohemia River. It was Papa's map that had a number one placed at the Bohemia River. Ben's note had a number one associated with OGM.

"Randy never mentioned the droll, yet unsophisticated, side to your humor."

"And you spoke to him when?" Alex asked.

"Oh, frequently."

"Frequently, five decades ago." Alex closed her eyes. Water Dog inched next to her on the towel and put his head on her belly.

During their cruise down the Glen River and out to the Chesapeake, Julia blabbed about backstage visits from Sir Paul McCartney, David Bowie and Mick Jagger. Of course—how could Julia Hale not be best friends with Madonna? If nothing else, her grandmother had imagination.

"The GPS says we're at the mouth of the Bohemia River. You drive, while I look around," said the confidante to wizards, kings, sultans ... and rock stars.

Alex opened one eye from behind her sunglasses. Julia had slowed the boat to a near idle. It was possible that the tugboat had once been hers. She drove it expertly, though the electronics confounded her.

"I'm sound asleep," Alex grumbled.

Julia stepped onto the deck and stretched her arms upward as if to touch the sun. " 'One touch of nature makes the whole world kin!' "

The beauty of the quote struck a chord and Alex sat up. "Let me guess ... Ibsen? Albee?" She paused for effect. "Shakespeare."

"Yes, brava. *Troilus and Cressida*, Ulysses in Act 3."

Alex jumped to her feet and dashed to the helm. "We're drifting into the lily pads!" She steered the small tugboat back to the middle of the channel. While holding the wheel steady with her knee, she typed, "One touch of nature ..." into the search box on her smartphone. She glanced over her shoulder. It was possible that Julia actually had been an actress in Britain. She exuded big, confident everything: voice, gestures, and ego.

"What are we looking for?" The humor was gone from Julia's voice and the sly green gaze reappeared.

"I wish I knew," Alex said honestly. "There's only so far we'll be able to go before we hit the bridge."

"So you've been here before?"

"Yes, many times. Papa, Ben and I fished and crabbed all over. I know every bend in the coastline from here to Annapolis."

The *Vital Spark* plodded up the river, through heavy, hot humidity; then Alex jerked the throttle into neutral. "OGM!"

"Oh my god." Julia frowned with disgust. "Soon the entire English language will be reduced to dreadful American acronyms. POTUS, CIA, KFC ..."

"No, not OMG. OGM." She pointed.

Up a scrub-covered embankment was a dilapidated outbuilding, caved in except one precarious wall, standing due to some invisible, indefatigable force. In the fall when the leaves dropped from the trees, the wood skeleton was visible from the river, but at the moment vines twisted between its broken planks, green snakes camouflaging its presence. The building was part of a farm, now long abandoned, the climbing plants erasing its memory of distant dreams and toil.

On the swaying, lone wall was a metal sign. A few more seasons of sun, rain, and frost would forever obliterate the sign's fading colors. Just visible amidst the dripping rust and curling paint was a green field and a grinning gray horse. The ancient sign faintly revealed the words "The Old Gray Mare Dairy."

"There's something that I need to check out, down the bay, that might be relevant to the case," Jay said urgently to Laura and Mrs. Pulacki.

Lie Number Two.

He grabbed the keys to the Boston Whaler from the key hook in the kitchen and hurried across the lawn. His fishing gear was now permanently stored on his boat instead of in the storage shed. If he could just retreat to his hidden fishing hole for an afternoon and mindlessly watch the bobber float on the still green water, he wouldn't be preoccupied by a bloody nightshirt, a wife intent on rearranging the garden flowers, according to color, of course, and fantasies of a naked Zera Lim in his hot tub where his beloved Laura had once been. It was no use ... it was he who was going mad ... it was he who should be talking to the psychiatrist, Dr. Richmond. He threw off the lines and started the engine. The gas tanks were filled, the way they were always kept these days, so that at any moment he might escape the tumult welling in his head. He turned briefly. Laura was on the dock, spade in hand, waving a good-bye. The image crystallized in his thoughts; she was leaving him.

But never—ever—would he commit her, no matter what Zera found on the shirt! But what if the blood on the shirt belonged to Randall Allaway? What if it was Laura who'd killed him? The murder had occurred in the evening. What if she'd snuck out of the house and taken a swim? There had been recent outbursts of temper. She'd smashed up the TV with a hammer, and thrown a blender through the kitchen window. But no one knew about that but him. He'd cleaned up the mess before Mrs. Pulacki had arrived the next morning. The story was that the TV had gone in for repair. A bird, a very large seagull, had crashed through the kitchen window. Never would he put Laura in a state hospital; he'd quit his job, tend to her for the rest of her days. Her family had money, lots of it, in fact. Her father had been a CEO of a large insurance company. They would help.

His impulse was to yank down the throttle of the Boston Whaler, scream under the bridge, and fly across the water to his serene place in the marsh. But he was a police officer. Before this mess with Laura, a highly successful, highly decorated one. No case had eluded him. Now he didn't give a shit. His singular obsession was to sit alone and fish, downing a large thermos of gin and tonic. He motored slowly through the no-wake zone, passed under the bridge and wound carefully through the tourists' boats in the harbor. The town was still congested with tourists, but not like yesterday when bands had played on the pier. On his way out to the bay, he passed Allaway's house and Old Ben's cottage. On the other side of the Point, he noticed the *Vital Spark* cruising up the bay. He lifted his binoculars. Strange, Alex Allaway wasn't driving. Instead, she stood at the transom, arms folded across her chest, her face brooding. Who was driving the tug? Another person was inside at the helm, but his binoculars didn't have the resolution to identify who it was. He fumbled through his fishing vest's numerous pockets until he found his ages-old khaki hat with the large brim. He pulled it low over his eyes, adjusted his Ray Bans, and followed Alex Allaway and the mystery pilot up the coast.

Ben Hancock had left Alex some message in code that Will had found in Ben's belongings. She'd feigned ignorance as to its meaning. And she, upon Ben's death, was to inherit his property. Though no will had been found amidst Randall Allaway's papers, presumably she'd inherit his property too. Two adjacent waterfront lots near the scenic River Glen Point had considerable value in today's real estate market. At

Randy and Ben's death, Alex would make a tidy little profit. Jay placed a call.

"Will, I want you and Lisa to check the camera footage on the bridge again, this time looking for Alex Allaway's car coming over the bridge on the night of Allaway's murder. I want to know her whereabouts that night. I want to know everything about her, police records, drug use, sex partners, where's she's been for the last few years, anything and everything. And I want to know where Ben Hancock is." He hung up.

The murder unraveled in his mind's eye. Alex plying her grandfather with alcohol laced with OxyContin. An impaired old man would put up no fight. Perhaps Laura had wandered onto Allaway's porch and witnessed the crime? Perhaps Alex had convinced Laura to put on the bloodied nightshirt? Who would believe a delusional woman? His oppressive guilt began to lift. He *was* working on the case, as he'd told Laura and Mrs. Pulacki; that was the truth. He was exonerated of Lie Number Two. He steered his boat into the Bohemia River. A tree bending over the river provided a dark, cool anchorage. On the opposite bank of the river was a camouflaged jon boat, its owner bowed over his tackle box. Jay turned his binoculars back on the *Vital Spark*, idling near the lily pads. An older woman and Alex gazed up an embankment. He moved his binoculars toward the shoreline. What was so interesting about that old wrecked barn in the woods?

Headquarters

"Jay thinks it's Alex Allaway," Will said to Lisa. This news and his brief encounter with Penny Bannister while dropping off Carly caused pressure to surge behind his temples. When he'd glanced into Penny's apartment, a mangy guy in boxers had been sprawled across her sofa, and empty beer bottles and ashtrays covered the coffee table. He could give a shit what slime-balls Penny was fucking; he just didn't want the slime-balls around Carly. Christ ... if he could just get custody! But if he broached the subject, Penny would certainly change her story. She was capable of anything. He could hear it now. "Now I remember everything from that terrible night. He plied me with booze, some drug, things turned violent. It was rape." Then there'd be no hope of ever seeing his daughter again. And there were the bags from the mall in the hallway. Penny had been shopping again, and to the nail and hair salon. Her fingernails were now bright red and her hair dark brown.

"Are you okay?" Lisa asked him.

"Fine. Jay wants us to see if Alex might have been in town on the night of the murder. We need to review the footage from the bridge camera. How about you check the footage and I'll check for any criminal background?" He dropped listlessly into his chair. "The whole thing's absurd."

"Do you know her from somewhere?"

"We were in school together, since elementary school. She loved her grandfather. She didn't kill him. There's a killer on the loose and this is a complete waste of time!"

The Bohemia

Alex waded through the lily pads. "This was a lame-brained idea. We'll never get you back in the boat."

"I'm as agile as a cat, darling," Julia said with irrepressible confidence. "Don't worry about me. I can fence with sabres, foils, épées, swing from chandeliers, climb anything, and dance brilliantly ... the waltz, the tango, you name it. I've even danced the hula in that dreadful American musical *South Pacific*. I've never understood the appeal of Rodgers and Hammerstein. Now Andrew Lloyd Webber's musicals ..."

"Are far superior because he's British," Alex said preemptively.

"Yes! Exactly. So we agree on that point."

Alex climbed on shore and turned to watch. Julia's long skirt floated around her waist as she struggled through the mucky bottom. "If you don't get out of the water soon, Your Pokiness, you're going to be eaten."

"What?"

Alex couldn't resist. "There are all sorts of voracious creatures in these American waters, but the most dangerous is the Bohemia Ness Monster, Bessie, who has a particular taste for Scottish flesh."

Julia grinned. "Touché."

Alex followed an overgrown trail up the embankment. "We need a machete to get through this jungle."

Julia caught up with her and they climbed over a crumbling stone foundation and ducked under fallen beams. It was an eerie place, a canopy of swaying ivy and vines, lush green penetrated by beams of yellow light. They kicked amidst seasons of leaves and weeds, through oppressive heat, only to find a plastic bag full of crushed beer cans, discarded tires, and rusty plows.

Alex flicked a tick off her leg. "That's the third goddamn tick on me! I hate ticks! I have no clue why I'm here ... what the hell am I supposed to be looking for? Papa's dead. I have no clue who you are. You could be the murderer!"

"That would be murderess, love."

"I could be alone in the forest with a psychopathic Scottish murderess for all I know! How do I know who you really are? Why did you come?"

"Ben told me to come and visit Randy and you. But he didn't elaborate."

"After fifty years you decide to visit your husband? Why didn't Papa contact you? Why Ben? Why didn't Ben elaborate? How did he contact you?"

"A letter and an email."

"Nothing makes sense!" Frustrated, Alex kicked at a milk canister with "OGM Dairy" embossed on it. It rolled with a weird thump and clanged to a stop against a milking stool.

They stared warily at the milk canister.

"There's something in there," Julia said uneasily.

"No shit." Alex stepped nervously forward. "With my crappy luck, it's a skunk." She lifted the milk canister and gave it a quick shake. She leapt backward. A dried skull with an ancient dagger lodged in the occipital bone rolled into the leaves.

That fisherman in the camo jon boat definitely has the right idea, Jay decided. After catching one fish, the man had stretched out between the seats and pulled his camo ball cap over his eyes to snooze. Jay moved the binoculars back to his eyes. It was impossible to see what Alex and the black-haired woman had been doing in the collapsed barn, but they'd obviously found something. Something in a white plastic bag. Alex waded through the shallows holding the bag over her head, handed it to the other woman, and climbed up the boat ladder. The woman handed the bag to up Alex, who rushed it inside. Alex then returned to assist the woman up the ladder. They quickly lifted the anchor, and the *Vital Spark* made a U-turn in the middle of the river. The sudden urgency to the women's gestures raised red flags.

It was improbable that Alex would recognize his boat. He'd moved to River Glen long after she'd moved out of her grandfather's house. Besides, she'd only been back home for two days; during that time his boat hadn't moved from his dock. No way would she recognize his boat anchored in the shadows. As the *Vital Spark* chugged down the river, he turned his back to them and dropped his fishing line amidst the tree roots.

Will and Lisa had been busy at headquarters and apprised him of details throughout the afternoon. It was Will who had called, each time with a frantic edge to his voice. Alex Allaway had no police record, Will said. Will clearly had some emotional attachment to Allaway. Like he should talk— his thoughts were on bedding Zera, the medical examiner. Allaway had attended the University of Maryland and received a B.S. in Environmental Sciences (Biodiversity and Conservation option) and an M. S. in Fisheries Science. She'd then spent some months working at the Scripps Institution of Oceanography in La Jolla, California, before moving to Washington, DC. There, she'd worked part-time as a fisheries consultant for an environmental watchdog group, and taught an Introductory Ecology class at a community college in northern Virginia. While in Washington, DC, she'd been living with a boyfriend, a patents lawyer, Richard Wells. After their breakup, she'd been sleeping on the sofa of Courtney Raney, a former friend from UM and medical student at Georgetown.

According to Allaway's statement, on the night of Randy's murder, she was shopping for a business suit and got a hair cut in DC. Will—again vehemently—said that her alibi checked out. Raney corroborated the story, as she was with Alex at the mall. The VISA company had confirmed charges on Allaway's credit card at the Hair Cuttery and Macy's. Nor was Allaway's car on the River Glen that night; Lisa had checked the camera footage twice. None of this explained how Alex Allaway's nightshirt had ended up behind his dryer.

"'Alas, poor Yorick! I knew him, Horatio: a fellow of infinite jest, of most excellent fancy,'" Julia said, holding the skull aloft.

"How did I know that quote was coming?" Alex replied. "Hamlet, the graveyard scene."

Alex had read the tragedy in high school, during the same semester that Will Wilkins' assigned seat was directly behind hers. His giant high-top sneaker infuriatingly jiggled her chair ... for an entire freaking semester. That same semester the asshole had almost gotten her suspended! It was a miracle that she'd learned anything in high school.

"I don't know how you can touch that repulsive thing," Alex said. "That was someone's head, you know. Holding their brain, their personality, their thoughts!"

"Yes, fascinating. And someone quite diabolically drove a knife into his skull from the back. The poor sod didn't even have a chance to defend himself." Julia turned the skull in her hands. "The skull's quite old. The dagger's completely fused into the bone." Her eyes narrowed. "My goodness! There's something written on it. Carved into the bone!"

"What?" Alex spun on the old barrel seat at the helm.

"Look!" Julia pointed, astonished. "Right there!"

"What's it say?"

"It's hard to see it."

"Hold the wheel." Alex rushed to the galley, took a morsel of dry dog food and crushed it into a fine brown powder between her fingers. She rubbed it into the faint lettering etched into the bone. The words appeared light brown.

"I have no idea what it says. It's not English. " Alex handed the skull to Julia.

"Memento mori 1694," Julia read.

Alex shook her head. "I don't know Latin. 1694? A year? A PIN?"

"The words mean 'remember that you must die,'" Julia said quietly.

Jay decided to place another call to Old Ben's girlfriend, Dott Garski, and this time talk to her himself. He reached into his fishing vest for his smartphone. Too many pieces of the case just didn't sit right. Too many 'hiccups' as Lisa Paco called them. Randy's death—stabbing or overdose? Will had mentioned an appearance of a long lost grandmother. Why were she and Alex rambling around an old ruin? Doing what? What was in the plastic bag? Did it have anything to do with Ben's message for Alex? Ben had been a student at the community college with Frank Whitby. Ben had missed the bridge game, and taken an alleged cruise down to Norfolk, yet he never passed under the Bay Bridge. Ben, Ben, Ben ... it all kept coming back to Old Ben Hancock.

The computer forensics team had discovered on Ben's laptop a series of emails made a few weeks ago between BHancock@comcast.net and DGarski@gmail.com. The couple had discussed at length different cruise lines ... do they go for ten or fourteen days? Should they go to the Bahamas, Bermuda, or the Mayan Riviera? Should they get a standard room, or splurge for the deluxe room with a balcony? They'd decided on the balcony room. Dott wanted to go on the Dolphin Adventure and Ben wanted to ride on the glass-bottom boat over the fringe reef. More excited emails about Casino Night and the Mardi Gras Dance Party on the Promenade Deck. Would she need a long dress or would a knee-length cocktail dress suffice? Over three days and thirty-some odd emails, the couple had planned their vacation down to the tiniest detail. After reading the affectionate email exchange sent to his smartphone from Norman in the IT unit, Jay wasn't sure if he had the heart to tell Dott Garski that Ben's sailboat had never made it to the Bay Bridge.

A pleasant woman with a melodious southern drawl answered his call.

"Ben hasn't arrived yet, but then again, he always takes his sweet time," Dott explained.

"And has he called you recently?" Jay knew the answer to that question. There'd been no activity on Ben's cell phone since the day of Randy's murder.

"No. We usually communicate by email. I doubt he took his laptop onto his boat. When he sails, he doesn't call. I think he likes his peace, the solitude of the water."

"And how long does it usually take him to get to Norfolk?"

"A few days, up to five or six days, depending on the winds and currents, of course. And he stops to take naps when he gets tired. He's not a young man, Detective."

"Mrs. Garski ..." he paused before breaking the bad news, "... we have no evidence that Ben made it as far as the Bay Bridge. We've been watching the cameras on the bridge for days. We've been trying to reach him. It's very, very important that we talk to him about Randall Allaway."

There was a protracted, uncomfortable silence on the other end of the phone. Dott's voice quavered. "Oh Lordy ... he should have at least made it to the mouth of the Choptank by now! Have you notified the Coast Guard? Please look down the eastern coast of the Bay. He usually goes by Deal Island, Tangier, Onancock, to Cape Charles. Are you sure he didn't slip under the Bridge unnoticed?"

"Yes. Quite sure. Will you please call Ben? His cell phone seems to be off. He might think our calls are courtesy calls so he's not answering. Please leave a message for him. Have him call us immediately."

"Yes, yes! I'll do that the second we hang up!"

"Thank you, and please stay in touch."

"I will. I will. And please call me the second you hear anything."

"Yes, of course," he said, ringing off.

Jay waited for five minutes before calling Norman, who was tracking Dott Garski's phone and email traffic. "Did she call Hancock's number?"

"Yup, ten seconds after you two hung up."

"And where did her call come from?"

"A cell phone at the Hampton Haven nursing home in Norfolk, Virginia. The same place the emails came from."

River Glen

"In the fall, they have Ghost Walks through this cemetery," Alex told Julia. "I did a Ghost Walk once, and only once. It was terrifying. The Halloween Ghost Walks and Giles Blood-hand Day singlehandedly save this town's economy." They passed under the black wrought iron gates of the River Glen cemetery and weaved between the headstones. "Water Boy, you have my permission to attack, bite, accost any ghosts or zombies that you see."

"Are you sure you know where we're going?" Julia looked cautiously about. The sun was settling behind the trees. The cemetery was empty except for the crickets and the startling flutter of a crow.

"Yes. The oldest graves are in the back."

"Curious," Julia said. "There are the same names again and again. Collinses, Smyths, Wilkinses, and Whitbys."

"The Allaways are over there. " Alex pointed.

They approached a marble obelisk about eight feet tall. It read "Todd and Janet Allaway," and the next line, "David and Debra Allaway." Under that, "Jason Allaway."

"Papa's grandparents, parents, and brother. Did you know Jason?" Alex asked.

"No, he died in the war, before I meet Randy."

Alex was moved and teary. "I'll bury Papa here with his family." She pressed her t-shirt collar into her eyes.

Julia patted her shoulder. "This is where he'd want to be, lass."

They continued wordlessly through the trees and gravestones, moving back in time through the 1800s, 1700s, to the 1600s, their walk delayed by Water Boy, who sniffed at each tombstone, intrigued by the scents in the ground.

In the back corner, bordered by a crumbling stone wall, the gravestones appeared like an old man's teeth: chipped, cracked and toppled. Some inscriptions were shrouded with moss, others worn away by the revolutions of time.

"What is this place?" Julia whispered.

"The pyrate burial site."

"They must have had an organized community by then if they were cutting headstones."

Alex stopped in front of one singular stone. "They always keep this headstone clear of moss for the ghost walks." A cold shudder blew through her.

It read:

> *Charles Innes Allaway*
> *1663-1694*
> *Here lies a pyrate rotten and dead,*
> *Rest for eternity without ye head*

"According to the man who led the ghost walk, Neville Whitby killed Charles Allaway, then put his head on a pike," Alex said. "The tour company had someone dress up as a headless pyrate and roam the graveyard. It scared the hell out of us."

Alex walked to a gravestone at the end of the row that, until the conversation with Levon Bakanian, had made no sense.

> *Neville Whitby*
> *Wife Emmaline*
> *Children John and Sara*
> *Memento mori 1694*

"Those four murders were the handiwork of Giles Blood-hand," Alex said grimly. "The Avenger."

Headquarters

Will disconnected the call to the administrator at the Hampton Haven Senior Living Center in Norfolk, Virginia. "What the ...? I feel like a dog chasing his tail. Jay's going to explode when he hears this!"

"It's important information," Lisa said. "We just haven't figured out how to interpret it yet. It will come to us, Will. It always does. There's no such thing as a perfect crime. Human error trumps all. Always."

He nodded, hoping to absorb some of Lisa's unshakeable optimism. Her whole life, besides school and the police force, had been spent caring for a mother debilitated by MS, their singular hobby discussing the intricacies of murder mysteries on TV. The sole ambition of his youth was to be a player or coach in the NFL, but his left knee had figuratively and literally let him down. At times, and this was one of them, his choice of a career as a policeman was befuddling.

He glanced down at his notepad, bewildered by the dangling bits of information. Things stuck better when he wrote them down. His yellow legal pad was a scrawl of names, events, arrows, bubbles and question marks. Maybe if he articulated his thoughts, something—anything—would appear to him.

"Dotthea Garski, formerly Dotthea Gunnarson, met Ben Hancock on a cruise to Cancun three years ago," he read aloud. "She's the widow of Captain Donald Garski of the U. S. Navy, who died of a heart attack five years ago. Gunnarson met Donald Garski when he lived in Stockholm and worked as an attaché to the Swedish Navy. Both Donald and Dott were career navy, both officers, married later in life; neither had children. The couple bought a motor sailer, *Njörőr* in Sweden and sailed it back to the U. S. They settled back in Norfolk where they both retired."

"Njörõr is the Norse god of the winds," Lisa said as an aside. "I once read this sick Norwegian mystery where the murderer named Njörõr used ice picks to—" Will stared at her balefully. "Okay, okay, I'll stay on task."

He continued aloud in his plodding way. "The couple sailed all over the Atlantic and Caribbean before Donald's death. All that seems straightforward enough. But here's where things start to get funky," he said, his eyebrow cocked. "Jay said that Dott Garski had a southern accent."

"Right. That's what he said." She spit her gum into the trashcan.

"Would someone develop an accent after living in Virginia for less than ten years?"

"Don't-know."

"The administrator at Hampton Haven confirmed that Dotthea Gunnarson-Garski was a resident there. She's been a resident there for the past six months."

"And this is funky also. She's very ill," Lisa added in a suspicious tone. "So ill that she had her right foot amputated due to blood clotting and severe diabetes two weeks ago. Garski's also morbidly obese, well over two hundred pounds. Answer me this, Will. Is a sick, old amputee really going to be thrilled about going on a cruise, dancing on Mardi Gras night, and swimming with dolphins?" She giggled at the absurdity.

"Norman verified that the emails were sent from the nursing home. The emails came through their hub," he said as a reminder.

"And the other weird thing," she said, snapping her new pieces of gum. "Her phone cell. Only calls to Ben. What person doesn't call other friends and relatives? Garski has four sisters in Sweden, and she never calls them? I bet she has two phones. One for friends and family, and another to speak to Ben, probably in code."

"But we read the transcripts. Their conversations were about the upcoming cruise, movies he and Randy had been watching on *Netflix*, and some work he'd been doing on his boat."

"I bet they were speaking in code," she insisted. "I'll figure it out." She handed Will her tablet. "Look at this."

He studied the timeline of events.

1966: Ben and Randy return from Vietnam, both discharged due to injuries.

1968: Colin Allaway born to Randall Allaway and Julia Hale

1969: Julia Hale returns to Scotland

1991:

July—Alexandra Allaway born

November—Colin Allaway and Carole Lowe-Allaway killed in hit-and-run

Fall—Ben Hancock and Frank Whitby attend same community college

2017:

May 21—Frank Whitby disappears

June 15—Randall Allaway murdered

With a pencil eraser, she tapped two points on her tablet. "The key dates in all of this are 1991, the year of the hit-and-run, and this year, obviously. Especially May 22, the day after Frank Whitby's reported as a missing person. That's when Ben and Dott Garski begin to plan their cruise via email. That's more than coincidence."

He stood abruptly and grabbed his car keys. "If I leave now right now, I can be at Hampton Haven in four hours and talk to the one-footed Swede."

"Good luck," Lisa said doubtfully. "You're chasing a phantom."

Norfolk

It was an uneventful drive down Route 13 South. Will stopped for coffee and a bagel at Dunkin Donuts, and made a rest stop, all the time checking his phone for a call from Alex Allaway. How could it be possible, after so many years, that one person could still have such an effect on him? There were many nice women from the gym that he could date. The whole thing was ridiculous ... beyond ridiculous. Teenage crushes were one thing, but he was now an adult, a parent, and a police officer. Who was he kidding? Retrieving Old Ben's computer had been a convenient excuse to talk with her.

It had all started when they were in the same English class, the first period of the day. Alex was always late, every single morning, late. This was when he had amazing luck, before bloodthirsty cheerleaders, drugged vodka and blown-out knees. His assigned seat was directly behind hers. For an entire wonderful semester he'd looked over the edge of his desk to see her pink or purple, on some days, black lace thong peeking over the edge of her jeans. One morning she leaned forward on her desk, dozing. Her butt was pressed back toward his desk. Her jeans had slid down. Her butt crack beckoned. Eddie Richmond, the good-natured stoner in the seat next to his, had noticed, too. Will had inched his eraser toward the edge of his desk. Eddie nodded and giggled. The eraser hung poised at the edge. "Do it!" Eddie mouthed silently. He'd nodded devilishly. The temptation was too great. He gave the eraser a tiny nudge. The eraser found its intended target and slipped down her pants. She sprang to her feet and hurled her notebook into his chest.

"You idiot, you pinhead!"

Alex's desk tipped over, spilling the metal desk can. Blood vessels popped in the English teacher's forehead. The teacher, Mrs. Maury, shouted and pointed toward the door. Alex was banished to the principal's office for the rest of the day. The story relayed back to him was that the principal had threatened to suspend her, hold her back for another year. All of her detentions for tardiness—and now this—could never be made up before graduation. "I'm already twenty!" she had pleaded. "I'm already the oldest senior in the state of Maryland!" Eventually Randy arrived, charmed the frumpish principal, and all was resolved.

Will checked his phone once more before he entered the Hampton Haven nursing home. Not even a text from Alex. Ms. Jennings, the nursing home administrator, ushered him down a waxy hallway and through the locked doors of the Special Memory Neighborhood.

"Dott Garski has Alzheimer's?" he asked.

"Oh yes, she has many health issues. She's healing well from the surgery, but of course she has no knowledge of it or her whereabouts. We're trying to make her as comfortable as possible."

They entered a lounge with a TV and card tables, and Ms. Jennings pointed to a large woman seated in a wheelchair. "That's Dott right there."

"Do you mind if I talk to her?"

"Good luck with that. She hasn't spoken since she got here."

"And that was about six months ago?"

"Yes. She's completely non-communicative."

He knelt in front of the wheelchair. "Ms. Garski?" He moved his face into her vacant gaze. "Ms. Garski?" Nothing, absolutely nothing but a blank stare. He nudged her hand. No response. He slipped his cell phone from his pocket and took a photo of the absent woman. "Ms. Jennings, I know this is an absurd question, but does Ms. Garski have a laptop or cell phone?"

She shook her head. "If she did, she wouldn't know how to use them."

"Any regular visitors?"

"No. None. She has a special friend who also lives here, Libby Hinchcliff. She watches out for all of the Alzheimer's patients."

He checked his watch. It was 9:18 pm. There was one more stop to make. He jumped into his sedan and sped over to a marina on the Lynnhaven River in Virginia Beach. Stewart Jones, the marina manager, was closing down the marine store when he arrived.

Jones knew both Don and Dott because they'd rented a slip there for years. A lovely couple, but both of them intense. Perfectionists. Meticulous where the *Njörðr* was concerned. Type A personalities, typical of the naval officers that he knew, and Norfolk and Virginia Beach were full of them, mostly surface warfare officers. Athletic for an older couple. Walked the long loop, about nine miles, around First Landing State Park together every weekend before Don's death.

"So Dott was not obese and did not look like that?" Will held out of the image of the woman in the nursing home.

"No. There's a photo of her there. " Jones stepped from behind the cash register. "When she won the bass tournament."

Will followed Jones to the front door where a bulletin board held seasons of photographs of fishing tournaments, as well as ads and flyers for boats, beach houses and condos for sale or rent. "Weird." Jones scanned the board. "It was here." He searched the floor and the board once again. "It must have fallen off and got swept away as trash."

"And she lived here?"

"Yes." Jones pointed out the door to a condo over the dock. "Right there, but she sold it about five months ago and lived on her boat. Then one day she filled the boat with provisions and sailed off. Said she was getting married and sailing to South America. She was all excited about seeing the Amazon. She'd been all over the world, but had never seen South America."

"When did she leave?"

"A few months ago. Don't remember exactly. Two, maybe three?"

"Who was she marrying?"

"Her boyfriend, Ben, I guess. He sailed down here to visit her every few months."

"Does Dott speak with a southern accent?"

"No, she has a heavy accent from somewhere."

"Can you think of anything else? Anything that seemed unusual?"

"Nothing really. She was preparing for a long voyage. She'd covered *Njörðr* with solar panels and took two heavy-duty Honda generators."

"For what? Why carry the extra weight?"

Jones shrugged. "Ballast? Who knows?"

After 10 pm Will left the marine store, with a lukewarm cup of burnt coffee and days-old pastry in hand—gratis from Stewart Jones. There was no way he was going to make it back to River Glen without falling asleep at the wheel and careening into some pine forest without coffee. Carly had awoken him that morning at 6:30 by jumping on his foldout sofa bed. Then came the turmoil of dropping her off at Penny's. That invariably elevated his blood pressure for hours afterward. This had been followed by his compulsive checking to see if Alex Allaway had called or texted him. Not.

That long ago double date between him and Gillian, and Eddie Richmond and Alex kept bubbling to the surface, a distracting background noise in his thoughts—all freaking day long. He pulled off onto a narrow dirt road in the Eastern Shore National Wildlife Refuge and reclined his seat. He was emotionally exhausted and mentally spent. After a short nap, he'd be good for the four-hour drive up Route 13. His journey to Norfolk had not been for naught. One more date needed to be added to Lisa Paco's timeline. January of this same year. Six months ago. Something crucial had happened six months ago that caused a mysterious old woman, alias Dott Garksi, to be deposited at a nursing home, and another Dott Garski to suddenly sell her condo and prepare for an Amazonian cruise. None of it made sense, but all of it had significance. After all, he was chasing phantoms.

Middletown, Delaware

"I'm so fucking tired of hearing about the pyrate festival that I could just scream," Penny Bannister said to her image in the bathroom mirror. "Daddy this and Daddy that."

That fucking Daddy was supposed to be a tight-end in the NFL! Not some cop in a backwater town in Maryland making just above minimal wage! She'd done her homework on all of the Maryland players that year. Of all the Maryland Terrapins, it was Will Wilkins who was supposed to go highest in the draft. Scouts from the Rams, Redskins, and Seahawks had all been talking to him. He reputably had the size, speed and hands of the best tight-ends in the NFL. And now he was a no-name cop ... please.

Her lawyer was equally useless. 'No, Ms. Bannister, you can't go after him for more money. You need to leave him something to live on. The man has to eat. Have you thought about getting a job?'

Well fuck you, asshole.

She gazed into the mirror and wiped away the lipstick with a tissue. That shade didn't quite match her new hair color, Parisian Brown. She tried another. No. And another. No. Yes, finally. She smiled widely at her herself. She liked what she saw. The in-office teeth whitening treatments worked so much better than the white strips from the drug store. If the lawyer would do his fucking job, she might be able to have in-office teeth whitenings once a month. But no, Ms. Bannister ... you have to leave him something to live on.

Oh, and there was another annoying thing. Carly's relentless chatter about dancing, face-painting and pony-rides. Leave it to Will to spoil her. But most irritating of all was talk of a beautiful pyrate with a black dog. Will's girlfriend? If he had money to date someone, he certainly had the money for another teeth whitening session every month and extra sessions with her personal trainer.

"What color were her hair and eyes?" she'd cleverly asked her daughter.

"Black hair and green eyes, like Giles Blood-hand," Carly had said.

Penny remained at the mirror, imagining herself with black hair and green eyes. She'd look awesome; she always did. She grinned at the cup of urine and dipstick on the back of the toilet. A purple dipstick! A positive! In a few months, after the court deliberations, her monthly income would double. So, the trade-off was pushing out another brat. Thank you, colorless, tasteless gamma-hydroxybutyric acid! An aphrodisiac, cleared from one's system in only a few days, so absolutely impossible to detect months later. Better living through chemistry.

It had been ridiculously easy, just as it had been with Will Wilkins. She was no longer a student and a cheerleader, but all that was necessary was to find the clubs that the athletes frequented and closely monitor the calendar for her time of ovulation. That basketball player from the University of Delaware, she'd read, had been talking to the Lakers. The days of nickel and diming her puny cut of a cop's puny salary were over; her appetite was for a big slice of a big pie, an NBA contract. She'd dropped next to the unwitting power forward on the barstool and jiggled her knee against his. That worked every time. It showed sexual eagerness and excitability.

She'd flashed her most demure smile to the bartender. "Some vodka shots, please. My treat ..."

Chapter 5

Day 5

The Morgue

Dr. Zera Lim extended and flexed her fingers over the keyboard of her laptop. Yesterday afternoon, she'd really overdone it, and today she was paying the price. With every slide of the mouse or tap on the keys a dull pain coursed through her hands. With any luck, no bodies would come in today, as grasping a scalpel or forceps would be a challenge. She pulled a bottle of extra-strength aspirin from the top drawer of her desk and swallowed down two tablets with a cup of Sumatran coffee that she'd brought from home. No watery, bitter coffee from the dispenser in the hall for her. She'd worked hard to get to this stage in her life, tending to children, a husband, pets, all of them now gone. It was time to indulge herself with life's finer treats. She stretched her arms over her head, as her shoulders and elbow joints also ached. No one else arrived as early as she did, so she indulged in a groan so forceful that it echoed from her office, all the way to the morgue at the end of the hallway. It was a groan of inexorable pleasure and satisfaction. The pain was so worth it. After months of trying, she'd done it. She'd mastered The Barrel.

She had no idea what had compelled her in the first place, but there was no going back now. Maybe she'd just seen too much at work that week. Too many people were involved in that boating accident, four of them children. The Boat, from her perspective—slicing propellers, flammable gasoline, no brakes, add beer to the mix—was the most diabolic invention known to mankind. As usual her office had been understaffed, and on top of it all, she'd been supervising two medical students and one college intern. And of course the press had clamored outside like a pack of wild dogs, flustering her secretary. Zera had been at work for over forty-eight hours straight, catching catnaps on her office sofa, before moving to the next body. That same week, she'd had to put down her beloved dog of fifteen years.

Driving home late that afternoon, the advertisement in front of an old airplane hangar in an abandoned airfield had caught her eye. Though exhausted, she'd turned her car into the parking lot. She'd walked numbly inside and handed the teenage boy at the counter some bills.

"Just one," she must have said.

It was a quiet evening. Other than her, the only people in the place were the two teenage boys behind the cash register listening to rock music. She'd proceeded to a bench, removed her suit jacket, pulled the shirttails from her slacks, removed her pumps, and slid on the pliable shoes, a bit like ballet slippers, that the boy had given her. He asked her to step into a harness, which he tightened between her legs and around her hips.

"Is this your first time?" he'd asked.

"Yes."

"It won't be your last. Try that one." He had pointed to a flat wall. "It's perfect for beginners. Just follow the green hand holds." He clipped the climbing ropes hanging from the ceiling to carabineers on her harness, and to carabineers on his belaying harness. "Ring that bell."

The silver bell, she'd estimated, must have been at an elevation of fifty feet, just at the roof the hangar. What had she gotten herself into? She was anything but impulsive. What insanity had prompted this?

"You can do it," he said. "You have the perfect climber's body. Tall and skinny."

A sixteen-year-old boy was checking out her body, a thought that at the moment didn't offend in the least. Her husband of twenty-eight years had replaced her for a newer model, the young partner in his architectural firm. For the past two years, since the divorce, she'd felt like a used car forgotten in the lot behind the car dealership.

She'd stalled and grappled for an excuse to escape this nonsense. Looming above her was a perpendicular wall. To her right was an inclined wall. To the left ... yeah, right. It looked like a giant cask of beer.

"That's the Barrel," the boy had said.

"That only Spiderman can climb."

"And me," he boasted.

"Really?"

"Yup. So you can definitely do this easy wall. It's part of my job to instill confidence. That's what the manager told me to do. Just take it one handhold at a time. Don't look down at the floor, or up at the bell. Find only the next available handhold."

The boy's pep talk was well rehearsed and delivered in a reassuring tone. She appreciated the message, the live-in-the-moment metaphor that at the moment was important to hear.

"Put out your hands," he'd said.

She did as told.

He sprinkled white powder into her hands. "The chalk will give you a better grip."

She reached tentatively for the handholds and stepped on to one. The rubber-soled slippers had tremendous grip. Perhaps she could do this. One handhold at a time.

"Three points of contact at all times. Always three points. Never, ever, two."

"Got it." She ascended to the next. Three points of contact, three points of contact, she whispered to herself—more invaluable advice from this unexpected fountain of wisdom, a pimply boy with purple and blue spiked hair.

Instantly the world simplified ... to a mosaic of colorful handholds, textures, and shapes. Her heart danced.

It would occur to her later when driving home that night, that not once during her exhilarating climb, and the two climbs that followed, was there a thought of drowned children, absent flotation vests, inebriated parents, or a bilge that had not been purged of gas vapors. Diminished also was the ache for a precious dog that would never again take her on an evening walk.

Her hand had swiped through the air three times at the Rock Gym, hitting its mark. DING. DING. DING.

The cell phone dinged on Zera's desk and drew her back to the present. It was a text from Jay Braden. That was a conversation she didn't want to have at the moment. She walked down the hallway to the changing room with the lockers. Before putting on her scrubs, she glanced down at her arms and hands. The pushups, the chin-up bar across her bathroom door, and hand-weights to improve upper body strength had really paid off. She was the Empress, the Queen, la Conquistadora of The Barrel!

The arrogance of men to assume that the breach of divorce need be filled by another man! There were so many interesting things in life to fill breaches, like joining a climbing club. Attempt real cliffs, real mountains! The Alps? Rockies? Andes? Dare she be so bold ... the Himalayas? Not that there was anything wrong with Jay Braden. He was intelligent, sophisticated, and handsome, a catch by any standards ... and married. But he was clearly drinking too much, his face bloating, his trim waist beginning to thicken. A fling with her would not fix his ailing heart, nor restore the neurotransmitter imbalance in his wife's brain. Alas, the irrational male libido, intent on miring itself deeper into the quicksand.

No, she'd found her life's passion, at the glorious, menopausal age of fifty-three, in the form of curves, angles, crevices, lines, carbineers, and chalk bags. But it was time for work. She lifted her phone and pushed Jay's number. There was no delicate way to put this to him. The swipes of blood from the nightshirt behind his dryer were not from Laura Braden or Randall Allaway, but from Frank Whitby.

River Glen

"Wakey, wakey, lass. We have work to do." Julia nudged Alex's foot.

Alex swiped her hair from her face and checked her smartphone. "I'm late for work."

"And I bet you forgot to call your boyfriend last night," Julia said. "I left his card on the galley table."

"What boyfriend?" Alex twisted her legs over the side of the berth.

"How many do you have?"

"None. Who are you talking about?"

"The policeman, Will. It's always useful to have a good, working relationship with the police. You need to call him and find out what they know about Randy's killer."

"Coffee, coffee," she groaned.

"We need to find the second clue." Julia stepped aside as Alex lumbered to the galley.

"Today I'm going to my job." Alex started the coffee machine and watched the mug fill.

"Yes, but we can do both. Don't you need to do some sampling, whatever you do, on the Sassafras River?"

"We? There is no *we*. Today *I*—singular—go to work and *I*—singular—actually do my job. It's my first full-time job. *I* need to do a good, no, a great job."

"Randy and Ben's code was mindlessly easy! 1 in 1OGM corresponded to the 1. Bohemia River. The means the 2CC can be found at 2. Sassafras River. Think, Alexandra, think. What's CC?"

"I have no clue. This whole bizarre scavenger hunt creeps me out. Who knows what we might find next? A severed arm, a leg?" She grimaced at the plastic bag containing their morbid find sitting on her galley table. "We have a skull with a dagger stuck in it. Charles Allaway's skull. And Papa and Ben wanted me to have it why? How the hell did they get that thing? I'll never be able to eat at that table again, I'm so grossed out."

Julia rolled her eyes. "I'm doubtful that grossed out is even a real verb in the English language. When will Americans learn to speak English?" She stepped onto the deck, put her fingers between her lips, and whistled shrilly. Water Boy scrambled onto the dock and dashed toward her. She stepped back inside. "He's been fed." She started the engine. "Now get yourself dressed, and get your breakfast. I'll drive."

"You're so not going to work with me."

"Yes, I am. Until they catch this killer, I'm watching your back."

"My back! What have I done to anyone?"

"What did Randy do? He still got it."

"So, you're going to fend off some thug with an assault weapon using your Shakespearean sword fighting skills?"

"Yes, if it comes to that. Now cast off those lines. It's Bring-Your-Grandmother-To-Work-Day."

A Duck Blind

"Fuckin' teenagers," Clyde Whitby grumbled.

Fuckin' teenagers had found the secret duck blind that he and Frank had built in the marsh, strategically positioned behind a screen of marsh grass, and directly across a channel from Frank's marine lab. Clyde searched the wooden platform. Fortunately, this morning there were none of the telltale signs of a teenage tryst: the condom wrappers, empty bottles of Wild Turkey—probably stolen from Daddy's liquor cabinet—and empty snack bags. The teenagers had been absent for weeks; perhaps they'd taken summer jobs at the shore. That past spring, when he'd first noticed the muddy sneaker prints and debris, he'd crouched stealthily in the grass with his shotgun, awaiting their return. Despite the long waits, he was never able to determine who they were, or when they came and went. Maybe they worked a late shift and came in the middle of the night. No way could his wife be left unattended in the evenings; he had to watch her every move. The man who rotated her tires was a bit too friendly. So was the manager of the grocery store.

He lifted the lid of the old milk container, the metal type from the days when the milkman delivered bottles to one's back door. He checked inside. Miraculously, his battery-operated CD player hadn't been stolen, nor any of his tapes. If those teenaged fuckers had stolen his ZZTop or Lynyrd Skynyrd, he'd have tracked them and the spartina grass would have been spattered with blood and grey matter. But never would he leave his tripod and high-resolution camera in the duck blind. That equipment he always returned to his truck.

How he missed the photo shoots with Frank! It was impossible that Frank would run off and not tell him where he was going. They were joined at the hip. That bitch Alex Allaway had everything to do with Frank's disappearance, he was certain. He checked his watch. Where the hell was she? What a slacker—second day on the job and already showing up late. But there was no on-site supervisor, so no one would ever know. Frank had the perfect job and she wanted it. It was that simple.

The remoteness of the marine station made it ideal for the photo shoots, allowing Frank to entertain his guests in absolute privacy on the back dock. The picnics were always an overwhelming success. Sultry, romantic music wafting through the screened windows of the grey building. Wine and finger sandwiches leisurely enjoyed on a soft blanket at the dock's edge.

"How about a swim, my beauty?" Flattering whispers and a massage with sunscreen melted away any lingering reservations.

Some of the women had heated to boiling point while bobbing in Frank's arms in the glistening water; another had tried to pull him back onto the blanket even before the swim. But each time he'd insist on the outdoor shower, a mere spigot projecting from the back wall.

"Pleasure's my middle name, beauty ..."

Frank's tacit smile over the woman's bare shoulder was the cue. Roll 'em, Clyde. The wife was filmed in every possible position from the unobstructed shower.

The X-rated film footage—such incriminating angles and zooms—could be quite an embarrassment to the husband, his business associates, the mother-in-law, not to mention the friends at the golf club, if posted on social media. How fast might such a video go viral?

Thank you Mrs. Weinstein, Mrs. Chandless, Mrs. Rockwell, and Mrs. Hawthorne for the monthly cash deposits! How wonderful to be self-employed and alone in one's duck blind on a pristine Monday morning, listening to the Allman Brothers sing "Sweet Melissa."

Lisa Paco unwrapped two sticks of gum and stuffed them in her mouth. She studied the white board with the timeline of the Randall Allaway case. #pacolivingthelife Most murder investigations were cut and dried, the killer captured within hours. But this case was intriguing on so many levels. This killer was very clever, having created smoke screens at every step to confound the police. What if they were dealing with a criminal mastermind like Professor Moriarty, who'd decided to operate his criminal syndicate from the eastern shore near River Glen? River Glen, after all, was ideally situated near the major cities of Philadelphia, Baltimore and Washington, DC. Had Randall Allaway been supplying *Cannabis* to

Moriarty's drug ring? #hmmpaconotsure There was no indication that there'd been any weed in his grow house for years. You're getting carried away, she told herself. Which were actual clues and which were red herrings? She tugged a long string of gum from her clenched teeth and twisted it around her finger.

1966: Ben and Randy return from Vietnam, both discharged due to injuries.

1968: Colin Allaway born to Randy Allaway and Julia Hale

1969: Julia Hale returns to Scotland

1991:

July—Alexandra Allaway born

November—Colin Allaway and Carole Lowe-Allaway killed in hit-and-run

Fall—Ben Hancock and Frank Whitby attend same community college

2017:

January—Dott Garksi admitted to Norfolk nursing home

May 21—Frank Whitby disappears

June 15—Randy Allaway murdered

At Will's suggestion, Lisa had added January 2017 to the timeline because he was convinced that that date, too, was important. During that one month a mysterious Alzheimer's patient had appeared at the Hampton Haven nursing home under the alias Dott Garski, and the real Dott Garski had put her condo up for sale. Soon after, Dott had told Stewart Jones at the marina that she'd be sailing to South America and then disappeared on her boat, all the while emails using the wifi at the nursing home were sent back and forth to Ben about a cruise to the Bahamas. Was Dott planning on sailing back from South America to hop a cruise ship to the Bahamas? Or was this just a ruse? And who was sending the emails from the nursing home on a smart phone registered to Dott Garski? Since Jay Braden's phone call and Will's visit to the nursing home yesterday, Dott Garski's phone had, not surprisingly, gone dead.

And January was important for another reason. She and Norman had identified interesting transactions on Randall Allaway's VISA card. Over New Year's Eve, Allaway had rented a beach house in Bethany Beach, a location not coincidently half way between River Glen and Norfolk. There were purchases on his VISA at a gas station, grocery store, and liquor store. Ben Hancock was also in attendance: dinner at an expensive seafood restaurant and groceries appeared on his credit card from locations in Bethany. Dott Garski may have been there as well, since Ben had purchased flowers from a florist in Bethany, twice. It was doubtful that Ben was buying them for Randy. Lisa also sensed some superior intelligence in Dott, as no expenditures occurred on her credit card during that time, but she'd taken three hundred dollars from the Lynnhaven marina's ATM just before New Year's Eve. Cash left no trail to follow, unlike credit card transactions. Could this have simply been a holiday party of a few senior citizens? Doubtful. The events that followed it were too weird.

One other person was there, Lisa suspected, though not in body, but in spirit ... the long-lost wife, Julia Hale. She and Norman had done an extensive investigation into Hale's past. Hale was an actress, as she'd claimed, and one of minor fame in Britain and Europe. She'd been a member of the

Royal Shakespeare Company for over fifty years, though intermittently, as she had an ill daughter, Cecilia, who'd required her constant attention. Hale had lived with her elderly father Clive (now deceased), aunt Beatrice, brother Ian, and Cecilia on an estate outside of Aberdeen, Scotland; the Hale Clan was an ancient family of some wealth. Last fall Cecilia, at the age of fifty-two, had drowned herself in a pond on the estate. Julia Hale had then moved to a flat in the Bloomsbury section of London. With the exception of two minor infractions, Hale was a law-abiding citizen. In her late twenties, there had been a drunk and disorderly charge—partying with two other actresses in a London club (apparently too much bubbly after an evening performance of *Much Ado About Nothing*). When Hale was forty-one, a civil suit had been brought against her by the wife of a lord with whom she'd been tangling. A savvy, silver-tongued barrister from Edinburgh had extracted her from that mess. That was the totality of Julia Hale's mischief.

She and Norman found no emails, texts, or phone correspondence between Randy and Julia, or between Ben and Julia until ...

The blue crabs are moving to deeper waters.

That email was sent on the same evening as Allaway's murder and it was the last communication of any kind sent from Ben Hancock's smartphone. The next day Julia Hale booked a flight, boarded a British Airways airplane at London Heathrow, and arrived at Baltimore-Washington Airport seven and a half hours later. The day after that she was spotted on the security camera at the River Glen bus station, pulling her rolling suitcase into the midst of the Giles Blood-hand festivities. She and the other blue crabs were moving to deeper waters.

Leah Devlin

The Sassafras River

Alex would never admit it aloud to the grandmother with indefatigable optimism who could combat villains with épées, as well as advise kings, sultans and wizards, but it was helpful to have another pair of hands onboard. And it was smart to use the *Vital Spark* rather than the work skiff at the marine lab. First, the tugboat had more deck space to hold the dredging equipment, nets, rakes, collecting jars, and buckets. There was space for the clingy dog that rarely left her side; at least Water Boy no longer feasted on her earlobes and ankles. There was a galley for preparing lunch and a head to relieve oneself after countless cups of coffee; this meant that they could stay out indefinitely, or at least until they ran out of diesel. The only negative was that the tug had no shower, but that was a minor inconvenience. When she got hot, she could adjust the pressure on the water cannon—in a former life the *Vital Spark* had been a fireboat—and spray herself off. Or, when dropping off the equipment at the marine station at the end of the day, she could wash off the silt and sweat at the outdoor shower.

While heading in the direction of the number 2 on the map, Alex collected water samples, looking for the larvae of the Atlantic blue crab, *Callinectes sapidus*, and the eastern oyster, *Crassostrea virginica*. Larval numbers would predict population sizes and the success of those industries in upcoming years. She also dredged the bottom for marine invertebrates burrowing in the muddy sand. The specimens were labeled and jarred to go to a lab monitoring environmental pollutants. She recorded the various bird species spotted, their density and location for a University of Maryland ornithologist whom she would assist in a seabird population survey. Her plan was to keep busy, incessantly busy, to distract herself from Papa's death, but every inch of the *Vital Spark* was a reminder of him and his eccentricities. The water cannon mounted on the bow was case and point.

Papa had broken the original cannon years earlier on a Giles Blood-hand Day, when he'd directed it skyward to act as a fountain for the tipsy tourists floating on inner tubes and kayaks. By the end of that afternoon, the cannon's motor, which drove the impeller, was red-hot and smoking. Papa and Ben had remounted a new cannon on a swiveling bar stool donated from Miles Harlow. It now had a tremendous range of motion and could blast water halfway across the river.

The remodeling of the *Vital Spark* occurred just after Papa, Ben, Alan and Jacob took her to Disney World for her tenth birthday. It had taken Papa years to save for the trip. The Pirates of the Caribbean ride left quite an impression; immediately upon their return, Papa and Ben had converted the tugboat into a pyrate ship. Since money was scarce, supplies for the renovation consisted of junk salvaged from the back corners of the boatyard and Smyth's Marina. The two faded nylon seats at the helm had been unscrewed and replaced with two wooden barrels. The sickly green linoleum table in the galley was replaced with a heavy wood table bound by wooden benches. The walls were covered with knotty pine planks. From the ship's wheel lamp over the galley table dangled toy parrots (Gillian borrowed one every Giles Blood-hand Day), plastic skulls and shrunken heads, which, according to Papa, came from a South Pacific island inhabited by cannibals. By ten, she had known better but just went along with it.

The centerpiece of the renovation, and possibly the only artifact of any value, was bolted over the hatchway into the cabin. Papa had won it off some unwitting sap in a poker game. It was an authentic eighteenth century figurehead of a woman in a low-cut, blue gown. She had ample breasts and her eyes were green glass. Around the figurehead's neck Papa had draped plastic Hawaiian leis and gaudy necklaces from Mardi Gras.

"We're at the Sassafras River," Julia announced.

Julia had been mercifully quiet that morning while Alex worked on the aft deck. Julia seemed baffled that people got paid to collect water and mud, and to watch birds.

"Dot number two seems to be in that inlet." Alex looked at the GPS. "There's nothing there but Chance's place."

"Chance is still alive?" Julia said.

"You know him?"

"Yes, of course. I remember him very well."

"Chance's inlet's very shallow. We'll take it very slowly. I'll drive."

"Suit yourself." Julia lifted herself off the barrel at the ship's wheel. "Horrid seat. Hard as a bloody rock."

The tugboat cruised slowly into the lily pads. The inlet was silent except for the chirp of crickets and the steady chug of the inboard. Alex cut the engine and they drifted toward a rickety dock. An old man with a walking stick limped down the dock. He lifted his arm in a stiff wave.

"Hey, Chance," Alex called through a porthole.

"Annie, hello!"

It was no use correcting him; he'd forget in two seconds. He'd done way too much LSD. He looked his usual self, white-hair flying off in all directions, sleeveless t-shirt, cut-offs and flip-flops.

Julia leapt off the boat, threw her arms around his neck and planted a kiss on his mouth. "It's me, Chance! Julia!"

"Julia ... oh my goodness!"

Julia pressed another kiss onto his mouth, this one longer than before. He smiled distantly. Wild parties were rumored to have occurred at Papa's place in the sixties; the second kiss confirmed it.

"Chance," Alex said, interrupting the love fest, "did Papa and Ben come by here and leave something for me?"

"Yes."

"What was it?" she asked urgently.

He shook his head, confused. "Hmm ... I don't remember."

"When was this?"

"Some time ago."

"Days ago or weeks ago?"

"Yes." He smiled pleasantly.

"Good," she sighed. "Can I look around?"

"Of course, darlin'."

Alex headed down the dock. Chance's common-law wife, Fat Theresa, burst from the cottage at the end of the dock. Everyone always called Theresa Fat, just as Ben had always been Old. No offense was taken. Theresa was in fact spherical. She waddled excitedly down the dock. Alex panicked. Fat Theresa's tremendous tonnage would certainly buckle the dock. The planks groaned with each descending step. Alex dashed down the dock and jumped onto the spartina grass. She turned. So far so good ... the planks were holding. Oblivious to their precarious state, the senior citizens howled in laughter at some antic decades before her birth.

Chance and Fat Theresa lived off the grid, subsisting on crabs, oysters, fish, deer and a garden in a clearing in the woods. There were no power lines running to their cottage. In his younger days, Chance had been a skilled wooden boat builder. Now boats in various states of disrepair lay in the marsh grass, his hands too knotted by arthritis to work. Alex wandered around his workshop. It had the wonderful scent of dry wood and oils. Saw horses, drills, bits, saws, caulk, and paint filled the cluttered space. Cobwebs draped kayaks in the rafters above. But nowhere did she see the letters CC.

She followed a narrow trail into the clearing with the vegetable garden, summer corn, and apple trees. No CC there. The smell of burning logs drew her farther into the woods. The air around the whiskey still was thick with smoke.

"Better than from CAN TUCK KEY," Papa had once told her, holding a Mason jar at the tap from the worm box.

She circled the still, turning over wooden crates and rummaging through the log pile, until her eyes burned from the ashes and heat. No trace of a CC there, either. Her frustration mounted. What was the point of this ridiculous scavenger hunt that Papa and Ben had sent her on? She should be back at the marine station, cleaning mud from the collecting equipment and entering the data in spreadsheets.

She wandered back through the woods and the clearing and came upon the green inlet once again. Bursts of laughter rang out from the dock. The planks were miraculously intact, so it seemed unlikely that she'd have to drag three old people through the lily pads and onto the shore after all. Water Boy sniffed through the grass, collecting as many ticks as possible in his black coat. No doubt he was looking for some fetid morsel to eat, whose repulsive odor he would breathe into her face during the inevitable tick plucking session.

There were two areas left to search. She didn't feel much like rummaging through the couple's cottage. She'd seen it before. It was a hoarder's paradise, with decades of books, newspapers, and magazines, and Theresa's potter's wheel and ceramics. Instead, she headed for the abandoned boats.

The first one was an O'Day day sailer that was missing its mast. She peeked into its hull. The only things present were a broken rudder and an orange flotation vest that was nearly black from mold. The next boat was a wooden rowboat filled with so much soil that *Rudbeckia hirta*, aka Black-Eyed Susan, the Maryland State flower, sprouted from it. And of course there was the Viking longboat that Papa, Ben and Chance thought might be fun to sail into the middle of the Giles Blood-hand festival. A Viking invasion on the Chesapeake! Unfortunately, the money had run out before they'd finished the hull. They'd never gotten much work done on it anyway; they'd spent too much time by the still. The remaining strakes from the ship were now fueling Theresa's brick kiln.

The last boat was a flat-bottomed marsh skiff, sitting amidst the grass and other scrub plants. She walked tentatively to the upside down boat, avoiding the poison ivy and scratchy ragweed. She bent her head to read the faded letters on the transom.

"Crabby Crab," she said in a pleased whisper.

She paused before turning the skiff over. It might be home to a snake, or worse, a skunk. "Water Boy, come!" He tore through the grass and leapt up, covering her shorts with muddy paw prints. "Down, down!" She held him by the collar and pointed his muzzle at the boat. Nothing held his interest, which meant it was safe to upright. She dug her fingers into the sandy soil and lifted. In the matted, yellow grass was a moldy backpack. She peered inside, her heart pounding, half-expecting—dreading—a frightening body part. Odd. The backpack held nothing more than a River Glen High School yearbook. From 1987.

She glanced westward. The sun would be setting in an hour or two. It would take at least an hour to motor back to the Glen River. She'd look through the book later. She and Water Boy returned to the dock, Alex stepping gingerly from plank to plank, the dog romping alongside.

"Julia, let's go."

"You found something on your shufti?" Julia stared wide-eyed at the backpack.

"Yup. Chance, Theresa, thanks for letting me have a look around."

Chance patted her cheek. "Of course, Amy."

The inlet was too narrow for a U-turn, so Alex backed the boat toward the river. Julia squinted westward toward the bay. A camo jon boat was fleeing into the late afternoon haze. Julia held out her smartphone. Two boats, a Boston Whaler and a jon boat swiped before Alex's eyes.

"Call Will tonight," Julia said, her voice sizzling. "I want to know who the pillocks are that have been following us."

Headquarters

Will couldn't think straight. Alex Allaway had asked him to come by. That same evening! The actress grandmother had given Alex his business card after all. There'd be no time to run home to shower and shave. Maybe he had a clean shirt in his gym bag that he could change into? Would it be appropriate to ask her out after they talked? Terrible idea. He couldn't to afford to take her for a pizza. And Jay would be pissed if he fraternized with witnesses. She hadn't been interested in him back in the day and she wasn't interested in him now.

When he'd found out that Alex was also attending the University of Maryland, he'd wandered by her dorm numerous times that September. They were from the same hometown. They could at least be friends. Who was he kidding? He wasn't interested in friendship. He had a zillion friends. He was a football player. Teammates, coaches and trainers were in his face all day long. He wanted her in his bed. *And that's changed how?*

Every time he went by her dorm, Alex was never there. Every time her blonde roommate would pop out from the room next door. "Sure, I'll tell her you came by. Sure, I'll give her your number."

You're a police detective and Alex's not interested ... focus, focus, focus! Lisa's unwavering attention to the case was impressive. Nothing could distract her, whereas his mind scrambled in a thousand directions at once. But it had been a day of interesting revelations. Dr. Zera Lim's team had been busy. Hairs obtained from the recliner were, of course, Randy's. Hairs from Old Ben and Alex were obtained from the collapsed sofa.

From the pattern of fingerprints in Randy's house, it seemed certain that Randy had opened the door for the perpetrators, since the perpetrators' prints were not on the doorknob. One perpetrator had handed Randy the Allman Brothers CD, and Randy had put it into the CD player. Randy had drunk scotch, while one perpetrator had drunk beer. A second perpetrator had drunk coffee. These behaviors would imply a friendship, as one is not going to listen to music and drink with one's enemies.

The fingerprints from the perpetrators were not in the FBI's central database. Nor was the DNA from the saliva on the beer cans in any database. But then came Dr. Lim's startling discovery. Frank Whitby's fingerprints were on the CD case, and the coffee cup. Some of his hair fibers were found near the recliner. His saliva was not on the beer cans, only the coffee cup. Two men had visited Randy Allaway that night, and the coffee drinker was Frank Whitby.

And there was one other bit of stunning information. A Coast Guard patrol boat had seen Ben Hancock's sailboat pass through the Chesapeake and Delaware Canal on the evening of Randy Allaway's murder. Ben had never headed south down the Bay, but instead had gone north, through the canal to the Delaware Bay, and out into the Atlantic. Had the timid Old Ben witnessed the murder, perhaps through a window, hid until Whitby and his partner left, then fled for his life?

River Glen

"Is that what you're wearing tonight?" Julia frowned while she kneaded mush in a mixing bowl.

"My Dior gown's at the dry cleaners." Alex flew through the kitchen and pushed through the door. There was no need for more chitchat with the grandmother that she'd been with since the crack of dawn—well, actually nine o'clock, but close enough. Nor had there been time to return to the lab to deposit the equipment. Instead they'd returned directly home. She'd combed the ticks—four of them—from Water Boy's coat, and shampooed him under the hose, only for him to trot down to the beach and roll in goose poop. She'd then dashed upstairs to shower in the house, and changed into gym shorts and her favorite t-shirt. So what if the red shorts and orange shirt didn't exactly match? At least she'd be comfortable. She passed on a dinner of Scottish Entrail Delight—haggis—and opted for peanut butter and jelly on the *Vital Spark*.

Finally, a moment's peace before Will came over ... a disconcerting thought in itself. The plastic bag with the skull was banished to the corner and she wiped the galley table with disinfectant. She prepared herself a sandwich and hot tea, sat under the parrots, skulls and shrunken heads, and opened her father's yearbook.

1987 was Colin Allaway's senior year in high school. She found him immediately, as he was with the As. He had a pleasant, thoughtful face, and looked more like Papa than Julia, though he lacked Papa's rakish smile. There was a Denniston in her father's class, the Hoffman's daughter, Harriet; and Curtis Smyth, now the business manager at the marina. She also spotted Will's mother, Belle Stanton, now the village's travel agent, before she'd married John Wilkins, the notary who owned the auto tags shop. She thumbed to the end of the alphabet—and gasped. The student was exceptionally handsome and keenly aware of it. His light eyes seemed to stare brashly into hers. Never had a mere photograph had such an effect. Frank Whitby raised goose bumps on her skin.

There was a commotion on the beach. She stood and banged her head into the lamp. "Ouch!" She peered out a porthole. Will held a tennis ball just out of reach of Water Boy's snapping mouth. He thrust his arm back and heaved the ball outward. "Fetch!" It landed almost half way across the river. The dog jumped joyfully into the water.

Will walked the dock toward the *Vital Spark* and Alex's temperature spiked.

This would be the first time they'd been alone since that double date at the Point. Her date that night had been Eddie Richmond. Will had been Gillian's boyfriend. That night had been a mess at so many levels. Hopefully he'd forgotten the whole evening. Yes, she was completely forgettable. He'd certainly forgotten. Maybe they could move this discussion into the house and let Julia explain about the creepy boaters? Yes, yes, perfect. Julia could handle this. Then he could go on his way; she wouldn't have to say a word. Suddenly it was too late. He stepped onboard, weaved between the crab pots and trotline, and knocked on the hatch door.

"Alex?"

She cleared her throat. "Yeah, come on in."

He ducked under the figurehead's breasts, leis and Mardi Gras necklaces, and grinned at the pyrate decor. "Yo ho."

"Papa never got over his visit to Pirates of the Caribbean."

"Carly would love this. She's already talking about next year's pyrate festival." He swatted a shrunken head and looked at her plate of food. "I'm not interrupting your dinner, I hope."

"It's okay. Just P B and Js. Want one?"

"You don't mind?"

"No. How many?" His dress shirt looked as though it had just been removed from a bag. It still had the new fabric-plastic bag smell.

"Two, if you have enough. I'm starved."

She slathered up slices of bread at the counter. "I have tea, coffee or water."

"Water's fine."

She pulled a water bottle from the fridge, placed the plate in front of him, and dropped onto the bench opposite him.

"So you're looking at old yearbooks," he said.

"My father's. Look who his classmate was." She turned the book toward him.

The smug face stared into Will's. Thoughts moved rapidly behind his eyes.

"Is Frank Whitby involved in Papa's death?" she asked. "Are you all close to catching someone?"

"I can't say what we're …"

"I know, I know." She fumbled with her teacup. "A lot of things feel wrong." That was an understatement. "Julia?"

"Julia Hale is who she says she is. A Scottish actress. Actually of considerable talent, apparently. And we checked the land records. She and Randy were co-owners of this house, so this place is hers. There's nothing questionable in her background, as far as we know. She flew from Heathrow a day after Randy's death."

"So she's definitely not the murderer … murderess?"

"No."

Alex's watch vibrated on her wrist. Another Hot Yoga class in thirty minutes.

"Do you need to do something?" He strained to read her watch.

"No."

There was an awkward pause, so they both grabbed their sandwiches.

"Your text," he finally said. "You wanted to show me something."

"Yesterday and today Julia and I were out on the boat. We were followed both days. I didn't notice, but she did."

Will's eyes widened.

"Here." She reached for her smartphone. "Julia took photos with her phone. Yesterday it was these two boats."

She swiped the photos of the Boston Whaler and the jon boat before his eyes. "And today it was the jon boat again. Can you check those boat registration numbers for me and find out who those creeps are?"

He hesitated. "Can I send these to myself?"

"Yeah. Of course."

He forwarded the images to his email and handed her the phone. "Where were you two?"

She stalled. "Yesterday we were on the Bohemia, and today on the Sassafras."

"What were you doing there?"

She stalled again. "Just boating."

He wasn't buying it and frowned. "Really, Alex. What were you doing? I can't help you if you're not honest with me."

Randy's map had said, "Tell no one Alex. No one! JAllaway might come." And there were the numbered dots: 1. Bohemia River, 2. Sassafras River, and 3. Mutter Island.

JAllaway had come. There were messages at the Bohemia and Sassafras Rivers. Papa and Ben were trying to tell her something. Something vital. But it was for her alone.

"Just boating," she repeated obstinately.

"Right." He stood abruptly, put his dish in the sink, and ducked under the figurehead on his way out. Then he bent his head back in. "This isn't the first time you've lied to me."

"What the hell are you talking about?"

"That night at the Point. 'I'm going to the University of Delaware,' you said. You were never intending to go there. You just didn't want me to know that you were going to Maryland. What a fool I was, wandering by your dorm room to see if you wanted to go out for dinner!"

"You never came by my dorm! Who's the liar?"

"Yeah, I did. A number of times. And every time your roommate would appear and take the message. She's was running interference for you."

"What roommate? I had a single. My whole floor was singles."

"Yeah, yeah, whatever," he muttered, rushing off the boat.

The Atlantic

Old Ben tightened the bungee cord around his arm and the tiller. If he could just get twenty minutes of a deep sleep, he'd be alert enough to get through the next few hours. Thankfully it was a calm night. *Star Gazer* moved silently over the swells. Despite the salty film coating his glasses, Sagittarius, Hercules and Aquila were visible in the June sky.

When he'd entered the classroom for his first college course, College Algebra, he'd realized that it was the astronomy and physics lab. Constellation globes, pendulums, oscilloscopes, weights, balances and pulleys were locked in glass cabinets. NASA posters of the planets covered the walls. The class before his math course was ASTRO 101. He'd hurry from the boat to catch the tail end of the astronomy lecture from the hallway.

On the first day of class, he'd strategically chosen the seat in the back, hoping that he wouldn't be called on. The seat was strategic for another reason. Next to it was a poster of the constellations. On countless nights he and Randy sat on the porch, looking up at the sky. Now he'd be able to identify the star patterns.

The thought of returning to school after so many years drove his anxiety through the roof. He smoked weed around the clock that August.

"You're a genius with numbers, Ben," Randy had said. "You can do this. Piece of cake."

"But I haven't been in school since I was seventeen."

"You'll be the top student in the class. Dean's List, I'm sure. Every semester."

Randy had a piece-of-cake philosophy about the world. Everything was easy, delicious, and satisfying.

It had been Randy's encouragement that induced Ben to enroll in the math course. Just one course. He might be able to handle one evening course after a long day on the water. Surprisingly, on the first quiz in September Ben had earned a nine of out ten. On the pop quiz, he'd gotten a ten out of ten. On his first exam, in October, he'd gotten a 93%. He was on a roll. He no longer smoked weed before class, as it was important to be as alert as possible. He went to Registrar's Office to enroll in another evening math course for the following semester with the same excellent math professor, and bought the textbook in advance.

A pretty, young freshman and a loud, handsome boy in designer sweaters sat in front of him that semester. They'd chattered too much, but he wasn't about to move from his favorite seat next to the constellations. He'd almost memorized all of them.

In late November the professor had wandered the classroom, handing back exams while Ben's head pounded. It had been an unimaginable week since the car accident. He'd slept on Randy's concave sofa most of that week to assist with the baby. The infant was used to Carole's breast milk. They'd had to switch to formula. She cried incessantly.

Randy was half drunk and despondent while muddling with the funeral arrangements. The Lowes were adamant that the couple be buried together in Philadelphia, Carole's hometown. Randy was hoping to bury Colin in the River Glen cemetery. Randy finally relented, as Colin had adored Carole and would want to spend eternity with her. Then was the back and forth about who was going to care for the baby. The Lowes travelled extensively, but there was that second cousin in Ohio.

That was the tipping point. Randy rarely exploded. "There will be no second cousin!" he'd yelled into the phone. "I've made concessions about the funeral arrangements and burial, but Alexandra is staying with me in River Glen!"

Ben had been preoccupied with cribs, diapers, black suits and flowers, when the math professor went to the board to review the test problems. He had earned a 98%, while the obnoxious boy in front of him complained about his 67%.

"What an unfair test! What a prick of a professor!" the boy had said to the girl. He flipped hotly through the pages of the test. "Everything fucking sucks. I can't go out this weekend. My car was in an accident last week. It's totaled."

Maybe it was just a coincidence, but Ben's blood ran cold. He couldn't help himself. He leaned boldly over the boy's thick shoulder, scanning the test for the boy's name.

"Back off, Googan! You smell like low tide at the docks," Frank Whitby had growled.

River Glen

"What the hell just happened?" Will asked himself. That meeting had gone just about as badly as possible. Alex pushed his buttons like no one else. Now he was lost in weird

Allaway Land. Between Randy's porch and the small beach were the lawn ornaments: gnomes, a faded blue dolphin from Florida, a statue of Neptune, a pink sea horse, and a sinister-looking Baltimore Raven. Who in their right-mind had a Baltimore Raven lawn ornament? Ravens Bigheads, yes, but a lawn ornament? Hanging from the porch railing were pyrate flags, Baltimore Ravens and Orioles flags, and a yellow "Don't Tread on Me" flag. And there was the old VW Bug with a birch tree growing through the engine block. The Harley motorcycle was rusting into the ground at the side of the house. On the porch was the barefooted grandmother, smoking from a 1940s cigarette holder. He turned back toward the tugboat, half expecting Alex to have her middle finger in the air, but there was no movement. For their meeting he'd stopped at Target to buy a new shirt and aftershave for thirty bucks, which he didn't have. She'd put on a garish South of the Border t-shirt that a five-year-old might wear. And he wanted be part of this freak show why?

He backed his car out of Randy's driveway. But where to go? The Point? No, any place but there. His apartment? It was too early to go home to the claustrophobic box, a stuffy, un-air-conditioned room with a foldout sofa bed, a cube fridge and a microwave. The lights were on at Jay's house on the promontory across the river.

Jay had been silent and surly all day. The only time he'd spoken to Will had been to tell him to ask Alex what was meant by b'lue crabs moving to deeper waters'. She was a fisheries biologist; she'd know that. But Will's mind had been on other matters. He'd completely forgotten. Where Alex was concerned, he'd lost all objectivity. It would be a setback in his career—it wouldn't be the first. And he'd probably be assigned to desk duty for eons—but Jay needed to remove him from this murder investigation.

Newark, Delaware

Clyde Whitby pressed his Spy Ear listening device against the wall in his home office and sat motionless. On other side of the wall, in the family room, his wife, Francine, was on the phone with their neighbor Deborah, yacking about the PTO bake sale. Before that they'd bantered about the Father-Daughter dance that he'd be forced to go to with his middle daughter, and which would mean shelling out money for her new dress. And then Francine and Deborah quibbled about who should be the next president of the Decorations Committee. So far, so good. No indication that Francine had been talking to Rufus Tucker, who rotated her tires. But one could never be too sure. He listened intently for a moment longer. His worries assuaged, he sat upright and put the device into his desk drawer.

It had been a vexing evening. Francine had nagged him about being late for dinner again.

"I worked all afternoon to prepare that beef stroganoff recipe from the Cooking Channel," she'd said.

"I was delayed at the new shop in northern Maryland," he'd muttered, lumbering past her to the shower.

"You're looking very tan," she'd said doubtfully.

"I stopped at a rest stop for lunch and to stretch my legs, if you don't mind. Exercise is important. I spend my whole day in the car. That's how I can afford to buy you an executive home in Newark. What else do you want?"

That shut her up.

Things were disturbingly quiet in the next room. Clyde rushed the listening device from the drawer and leaned again toward the wall. A male voice was heard in the next room. A

British voice. Oh thank God ... it was only Gordon Ramsay. Francine had switched from the Shopping Channel to *Kitchen Nightmares*.

He clicked open the Whitby family genealogy folder on his laptop. There was one particular document he needed to re-read. Never, ever would he mention the rare document to Professor Levon Bakanian or other historians. The knowledge in it was for Whitbys only, passed from father to son since the 1690s. It bothered him that he'd only produced daughters, three of them, but he'd keep trying. It was he, Clyde Whitby, not Levon Bakanian, who was the world's expert on the pyrates of the northern Chesapeake! He, Clyde Whitby, was the keeper of Conall Whitby's diary.

Both Conall and Neville Whitby had been illiterate men, but they were shrewd enough to befriend Brother Guillermo, a scribe. The errant priest, unable to resist rum and women, had found refuge with Jack Black-Tooth and his band of coastal brigands in the Carolinas. When the *Raven* stopped to trade for beans and pigs and resupply their water, Jack Black-Tooth had told Giles Hale of a farm up the coast, in the colony of Virginia, with indentured field hands from Newgate Prison. The news of "fierce, dirty women" enthralled Giles. It was time he took a wife. At the mention of women, Brother Guillermo enthusiastically volunteered to join their crew. The *Raven* hurriedly weighed anchor. En route north, behind the barrier islands, they pillaged a coastal farm for cattle and more pigs. Near the Pamlico River, they stole the mainsail, cables, topsail, spritsail, rigging and anchors from a tobacco trader. The women convicts were, as Jack Black-Tooth promised, at a tobacco plantation near the North Landing River. The women were happy to cast their lot with the *Raven*: pyrates were preferable to the ceaseless lash of the sadistic foreman.

The *Raven's* hull was taking on water. It was doubtful that the ship would make it as far as the pyrate haven of Rhode Island. A closer sanctuary was necessary to make repairs. She sailed northwest into the mouth of the Chesapeake, a region squabbled over by the new colonial governments of Virginia and Maryland. The fortifications at St. Mary's City and the James, York, and Rappahannock rivers were little more than earthen berms and pikes, occasionally manned by starving colonists. In the dead of night, the *Raven* slipped unnoticed by these laughable defenses, and hid in the labyrinth of islands on the eastern shore during the heat of the day. Next, the *Raven* snuck by the Kent Island settlement and continued north.

In the northern Chesapeake, the *Raven* came upon a remote river, impassable but for one narrow channel. A scouting party set out to shore and found the area uninhabited except for a few runaway slaves and Nanticokes who, upon seeing the ferocious men with blunderbusses and sabers, retreated into the forest. It seemed the perfect place to repair the ship, because the waters teamed with herring and blue crabs. Rotting ropes around their waists, the men and women dragged the *Raven* between the oyster beds and sandbars to a beach upriver. They unloaded the supplies and readied the tar and pitch. But the *Raven's* sailing days had come to an end. The planks were riddled with shipworms and crumbled under their hands. At best, some boards might be salvaged to construct huts, but unless they stole another vessel, their pyrating days were over.

Clyde whipped his Spy Ear from the drawer and leaned toward the wall. His oldest daughter was talking to Francine about getting her learner's permit. Fuck! Now he was going to have to shell out money for driving instruction. He returned his attention to the invaluable family document that he'd scanned on his home scanner. The original document was locked in his attic's sturdy safe.

Clyde's heart convulsed when he got to this section of the diary. Thankfully Conall had survived Giles' massacre to describe the events as they truly happened, accurately documenting this essential piece of Whitby family history. Charles Allaway's accusation was entirely unfounded. Neville Whitby was a respected founding father of River Glen. Never would he have stolen gold from the community treasury!

It was that lying Charles Allaway who had stolen the gold allotted for boat repairs, nets, saws, and blankets and herbal medicines for the children. Neville was no thief! It was Allaway who was the thief, and Allaway's accusation had publicly humiliated Neville and tarnished the Whitby name! For that offense Allaway had paid in blood, paid with his head on a pike in front of the village tavern, a dagger lodged in his brain.

Now another Allaway had struck a blow to the Whitby family honor. Alex Allaway was responsible for Frank's disappearance, and possibly his death. Before killing him, had she tortured him? Had Frank in his agony divulged the contents of Conall Whitby's diary? What were the objects that she found while roaming the banks of the Bohemia and Sassafras Rivers? Something Frank had hidden ... some incriminating lingerie or sex tape from one of his married playmates that Alex might turn over to the police? Frank's body was not in Randy's basement or attic. Otherwise the police would have located it during their search for Randy's killer. If the boneheaded police were unable to find Frank, dead or alive, then by God, he would.

Middletown

Vital Spark

Penny Bannister glanced at the calendar on her new 6G ultraflex smartphone and blew on her wet finger nails. By next year at this time, she, Carly, Baby X and the nanny would be residing in a beachfront house in Ocean City, Maryland. Goodbye puny two bedroom apartment in Middletown, Delaware. The beach house, she'd insist to the Realtor, must have an open floor plan with hardwood floors, double sinks in all the bathrooms, granite countertops in the kitchen and stainless steel appliances. She'd probably design the pool and hot tub herself. No boring rectangle or oval-shaped pool for her, but something artistic and zany that would be the talk of her parties. Her OB/GYN had confirmed it that morning—she was pregnant. Soon her lawyer would be contacting Darren Darien, the power forward for the Delaware Fightin' Blue Hens, with the good news. Congratulations Darren, you're going to be a father!

A coalescence of fortuitous events during her freshman year in college had led to her profitable entrepreneurial scheme. First was an article she'd read about a groupie who'd gotten herself pregnant by three different rock stars and never had to work a day in her life. Never working a day in her life sounded good to her. The idea was brilliant in its simplicity. She had no access to rock stars, but she was a cheerleader, and a beautiful one at that. Athletes there were aplenty.

More divine luck. During the first week of school an athlete literally delivered himself right to her door—well actually, the door next to hers. It was destiny. Here was the new tight-end, the giant freshman with the great hands who never dropped a ball. She'd seen him over the summer at the scrimmages. He'd walked right passed her room and knocked on Alex's door. How did he know Alex, the scatterbrain from a nameless fishing village who dashed out of the dorm every morning, hair uncombed, flip-flops flapping, buttoning her shirt as she ran?

Quick thinking had been in order. She'd sprung off her bed. "Alex is in class. I'm her roommate, just studying next door."

"Oh. Can you tell her that Will came by? Just to say hi."

"Sure, no problem." The dolt didn't even realize that these rooms were singles.

Then she'd hung around her dorm around-the-clock with her door open. "I gave her your number. I don't know why she didn't call."

The clincher: "Alex is away for the weekend with her boyfriend." After that, he never reappeared.

Penny then dyed her hair auburn so that he wouldn't recognize her at the games. Should he run into Alex somewhere else on campus, discover the ruse, and an accuse her of subterfuge, her line would be, "I have no idea who you were talking to. What blonde?"

She had watched him at the games and followed his statistics. Yes, he was the one. She discovered the frats that he attended after the games, the clubs he frequented. She waited until sophomore year, in case his freshman performance was a fluke. It wasn't; in his sophomore season he set more records. Scouts were talking to him after every game. Mr. NFL would be her meal ticket.

Also helpful in her scheme were the two science nerds in the two rooms next to hers freshmen year. The pre-med, Courtney Raney and the scatterbrain, Alex, were in the same Intro Biology class. For the entire fall semester they'd studied together, talking about cells, DNA, and natural selection. In the spring semester they'd taken physiology together, and Penny could overhear them discussing the oscillating female hormones. Day 14, the magic day in the ovarian cycle, was when ovulation occurred. The few days after her Day 14 was when she'd tracked down Will. It was too easy.

Penny blew on her fingernails again and held the nails next to her eyes. For some time she studied herself in the bathroom mirror. Her green nails and the new green contact lens were a perfect match. The Parisian brown had gotten tiresome. She'd never had raven black hair until now. It was a great look on her. Carly loved it too. "You look beautiful, Mommy, just like Giles the Pyrate." Carly's persistent chatter about the pyrate festival was soooo irksome. The reputed girlfriend ... her name was Gillian ... had an adorable black lab puppy. Carly had been dancing with Will, Gillian and the puppy. Was the dog a gift from Will? If he could afford a puppy, he could afford a larger living allowance for her and Carly. And the girlfriend had a beach house near River Glen Point, plus a boat. Was Will financing the girlfriend's lifestyle with some funds she didn't know about, or was Gillian some sugar mama who was independently wealthy? In college Penny had majored in Business, as it was important to know how to invest one's fortune. "Any successful businessperson has to gauge the strengths and weaknesses of competitors," her business professors had said time and again.

It was time for a drive to River Glen Point to check out the competition.

River Glen

Julia ducked through the tugboat's hatch door with two glasses and a bottle of scotch in hand. "Randy told me that you loved stories." She dropped down on a bench seat at the galley table.

"When I was five," Alex said. "I don't like hard liquor."

Julia poured two glasses and pushed one her way. "But I do. Once upon a time. Oh, by the way, this is a true story—"

"Next time you want to talk to the police, you can talk to them yourself!"

"But you did show Will the photos of the boats, didn't you?"

"Yes. He sent them to himself."

"Good."

"But you can talk to him about it. I'm not talking to him again. That jerk called me a liar."

"Did you lie to him?"

"Whose side are you on?"

"I take no sides, until I have information. Every story has two sides."

"Okay, I did lie about where I was going to college—"

"College?" Julia cut in. "And when was this?"

"Maybe six years ago."

"You've known him for a while."

"Since forever."

"So why'd you tell him that?"

"I didn't want to hang out with River Glen people in college and have a repeat of high school. High school was a disaster in every way. I barely graduated. I wanted a fresh start. He said that he came by my dorm room looking for me, and that my roommate told him that I wasn't there. Every time he came by, she said I wasn't there. He as good as accused me of putting her up to it. I lived by myself! I didn't have a roommate! I told him that. He said that I was lying about that too. Then he made me doubt myself." She fumbled with her smartphone. "So I even went to the Residential Life website and found the floor plan of my freshmen dorm." She pointed vehemently. "Look, look! That was my room. A single. The person to my left was Courtney Raney. We're still great friends. Will mentioned a blonde girl. It must have been the girl to the right, who I hardly remember. Why would she do that?"

"I don't know, lass, but send him that floor plan. Defend yourself."

She shook her head. "I don't give a shit. I'm having nothing more to do with him."

Julia twisted a cigarette into the black holder and lit it. She inhaled deeply then blew the smoke into the mix of parrots, skulls, and shrunken heads. "This is just a misunderstanding, and easy to fix if you send him the floor plan. He seems quite nice."

"He's not. He pushed a bee, no, an eraser down the back of my pants in English class. I don't want to talk about this. Aren't you here to tell me a bedtime story?"

Julia laughed. "It sounds like he put more than bees and erasers into your pants."

"Thanks for the sympathy," Alex said sarcastically.

"Have a drink, love." Julia nudged the scotch her way. "Lighten up."

Alex considered the glass for a moment. "Maybe it will numb my headache." She took a giant gulp, her face scrunched.

"Highland scotch whiskey is a cure-all. Here's my story, and remember, it's true. Once upon a time there was a Scottish lord named Sir Edmund Hale. One day in 1695, he was up in the hills with his hunting dogs and old gillie when a black speck appeared below in the valley, moving slowly next to the river. Edmund and his gillie hid behind a boulder and watched, their rifles readied. The black speck took form. It was a man and woman in tattered cloaks, each carrying a small child in a sling. These were no highwaymen or poachers on the estate, just a beggar and his family. Since it was the Christian way to feed the poor, Edmund and the gillie strode down the hill. As they approached, the young man raised his hands to indicate that he was unarmed and meant no harm. He pulled back the hood of his cloak. Edmund nearly collapsed. The old gillie grasped his sleeve., exclaiming, 'Giles is alive, Master! Giles is alive!'"

The Atlantic

Ben pulled a tarp over his head when it began to drizzle. Even if it poured buckets, he'd remain on deck. It had been drizzling that November night in 1991 when he'd walked out of the science building after algebra class and waited in his pickup. Frank Whitby had paced in annoyance under the overhang of the building, glaring repeatedly at his watch. Finally, a glistening red Corvette had pulled up to the curb; Frank climbed in, hissing and sneering at the driver. Ben followed the sports car from a distance, up the highway, and onto the coastal road where there was a development of executive homes. The Corvette had turned into the driveway of a home with a groomed lawn, spiraled topiaries and a stained glass front door. The garage door opened and the Corvette disappeared into the bright space. Ben motored by, noting the house number on the mailbox.

Ben had returned home to find Randy in the rocking chair, Alex asleep on his shoulder. Randy's face was gaunt and his eyes stared beyond the evening news display on the tv screen.

"I don't know if it's anything ..." Ben lifted a burning joint from the ashtray. "But there's this kid in my class ..."

Randy turned slowly in his malaise.

Ben exhaled the smoke up to the ceiling, away from the baby. "...who cracked up his car last week."

A glimmer of interest sparkled in Randy's glazed eyes.

"His name is ..."

"Let me guess," Randy said bitterly. "Whitby."

After that Randy was on a mission. Dressed in his black leather jacket and helmet, he'd set off every evening on the sputtering old Harley and park in the woods at the edge of the development, returning exhausted at daybreak. They prayed that the right house was being surveilled, and that the wrecked car had not already been disposed of. It was unlikely that the thugs would have dumped the car during Thanksgiving week, a time occupied by relatives and festivities. Besides, the police were combing the back roads of River Glen looking for a damaged vehicle.

Then, one night, the garage door opened and the red Corvette motored through the neighborhood. Randy checked his watch; it was just past three. He kick-started the old motorcycle to life and followed with his headlight off. The Corvette turned into a farm. A tow truck was waiting next to the barn. A wrecked car had already been loaded onto its bed. Another car had also been present, a dark sedan of some kind. The caravan of cars left the farm and eventually stopped at a dirt road near Cooper's Creek. Men had worked feverishly to remove branches and scrub bushes from a long overgrown road, and then the tow truck backed into the darkness. There was a grinding of gears and moan of metal, then a hollow splash. The tow truck had rapidly departed and the remaining men had moved the branches and bushes back into place to obscure the entrance to the dirt road. Randy waited motionlessly in the woods, the motorcycle hidden in a gulley. The red Corvette had passed by, and then the dark sedan—an unmarked police car.

River Glen

Jay answered his front door with a brusque "What?"

Will shuffled on the step, unsure, unsure of everything. "Um, can we talk for a moment, sir?"

Jay glanced over his shoulder, at what, Will couldn't see. He finally motioned him in. "Drink?"

"Yes, okay." Will tentatively entered.

An Italian opera played from some room. He followed Jay into the foyer. Oddly, the dining room housed the living room furniture. Even more peculiar, the furniture was positioned against the walls according to color, transitioning from warm to cool colors. The pictures on the walls were arranged in the same general color scheme. The dining room table and chairs were lined up against living room walls and white painting tarps covered the living room carpet. None of the lamps had shades. Laura Braden stood in a white smock in front of an easel, opera coming from her CD player. She looked blankly at Will, and then returned to the canvas. It looked as though she were painting a still life, reminiscent of van Gogh's "Sunflowers." She must have been painting from memory, as no still life arrangement was present in the room.

"Dr. Richmond had her start art therapy," Jay said, en route to the kitchen. "She used to paint all the time. She was a commercial artist before ..."

Jay pulled a pitcher from a kitchen cabinet and dumped a bottle of gin into it, followed by tonic water and ice cubes. Will followed Jay through the den, where the books on the shelves were arranged according to color, and onto the back deck.

The Bradens had an amazing view of the Glen River. To the right, the river disappeared into a lush forest. To the left were three riverside houses, the Dennistons' B&B, the bridge and the village. Directly in front of him, at the tip of the promontory, was a dock with the Boston Whaler that he'd pulled like a mule up Cooper's Creek. He itched just thinking about it. A pack of Marlboros and a perspiring beer mug of gin and tonic sat on the table. There was also a pair of binoculars.

"I can see the Allaway's place from here. Just barely." Jay dropped into a chair and filled a beer mug of G&T for him.

Will held out his phone to Jay. "The grandmother photographed your boat on Sunday."

Jay lit a cigarette. "I don't smoke," he said ironically.

He swiped to the next image. "This jon boat followed them yesterday and today."

Jay looked at the image and nodded. "Yeah, I saw it."

"I just called in the boat registration number to headquarters. The grandmother's definitely paying attention, but Alex is Alex, completely out there. The murderer could come right up to her and ..."

Jay noticed the despair in Will's voice and downed half of his mug.

"The women were at the Bohemia, where you saw them, and at the Sassafras today," Will said. "And Alex wouldn't tell me why!"

"She's definitely withholding something," Jay grumbled. "I'm still wondering about the message Ben Hancock left her, with the numbers and letters."

"And I blew it tonight! I forgot to ask her about the blue crabs. And we fought about—shit—it doesn't matter. You need to take me off this case."

Jay kneaded his temples and downed the rest of his drink. "I need to check on Laura." He left.

Will grabbed the binoculars off the table. The portholes on the *Vital Spark* were yellow dots in the darkness. Beyond the tugboat was a black spit of land, the Point. The Point...

That night at the Point didn't start out as a double date; Alex would never have agreed to it if she'd known that he'd be there. It was the Fourth of July after graduation. That spring the expected senioritis had set in, and the students had partied at the Point every weekend while waiting to hear from colleges.

From the moment he was born, his life's ambition had been to be a Maryland Terrapin and then play for the Baltimore Ravens. Bigheads of Ray Lewis and Ed Reed, his heroes, were on his bedroom wall. Every night of his boyhood he'd slept under Ravens sheets and a Ravens comforter. There were offers from Oklahoma and Florida State, but he'd decided to stay in Maryland so that his parents and sister could attend his games, and so that Ravens scouts might visit him.

He'd been dating Gillian White off-and-on all senior year for all the wrong reasons: she was horny and he had no shot at Alex Allaway, who referred to him, when she considered him at all, as The Pinhead. Alex had been dating off-and-on Eddie Richmond, the son of the famous psychiatrist, Terrence Richmond. Eddie was not interested in Alex's body per se, because he was certainly gay, but rather, access to Randy's weed harvest in the grow house. Gillian and Eddie were first cousins. In one way or another, all of River Glen was related.

Gillian had spotted Alex and Eddie on a beach blanket at the Point. She had insisted on sitting with them to watch the fireworks. Will had expressed his reservations that this was a bad idea, no, a terrible idea, but Gillian had been adamant. She'd grabbed his hand and pulled him across the beach. "Eddie's my favorite cousin. I want to party with Eddie. I won't be seeing him much after he goes to Colombia, Uncle Terrence's alma mater." Gillian had no college aspirations and was staying in River Glen to become a zumba instructor and certified personal trainer.

It had been a steamy night. The people on the beach blankets were in bathing suits, including Eddie, who also wore a red, white and blue party hat. He'd bought beer and rum from Boyd Fleming, a local scumbag, who parked at the Point most weekends and sold booze at obscene prices to the under-age students. Eddie's preparations for the date were impressive. Citronella candles lined the blanket to keep at bay the man-eating mosquitos emerging from the marsh. In addition to the booze, his rolling cooler was stocked full of snacks and soda.

The River Glen town coffers could not afford their own fireworks show, but the Point strategically faced Elkneck State Park, where an amazing firework display was held every summer. As fireworks showered the sky, the cousins chugged beers and gulped down rum shots, laughing hysterically at the expense of defenseless relatives: their grandmother's farting at Thanksgiving dinner, Uncle Jasper's topiaries, and Aunt Judy's cockeyed breast implants. Will wasn't drinking that night because summer mini-camp started in a few weeks and he needed to be quick and lean. Instead he drank from a water bottle and munched on popcorn. Alex sipped a Coke, said little because he was there, and gazed up at the bursting fireworks. Among Eddie's sundries were neon glow sticks that all four of them had looped around their necks. The green shadows accentuated Alex's elegant cheekbones, smooth jawline, slender neck and perfect breasts under her bikini top. He chomped down more popcorn.

"It just occurred to me," Gillian had said out-of-the-blue. "You're both going to Maryland."

At the words, Will's hopes skyrocketed like a firework. College might be a new start for them both. Perhaps they might drive back and forth together for holidays. If he got her season tickets, would she go to his games? Maybe they could take some classes together? Study together? Study in her dorm room ... on her bed ... During study breaks they might ...

"No," Alex said quietly. "I decided to go to Delaware. They have a good marine science program."

Will's hopes fizzled.

"Oh," Gillian said. "When'd you decide that?"

"Recently," Alex answered obliquely.

"We're out of beer, Gill," Eddie complained. "Let's go find Boyd. Come with me. I'm so fucked up. I can't walk straight."

"Okay." Gillian struggled to her feet.

The two cousins stumbled around searching for their sandals and Eddie's wallet. After fumbling, laughing, burping and more fumbling, they staggered arm in arm toward the parking lot, giggling about Aunt Carmen's toy poodles.

Will sat in tense silence, separated from Alex by a vast, un-navigable ocean of blanket. What to say? What to say? His mind was parched of words.

"Popcorn?" He extended the bag across the blanket.

"Yes, thanks." Her hand quickly shot into the bag, grabbed a handful, and pulled back.

She'd spoken to him! Albeit two words, but polite enough. Her previous words had been, "You idiot! You pinhead!" while her desk collided with the trashcan.

She suddenly put the whole handful of popcorn into her mouth at once, sprang to her feet, and jogged toward the water.

He scrambled to his feet as well. An unrelenting force beckoned him to follow.

Chapter 6

Day 6

River Glen

Colors from warm to cool on the bookshelves came into view as Will stirred. And he was slightly chilled. At his apartment, the Box, he awoke every morning sweaty and sticky, the fan unable to budge the hot block of air, but Jay had this marvelous technology called central air-conditioning. Will pulled himself from the leather sofa in the den. The leather also was cool. He opened the slider to the deck and found his shoes and socks. At some point during the evening, he'd rolled up his pants and stuck his legs in the hot tub, watching fireflies flicker over the lawn. The three G&Ts had gone straight to his head, so Jay had pointed him to the sofa. Who knows how many drinks Jay'd had? He had hollow legs.

Will's new dress shirt from Target and his tie were located on the back of an Adirondack chair, but there was no point in putting them on. He wouldn't be in a shirt and tie that day. Jay was not taking him off the Allaway case because they were stretched for manpower. Instead, Jay was giving him another assignment, one that filled him with elation and dread. A special assignment.

He dropped into a chair and pulled on his shoes and socks when Jay stepped outside and handed him a cup of coffee.

"Thank you, sir."

Jay looked out to the river. The water was still, like olive-green glass. Mist hovered on the surface. "Don't you wonder what's under there?"

"Mud and sand?"

"Come." Jay waved him inside.

He followed his mentor to the living room. The floor tarps had been moved along one wall. He gasped.

Laura Braden had had a busy night, a very busy night. The easel with the Sunflowers had been relegated to a corner. She was asleep, curled into a fetal position, in another corner.

A mural had been painted across an entire wall of floral wallpaper. Two old men were seated on beach chairs, drinks in hand. The likeness to Randy and Ben was remarkable—Randy's snow-white hair, Ben's grey ponytail and beard. A fierce-faced, young blond man stood over them. In one hand was a black puppy. His other hand pressed a pistol to the dog's head.

Headquarters

The night before, Lisa Paco had figured out the murderer in *Death in the Tropics* within the first eighteen minutes. Her mother was sure that the murderer was the daughter-in-law, but Lisa'd argued that it was the business partner who'd been hiding behind the statue. It was so obvious that that was where the gunshot had come from—the sculpture garden. The tropical island was breathtakingly beautiful, but such places were best viewed through one's TV screen, so as not have to deal with congested lines at airports, fat tourists spilling into one's seat on the airplane, sand in one's bathing suit, and skin cancer from an equatorial sun.

Lisa was eating breakfast at her desk, a Monster energy drink, bag of Doritos, and an apple—#tokeepthedoctoraway—when Jay called. He would be late, as he was driving his wife to her appointment with Dr. Richmond, and Will would be out of the office for the day. "Woo hoo! Quiet time to myself!" She could hardly contain her glee. It's not that she didn't like her partners; she did, immensely. Jay was a bit like the cranky Inspector Morse, and Will was unwaveringly decent, like Morse's foil, Robbie Lewis. But now she'd be able to study the .jpg of the mural that Jay had attached to his email *on her own*, and review what Frank Whitby did on the day he went missing *on her own*.

"Go back through everything, Paco," was Jay's gruff order.

She decided to start with Frank Whitby's estranged wife, Donna. She reached Donna's cell phone while the wife was out in the neighborhood, walking her dog. Donna was in remarkably good spirits and asked quite happily if they'd located Frank's body yet.

"No," she answered. "You expect him to be dead?"

"Of course. A bigger asshole never lived. He was a thief, con man, swindler, you name it. Every husband on Maryland's eastern shore had reason to kill him."

"Why didn't you divorce him?"

"He refused. Frank pay for his own apartment? You gotta be kidding me! The man was a tightwad. He expected everyone else to pay his way through life."

Lisa glanced through the missing persons report. "So he left for work on May 21st and never came home that night."

"Apparently. I didn't realize it until the next morning. We lived in different parts of the house. Our neighbor, Jim Loften, came to pick him up for golf. I told Jim to go up and wake Frank, as we were beyond the point of talking. Jim came down and said that Frank wasn't there. We walked out to the garage. Frank's car wasn't there, either. Jim suggested we call the police. I said that he was probably at a girlfriend's house. Jim said that Frank was never late for golf. That's when we made the call."

"Do you have any children that were also around?"

"No. We have a grown son, Zachary, who lives in Oregon."

"What does he do?"

"Zach's a nutritionist for a company that sells vitamins and herbal supplements."

"And his relationship with his father?"

"Zach couldn't stand him. As I said, Frank had a million enemies. He offended and pissed off people wherever he went."

"Was Zach around when Frank went missing?"

"No. He hasn't been out to the east coast for years. To avoid Frank."

Lisa glanced at the police report once again.

"You mentioned in the original report that he was wearing a blue and white striped sports shirt the morning he left for work? Why would you have remembered that much detail?"

"Because I didn't buy it for him. And he was so cheap, he'd never have bought it for himself. It was probably a gift from some girlfriend. Or he shoplifted it."

"Did he have any firearms?"

"Are you kidding? He was a gun freak. I'm amazed that there's any wildlife at all left on the east coast."

"Did he keep the guns at home?"

"In the garage. I'm almost home. I can check."

"Whom did he hunt with?"

"His brother, Clyde, mostly. Sometimes his cousin, Desmond."

"Do you know where they hunted?"

"No clue. The less they told the wives, the better, in their view. They're three peas in a pod, all assholes."

Through the phone, Lisa heard the grind of a garage door and the jingle of keys.

"I'm at the gun cabinet," Donna said. "All of his hunting rifles are present, but his handgun's missing."

"You know what kind it was?"

"No, sorry. I never had much interest in firearms."

Lisa studied the image of Laura Braden's mural once again. The sick bastard holding the dog in a death grip was possibly Frank Whitby, because the man was wearing a blue and white striped shirt.

The jon boat that Will had called about was registered to Frank Whitby.

"One last question, Donna. The jon boat that your husband owns. Where does he keep it?"

"Thank God for that boat. It got him out of the house and far away from me. He extorted it from some teenager at the boatyard. Frank pay for a slip at a marina? Never! He kept it at the marine station. He filled his outboard illegally with the marine lab's credit card, funded by the Maryland taxpayers, the swine."

The Duck Blind

Clyde's ears strained and sifted through the seabird caws and chirping insects. There'd be no listening to music from his CD player that morning. He needed to be ready to go. Any minute now he'd hear the rhythmic chug of the *Vital Spark* motoring to the marine station to pick up supplies for a days' work.

The jon boat in the marsh grass was stocked up with water, sandwiches, bug repellent, and sunscreen. Because fucking Alex Allaway had offed Frank, he now had to purchase gasoline out-of-pocket! The days of filling the red gas canisters at cousin Desmond's service station and returning to the marine station to fill their cars and boats were over. Fuck her. He and Frank hadn't bought gas for years. That morning he'd had to fill his car and the canisters for the jon boat with his own credit card. The good news was that he'd be receiving payments from Mrs. Weinstein, Mrs. Chandless, Mrs. Rockwell, and Mrs. Hawthorne later in the week. His second income would cover his oldest daughter's driving school and his middle daughter's dress for the dreaded dance. Girls, he groaned.

If only Alex Allaway would find whatever the hell she was looking for! He really should be a presence at the new shop that just opened in northern Maryland. The store manager who'd taken the job for minimum wage and no benefits seemed competent enough, but who knows what the employees might steal while the owner was away. A green fly bit his neck, and he cursed and slapped himself. He pressed the binoculars back to his eyes. Through the slats of the duck blind the bay sparkled green. What was that Allaway bitch looking for out there?

River Glen

Julia poked her head through the hatch door. "You have a visitor, lass."

"Quick! Cast off the lines!" Alex dashed to the helm and turned the key.

"You need to let the engine warm up."

"Not this morning! Never mind, I'll get the lines." She shoved pass Julia, hopped over the crab pots on the deck, threw off the fore and aft lines from the bollards, and ripped off the spring line.

Julia smiled in amusement.

"Shut-up. It's not funny!" Alex dashed back to the helm.

"I didn't say anything," Julia chuckled. "You better hurry. He's quite swift."

In a panic, Alex looked through the porthole. Will sprinted along the dock at full speed. He was not in his khakis, dress shirt and tie, but in shorts, sneakers and a t-shirt. A backpack thumped against his back. Water Boy was leaping and barking, paws scratching on the gunwale.

"Come on, baby," Alex urged as she tugged on the throttle.

The boat lurched away from the dock. Her face pressed against the porthole again. A foot, two ... a yard at least, from the dock. Any second, he'd slow his pace so as not to plunge off the end. What? The lunatic had increased his frantic pace. Five feet at least now. No way would he make it. Six feet. She yanked the throttle to increase the speed. Maybe eight feet. At any second he'd splash into the river. He took a flying leap, arms and legs swimming through the air. With a shock she felt the back of the boat dip down. Two hands grasped the gunwale, and then a neon sneaker appeared over the edge. He spilled into the crab pots, while the delighted dog pinned him to the floor.

"Bravo! What a wonderful display of athleticism!" Julia clapped.

"Julia, I'm not talking to him," Alex threw the tug into reverse. "See what he wants. Then he's getting off."

Will removed the dog from his chest and righted himself. "I'm your police escort. Detective Braden's orders. The boat that was following you belonged to Frank Whitby. Whitby was in Randy's house on the night of his murder."

That silenced them.

"I thank Detective Braden for the special protection." Julia stepped toward the coffee machine. "It gives me peace of mind to have you onboard. Coffee?"

"Yes, ma'am," Will said.

"Alexandra, don't you want to show Detective Wilkins a certain floor plan?"

"What floor plan?" he asked.

Alex wordlessly pulled on her headphones, adjusted her sunglasses and motored the boat into the channel.

"I've been telling Alex pyrate stories. Cream and sugar, Detective?"

"Yes, both. Thank you."

"Pyrate stories about her and my great-, great- ... who knows how many greats ... grandfather, Giles Blood-hand." Julia handed him a coffee and sat down at the galley table.

He joined her under the parrots, skulls, and shrunken heads. "You're kidding me. You're related? I was never sure if Giles was a real person."

Alex discreetly turned down the music and listened.

"Yes, his name was Giles Hale," Julia said. "There was a Barnaby Wilkins in the pyrate camp of early River Glen, but I don't believe he was involved in the raids in Florida and the Carolinas. He was a carpenter. Pyrate crews and the Royal Navy often pressed carpenters into service against their will. Carpenters were highly valued in the days of wooden ships."

"How do know all of this?" he asked.

The *Vital Spark* rounded the Point; Alex fumbled awkwardly with her vibrating watch.

"When Giles returned to Scotland in 1695, his father, Sir Edmund, was intrigued by his son's adventures and had him describe them to a local scholar, who wrote them down. The memoir is badly faded, almost illegible at this point. My Aunt Beatrice, who's quite fascinated by Hale history and genealogy, is having these documents transcribed and digitized. It's quite a long document and describes the journey that teenage Giles and his best friend, Charlie Allaway, made to the city of Edinburgh, the tavern brawl that landed them in the prison at Old Tolbooth, their escape and trek to Ayr, where they hopped a ship to the West Indies, and then the brutality of Captain Bart Dodd on the *Raven*, the mutiny and so on."

Levon Bakanian would love to read this chronicle, Alex thought.

"Things got particularly interesting when the pyrates absconded with the women convicts at the North Landing River plantation. Giles set his sights on a beautiful prostitute named Kathleen Noonan. Neville Whitby was also interested in Kathleen, but she was not interested in him. Charles Allaway hooked up with a pickpocket named Shannon O'Malley."

"Did you say Whitby?" Will cut in.

"Yes, Giles and Charlie Allaway were traveling with the Whitby brothers, Neville and Conall. Kathleen preferred the handsome Giles, so Neville took up with a woman that the other women referred to as Poison Emmaline. Emmaline was completely daft.

"When they reached the river that the Scotsmen named the Glen River, they found that most of the planks from the *Raven* were rotten, so they hurriedly cut down trees to build dwellings before the onset of winter. That is how Allaways and Whitbys ended up at River Glen.

"The following spring the colonial governments of Virginia and Maryland, far to the south at the mouth of the Chesapeake, heard rumors of a pyrate village that had taken root along a northern river, but they had bigger concerns, such as attacks by Dutch warships that interrupted the tobacco trade to England. Skirmishes with homegrown pyrates on the Atlantic coast near Accomac and the barrier islands of the Carolinas were another headache.

"The Hales, Whitbys and Allaways had settled down to become fishermen, farmers, and craftsmen, and fathers to a growing population of children. They had no ship with which to terrorize the colonists of the Chesapeake. The rigging, sails and beams of the *Raven* found a second life in the form of fishing skiffs. River Glen was of no consequence to the government officials in the south, and so was ignored.

"Charlie Allaway and the Whitby brothers became watermen and supplied the community with crabs, oysters, and fish. Giles and Kathleen brewed beer and built a tavern. The tavern served many functions for the community. For one, it was a meeting hall of sorts. The pyrates developed their own economy based on a barter system and used pieces of eight from the Spanish galleon for their currency."

"When I was a boy I was told that one could still find an occasional piece of eight on the shoreline," Will recalled. "But I thought it was just legend, like Giles."

Alex's piece of eight was sequestered under the insole of her sneaker. So ... apparently Papa and Ben had found one. Until their reason for sending her on this time-wasting scavenger hunt for skulls and yearbooks became clear, nothing—absolutely nothing—would be said about the gold piece.

Julia went on. "Everyone in the village contributed to a treasury for the purchase of communal goods when traders passed through, for items they couldn't manufacture on their own. The treasury was located in a locked room at the back of the tavern. The village was happy and prosperous for a time. Until ..."

Julia's dramatic pause reeled Will in. He leaned forward, his eyes wide and waiting. "What?"

"Two women were found inexplicably dead, the wives of Huw Collins and Angus Smyth. Fine one day ... dead the next. The villagers rushed to the tavern, fearing that a plague had struck River Glen, perhaps carried by one of the traders. But the women who had been in Newgate Prison together suspected the poisoner, Emmaline Whitby."

"Did she do it?"

"Poisoning was difficult to prove in those days, but the untimely deaths caused an atmosphere of distrust. Everyone started to watch everyone else."

The pyrate history was fascinating to Alex also, but there was work to do. Mr. Ward from Annapolis might check on her any time to see what she'd accomplished. She rose off the barrel seat and pulled off her headphones. "Julia, you need to drive now. I'm going to start collecting at regular intervals across the channel."

Will stood also. "Alex, do you need any help?"

She pretended not to hear, returned the headphones to her head and stepped outside. For the next few hours she affixed the collecting nets to the transom and hauled in specimens, measured them, and threw them back overboard. Invertebrates were collected and placed in jars. She took water temperature and specific gravity readings. Work, work ... work incessantly. Record, record in her lab notebook every variable possible. Work, work to distract, distract ... from Will removing his shirt ... bending over to search his backpack for binoculars ... slathering his bare chest and arms with sunscreen. She noticed none of it. Really. To distract from Julia smiling smugly at her discomfort. Work, work. Finally, Mutter Island appeared in the distance.

Headquarters

"Patient-therapist confidentiality. I hate that goddamn policy," Jay Braden said to Lisa Paco. He slumped into his office chair and sipped lukewarm coffee. "Dr. Richmond told me basically nothing. Laura had recently reported having bad dreams, but he divulged nothing of their meaning or content. Those were no dreams. Who's he kidding? Laura definitely saw something."

"And Donna Whitby's description of Frank's shirt was identical to that in Laura's painting." Lisa pulled her gum from her mouth and stretched it in front of her.

"Disgusting, Paco. Do you know how many germs you're putting on the gum, playing with it like that?"

"It helps me think. And I'm bolstering my immune system so I never have to take a sick day."

He grimaced.

"What I'm wondering," she thought aloud, "is how does an ecologist making 42 K a year afford a house in an executive development and a membership at the Tidewater Greens golf club? According to Whitby's bank statements, he lives from paycheck to paycheck like everyone else. He has hardly any savings and no money from an inheritance. Donna, the trophy wife, has never worked. It doesn't add up."

"What did Norman find in his computer?"

"Golf videos, business-related emails, a few half-written reports for Mr. Ward, his boss in Annapolis. Some photos from vacations. Nothing out of the ordinary."

"Unusual charges to his credit cards?"

"Not really. Ammo from the outdoor outfitters and fishing gear. No gasoline. His wife mentioned that he bought gas illegally on his work credit card."

"Other expenses on his work credit card?"

"Lots of gas mainly. Seems like he was filling both his boat and his car. The dirtbag. There was the typical office stuff. Reams of papers. Memory chips for a digital camera."

"What was he photographing?"

"Birds, wildlife? Who knows?"

"Were there photos of wildlife in his computer?"

"Nope. The computer from the marine lab was an antiquated piece of junk. Norman found nothing in it. Frank was using his personal laptop at work since it contained the fishery reports."

"Yeah, that's what Alex Allaway was doing when we dropped by the lab. I can't watch you play with your gum a minute longer," he grumbled. "I'm going back to the Allaways and walk around that beach. Frank obviously didn't kill the dog. But he was threatening Randy and Ben about something."

"On your way to the Allaways, you might want to swing by this place." Lisa handed him a business card. "Both Randy and Ben had the same card in their belongings."

Jay read the card. "McKibbin's Apartments? It's usually occupied by itinerant agricultural workers."

River Glen

Alex scowled. A skull, her father's yearbook, and now a gas canister from the Gimpy Gull gas station and gift shop. "How am I supposed to make sense of this?" she muttered. Each clue was somehow linked to a Whitby, that much she had figured out. Neville Whitby plunged the knife into Charles Allaway's skull. Frank Whitby was in her father's graduating class in high school. And Desmond Whitby owned the Gimpy Gull service station up the highway. So what? What did any of this mean? OGM, CC, GG. She'd found all the clues. Now what? The scavenger hunt was over. Why had Papa and Ben wasted her time by sending her on such follies?

The good news was that Frank Whitby wasn't following them on his jon boat today. He'd likely spotted the cop on board and decided to scram. It actually gave Alex some peace of mind to have Will around. He'd pretty much left her alone all day. After all, who could compete with a dazzling actress who'd been whisked around the globe by sultans—probably on magic carpets—and wizards —probably on unicorns? Nor did Alex tell enthralling tales of poisoners and pyrates.

Besides a brief stint researching sea urchin embryos in La Jolla, California, she'd pretty much been nowhere off the Atlantic seaboard.

While she'd traipsed around Mutter Island searching for the GG clue ... fortunately the island was little more than a muddy sandbar with trees and bushes ... Julia and Will had decided to take a walk and swim together. By evening they'd probably be announcing their engagement.

Mutter Island was much like the Old Gray Mare ruin, a place for secluded picnics, teenage beer parties, and trysts. The evidence of human habitation were crushed beer cans, a sand-covered beach blanket, an empty marshmallow bag, and fragments of an old barrel. Nearby was a rusty gasoline container embossed with the words "Gimpy Gull Service Station." GG. She'd excitedly shaken the container, and looked inside, hoping it might reveal some important clue, but it was empty. Only sand spilled out. Of all Papa and Ben's clues, this was the most baffling. As a child, she'd begged Papa to stop at the Gimpy Gull service station because its gift shop advertised fireworks, pyrate trinkets, peanut logs, and homemade ice cream, but he'd outright refused to patronize that establishment. Even if his gas tank was bone dry, he'd have pushed his pickup truck down the highway to the next gas station rather than stop at the Gimpy Gull. Desmond Whitby and his wife, Blanche, who ran the gift shop, seemed nice enough. Eddie, Gillian and Alex used to stop there for sodas and Old Bay-seasoned peanuts after they'd gotten their driver's licenses.

Julia and Will resumed their animated conversation about, what else, poisoners and pyrates, while making peanut butter and jelly sandwiches. She meanwhile drove the *Vital Spark* back to River Glen. She'd collected a ton of data in just these couple of days. Tomorrow she'd enter it into spreadsheets and perform some chemical tests in the lab. The lab, once and for all, would be cleaned and organized. Enough cruising around the bay. She'd found the three—meaningless—clues. Tomorrow would be spent in the lab. But for now she was drowsy and just needed to relax. She was sandy, salty, and dehydrated. How perfect would it be to have a bubble bath, then crab cakes and white wine at the Dockside Café, capped off by great sex and a deep slumber in the berth? She'd had lots of mediocre sex with Richard, but she hadn't had great sex for what—almost seven years. And only once. Pathetic.

"Did you say something, lass?" Julia said.

"No."

"Oh. I thought you said 'pathetic.'"

Will stepped over to her with a sandwich and a water bottle. His flat, bare belly was inches in front of her face. "Here, Alex."

"Thanks."

Will's phone buzzed so he stepped outside.

"The floor plan!" Julia whispered.

"You're meddling!" she whispered back.

Will's face darkened. He pushed the phone back in his pocket, and scanned the horizon with his binoculars. He ducked under the figurehead. "Jay Braden's assigned me to be your security again tomorrow."

"Fucking patient-psychiatrist privacy." Jay Braden traipsed irritably across Randall Allaway's front porch. How many murderers, rapists, and assorted perverts were walking free because of confidentiality laws? Terrence Richmond knew exactly what Laura had seen!

Jay wiggled Allaway's doorknob. It was locked. He looked under the doormat. No key. He peered in the front window. It appeared as though the first wife, Julia Hale, had rearranged the furniture in the living room and organized Randy's clutter. The piles of books on the floor had been placed back on shelves. The old wood floor had been swept. Vases of wildflowers graced the coffee table and brightened the shelves by the windows. Large, bright candles from the candle shop in town had been placed around the living room.

He left the porch and circled behind the house. On tiptoes, he looked into Randy's bedroom on the first floor. Julia Hale's rolling suitcase was on a chair. Her perfumes and powders were on Randy's dresser, beside them was a photo of a black-haired woman and a young Randy. Whoa... if that woman was Julia Hale, then she'd been gorgeous. He checked for texts from Will. There'd been no sign of Frank following them on the jon boat that day. Frank was probably hiding out at some girlfriend's place, surveilling the police activity at Allaway's house from afar. He might be watching him at this very minute.

Next Jay walked Randy's riverfront beach and pointed his binoculars toward the promontory. Laura and Mrs. Pulacki were having lunch on the deck. Tonight he'd encourage Laura's painting. Praise her—tell her the mural was wonderful. Paint, Laura, paint! Paint on any wall, all the walls if you like! If Frank had menaced Randy and Ben on the beach, maybe he had come back with a second man and stabbed Randy in his living room weeks later. Frank had also threatened Water Boy. Jay felt a pang of regret at manhandling the dog, grabbing him by the scruff of the neck and lassoing him with a rope. No wonder the dog was a basket case.

Jay zigzagged across the beach but found nothing in the sand except tennis balls, a chew toy, and reeds and sticks that had washed up on the shoreline. He placed himself in the exact position where Laura must have seen Frank talking to—glaring at—Ben and Randy. The two lawn chairs were still in the same position. She must have been standing at or near the dock and the canoe. Perhaps she was crouched under the dock, hiding, so that Frank didn't see her? If so, many tides since then had washed away any footprints.

He flipped over the canoe. Nothing in or underneath it. He checked Randy's storage shed. There were a number of signs for parking on Giles Blood-hand Day, a dusty pink bicycle, roller skates, flotation coats, and oily tools. He strolled back to the grow-house-turned-greenhouse. Odd. There were no oars to the canoe anywhere on the property.

He climbed into his unmarked police cruiser and headed down the highway. McKibbin's Apartments never failed to depress him. They were rundown cottages occupied by agricultural workers who crammed themselves into squalid rooms while sending every penny of their wages back to wives and children in Central America. If lucky, these men saw their families every few years. The workers were hardworking, law-abiding, and kept to themselves. It was Morris McKibbin, the owner of the apartments, that made his skin crawl. Twice in the past year the police had been called to the apartments for domestic disputes between McKibbin and his wife, Agnes.

A sign with missing letters advertised room rentals for the day, week, and month. Free ice, refrigerators, wifi. Doubtful. Nothing was free at McKibbin's dump.

McKibbin and Agnes peered through the office door the second the sedan pulled into the gravel parking lot. They stepped outside, already on the defense. A slimy cigar dangled from the corner of McKibbin's mouth. The buttons of his stained shirt strained across his protruding beer gut. Agnes scowled while adjusting the curlers in her bleached blonde hair.

McKibbin waddled toward Jay's car. "I haven't done nothin'! Absolutely nothin'!"

"I didn't say you did, Morris," Jay said. "Have either of these two men come here before?" He held out photos of Randy and Ben.

"Never seen 'em." McKibbin's head twitched in a negative.

Two men in jeans and white t-shirts watched curiously from plastic chairs in front of a cottage. One worker's foot was in a boot. The other man's arm was in a sling. Fast food bags were at their feet.

"And this man?" Jay held out Frank Whitby's photo.

McKibbin blinked quickly and chewed his cigar. "Never seen 'im neither."

"You sure?"

"Absolutely sure." McKibbin sniffed.

Jay nodded and returned to his sedan. He tossed the photos in the front seat and grabbed a baton. He walked back to McKibbin. "Then let's do this hard way."

"I, I remember him now!"

"I thought you might."

McKibbin pointed to the cottage at the far end of the parking lot. "Th-that's his cottage there."

"Is he here now?"

"I haven't seen him for weeks. He hasn't paid me for weeks!"

"And I bet he only pays in cash."

"Yeah."

"Open it, Morris." Jay strode across the parking lot. "Does he come here with other people?"

"Women. Women love this guy."

"No men?"

"Never. Just women."

McKibbin jiggled the master key in an old lock and pushed open the grimy door.

Jay stepped into the room. His blood pressure soared. He whipped his phone from his pocket. "Zera, send forensics to McKibbin's Apartments ASAP." He rang off and called Will. "You're on security detail with the Allaway women until we catch this bastard." He turned back to McKibbin. "What's the name of the guy who rents this room?"

"A big handsome fella. Connor Whitebay."

Clyde Whitby seethed. All day he'd waited for Alex Allaway to appear at the marine station. The lazy bitch was a no-show! It'd been less than a week and already she was shirking her responsibilities, skipping an entire day of work, all while he roasted in the steamy marsh and was devoured by mosquitos and green flies. A snake had the audacity to slither across *his* duck blind, so he'd hacked it to pieces with his hunting machete and cast the bloody chunks into the marsh.

But the day wasn't a total write-off; he was able to manage the inventory of his plumbing supply stores via his tablet. Plus, he'd done part of the payroll for Store Two in Wilmington, and found a great deal on garbage disposals and shower heads that would be marked up for an enormous profit.

He passed over the River Glen Bridge and turned down the river road, planning to park at the Point. From there he could sneak through the pine forest to the Allaways' house and creep around the back. With his listening device in his ear, he might overhear some conversation about where the women had been that day. What had they found at the Bohemia and the Sassafras? That was bugging the shit out of him. What was in the plastic bag and the backpack? So fucking frustrating not to know! With any luck, Alex might tell that older woman what she'd done with Frank, but more likely the woman was an accomplice. She'd probably assisted in killing him. Maybe they'd done it by poison. Poison, he knew, was a frequent and effective method of murder used by women.

Clyde drove past the Allaways' house. He'd been there once before, with Desmond. The house of the Enemy. Hideous lawn ornaments and flags, and a rusted out car and motorcycle littered the yard. Red hot chili pepper lights lined Randy's porch. Such humans—sub-humans—should be sterilized and not allowed to reproduce and infest the planet. Lights were on in both the house and the tugboat. The black dog, should it appear, would be quickly silenced with the machete.

Only one other car was parked at the Point. The beach had been vacated and the lifeguard chair was abandoned for the day. He selected a space in the corner, bordering the pine forest. It was now completely dark. In moments he'd creep through the forest and make his way to the Allaways' through the backyard. He ate his last sandwich and checked that his supplies were ready. Machete, check. Gloves, check. Spy Ear, check. Balaclava, check. Black hoodie, check. Night vision goggles, check. The night vision goggles had been a gift from Frank. His brother had shoplifted a pair for both of them from the outdoor outfitter store when they were teenagers. What fun they had with the goggles while skulking around the shadows at the drive-in and Point, photographing couples in various tangled positions!

A flicker of light appeared in his peripheral vision. The door on the women's side of the bathhouse opened. A light over the door, circled by frenzied moths, illuminated a young woman, shining on her dark hair. Clyde's heart jolted. The woman walked toward the lone car in the parking lot. What fucking amazing luck! He leapt from his car to confront Alex Allaway.

"Competition ... what a joke!" Penny chuckled to herself. Will was dating river trash. Carly's description of the house with the plastic gnomes, black bird and blue dolphin lawn ornaments made it ridiculously easy to find. All that was missing was a tacky pink flamingo. Nor did the girlfriend have a luxury cruiser. Instead, the boat was a faded red and blue tugboat. The beach ... really? It was no more than a narrow strip of sand lined with dilapidated lawn chairs and a leaky canoe.

Penny pushed through the door of the bathhouse and headed through the darkness toward her car. Hers was a dreadfully mundane car, but her father had insisted that she buy it because it was safe for Carly. By next year she'd be driving something flashy, like a Cadillac Escalade with plenty of room for two child seats and the nannie. For nights on the town, she'd get herself something sexy and sporty. It would definitely be a convertible, bright cherry red with an all-leather interior. She glanced at her cellphone to check the time. Sweet ... there was time for a margarita or two at Jox before picking Carly up from her next-door neighbor's. She pulled a perfume bottle from her purse and applied a spritz to her neck and wrists. One never knew whom they might meet in a sports bar.

"Alex ..." a voice said.

She turned. It was a man. Homely, weaselly, fiftyish. "You got the wrong person."

"Don't be smart with me. I want to know what you did with Frank."

"I don't know any Franks." She continued toward her car.

"You stop this instant! You tell me right now what you did with Frank!"

"Didn't you hear me?" she said over her shoulder. "I just said that I don't know a Frank. Now get yourself back to the Alzheimer's ward."

The man tensed. "You fucking rude bitch!"

She spun, her hands on her hips. "And you're a retarded old geezer! Now get lost!"

"You're not going anywhere until you tell me what you did with Frank!" the old retard snarled.

"Oh, I get it. Frank's your boyfriend. Is that it, you old queer?" She smirked. "So you want to know what I did with Frank? I fucked him, again and again, fucked his brains out. He was screaming in ecstasy. Screaming that he'd never fuck you again, only me, forever!"

He visibly quaked and his eyes popped. "No, no, that's not possible! He'd never fuck an Allaway! Never!"

Now to really rile up the creeper. Maybe she could induce a heart attack, and then drive away, leaving him to croak on the pavement. "Yeah, I tied him up in my basement. Just fucked him for days on end, fuck, fuck, fuck ..."

"No, no, impossible!"

Penny dug through her purse. *If this worthless excuse of a man steps a foot closer, the perfume is going straight into his beady little eyes ...*

Will stepped out of his shower, a cold one, because his apartment was ninety-two degrees and he was sunburned from his day on the water. Not even a hint of a breeze passed through the single, slit-like window of the Box. It would be another evening of sleeping on top of his sheets with a cold washcloth over his face. By morning he'd have drunk two liters of ice water. He lay down on his sofa bed and turned on the fan. "So pathetic," he said aloud. A dusty fan occupied the other side of his bed, where lovely Alex Allaway might be.

Over the course of the entire day that they'd been on the boat together, she'd uttered ten words: no, collecting jars, net, water bottle, Gimpy Gull, pathetic, thanks. And something about a floor plan? Floor plan to what? It was obviously a touchy subject between Alex and Julia, so he'd decided not to push it. His phone vibrated. The number for Rosa Cabrera, Penny's next-door neighbor, glowed on the screen.

"*Hola*, Rosa," he said. It was unusual to receive a call from Rosa at this time of night.

"*Hola*, Will. I was wondering if you'd come by and get Carly. Penny's not back yet and she's not answering. I need to get to bed soon. I have work very early and need to get the twins to bed. They have camp early tomorrow morning."

He glanced at the time. It was 10:43. "Yes, of course. I'm leaving right now."

He rushed on his clothes and sped up 301 North to Middletown. All day he'd felt a nagging unease that Rosa's call just compounded. Penny was never late; never would she jeopardize her standing, her competency as a parent, in the eyes of the court. If she told Rosa she'd pick up Carly up at 9:00, then she'd be there at 8:55.

Rosa answered the door, an exhausted smile on her face. Carly and the four-year-old boys were on the sofa, a Disney CD playing softly in the background. Roberto and Manuel were in matching pajamas. Roberto was slumped over the armrest, snoozing. Carly hugged Manuel and Rosa goodbye, kissed the sleeping Roberto, and climbed into Will's arms. By the time he placed her in the car seat in the parking lot, she was fast asleep.

Neither Rosa nor he had a key to get into Penny's apartment to get Carly's clothes, lunchbox, and backpack for summer day camp the next day. Nor did he want to wake his daughter by going into a 24-hour Walmart to get those items. Besides, he was too tired to think straight. He'd be lucky if he could stay on the road. He returned to River Glen, bypassing his apartment building; the Box was too stifling hot for two bodies. Instead he headed to his parents' house, where his mother would have a clean change of clothes for Carly and a toothbrush from their sleepovers. His mother let them in and offered to heat up a casserole, but he just needed sleep. He carried Carly upstairs to his sister's old bedroom and tucked her into bed. She hadn't budged since the car ride. The evening of play with the twins had been too exciting.

He dragged himself down the hallway to his old bedroom. Baltimore Ravens everything—lamps, curtains, Big Heads, bedspread—assaulted him from every angle. It was the bedroom of lost dreams. But there were two positives in his life: this would be the second night in a row that he'd get to sleep in air-conditioning, and his precious daughter for one evening was out of the conniving clutches of Penny Bannister.

Throughout the evening, Jay had confined himself to the upstairs. It would be impossible to sleep, he realized. Laura's muted humming rose from the living room. "Paint me another mural, Laura. It's wonderful. What happened next?" he'd said before heading up to bed. His impulse was to creep downstairs and watch from the next room, but he feared that he'd interrupt the creative flow, that she'd shout and stop painting.

He squirmed in the sheets, thinking. His team of detectives had made huge strides that day. The case was finally gaining momentum. The McKibbin's hideaway had revealed volumes about Frank's character, or lack thereof. Whitby's fingerprints had been found throughout, but that was no surprise. There were numerous other prints, presumably from the assorted girlfriends. Again, to be expected. The only other prints that could be identified in the fingerprint database were from Marie Chandless, a notorious kleptomaniac who'd been repeatedly arrested for shoplifting until the police realized that she'd always return the items the next day. She was an adrenaline addict.

The bathroom at McKibbin's place contained bubble baths and massage oils. His team had also discovered tiny cameras hidden around the room, all pointing, not surprisingly, toward the bed. There was a well-stocked bar. Apparently Frank liked his women lubricated with both liquor and sex oils. In the drawers were computer memory sticks and a travel-sized laptop. Lisa and Norman in IT had found that the laptop contained very interesting footage of Frank and the wives of the president of the country club (that explained the free membership), the golf pro, the director of the historical society, the mayor, and on and on. Frank had been trolling the Tidewater Green Club for wealthy, lonely women who paid dearly for his silence. A veritable Bank of River Glen, all in hundred dollar bills, was stashed under the carpet in the cottage.

But what had startled Jay when Morris McKibbin first opened the cottage was a series of pictures tapped to the wall. There was a hand drawn map of Randy and Ben's houses and the woods beyond. His eyes had been attracted to the color red. It was not blood, but red acrylic paint, like Laura used. What had prompted him to call Zera and Will was that "Connor Whitebay" had painted red bull's-eyes on the photos of Randy and Alex Allaway, and Ben Hancock.

No matter how Alex positioned the fan, she couldn't sleep. All of the portholes were open, the fan blew directly at her head, yet the berth was still a pocket of suffocating heat. She could take off her t-shirt and panties and lie naked on top of the sheets, except that the *Vital Spark* had become Grand Central Station to everyone in River Glen. And every time she moved, Water Boy felt compelled to lick her face. Dog tongue and dog breath in her face were bad enough. If she took off her clothes, there'd be dog tongue on ... no, no way. The clothes would stay on.

"Better dogs than men." Ha, ha ... thanks, Julia.

It was too hot to sleep, think—do anything. She rose and looked out a porthole. Something was up. Something was definitely up. Will had been given the order to return tomorrow. Before leaving for the day, he'd wandered through Papa's house, searching all the rooms. He'd also gone through Ben's place one more time. He hadn't left until an anonymous black sedan driven by a police officer had parked between Ben and Papa's houses. The sedan was still there, even at this late hour.

She grabbed a water bottle from the fridge and went to the deck to cool off. She dropped onto a crab pot and looked down the black river toward the Point. That night had messed her up forever. She couldn't pass the Point without feeling aroused. It was probably the reason for the breakup with Richard. It's not that she had anything against having sex in beds. Beds were fine. But so were bathtubs, showers, rivers, lakes, oceans, and bays. During that vacation with Richard in the Poconos, that babbling brook had looked so enticing, but "No Alex, we have to wait until we get back to the cabin." And there was the time they'd been kayaking in that back bay near Assateague; that secluded little cove had been perfect. "Jeez, Alex, it's broad daylight! Can't you wait until we get to the hotel?" (No, I don't think I can!)

All because of that night on the Point.

It didn't start out as a double date, as she never would have agreed to it if she'd known that Will would be there. But that Fourth of July weekend she'd been celebrating the fact that she'd actually—finally!—graduated from high school, and had an acceptance letter from the college of her dreams.

It felt to Alex as though from the moment she'd been born, her life's ambition had been to study fisheries at the University of Maryland. Countless times, she'd read books by Rachel Carson, Sylvia Earle, Jacques Cousteau, and Maryland's own Eugenie Clark. She'd volunteered for summers at the bay's environmental center, between assisting with the haul on Papa and Ben's workboat, *High Tide*. They'd taught her everything about finding the sooks (females), the picking crabs, and the large Jimmies (males) to be served up as steamed crabs in restaurants along the eastern seaboard. She knew the best baits (herring, not menhaden), in which shoals and channels the sooks and Jimmies hid, how they molted, their courtship and mating behaviors, and their migration patterns down the bay once the fall chill descended upon them. She knew everything about *Callinectes sapidus*, both from a waterman's and a biologist's perspective. That was why she'd received offers from Delaware, North Carolina, Virginia, and Maryland. But Maryland was the school for her. She could pay in-state tuition—money was a perennial problem for Papa, Ben and the other eastern shoremen. Their fortunes, or misfortunes, were at the whim of climate and the market; there were no government subsidies for shoremen, as there were for farmers. Routine boat maintenance, diesel, crab pots, line and bait cut deeply into the profits at the end of the day. During the height of crab season, one went through a pair of gloves and rubber aprons every few weeks.

While applying to colleges her senior year, she'd been dating Eddie Richmond off and on. He rarely made passes at her, except to occasionally make out, which made her more than a bit insecure about her relative attractiveness. Their friendship was based on their love of the same music and movies. While sweltering in her cap and gown in the processional line, it had dawned on her that she was graduating with two distinctions: the Oldest High School Graduate in the State of Maryland (yay! ... she was nearly twenty-one) and the Only Graduating Virgin.

Eddie was also a distraction from Will, who sat behind her in English Literature class and jiggled her chair with his gargantuan sneaker. While most teenaged boys smelled like stale sheets or their gym locker, every morning the alluring scent of Will's body wash wafted over her shoulder. How was she supposed to concentrate on Mrs. Maury yacking about "A Good Man is Hard to Find" or "The Cask of Amontillado," when some aphrodisiac in Will's body wash tingled every particle of her being? That set her own foot to jiggle.

The arm of the obnoxious cheerleader in the seat in front of hers had shot up. "Mrs. Maury, Alex is kicking my chair!"

"Sorry, sorry!" she'd cried. "I wasn't aware of it. It wasn't intentional."

"Alex, would you like to serve another detention?" Mrs. Maury had asked with cloying pleasantness. The bitch always sided with the cheerleaders and jocks.

(SHIT!) "No, please, no," she had pleaded. The whole class snickered. Worse, someone had recorded the incident on a smartphone. By lunchtime a zillion viewers had seen her groveling/whimpering/begging on You Tube.

Then, to her utter horror, she found herself on a beach blanket with Will Wilkins on the Fourth of July.

"It just occurred to me," Gillian said out of the blue. "You're both going to Maryland."

At the words, Alex's anxiety had skyrocketed like a firework. What if he sat behind her in freshman Biology or Inorganic Chemistry and jiggled her seat? She'd never learn a thing. She'd never be accepted into her major. She'd never be a Chesapeake Bay fisheries expert. All was lost. What to say? What to say? Maryland was a huge university ... it'd be easy to get lost if he never knew that she was there ...

"No," she'd said. "I decided to go to Delaware. They have a good marine science program."

"Oh," Gillian had replied. "When'd you decide that?"

"Recently," she'd answered, trying to think of a way to change the subject. She'd fixed her eyes on the fireworks once again to distract herself from the neon glow stick around Will's thick neck ... how it accentuated his strong jawline, the depression in his chin, his wide shoulders and chest, muscular stomach, and baggy surfer swim trunks.

Were girls even supposed to have wet dreams? Was that even physiologically possible? Or was that some freakish abnormality of Maryland's Oldest High School Graduate and Virgin? A reaction to the pheromone in his body wash, maybe? A number of mornings, she'd awoken ridiculously wet, having dreamt of herself and the Pinhead in some twisted position or bizarre location, usually both.

"We're out of beer, Gill," Eddie had complained. "Let's go find Boyd. Come with me. I'm so fucked up, I can't walk straight."

And leave me here on the blanket alone with Will? I'll go with you, Eddie. Please let me go! she'd wanted to cry. But the cousins were having too much fun laughing about farts, breast implants, poodles and topiaries. Plus, their ulterior motive was to sneak into the pine forest to smoke a blunt.

She'd watched in muted panic as Gillian and Eddie had staggered down the beach. She'd felt herself break out in a sweat. The air over the bay was already two hundred degrees. Also, the beach blanket was smothering and microscopic. What to say if he spoke to her? No way was she initiating a conversation with him. Besides, her mind was devoid of words.

"Popcorn?" he'd asked, pushing the bag toward her.

She'd just managed, "Yes, thanks." Her hand had shot into the bag, and she'd grabbed a handful. She was ravenous.

She'd spoken to him! Her voice hadn't shaken, nor had she stuttered. Her last words to him had been, "You idiot! You pinhead!" after her desk had collided into the trashcan. That outburst had been posted on Facebook; by third period it had had over two hundred "Likes."

Escape was imperative. She'd put the whole handful of popcorn into her mouth at once, sprung to her feet, and jogged toward the water.

If she could just get into the water, that tightening, tingling feeling in her … everything … might disappear. It was the same sensation she'd had when she, Gillian and Linda Morgan had watched the CD *Biker Sluts* that Linda had snuck from her mother's dresser. How do things tighten and tingle at the same time? Is that possible, or just another freakish physiological defect of Maryland's Oldest … she heard splashing behind her and spun, alarmed.

"What, Pinhead?"

"You shouldn't swim alone. There are no life guards on duty."

"Because of you, I almost didn't graduate."

"But you did graduate."

"At first I thought it was a bee, that you'd pushed a dead bee down my pants. Dead bees can still sting."

"A bee?" he laughed. "It was just an eraser."

"I'm terrified of bees. One flew down my shirt on the boat once. I got stung. It was horrible." And she told him this why?

By now he was grinning outright at her idiotic rambling. The glow stick cast him a neon green. He was a shimmering, green sea monster with a beautiful body.

"Why's that funny?" she'd asked.

"It's not funny." He still grinned ear to ear.

"It's not."

"That's what I said. It's not."

"Jerk. " She splashed him. He approached. She splashed him again. He laughed. She dove away like a porpoise, but he caught her ankle, pulled her backwards through the water, and tickled her foot. Then there'd been more splashing and wrestling. A kiss? Who kissed who? Twisting, shoving. More kissing. Hugging, grabbing, gasping, panting oh, oh, oh. Their glow sticks faded and they'd stood in the black water, embracing. This ... can never be surpassed.

Gillian and Eddie had stumbled from the parking lot, shrieking with laughter. She and Will had pulled themselves apart and wandered wordlessly from the bay.

"What were you two up to?" Eddie asked.

"Swimming," Will had said, dazed.

She'd nodded, bewildered. "Swimming."

Chapter 7

Day 7

River Glen

Zera Lim's call to Jay Braden came just as he was studying Laura's second painting. As on the previous morning, Laura was asleep in the corner. Other than Mrs. Pulacki frying up bacon in the kitchen, the house was still. He pulled the vibrating phone from his pocket.

"We're at the Point, Jay. There's a nasty piece of work out here." Rarely did Zera express any emotion, but her tone was tinged with a primal fear.

"I'll be right there." He took a picture of Laura's painting for Lisa and Will, bent down to kiss his sleeping wife, grabbed his lunch from Mrs. Pulacki and dashed out the door.

Jay's thoughts bounced between those neighbors who lived closest to the Point ... the Allaways, Hoffmans, Miles Harlow, and Luna the palm reader, who might have seen or heard anything, and Laura's newest work. The focus of the second painting was clearly Water Boy, as he was in the dead center of the action. As before, Frank Whitby was holding him aloft, the dog writhing in obvious pain. The pistol was still shoved into the dog's head. But Randy and Ben were no longer seated. Randy had stepped forward, reaching for the dog; he gazed directly at Frank Whitby. But a distraught Ben was looking off canvas, at something or someone on the dock.

Rubberneckers had congregated on the bridge, which slowed Jay's crawl through the village. The entrance to the river road had been cordoned off by police cruisers. Forensics vans were in the parking lot at the Point. Uniformed police combed the beach, parking lot, and adjacent pine forest, while Zera's team huddled around the body. Jay hurried from his car and ducked under the yellow crime scene tape.

Zera emerged from her group. Lisa Paco was also present. Only a dead body would draw Lisa from behind her desk.

"Paco, do we know who it is?"

"Not for sure, sir," Lisa said. "Young female. Very fit. No ID. No purse. No nothing."

"How?" he asked Zera.

"A knife with a very large blade. If I had to guess, a machete."

"When?"

"Sometime last night. Between seven and nine pm," Zera answered.

He eyed the vehicle. "Delaware plates."

"I called it in," Lisa said. "It belongs to a fifty-eight year old male, George Bannister. The glove compartment's been cleaned out. No registration, no insurance cards, nothing."

"Stolen?" he asked.

"It's not reported as stolen."

"Who found her?"

"Those two. Susan Denniston and Alan Johnston." Lisa pointed to a middle-aged, redheaded woman in running attire, and a middle-aged African American male, also in running attire.

Jay knew them both. Sue ran the B&B, and Alan was a co-owner of Nauticus, with his partner, Jacob Horrigan. Sue and Alan ran together frequently, along the coastal road, through the farmland, all over. Now they sobbed in each other's arms.

"They found the body behind the bathhouse at 6:52 this morning. They say it's their friend, Alex Allaway. I got their statements."

Jay exhaled sharply. "Zera, is it the same killer as Randy Allaway's?"

"It's too early to tell, but the two attacks are very different. With Randy, it was one well-placed stab to the heart. This was a frenzied, ferocious attack. The victim's face is almost unrecognizable. I'm doubtful that this was random. The perp was enraged. This was personal."

He swallowed. "Let's have a look."

They walked toward the body. A member of Zera's team uncovered it.

Jay's stomach roiled and his head jerked back. His arm flailed. "Cover it back up!"

Another unmarked car pulled into the lot. Will climbed out.

"Paco, keep him away from this."

"Yes, sir!" She hurried to intercept Will.

"Who is it?" Will asked her.

"A woman. Multiple stabs wounds. Some time last evening."

"Lisa, I asked who?"

She shuffled her polished black shoes in the gravel.

"Who!"

"Possibly Alex Allaway," she said weakly.

Will shook his head in vehement denial. A terrible suspicion bloomed in his mind; *What if ...?* He veered around Lisa and ran toward the body, but Jay stepped into his path. "Don't, not if she's a friend of yours."

"Just show me her right ankle!" Will shouted.

Jay looked curiously at Zera.

Zera nodded. The forensic scientist kneeling next to the victim pulled back the cover from her legs.

A Maryland Terrapin was tattooed on the dead woman's right ankle. Will went white.

"This isn't Alex Allaway. It's Penelope Bannister, Carly's mother.

A Marine Station

Will was absolutely positive that the dead woman at the Point was Penny Bannister. She had the telltale Terrapins tattoo and expensive designer clothes. She'd dyed her hair, yet again, had perfect fingernails, and was wearing green contact lenses. Penny had blue eyes under her ever-changing array of contact lens. The victim looked uncannily like Alex Allaway, which was why Sue and Alan had misidentified her. This unnerved all of them. What was Penny doing in River Glen, of all places, impersonating Alex Allaway? And on the same road as Alex's house? Had the murderer meant to kill Alex?

Will checked his watch. At this moment, Penny's parents, George and Danielle, were driving from their summer cottage on Fenwick Island to the morgue in River Glen. He'd only seen her parents once, in court, when they'd glared insanely at him as if he'd violated their "innocent daughter." that was probably what she'd told them. At this same time, police were combing Penny's apartment in Middletown. The police spokesman had told the swarming reporters only that a young woman had been found dead. Her identity would not be disclosed until family members were notified.

Carly was Will's sole priority. It was imperative to keep things as normal as possible for her. Upon recognizing the victim, he'd rushed to call his mother, who'd agreed to take Carly out of town, to his sister's house in Chestertown. For the day, she'd play in the backyard pool with her cousins. In the afternoon, when the victim's name was released to the press, his would be the horrible task of telling his daughter that her mother was now living with the angels. No way was Penny in heaven, but he could hardly tel his daughter that! All morning he'd been on and off the phone with his parents. It was settled, his mother had insisted; he and Carly would live with his parents until things calmed down. Thank God for take-charge mothers.

Now he sat in the marine lab with Alex Allaway. For the time being, it was all about normalcy, or at least the appearance of normalcy. He was on security detail again. He was grateful for the assignment, away from the clamoring press, hidden away at a remote location in a marsh. When the name of the victim was released that afternoon, he'd be allowed to go home. Another officer would spell him. He checked his watch again. His only wish was to embrace his daughter.

Alex had miraculously spoken to him that morning when he'd climbed into her car. "Good morning." Her voice was strained and she was wound tight, like everyone. It had taken them forever to navigate the police barricade, cross the bridge and get onto the coastal road to the marine lab. Julia had decided to stay in River Glen and was hovering around the edges of the barricade with Alice Hoffman and Luna. Thankfully, the drive to the marine lab was a short one, because Alex was a menace on the road. Twice she'd driven onto the shoulder when Water Dog had licked her neck. She'd swatted and cursed at the dog, then swerved into the other lane. Theirs was a love-hate relationship, like the one she had with him.

While Alex had set up her laptop, he'd inspected the lab building. Nothing seemed unusual or out of place. The marsh was a beautiful and serene place; the only movements were seabirds and insects in the tall grass. He'd returned inside and set up his laptop at a table covered with boxes, instrument catalogs and guides to the birds, fish, and invertebrates of the Chesapeake.

It was best not to appear too nosey and focus on his own work—on the items found in "Connor Whitebay's" sex den—but he wondered what a marine biologist did. Alex bounced back and forth between her desk and the lab bench. For a while she made spreadsheets on her laptop and wrote in a lab notebook. At the bench she mixed chemicals and cleaned the lenses on a microscope. She was clearly trying to organize and clean a disorderly and neglected space.

She spoke for a second time. "There's tea." She pointed to a coffee pot filled with teabags.

Progress! Two more words spoken to him! An offer of tea ... a hint of civility. He disliked tea, but he'd have a cup as a gesture of goodwill.

"Thank you."

They worked silently for a while. Sensing a presence, he twisted in his chair. She stood over him. Her breasts under her tight "Maryland Is For Crabs" tank top were inches from his face.

"I know you think I'm an outright liar, but here." She pressed her smartphone into his face. "The floor plan of my freshman dorm. I lived in a single. I don't know who the hell you were talking to, but I didn't have a roommate."

She left him her phone, grabbed the headphones off her desk, and fled out the back door.

He stared at the image. She was right. It was a single! In the heat of the moment he'd accused her of lying without even checking! He was a shithead, plain and simple.

Who the hell had he been talking to in her dorm? Who was that blonde who'd popped out of the room next to hers?

He followed Alex outside. She was in the skiff tied at the dock, fumbling with the outboard. He handed her the phone. Her stance was defiant, her hands locked on the hips of her flowered shorts. He dropped sullenly onto the edge of the dock, his legs hanging limply over the boat.

He inhaled. "Take off your headphones. Please."

She did grudgingly.

"Alex ... my God, I'm so sorry ... I don't understand why that girl would say ... I just don't know!"

She relaxed a bit.

"Do you remember her name?" he asked.

"Probably not. I barely knew her." She paused, trying to recall. "Patty, maybe. Weird last name. Patty Barnstormer?"

He felt the name catch in his throat. "Penny Bannister?" Why did he phrase it like a question? He knew the answer to his question. He'd asked himself a thousand times over the years ... why me, why me? Suddenly all was clear. He'd walked right into her web in the first few weeks of his freshman year.

A sickly pallor suffused his face and she asked, "Are you alright?"

"My head's going to explode."

"What, Will?" She climbed next to him onto the dock.

He struggled to slow his breathing. "You're going to know this by this afternoon anyway. The woman at the Point this morning ... we're pretty sure that it was Penny Bannister."

"What was she doing in River Glen?"

He had a number of ideas, but it was best to answer evasively. "That's what we'd like to know."

"Her murderer ... is it same the guy who killed my grandfather? Two murders in less than a week, and on the same road."

"We don't know yet. There's something else ... Penny is—was—Carly's mother. Now I understand what happened. When I came up to see you all those times, she must have recognized me. She was a cheerleader. She'd know who I was. I never paid much attention to them. I was focusing on football, on getting to the NFL. She set me up, stalked me. Drugged me at that party. There was no way I'd blackout from a few shots of vodka. I never drink much, anyway. I told that to my lawyer, and to her lawyer. No one believed me! I swear to God, she put something in my drink! All I remember was waking up alone in some unknown room in some unknown frat house. I had no idea who I was with, or how I got there."

"Wow." She remained quiet for a moment. "Wow sounds trite, but I don't know what else to say. Sorry seems inappropriate, because you have Carly."

"That's the part I have to remember." He stood. "We should get back to work."

"Yes."

They started toward the back door when he halted. He whipped his phone out of his pocket, took a photo of the outdoor shower and sent the image to Lisa and Jay. In the laptop in the McKibbin cottage were numerous photos of Frank and assorted playmates, Marie Chandless, Olga Hawthorne and others, in the throes of wet and soapy passion against a grey building. That grey building had just been located. He spun toward the marsh. But who had been taking the photographs?

"What, Will?"

"I need to check out the marsh, but I'm reluctant to leave you here by yourself."

"My fearsome guard dog will protect me," she said facetiously.

Laura Braden's paintings sprang to mind, the helpless, terrorized puppy with the gun to his head. Was it safe taking Alex into the marsh with him? He mulled it over. There was no choice. His job was to keep her in sight at all times. He dashed inside, pulled a pistol and shoulder holster from his bag, and returned to the dock.

"You'd better come with me. Does the boat run?"

"It should. I started the outboard a few days ago." She whistled. "Water Boy, come!" The dog splashed along the water's edge. "Get in the boat." He leapt off the dock into the skiff. She opened the gas lines and pumped the bulb, while Will scanned the channel with his binoculars. She pushed the throttle from neutral and the skiff cruised into the marsh.

River Glen

Lisa had returned to headquarters to look at security camera footage of the bridge and start a file on Penny

Bannister, uniformed officers were sent to work with the Middletown PD in Bannister's apartment, and Will was to watch Allaway. That left Jay in the village to interview his neighbors, shopkeepers, restaurant owners, and mechanics at the boatyard and marina. None of them had seen Penny Bannister around the pier or in the village the previous evening, or ever. Nor did any of them know her. The one person who'd conspicuously disappeared from the gawkers as he approached was the grandmother, Julia Hale.

He passed through the police barricade and walked up the river road to the Allaways'. Julia Hale was smoking on the porch, her bare feet outstretched from under a skirt. She had remarkably nice legs. Her dark hair was clipped in an unruly pile on top of her head. She was definitely the woman in the photograph with Randy that he'd spotted through the bedroom window. Her age, he estimated, must be approaching seventy, but she was a still stunner, a fact she was quite aware of. She was also a show-off, blowing smoke rings for his benefit. She stood when he climbed the steps. revealing herself to be a taller, more curvaceous version of Alex Allaway. She gazed directly at him and smiled a cool "I-tell-nothing" smile that he'd seen infinite times on the streets of Baltimore, usually from madams.

"Detective Braden, why were you following two innocent boaters on a Sunday afternoon?"

Innocent, unlikely. He smiled wryly. He liked the directness. Detective Braden. Familiarity. She'd been doing her homework. It was an attempt to disarm him with a question, while casting aside tedious social formalities. There was no need to display his badge.

"What did two innocent boaters find in a ruined barn on a Sunday afternoon?" he countered.

"A skull with a knife in it." She walked to the door. "Tea?"

Will had told him that they'd found a skull, a yearbook, and an old gas can from Desmond Whitby's service station. So far a truthful answer, but nothing that he didn't already know. "Coffee."

"Coffee, it is." She held the door open for him, but he insisted that she pass through first. "A gentleman," she remarked as if surprised. "I have Jamaican Blue Mountain."

"My favorite," he said pleasantly.

"Cream and sugar?" She stepped into the kitchen.

"Black."

She nodded approvingly.

"What were you doing last night between seven and nine?" he asked.

"You already know that."

"But I want to hear it from you."

"Not murdering a young woman. I was at Luna's cottage. She was telling me about her adventures at Burning Man. It sounded wonderful. I must go one day."

Luna had told him the exact same thing. They'd had some homemade wine, got quite giddy, and talked about their assorted travels.

"When you walked to Luna's, did you see any cars driving to or from the Point?"

"No."

"Why are Randy and Ben sending Alex to points on a map?" Will had informed him of the three locations: the Bohemia, Sassafras, and Mutter Island.

"Your guess is as good as mine. Perhaps their brains were addled from so much marijuana use."

Lie Number One. Randy and Ben were sharp as tacks. He'd chit-chatted with them numerous times in the village.

He circled the living room, observing all of Hale's changes to the décor. "You seem to have moved right in."

She handed him a mug of coffee. "I moved in over fifty years ago. My father bought us this house as a wedding present."

"Is your family wealthy?"

"Is that relevant to the case?"

"One never knows what bit of information might be relevant."

"Wealth is relative. If we're talking monetary wealth, compared to Bill Gates or the Sultan of Brunei, no, I'm not wealthy. If we're talking the intangibles, good health, passion, intellect, then I'm infinitely wealthy."

Another tactic: evasion. "Why return to River Glen after so many years?"

"It was time." More evasion.

"Time for what?"

"Time to meet my granddaughter, of course."

"You'd never met her before? Why was that?"

"Things were complicated in Scotland."

"How complicated?" He sipped the coffee. "By the way, this is excellent."

"I had a daughter, Cecilia, who was mentally ill."

"Who was her father?"

"An actor. I was very young, a teenager, still in acting school. It was before I met Randy. Then I got pregnant by Randy when I was passing through River Glen doing *Othello*. I came to the United States to have Colin. The original idea was for me to bring Cecilia here as well. But she had fits of violence. We were fearful that she might harm Colin. She was a very sick girl. We decided that I would go back to Scotland, where my father and aunt would help me with Cecilia. The doctors never expected Cecilia to live as long as she did. Her disease worsened drastically over the last decades. She was in tremendous pain. She drowned herself last year. The house in Aberdeen had too many difficult memories, so I moved to London. I finally had some freedom to travel."

"But only when Ben emailed you that the blue crabs were moving to deeper waters. It's code. What's it mean?"

There was no delay in her answer. Her answers to his questions were well-rehearsed. She was an actress, after all. "Ben and Randy referred to themselves as the blue crabs. The deeper waters should be interpreted literally. They were going on a cruise."

"But Randy never made the cruise."

"No."

"That's bullshit. Why not just say, 'Hey Julia, we're going on a cruise'?"

She shrugged and sipped from her mug.

"And you interpreted it as a signal to hop a plane to the United States the next day."

"Yes. Exactly."

"What did Ben mean, figuratively?"

She paused as if deeply pondering his question, but more likely she was concocting another bullshit answer. "The color blue usually connotes trust, wisdom, and truth. Other than a crustacean, a crab can be a grouchy person, but neither man was grouchy. Randy was quite free-spirited and funny, and Ben introspective and sweet." She paused again. "What do you think Ben meant?"

"Let me ask the questions."

"Yes. Of course."

He placed his empty mug on the kitchen counter. "Can you think of anything else?"

"No."

He handed her his business card. "My phone number. Call me if anything comes to you, or if you want to tell me the real meaning of Ben's message to you."

"Of course. Come by for coffee any time. Now that we're neighbors."

"You're staying?"

"'We are visitors to this time, this place. We are just passing though.'"

Another non-answer, another deflection. He headed to the door.

"Aren't you interested in who said that?" she asked.

"Minimally."

"At least make a guess," she urged.

"No."

"Come on, humor me ..."

"If you don't cooperate with me, I don't cooperate with you."

"The quote's from an Australian aborigine," she offered as a concession.

He found himself smiling as he pushed through the screen door. Never had he gotten less information from an interview, and never had he been so beguiled.

The Marsh

Will's heart pounded. What if Frank Whitby's partner, the fellow blackmailer who had filmed Frank with Mrs.

Chandless and others, had Alex in his sights at this very minute? He'd made a terrible mistake bringing Alex out to the marsh with him! What was the correct procedure for this? He couldn't think straight in her presence. He stood, causing the boat to teeter.

"What are you doing?" she said.

"Scoot over." He dropped onto the bench next to her.

"It's not big enough for two."

"Just move over. I want to sit between you and the grass."

"Do you think someone's trying to kill me? That's what Julia thinks."

"I don't know." Will's phone vibrated in his pocket and he read Jay's text. "You know a lot about blue crabs. What does it mean when they move to deeper waters?"

"During the fall and winter crabs move to deeper waters and burrow in the sand to ride out the winter."

"They're hiding?"

"More like hibernating, protecting themselves. Why?"

"Jay Braden was asking about blue crabs."

"Why?"

"Something he read in an email."

"In what email?"

"In an email Ben wrote to Julia on the night Randy was killed. Ben wrote that the blue crabs were moving to deeper waters. That one passage prompted her to come to the U.S."

"That's all Ben wrote?"

"Yes. We need to sit down with Julia and have her tell us everything in that Giles Hale memoir. That's why she's here. To tell you something."

"Every clue involves the Whitbys. Neville Whitby kills Charles Allaway. My father was the same class as Frank Whitby. The gas can is from Desmond Whitby's gas station."

"Look," he whispered. Hidden in the marsh grass was a camo jon boat. He read the registration numbers. "It's the same one. Frank Whitby's." He pulled the gun from his shoulder holster.

"That gun makes me nervous. There's no one around. Put it away. They would have shot me by now."

"Don't say that!"

"But it's true. Let's tie up over there."

Will leapt to the shore. She tossed him a line and he heaved the skiff into the grass. Water Boy jumped off the boat and disappeared in the marsh. Will reached out his hand to assist. She reached outward. He stared down at her palm, looked briefly into her face, and then stared at her palm once again.

"What?"

"Nothing," he said quickly. "This way. That path."

A path had been tamped down by hunters and fishermen's feet. A duck blind appeared amidst the tall grass. Will stepped onto the wooden platform and pulled his binoculars to his eyes. From the blind was a direct view to the marine station dock and Frank Whitby's outdoor shower. There were crushed beer cans and sandwich wrappers in the corner. He opened the old milk box with a pen so as not to leave fingerprints. A battery-operated CD player. CDs. ZZ Top, Molly Hatchet, Alabama and so on. An Allman Brothers CD—the same album that had been found in Randy's house.

"Blood," she noticed.

"Where?" he asked quickly.

"There. Snake blood, I think. See the scales."

He whipped out his phone and took pictures of the hacked wood and blood, the CDs, beer cans, and the view to the marine station. He attached the photos to a text to Jay and Lisa with the subject line, "More work for Zera's team."

"We should be getting back," he said. "I want to come by tonight, if you're not busy. To hear the whole story from Julia."

"Yes. Fine."

He held out his palm and grabbed hers. "I want to know why we both have the same cut across our left thumbs."

"Papa told me that I cut it on a sharp can when I was a little girl," she explained.

"Yeah, I bet. And my father told me I cut myself with a Swiss Army knife when whittling a stick."

Rush Hour Traffic

It was done! The last Allaway had been purged from River Glen! The Allaway line ... robbers of the pyrate treasury, defamers of the noble Whitby name ... were finally exterminated. He, Clyde Whitby, was the avenger of the Whitby honor. His praises would be sung for generations to come.

It had been an exhausting but glorious evening for the heroic knight of Clan Whitby. As before, during the hit-and-run, his ever-faithful squire, Desmond, had come through. Desmond had hosed him down behind the service station to wash off the blood, burned the black hoodie, pants, gloves, and Alex's purse in his ash can, and given him a clean change of clothes.

Upon returning home, Francine had nagged him about missing dinner, and his tan, accusing him of going to the beach without her.

"No one gets such a great tan from having lunch at a rest stop." Her voice grated as usual. "And where did you get those clothes?" she'd added suspiciously.

She seemed to buy his story that he'd left work early to work on his golf swing, changed clothes at the club, and then run into potential business associates and had drinks.

That morning, after a sound night's sleep, he'd awoken to find his daughters and wife hovering in front of the morning news. "Another body found in River Glen," Francine had said worriedly. "This time, a young woman. Still unidentified."

"Terrible," he'd said, filling his coffee mug.

"You're all dressed up," Francine had said. "Handsome."

He had to admit that he was a dashing figure in his new business suit. "Strategy meetings at stores 2 and 4." In actuality, he'd be at store 5, but it was always best to conceal his exact activities and destinations from his wife and daughters. They always wanted him for something.

At the moment, he was stuck in afternoon traffic on Route 273 in northern Maryland. He cracked open a beer and turned up sports radio. The entire day had been spent behind the books of the new shop. The accounts were in perfect order, the new manager meticulous and competent, but it was always smart to create uncertainty, to keep one's employees on their toes. A deliberate look of vexation had been on his face all day, to imply errors had been discovered.

In reality, the extermination of Alex Allaway had preoccupied him throughout the day. The final culling of the herd! What impudence to suggest that Frank had fucked her! If she was the last woman on the planet, Frank would never … she was delusional, it was wishful thinking, perhaps lusting after Frank, stalking him for years. Perhaps in her lovesick frustration, she'd finally trapped him. No doubt

Frank had refused her advances. It was then that she'd killed him, probably with some poison, like Emmaline had used on the wives of Huw Collins and Angus Smyth. How dare those women accuse Emmaline of staking out the treasury? Unfounded accusations of that sort had to be silenced. The Allaways were low-life crabbers. Perhaps Alex had cut Frank into pieces and sent the pieces to the bottom of the bay. She'd reduced Frank to fucking crab bait.

Then the powers-that-be had smiled on the Whitby Clan once again ... the opportunity to exact revenge. Alex had reached for something in her purse, probably mace to blast into his face. But he'd been quicker. His machete had struck her wrist, and her purse spilled onto the pavement.

"Fucking asshole!" she'd screamed at him, as blood coursed from her arm.

He'd wiped that haughty, indignant rage right off her face.

After the culling was finished, his first impulse had been to stuff her body into his trunk, but no way was he going to contaminate his new leather golf bag with Allaway blood. It was smarter to just leave her body to be fed upon by insects, foxes and birds until it was discovered. Besides, he'd worn gloves; he'd left no physical evidence at the scene. He'd dragged the body into the marsh grass behind the bathhouse. He'd then grabbed the car keys from her purse and snatched the papers out of her glove compartment, in case there was information on what she'd found at the Sassafras and Bohemia Rivers. Sadly, there'd been nothing helpful in the papers. Only a road map of the Delmarva peninsula, and an insurance card and car registration for a person, probably a boyfriend, named George Bannister. Clyde's next impulse had been to torch the car, like they did after the hit-and-run, but then there'd be no time to escape from the Point undetected. Besides, he felt no ill will against George. Lucky George had been rid of his arrogant girlfriend, but he would be sad if he lost his car.

Shit ... what a crazy night, twenty-six years ago! The whole family had been at their grandmother's birthday party, held annually the day before Thanksgiving. Uncle Bobby always made a potent punch. After the party, Frank had climbed into his Saturn, and he and Desmond had gotten into the van. "Last one to River Glen buys the beers!" shouted Frank through his car window. It had been a gloomy late afternoon when they'd raced down the coastal road, occupying both lanes. Suddenly a car appeared from behind the crown in the road. Frank had swerved to miss it, but his Saturn clipped its front end, spinning it off the road. The car careened off the shoulder and crashed into a pine tree; the hood popped open and steam hissed from the engine.

The Saturn and the van skidded to a stop on the shoulder, and the three of them crept forward. Both passengers, a man and a woman, were crushed behind the dashboard. The woman in the passenger's seat was unconscious. The man turned his bloody head. "Call for an ambulance," he rasped through the shattered window. "Oh, Frank, it's me. Colin. From high school. My wife ... she's hurt."

The three of them huddled in panic.

"Who's that, Frank?" Clyde asked.

"Colin Allaway."

"We can't help them! They're fucking Allaways!"

Frank looked frantically down the dark road. "We can't stay here. If we get fuckin' breathalyzers, we're fucked! I can't get a second DWI. Fuck! I've only made two payments on this car."

"That woman's a looker," Desmond leered. "We should take her into the woods."

"Shut-up, Des! We don't have time for that!" Frank yelled.

"We can't just leave them here. They'll rat on us!" Clyde said. "Des, do you still have gas for the Jet Skis in the van?"

"Yes!"

"Get it, asshole!" Frank ordered.

Desmond rushed to the van and returned with two canisters from his father's service station, the Gimpy Gull. Frank and Clyde snatched them and splashed the paralyzed car with gasoline.

"Frank, help us!" Colin implored. "Please ... my wife ..."

"Wait!" Desmond yelled. "Let's grab that woman!"

But the cry was too late. Frank had already pulled a matchbook from his jeans and struck the first match. It was a dud . Cursing, he tossed it to the ground.

The second match sparked.

Their three faces glowed orange. Frank held the flame to the matchbook to ignite the whole packet. He'd chuckled, tossed the fire at the car, and leapt backward.

Flames danced among the dark pines that November evening.

Headquarters

"The killer sure did Will a favor." Lisa reviewed the inventory of items from Penny Bannister's apartment. "Fifty shades of nail polish. Thirty lipsticks. Bannister was a Narcissist with a capital N. And a stash of date rape drug, just like Will suggested."

"The autopsy found that she was pregnant," Jay said.

"Bannister had a file folder on Darren Darien, the Delaware basketball star. He was probably the father. The killer did him a favor too."

"Anything else?"

"Nothing, really. She was unemployed. Will was sending her monthly child support checks. Carly was attending summer camp while Bannister was spending her days at the gym and mall. She was an exercise freak. There were lots of health and beauty magazines and some children toys around the apartment. Sex toys in her bedroom closet."

"What did Norman find in her laptop?"

"That she lived on Facebook. She changed her profile picture every day, posting pictures of her new nails, hairstyles, and designer clothes. No pictures of Carly. What parent doesn't post about their kids? It was all about her."

"Zera counted over twenty stab wounds with a large hunting knife. There were bloody smudges on the passenger's side door handle where the killer entered, and more blood around the glove compartment. The killer was definitely looking for something. But what?"

Lisa clicked on her keyboard. "Camera footage from the bridge last night at 7:52. Check out the driver of the Lexus. Black hoodie, balaclava. License plate covered up. This is our perp."

"Check to see if this car passed over the bridge on the night of Randall Allaway's death."

"Already did it. I ran all the plates from that night. This car wasn't there, but there was a tow truck registered to a Desmond Whitby. He owns the Gimpy Gull service station."

"Let's go." Jay grabbed his car keys.

The Gimpy Gull was located outside of River Glen, on the main highway coming into town. Behind the gas station was a fallow field; beyond that, a distant forest. Jay climbed out of the car, thankful to separate himself from Lisa's gum smacking. Smart young woman, huge asset to the team, but the stretching, twisting, and swaying of the bubble gum around and between her finger was enough to induce madness.

Rusty metal signs of products long forgotten covered the white building. Adjacent to the gas pumps and garage was a shop that sold tourist knick-knacks: t-shirts, peanuts, fudge, Maryland crab memorabilia, local ciders, and homemade ice cream. He pushed through the door, triggering a bell, and headed to the snacks aisle. After locating Laura's favorite, Old Bay-flavored peanuts, he returned to the cash register. A puffy-faced brunette in her fifties shuffled nervously around the storefront. She reminded him of a sausage, fatty meat stuffed into plastic wrapping, in this case a tight tank top and polyester shorts. She glanced through the plate glass window at Lisa, who was photographing the tow truck.

"Old Bay. Great with an ice cold beer." Jay pulled a bill from his wallet.

"Yes," she answered distractedly.

"Is Desmond here?"

"In the garage." She handed him the change.

"Charming shop."

"The family's owned it for generations. Since the nineteen thirties."

"Your name is?"

"Blanche. Whitby. Desmond's wife."

"Thanks for the nuts." The bell jingled once again as he left and approached the garage.

Desmond Whitby, a man in a gray jumpsuit with the sleeves cut off, left the garage in an irritated slouch. He had thinning grey hair, a scraggly mustache, and spindly arms and legs. A large, oily wrench was clenched in his fist, a gesture that made Lisa's steps falter.

"What's so interesting about my truck?" he snarled at her.

Jay stepped into his path and presented his ID. "I'm Detective Braden, and this is Detective Paco."

"I asked *her* a question," Desmond retorted.

"I'm asking the questions now. Your truck was seen on camera passing over the bridge in River Glen and turning down the river road last Thursday night. On the night of Randall Allaway's murder."

"I didn't know that River Glen was off-limits to tow trucks."

"What were you doing on the river road?"

"Taking a drive to the Point."

"To do what?"

"Watch the sunset."

"At 10:05. Who was your passenger?"

"What passenger?"

"The Point's where couples go for romance. Do you have a boyfriend, Desmond?"

"What? No!"

"Who's your boyfriend?"

"It was my cousin!" Blood vessels popped from Desmond's scrawny chicken neck.

Jay eyed him coolly. "Detective Paco, have a look around with the scanner."

Lisa pulled a small electronic device from a leather case.

"What's that thing?" Desmond asked anxiously.

"A wonderful bit of technology," he answered. "It scans for fingerprints on objects, or from individuals, and it goes right into the central database. Do you mind if we scan yours?"

"I have nothing to hide. I've never had any run-ins with the police." Desmond stepped threateningly close to Lisa and overtly stared at her chest. Blanche's face through the window was one of resigned disgust.

"I'll hold that." Jay reached for Desmond's wrench.

"Suit yourself." Desmond handed him the tool. Again he smiled at Lisa to intimidate. The yellow teeth had their intended effect, and she winced while she moved the scanner over his blackened fingers. Done, she darted away to scan the garage.

"One more time," Jay said. "What were you and your cousin, named … "

"Why's that matter?"

"The multitude of uses for a wrench." Jay turned the tool in his hands.

"Clyde," Desmond said quickly.

"… doing on the river road?"

"Fuckin' wastin' time! The whole evening wasted!"

"Why?"

"We were supposed to meet Randy Allaway."

"Why?"

"He contacted Clyde. Said he knew where Frank was."

"Really?"

"We drove down to Allaway's place, but it was dark. We knocked, but no one answered. He was playing head games with us."

"How did Allaway contact Clyde?"

"By letter to Clyde's house in Newark. It completely spooked him that Allaway knew where he lived. In a different state."

"Newark, New Jersey?"

"No, Delaware. Clyde worried that Allaway might hit on his wife and daughters."

"Did Clyde ever see Allaway around his home?"

"No."

"Did you see Ben Hancock around that night? Was his sailboat at the dock?"

"No boat, no Ben. His place was dark. We heard a dog barking from his place."

Lisa emerged from the garage and Jay glanced questioningly at her, but she shook her head nearly imperceptibly. Desmond's prints did not match those in Randy Allaway's house, the jon boat, or duck blind.

She disappeared around the side of the garage. Desmond's face furrowed with consternation. "Aren't we done here? I have to finish a tune-up before closing time." He rushed after her.

She wandered by empty propane tanks, old tires. Gimpy Gull-embossed gas cans from eons ago, bent lawn chairs, and other debris in the weeds. After crossing the gravel lot, she stood on tiptoe and peered over the edge of a dumpster. It contained empty cardboard boxes and plastic trash bags. A smoky smell permeated the air. She looked over the brim of a blackened ashcan. It was empty of debris. She knelt and felt its bottom. "Sir, it's still warm, but it's been emptied."

"Where were you last night between seven and nine?" Jay asked Desmond.

"Here. Until closing at eleven."

"Your wife? Was she here?"

"She leaves around five and meets her girlfriends for water aerobics at the swim club."

"There's no CCTV at your shop. Why?" Lisa asked.

Desmond's eyes crawled over Lisa; her jaw tightened. "Too expensive."

"Can anyone verify your presence here last night?" Jay asked.

"Yeah, the twenty-odd customers whose tanks I filled," he said petulantly. "And the mayor. I tanked his car and filled his tires."

"What were you burning back here?" Jay said.

"It wasn't me. I never come back here. Blanche takes out the trash."

Newark

"Dinner, Clyde," Francine called into his home office.

"I hate dinners at home," Clyde grumbled to himself. His daughters would inevitably chatter about clothes, dance class, or drama camp, where they were performing *South Pacific*. Francine would chatter about some home improvement project that she had in mind. Her current fixation was the purchase of a grandfather clock for the entryway, because the Judds and Holmeses down the street had one. Chatter, chatter, endless chatter. Every time he looked at his wife or daughters he felt money being sucked from his wallet as if by a giant, invisible vacuum.

He entered the kitchen and smiled at Francine. "Dinner smells wonderful." If he complimented the new recipe, he might get laid that night.

"Chicken tetrazzini," she said.

"Yum." He grazed his hand over her ass.

"You're incorrigible," she whispered.

He smiled again. He was definitely getting laid that night. His daughters stared at the TV in the family room. When they'd bought this executive home, Francine had insisted on a kitchen island, granite counter tops and an open floor plan. Fucking open floor plans. Open floor plans meant no privacy. Everyone could always see what he was doing and ask him to do some tedious chore.

If only he had the power to change one daughter into a son! With a son, he'd have a hunting buddy. What an amazing childhood he'd had with Frank for an older brother! They'd skulked around the fields and woods with their rifles. On secret safari, Frank had called it. They'd become crack shots by junior high. They'd killed countless squirrels, rabbits, chipmunks, and birds, but big game hunting was their favorite activity. They'd killed a few foxes, deer, and neighborhood cats, and even Mr. Gardner's German shepherd, but no one had found out about it. Rex had been weighted down with rocks and sent to the bottom of the river.

"Here, hon." Francine handed him a glass of white wine.

"Breaking news in the River Glen murder investigation," said the news anchorman.

"Turn it up," she called to her daughter with the clicker.

On the TV screen a middle-aged couple trudged listlessly up the front steps of the River Glen police station, a crowd of reporters pressing cellphones, microphones, and cameras into their distraught faces. Clyde watched curiously. Who the hell were these individuals?

"George and Danielle Bannister arrived in River Glen today. They identified the victim as their daughter, Penelope Bannister of Middletown, Delaware."

At sea

Near the edge of the continental shelf, Old Ben pulled a joint from a plastic bag, flicked the lighter and gratefully inhaled. The pain in his arthritic hip would be dulled within minutes. The cramped sailboat and lack of exercise weren't helping. One of the saddest times he could recall was disassembling the grow house in the woods. But there had been no choice. It had been only be a matter of time before the police would be swarming the property, and no blame must fall on Alex. So he, Randy, John Wilkins, and Luna had moved the fullest, most fertile plants into Luna's basement and installed ample lighting and a hydroponic system. This way, a steady amount of weed would still be available for the various aches and pains of the aging population of River Glen, for the Hoffmans, Smyths, and Dennistons. John Wilkins, who had no physical ailments, was an outright pothead. He simply liked to get buzzed every night after his boring job of filling out the applications for auto tags. And the weed helped Luna to sleep. That was the River Glen way —the pyrate way—to look out for one's neighbors.

Ben flicked at the lighter to pass the time. He'd brought books for his voyage, but it was too difficult to read with the wind flapping the pages. The solitude gave him time to think. He gazed at the sputtering flame. It wasn't the car crash itself that had killed Colin and Carole Allaway, but fire. That nightmare of a Wednesday when the two cops arrived, Randy had insisted that they take him to the scene of the accident.

Ben had stayed at home with the infant. He'd had nothing to feed a baby. In a panic he'd called Alice Hoffman, who'd had a number of children. Alice and Luna soon arrived with bottles, nipples, and formula. John Wilkins and his new bride, Belle Stanton, arrived shortly after, with a case of beer .... Randy returned hours later, ashen and red-eyed, and made a beeline for the liquor cabinet.

"Whitbys are behind this!" Randy poured himself a generous scotch.

Alex howled from the next room. Luna and Belle rushed away with a bottle to calm her.

Randy collapsed into the U-shaped sofa. "The car was hit! I could tell! The front bumper was smashed in. When I tried to look, the police chief, Stanley Whitby, shooed me away. Colin's arms were around Carole ... they were black, charred ... gone." He sobbed into his hands.

Alice dropped into the sofa and pulled him into her shoulder. John Wilkins filled a bong and passed it around the room. Belle and Luna reappeared with little Alex, and they sat in front of the fireplace. Luna jangled her necklaces and colorful earrings while the baby watched, fascinated.

Randy eventually composed himself. "When I asked the fire chief how the fire started, he could barely look me in the eye. He mumbled some bullshit and jammed his hands in his pockets. That's when the police chief stomped over and ordered all of us to leave. Those Whitbys will pay!"

"Look at this beautiful baby." Luna placed Alex in Randy's lap. "Make them pay later. For now, there's a child to raise."

River Glen

How could her grandmother move comfortably around a house where a murder had taken place? Alex wondered. Where Papa's recliner once was, Julia had placed a table with an arrangement of wildflowers picked from Ben's garden. It was a memorial of sorts. Eventually they'd have to arrange Papa's funeral, but she'd let Julia handle it. Some people thrived in the midst of disaster and turmoil, and Alex was not one of them. Julia clearly was. Carly Wilkins snoozed on Papa's sagging sofa. Water Boy was shredding one of Julia's bedroom slippers and scattering foam rubber across the living room floor. Luna circled the house outside, chanting incantations and waving branches and incense to ward off evil spirits. A police car was posted at the entrance to the river road. Another one was at the Point. And Will Wilkins was in the kitchen preparing snacks with Julia. He was enamored with Julia. Every male on the planet was.

The recounting of Giles Hale's memoir was an occasion for a party, Julia had decided. Somewhere, probably from the bar at Nauticus, Julia had acquired a bottle of sparkling wine. Its cork popped and flew across the kitchen, hitting the shell mobile that she had made for Papa when she was a Girl Scout. For whatever reason, that had some element of hilarity that made Will and Julia burst into laughter.

It was best to stay out of the kitchen, Alex decided, because Will was wearing a pheromone-saturated aftershave. It was the same scent she'd smelled when he'd pressed against her on the seat of the skiff that morning. That had made her uncomfortable for the rest of the day. Her only thought had been to pull, strip, tug ... pull him out the door and across the porch, strip off his clothes on the beach, and tug him into the water. She recalled Richard's castigation, "Alex, we'll get arrested if we do it outside." With so many cops around, an arrest was likely. And with one of their own

... great. More reporters, more publicity, a photo in the *Washington Post*, and a text from Richard. "Told you so."

"Let's talk on the porch. It's a gorgeous night." Julia held a tray of cheese and crackers. "Will, you light the chiminea. Alex, you get the wine and glasses."

She did as told, pushed through the screen door, and chose a seat as far as possible from the source of the potent love potion.

"The house is purified and safe now!" Luna called. She drifted down the river road, her long dress flowing and beads jangling on her fringed vest.

It was a gorgeous evening, Alex agreed, despite the terrible events of the day. The sky was rich with stars, fireflies flickered on and off along the beach, and a thin mist veiled the river. At the end of the black dock, a lone stern light illuminated the *Vital Spark*.

"Where did I leave off?" Julia asked. "Did I tell you about the treasury?"

"You mentioned a community treasury in the tavern," Will said.

"Yes, that's the one. Two men were elected by the community to watch over the treasury."

"This was a strange turn of fate," Julia said. "The treasurers were the carpenter, Barnaby Wilkins, and the fisherman, Charles Allaway. Abigail and Tess, the wives of Huw Collins and Angus Smyth, noticed Emmaline Whitby surveilling the tavern, watching when Giles and Kathleen, Charles and Barnaby were about or absent. Abigail and Tess confronted Emmaline and asked her what she was doing. Emmaline muttered something incoherent and ran off. Two days later, both Abigail and Tess were found dead, a horrible rash on their faces and necks. The women of Newgate Prison were aware that Emmaline had been convicted of poisoning her master's family in London. They were furious—and terrified.

"Barnaby checked the treasury and reported that the gold from the *Espiritu de la Virgen* was missing. Panic ensued. A band of men searched the dwellings in the village. A pouch of poison—foxglove—was found in Neville Whitby's hut. A tribunal was formed in the tavern, presided over by Charles Allaway. The citizens of the tribunal demanded that Neville and Emmaline return the gold, and that the Whitby family be banished. Neville and Emmaline were outraged and denied all knowledge of the foxglove and the theft. The tribunal gave the Whitbys one night to pack their belongings. Emmaline returned to her two children, but Neville lay in wait in the darkness for Charles Allaway, the judge at the proceedings."

"Later that night, Giles and Kathleen heard screaming in the street. They dashed from the tavern to find Charles's head on a pike. They rushed to Allaway's cabin, fearing for the lives of Charles' wife, Shannon O'Malley, and their children. Giles rowed the Allaways and his own family out to a nearby island for safekeeping. Then he returned to River Glen, only to find that Neville and his family had fled the camp, fearing the worst. And the worst was on its way. Giles tracked the family through the forest and found them boarding a small dory—a dory, incidentally, laden with the treasury's gold.

"On the beach the next morning were four dead Whitbys: Neville, Emmaline, and the two children. The gold had been returned to the treasury. But the dory and the Hale family were gone. And that's the story of Giles Blood-hand."

"But what happened to Shannon and her family?" Alex asked.

"Ah, Shannon." Julia said. "She's the mother of River Glen. There were more pyrates than there were female convicts in the village, so she lived in a progressive marriage of sorts with the widowers, Huw Collins and Angus Smyth. Shannon's the great, great, and so on, grandmother of the Allaways, Collinses, and Smyths."

"And Barnaby Wilkins?" Will asked.

"Barnaby would later marry a Spanish woman. It's rumored that she was part of the crew of Spanish pyrate, Juan Carlos de Castillo."

Will peeked through the screen door to check on Carly. "And Conall Whitby?"

"Conall convinced the tribunal that he had no involvement in Neville and Emmaline's activities, so they let him stay, but he was largely an outcast forever after. He befriended an alcoholic priest, Brother Guillermo. The two of them were drunk most of the time."

"And the treasury gold?" Alex asked.

Julia yawned and stretched. "Who knows? Giles and Kathleen didn't bring any treasure back to Scotland. They were destitute when they returned to Sir Edmund's estate. Now, I need my beauty rest." She pulled herself from the chair. "Sweet dreams."

"Wait!" Alex held her left thumb into the air. "Why do Will and I have the same mark on our thumbs?"

Julia held up hers. There was no mark. She gave a naïve shrug. "You cut it, I guess." She departed into the house.

Will lifted the bottle. "More wine, Alex?"

"Sure."

He filled her glass, then stuffed another log into the chiminea. All was dark except the crackling fire, the flickering fireflies, and the stars.

Sweet dreams. Dreams?

She stared at Will.

"What?" he asked.

"Dreams. Over the years I've had this recurring dream ..." She leaned toward the heat with her wine glass between her hands. "It's dark, night, just like this, but it's fall, not summer. There are candles and pumpkins. There are a number of people, all adults, unrecognizable in the shadows. I move, or am nudged toward a fire, and something else, that I can't remember. Someone holds my hand over something. Something shiny. I'm terrified and shaking. A knife glimmers in the darkness and swiftly cuts my thumb. I wail. Someone squeezes my thumb, dripping my blood onto shiny objects. Then I'm lifted up by one of the adults, and hugged. It must be Papa who comforts me. I feel warm flannel against my cheek and smell salt water in the air. "Shh, it's done," he consoles me. I open my eyes. The shadows part and a small boy appears, his hand shaky and outstretched. There's a flick of a blade, his cry, and dripping blood." She moved her eyes from the fire. "Will, that boy is you."

"It's not a dream, is it?" he said, mesmerized.

"No. All these years I thought it was just a dream based on a bizarre pagan ritual that Luna must have told me about as a child. Just now, I realized that it must have been real. Do you remember it?"

"No. My father has the same mark, but not my mom, because she's a Stanton. And Randy?"

"Yes. Not Julia, because she's a Hale. Only Wilkins and Allaways by blood, not marriage."

"We're the pyrate treasurers," he whispered. "But treasurers of what?"

"Let's find out. I'll be right back." She jumped to her feet and dashed down the dock to the *Vital Spark*. She flipped on the galley light, grabbed the white plastic garbage bag and her laptop. She lugged the items back to the porch.

She moved the laptop onto her knees. "I was talking to Professor Leon Bakanian, a historian at UVA, who suggested that the treasure was drunk and whored away in the Caribbean. But it clearly wasn't if pyrates were beheading each other for it in colonial River Glen."

She typed *Espiritu de la Virgen* into the search engine. A link to *El Archivo General de Mercaderes del Mar Caribe* appeared on the screen. "You can find anything on the internet."

"That's the truth." He pulled his chair next to hers and gazed at her laptop. "What's it say?"

"I can read Spanish but I can't speak it. The galleon was part of a regular convoy between Cartagena, Colombia, and Cádiz, Spain. It was one hundred feet long and thirty feet wide. Three masts, three decks, with thirty-six cannons. Sounds top heavy. Her normal cargo to the Americas was food, tools and weapons, and domestic animals for the Spanish colonists in the West Indies. Her cargo back to Spain was gold, silver, assorted other treasures, and spices. According to the ship's manifest of 1688, she left Cartagena with a cargo of emeralds from Colombia, rubies from Brazil, pearls from Margarita Island, and Peruvian gold and silver. For months she waited in Havana for three other galleons from Veracruz. The ships from Mexico were delayed by a disease that struck a mule train moving goods from Acapulco on to Veracruz. Finally, when the convoy was assembled, five heavily armed and laden galleons left Havana, their intended route the Florida Straits, and then the Gulf Stream back to Europe. Just after they left Havana, a killer storm hit. Two ships sank. The *Espiritu* got blown up the Gulf coast of Florida. They were forced to anchor in a shallow cove to make repairs to their masts and rudder. Most of the Spaniards were on the beach, tending to the wounded and sewing up the shredded sails, when a small, swift schooner, the *Raven*, appeared, her guns blazing. The small detachment of soldiers left on the galleon was no match for Captain Bart Dodd and his crew, and the galleon was quickly overtaken. Dodd turned the guns toward the beach, killing the wounded and scattering the rest into the mangroves. The pyrates offloaded the bounty onto the *Raven* and burned the galleon to the waterline. That's all that's written here."

She pulled the skull from the plastic bag. "Memento mori 1694, the year of Charles Allaway's murder." Then she removed the yearbook. "My father's yearbook from 1987. It was a small class. My father must have known Frank Whitby." The last object pulled from the bag was the Gimpy Gull gas canister. "This meant nothing to me until I hosed the mud off it earlier today and noticed this." She pointed. "This was scratched into the paint. 11/25/1991. The date my parents died."

"In a hit-and-run."

"What?"

"You didn't know that?"

"No! Papa told me that my parents drove into a tree after swerving to miss an animal. Did they ever catch the person?"

"No. But we're pretty certain we've found the other vehicle. It belonged to Frank Whitby. Randy and Ben have been leaving us very valuable clues."

"Like what?"

"Randy left a map of Cooper's Creek in his papers. When Jay and I checked it out, we found a sunken car. Whitby's.

Then, both Randy and Ben had in their belongings information about McKibbin's Apartments. That's where Whitby was filming women having sex, then blackmailing them. But he had a partner who was also filming him and the women in the shower at the marine station. Randy and Ben were deliberately tipping us off."

For a moment Alex said nothing. Will had been direct and honest with her, terrible as the news was. It was her turn to divulge her share of the information.

"They left me clues as well. Here." She pulled the two papers from her pocket. "Here's the one from Ben's things, that you gave me. 1OGM 2CC 3GG The numbers 1 2 3 correspond to this map Papa left me."

"Jay and I know about the three places. But where was this map?"

"Right on the table next to Papa, when I found him. In an envelope with my name on it. I was frightened. I thought it was from the killer. But it was in Ben's handwriting. The 1 was at the Bohemia River, the 2 was at the Sassafras, and 3 was at Mutter Island. That's how I knew to go there."

Will read the message along the edge of the map. *"Tell no one Alex. No one! JAllaway might come.* JAllaway is Julia Hale-Allaway, who comes when Ben sends her an email that the *blue crabs are moving to deeper waters."*

"That's why I didn't tell you the other day. I was following Papa's instructions to me. I was trying to figure out what all this meant. Up to now I thought they were sending me on a scavenger hunt to understand my family history."

"And it couldn't be figured out without all three pieces of information ... from Randy, Ben, and Julia. This is crazy."

"Oh ... it gets crazier." She took off her sneaker.

"Your foot? That's also a clue?" he smirked.

"The envelope that contained the map said *Alex, open my hand*. I pried open Papa's fingers. I was terrified. "

"What'd you find?"

She lifted the insole. "This." The piece of eight glistened in the light of the fire. "Papa and Ben aren't sending me on a scavenger hunt. It's a treasure hunt."

Newark

Francine's chicken tetrazzini churned like lava in Clyde's stomach, so he took another swig of antacid. He'd killed the wrong fucking bitch! On the laptop in his home office he'd watched the news stories on Penelope Bannister's murder on his favorite, FOX News, then ABC, NBC, CBS and even CNN, but nothing new could be gleaned from any of the reports. Bannister was an unwed, unemployed single mother living in Middletown, Delaware. She had a business degree from the University of Maryland; she'd been a cheerleader and made the Dean's List. Her reasons for being in River Glen were still unknown.

The Bannister bitch had it coming. He drained the rest of the chalky medicine. She had baited him, goaded him, pretended to know Frank, and disguised herself as Alex Allaway. His response was justifiable and her death inconsequential. But what was really upsetting was the sheer volume of police vehicles combing the Point. If Uncle Stanley were still alive, there'd be an ear inside the investigation, like after the hit-and-run. Uncle Stanley had been an exemplary officer and run the River Glen police unit with an iron fist. He'd always had their backs. The corruption charges that eventually forced his retirement, and contributed to his premature heart attack, were completely unfounded. With

Stanley gone, he knew absolutely nothing! His cell phone vibrated.

"Stan's peeps dropped by GG," read Desmond's text.

Stan's peeps equaled police, GG equaled the Gimpy Gull gas station.

Sweat broke across Clyde's face. How did the police connect Desmond to Bannister's murder? But if Braden and Wilkins were investigating, there was no need to worry. The dimwits still hadn't found Frank. Those two had a combined IQ in the negative numbers. Still, what had the police asked Desmond? Desmond wasn't the sharpest Whitby. What did the police find? What did they ask? It was urgent not to communicate electronically, in case Desmond's phone was being monitored. Despite a quaking stomach, a drive to Maryland—at this very moment—was imperative.

"Meet in two hours. The usual place," Clyde texted back.

"OK"

Clyde hurried to the bathroom to purge the molten dinner from his stomach, before rushing his laptop into his briefcase. He found his wife and daughters in the family room, giggling at the TV show *Dating Naked*.

"Honey, I just got a call from the man I had drinks with at the club. A group of executives are meeting tomorrow in Ohio. It's a huge opportunity. Think of it! Whitby Plumbing Supplies could go national! Hopefully I can catch a flight tonight."

Francine turned reluctantly from the TV screen. "That's exciting. Shall I help you pack?"

"No, no, I have a suit in my office at Store 1. I'll stop there for my things before heading to the airport."

He rushed to his garage. Indignant fury flowed through his blood. Alex Allaway had confounded him once again! She had killed Frank, effectively disposed of him, taken his job—simultaneously eliminating any new income from Frank's wealthy wives—and she'd cajoled an unwitting bimbo named Penelope Bannister to take the fall for her. He wouldn't miss a second time. He loaded his truck with his hunting gear. Desmond, his stupid but faithful squire, would go along with the plan; he did whatever he was told to do. A second pair of hands would be helpful. They were going on secret safari, he'd tell Desmond; big-game hunting for a rare, endangered species: the last remaining Allaway.

Chapter 8

Day 8

River Glen

Jay's thoughts hovered in that place between sleep and wakefulness, refusing to push through the portal of consciousness. His arm fanned across the bed, reaching for Laura. It was an old reflex from his college days, when she'd visited him on the weekends. His hand retracted from the cold sheets, empty on her side as they'd been for weeks, months, an eternity. The gloom of morning appeared before his eyes. He rose with a groan. His sciatica was flaring up again. No amount of gin could dull the pain in his left leg. He lumbered stiffly to the window and opened the blinds. The blast of sunlight roused him like a swift punch to his chin. The river beyond his lawn glistened like green gem stones. Canada geese paddled along the shoreline. His Boston Whaler floated silently at his dock. From his kitchen wafted the smell of bacon and coffee. Mrs. Pulacki had let herself in with her key. The evidence from Penelope Bannister's murder investigation cascaded upon him at once.

A person in a balaclava and Lexus GX SUV, the license plates covered. No CCTV camera at the Gimpy Gull. What business owner doesn't invest in one? A business owner who doesn't want his activities recorded.

The warm ashcan behind the gas station was covered with the fingerprints of Desmond Whitby, none of Blanche's. But Desmond's alibi checked out: he'd been at the service station all evening, not at the Point. The police had checked with the mayor and other persons who'd charged gas to their credit cards.

Charred remnants of the ashcan had been scattered throughout the fallow field behind the gas station, presumably that same evening. Burnt pants, sneakers, a hoodie, an apron with ice cream stains, a metal clasp to a women's purse, empty ice cream containers, a broken ice cream scoop, soda and oil cans, old spark plugs, and cardboard boxes were among the blackened debris. The fire had been started by an incendiary, probably gasoline. Desmond had rabidly denied any knowledge of how the fire had been lit, or how and why the debris had been tossed across the field. Yet no other prints were on the ashcan.

Also intriguing was the damp soil under a back spigot covered with Desmond's handprints. No hose was to be found. What spigot doesn't have a hose near by? More interesting still was that the dirt was new to that site. It had been replaced, raked into the surrounding soil, tamped down, and moistened. Someone had gone to great lengths to remove the original soil and the hose, burn the contents of an ashcan, and then hide them amidst a field of grass. The Gimpy Gull gas can that Alex Allaway had found on Mutter Island was identical to those discarded behind Desmond's gas station—another vital clue left by Randy and Ben.

Jay headed into the bathroom for a quick shower. It would be an insanely busy day for the understaffed rural police department of River Glen. The first priority was to interview Clyde Whitby, who'd allegedly received a letter from Randy Allaway about Frank's whereabouts. A dubious story, but one that needed checking out. Also, a Lexus GX was registered to Clyde's wife, Francine, while Clyde drove a Toyota pickup truck. The Lexus needed to be located and checked for Bannister's blood; Francine needed to be located and interviewed about her whereabouts on the night of Bannister's murder.

Zera's CSI team was at the point of exhaustion after performing Bannister's autopsy, searching the duck blind, then the gas station and field beyond.

Jay's young team was rattled. Lisa Paco, he noticed, was intimidated by bullying men like Desmond Whitby, which explained her zeal to work behind her computer at headquarters. She lived with a sick mother; there was never a mention of a father. What was the reason for that? Will was justifiably preoccupied with comforting his daughter. Will's other preoccupation was clearly Alex Allaway. Jay's wife was mad, and his Zera fantasies had been pushed aside by new ones starring a cagey actress with lovely legs and a musical Scottish accent. Two people had been murdered in River Glen in just a week. Other than that, everything in his world was just dandy.

After his shower, Jay wiped the steam from the mirror. Shit … he looked like shit … red-eyed, bloated, and pale. The latest men's fashion trend was the unshaven look. He could give a damn about fashion, but it was a convenient excuse not to shave.

"Paint, Laura, paint," he'd said before heading to bed. "Paint me one of your beautiful paintings." What had she painted last night?

He hurried into his clothes and headed for the living room … and stopped short. A wave of heat rose engulfed his face. He jerked loose his tie. Laura had been very busy.

In the third mural, Randy and Ben are standing once again on the beach, their faces registering panic and shock. The black dog is secure in Randy's arms. Frank Whitby is supine on the sand. Blood covers his blue and white shirt. His facial features are unrecognizable, as his head is portrayed as a nebulous red oval. A new character has appeared: Laura herself, in a blood spattered nightgown—the pink silk one he bought her in Paris—stands over Whitby's body, a red boat oar gripped her hands.

For the third time that morning Carly Wilkins climbed into Will's lap and asked him about Heaven. Each explanation was more fantastical than the one before.

"Heaven's a place of all of your favorite animals—dolphins, penguins, Chincoteague ponies and black lab puppies. All of the angels, both animals and humans, fly happily around trees of cotton candy and zigzag over cream soda lakes and ponds."

He looked at the breakfast table for inspiration. As long as he could remember, his father, John, ate Fruit Loops for breakfast every morning. "The inner tubes that float along lazy rivers are giant Fruit Loops. Everything is sweet and delicious." Carly thoughtfully considered his words. For the moment, the explanation of her mother's whereabouts seemed minimally plausible. Despite the lovely description, extra hugs, doting adults, and extra scoops of ice cream, she had an unspeakable awareness that something was terribly wrong.

"You'll see Mommy in Heaven one day," he said.

She fumbled nervously with the buttons on his shirt. "Soon?"

"Time moves faster with every passing day," he said.

"That's the truth," Belle, his mother, chimed in from the stove.

Will forced excitement into his tone. "Today you'll go to Rehoboth Beach with Grandmom and your cousins."

Belle placed a tall stack of pancakes in front of them.

"I want to eat here, on your knee, Daddy." Carly still clung to his shirt.

"Okay. Let's pretend we're lab puppies eating from the same bowl." He placed their pancakes on one plate.

Carly nodded and squeezed syrup over the stack.

"The Redskins are doomed as long as they have this owner," John muttered from behind the *Washington Post*.

"Horribly racist team name," Belle said. "They should call them the Washington Warriors. That way they don't need to change their wonderful logo." She peeked secretively outside the kitchen window. "What is going on? Another news van .... ooh ... this one from CNN ... I wonder why. Maybe there's some new evidence."

Belle had a ghoulish fascination with chaos and mayhem, as some people do. She'd closed her travel agency for the week and meticulously planned day trips with Carly, all strategically outside of River Glen. Her cell phone buzzed from the counter and she read the text.

"Aunt Dora saw our house on CBS. She said our begonias look lovely." Belle paused. "Carly, you're not eating enough, honey. How shall we decorate your new bedroom? With minions? Anna and Elsa from *Frozen*? How about a "Hello, Kitty" theme?"

A horn honked in the street, so Belle craned her neck around the curtain once again. "There's a traffic jam of news vans in front of the Smyth's next-door. Gary will have apoplexy."

"The quarterback situation's a mess," John said. "It's the start of minicamp and no starter? I've never seen such mismanagement in a front office."

Carly planted a sticky, syrupy kiss on Will's cheek. At that gesture he felt Penny Bannister's yoke of servitude loosen. For the first time in five interminable years, his dark mood blew out to sea and a glimmer of light appeared on the horizon. He'd witnessed all types of criminals in his few years as a cop. Most criminals acted out of silliness, folly, inebriation, lust, or the desperation to survive. Few people, he believed, were inherently evil and took pleasure in the suffering of others. Penelope Bannister fell into the latter category. Her gluttony was of the most dangerous kind. Of course she wanted objects, but she also wanted souls. For five years, she'd owned his. Had she lived, she would have owned that of another helpless sap named Darren Darien. The soul-robber was gone from his life. Not the slightest bit of remorse nagged at him. The newfound freedom was ineffable.

Will visualized his mental space as a pie chart: colorful slices of descending size had been allocated to Carly, family (mom, dad and sister), work, and Penny. Penny's unwelcome slice was black and sharp. Yesterday, at the sight of the Maryland terrapin tattoo, the black shard had vanished. He'd climbed back into the boat, a survivor, a free man, and, odder yet, co-treasurer of a mysterious pyrate treasure. A new slice, larger in magnitude and a beautiful incandescent green, had been inserted where the black shard had been.

"Now the FOX van! John, I'm glad you mowed the lawn last night," Belle said. "Ooh ... there's a cameraman on our sidewalk. I wonder why they're not at the Point."

Through the crack in the curtain, Will saw a spectacular summer day. Not a cloud was in the sky. It would be a glorious day on the water with his partner in their treasure quest. Their agenda, agreed upon the night before, as he'd carried Carly out to his car, was to return to the Bohemia and Sassafras Rivers and Mutter Island with the metal detector from Randy's closet ... and restore the pyrate treasure to the silent pyrates of River Glen. He placed a syrupy kiss on the cheek of his daughter and she threw her arms around his neck and squeezed.

Will's phone vibrated between the butter and lingonberries on the table. It was an unrecognizable number. Best to answer it, in case it was someone from headquarters.

"Wilkins, here."

"A reporter found your court deposition, and the lies you told the lawyers about the date rape drug. It's a total fabrication! This is defamation!" George Bannister yelled. "Penny told me, time and again, that you were an unfit father. You'll be hearing from my lawyer! We want full custody of Carly!"

The phone went dead. Will stared numbly into space. Then it dawned on him. The reporters and news cameramen on the front sidewalk, vultures on a carcass, were looking for him. Even in death, Penny Bannister refused to relinquish her chokehold.

Jay remained transfixed by the gruesome mural on his living room wall. Everything was finally clear. Laura had whacked Frank Whitby in the head for harming the dog. She'd had recent inexplicable outbursts of rage and violence —he wondered if they'd been triggered by what she'd witnessed, or if they'd caused her reaction. Randy and Ben must have given her Alex Allaway's nightshirt to change into, then disposed of Whitby's body. They had protected Laura.

As crabbers, they knew every inch of river, inlet and marsh of the Chesapeake. Whitby could be anywhere on the silty bottom of the bay. For their actions, another person, most likely a Whitby, had killed Randy. Before Old Ben could be targeted, he'd fled. But what about the anomalies, Lisa's so-called hiccups? The booked cruise? A fake Dott Garksi at the nursing home? These continued to baffle his team.

He struggled to contain his panic. What to do with Laura? They couldn't charge her if no body was found. The only evidence of foul play was a painting by a mad woman. Could this image possibly lead to Laura's arrest, her incarceration? It was urgent that he talk to her. Maybe she could fill in the details in her brief moments of lucidity. The place on the corner of the rug where she'd slept the past two nights was vacant.

He headed toward the kitchen. Mrs. Pulacki often put Laura's breakfast on the deck on nice mornings. He popped a waiting slice bacon in his mouth and glanced out to the deck.

"Where's Laura?"

Mrs. Pulacki turned from the stove. "I thought she was upstairs with you."

"Have you seen her at all this morning?"

"No."

Alarmed, he dashed to the top of the basement stairs. "Laura?" He tore down the stairs and flipped on the lights. No one was in the basement. He flew up the stairs, down the hall, and up to the second floor. "Laura?" He searched every room, bathroom, and closet upstairs. Nothing. He ran down the stairs and went outside.

"Laura? Laura!"

All the cars were in the driveway. Her bike was in the garage. He ran to the backyard. His boat was at the dock. So were the two kayaks.

He jogged along the shoreline trail, his lungs heaving from the cigarettes. There was no sign of Laura in the yards of the Wynskis, Larsens or Culps, or the Denniston's B&B. No Laura anywhere! He dragged himself back to the house.

"I can't find her! I didn't hear a thing last night. I have no idea when she left!"

What if Randy's killer had come for Laura to account for her killing of Frank Whitby? He had a murderer to catch, perhaps two, and now a missing wife! Dead wife? He was paralyzed with indecision and panic. A smothering pain constricted his chest.

"Laura's fine, Laura's fine ..."

"Yes, Laura's fine," Mrs. Pulacki said, unconvincingly.

Maybe a neighbor had invited her in for a cup of coffee ... unlikely, but he could always hope. Maybe she was taking a walk, or had gone for a swim up the river? He'd cruise the back roads of River Glen. He'd have his neighbors keep an eye out. Police patrols could look for her while on their rounds.

"Mrs. Pulacki, text me at the first possible sign of her. That's the plan. Laura's fine. Laura's fine."

Dazed, he moved to the extra room that he'd converted into an office. He paused in front of the safe, then opened the calendar on his phone.

Laura was clearly involved in the cause of Frank Whitby's death and disappearance. What the hell had he been doing that night? May 21st. There was nothing on this calendar for that evening. He'd probably been passed out in his recliner, after saturating himself with gin and tonics. He swiped the calendar to June. June 15th. One bit of good news—she hadn't killed Randall Allaway. On the night of his death, he and Laura had been together at the Historical Society for a lecture that she'd begged him to take her to and then proceeded to sleep through. It had been horribly embarrassing at the time, but now he was unspeakably relieved. Two nights ago, on the night of Penelope Bannister's murder, he had watched an Orioles-Braves game and drunk G&Ts, while she'd painted her own version of Edvard Munch's *The Scream*.

He turned the dial of his safe. The combination of numbers was the happiest day of his life, the date that he'd asked Laura to marry him and she'd said yes. He swung open the heavy door. His knees faltered and he grabbed the safe for support. Gone were his shoulder holster and service revolver, a forty caliber Beretta.

Julia looked up from her breakfast. "A shower before work this morning," she commented suggestively. "And is that perfume I smell?"

"No comment," Alex said. "You're not coming today."

"I wouldn't dream of stepping onto your love boat today, lass," Julia laughed.

Alex headed toward the *Vital Spark*. Love boat, she could only hope. It was probably pointless to have taken a shower. In an hour or so she'd be covered in sandy mud and sweat, swishing a metal detector across a leaf-covered, ruined barn at the Old Gray Mare Dairy. She'd even gone so far as to shave her legs, the first shave since her breakup with Richard. With her dismal luck, the moisturizer would attract ticks. Then she'd flail spastically about, flicking away the parasites, while Will would ask himself why he'd ever agreed to the silly treasure hunt.

Chill, Alex, chill.

"Come Water Boy!" The dog had moved into the almost-likeable category. He was good-natured and no longer nipped her ankles, but her morning wake-up call was horrendous dog breath panted into her face. He bounded down the dock and jumped onboard. "Drink." She pointed to his bowl. "Drink. Hydrate for our long day on the water."

She ducked under the figurehead and scanned the cabin, checking for everything: water bottles, laptop, towels, food, sunscreen, and metal detector. She'd never known Papa to have a metal detector, but Will had spotted it when the police had searched his closets. It was another helpful aid, amidst the clues that Papa and Ben had left her and the police.

She checked herself in a mirror. "Hopeless." Somewhere she'd lost her comb. She moved to the berth. With any luck Will might be with her in her bed, the river or the bay before her eightieth birthday. She shook the dog hairs from the blanket and swept sand from the sheets. Bummer, only one pillow.

Would Will even be interested? As a football star, he'd certainly bedded countless women. But she wasn't entirely inexperienced; she'd had sex with three men. The first time was unsurpassable. She'd wanted to shout her inexpressible pleasure, except that it would have alerted Gillian and Eddie in the pine forest. Papa and Ben up the river road might have come running, fearing that someone was dying on the beach. It amazed her to this day that the wave of orgasm that shuddered through her hadn't set up a tsunami that travelled down the length of the bay and capsized the aircraft carriers at Norfolk. The second time had been Nick at Scripps. He was more than willing to indulge her passion for the outdoors. All had seemed very promising with the supposedly divorced oceanographer. That relationship had ended the moment his wife and twins in a stroller appeared at the laboratory picnic. That was definitely awkward. And then there was Richard. Kind, intelligent, doting Richard, who only wanted sex indoors, always in a bed, and always in the missionary position. That was the deal-breaker.

"Planning your seduction?" Julia asked.

Alex turned. "What? No."

"You've been staring at the berth for minutes."

"Just straightening up."

"I just walked onto this boat and you didn't even hear me," Julia admonished. "Wake up, lass. Pay attention. Shag him later, but for now you need your wits about you. There be murdering pyrates and nutters about."

She nodded. "How much treasure are we even looking for?"

"Who knows what's left after three centuries."

A car door slammed. Jay Braden strode up the dock, staring at his cellphone. She and Julia stepped outside. Water Boy recognized the cop, and cowered behind the empty Clorox bottles that marked the trotline. Jay looked a wreck. His tie was loosened and his shirttails were out.

"Someone's a wee bit knackered this morning," Julia said coyly.

"A wee bit," he grumbled. "My wife's disappeared and she, or someone else, has my handgun. I need everyone keeping an eye out for her."

"I'm spending the day with Luna," Julia said. "We'll look for her."

He exhaled in aggravation. "Stay away from Luna's ayahuasca tea. We had to lock up two of her houseguests who claimed they were on a soul-journey with the Dalai Lama, on the pier, during Arts Fest.”

“No, never. My only vice is highland single malt whiskey.” Julia flashed him an engaging smile.

He smiled reluctantly.

Gary Smyth’s skiff motored toward the dock. Will was onboard, wearing the bright yellow ball cap and yellow t-shirt of the employees of the Smyth Marina. Gary was in the same yellow uniform. Will climbed onto the dock; Gary Smyth waved and headed back toward the village.

“What the hell is this?” Jay said. “Your leg’s bleeding.”

“I cut it climbing over Gary’s back fence,” Will replied. “Then we snuck down the bluff to get to the marina. Thanks to the disguise, I slipped by the reporters unnoticed.”

“What’s happening on Main Street?” Jay asked. “We don’t have the manpower for traffic control right now.”

“News vans at my parents’ house,” Will said guiltily. “It’s all my fault! Some reporter found my deposition, before I went to court, where I mentioned the date rape drug. George Bannister says it was a lie, that I’m unfit. He’s suing me for custody of Carly and for defamation!”

“That’s all we fucking need!” Jay said. “Do you have Bannister’s number?”

“In my recent calls list.” Will handed Jay his phone.

Jay punched the screen of the phone, his eyes narrowed. “Mr. Bannister? Detective Braden from River Glen PD. Yes, yes. Good morning to you also. Is your wife there?” He waited. “Good. Please put this on speaker phone. We have a bit of a bottleneck on Main Street due to your law suit against my detective, William Wilkins, who’s working diligently to catch Penelope’s killer.” He listened for a moment, his face reddening. “I might mention some of the objects the police found in Penelope's belongings. First a significant quality of a controlled substance called gamma-hydroxybutyric acid, in layman's terms, date rape drug. Equally interesting was Penelope's box of toys." He paused to escalate the tension. "It contained anal plugs, ball gags, dildos, cock cages, and the like. Oh, I nearly forgot to mention Penelope's smother box, homemade, no less. Her engineering skills will impress a jury. So will the Sybian machine. All of these items should be admissible in court. The jury will be fascinated by Penelope's interests. Now, if this information were to go viral, it would double the number of press vans in River Glen, and no way will our police cruisers get down to the Point to search for clues." He glanced at his watch. "Mr. Bannister, we have an extremely busy day ahead of us. I'm going to give you exactly five minutes to decide how you want to proceed, because that's going to dictate how we proceed. Please call us back at this number. You have five minutes." He hung up.

"Stunning performance!" Julia said.

Jay grimaced. "Ms. Hale, I'll bet you a highland scotch whiskey at Harlow's that Bannister calls me back in less than three minutes."

"You're on, love!" Julia stepped next to him and stared intently at his watch. Minutes ticked by. One minute, then two, and then three.

At three minutes and forty-two seconds Will's phone rang. Jay answered. "Braden here." He paused, listening. "Wise decision, Mr. Bannister. Now we can get to work without distractions." He rang off. "You're in the clear, Will."

Will slumped in relief against a gunwale. "Thank you, sir."

"Too much time has been wasted already," Jay said. "This killer's clearly after Allaways. Everyone must be with a buddy today. Will, you're with Alex, Ms. Hale, you stay with Luna, and keep an eye out for Laura." He stepped onto the dock.

"My brand's Royal Lochnagar," Julia called.

A slight smile passed across Jay's face. "I took you for a McClelland's lass." He hurried down the dock, stuffing his shirttails into his pants.

The Morgue

"Living the dream. Two murders in less than a week," Lisa said quietly. She climbed out of her mother's station wagon, its faux wood panels peeling off the sides, and circled Zera Lim's Boxster. It was a Spyder, 320 horsepower, 6 cylinders. It wasn't that she was a car geek, but automotive magazines were part of her bedtime reading. One never knew when some obscure car fact might be a vital clue in a crime. Besides, her mother got amazing discounts as a gold star member of an online magazine club.

Lisa peered into the front seat of the Porsche. The car was immaculately clean, like Zera's office. Examining the car, one could tell little about the owner's personality. Zera probably did that deliberately to maintain her privacy. All that could be deduced from the car was that the owner had some wealth, was a neat freak, and the Yankee candle air freshener revealed a preference for cinnamon. Not even one CD was visible to reveal the driver's musical tastes.

Reserved for the Medical Examiner read the metal sign on the building behind the Boxster. How cool to have your own reserved parking spot! The edgy London detective Jane Tennison on *Prime Suspect*, played brilliantly by Helen Mirren, and the fictional Virginia medical examiner, Kay Scarpetta, probably had reserved spaces as well. Such goddesses of crime never had to drive around a parking lot looking for a space, like mere mortals such as herself. At the moment Zera's was the only car in the lot because she always arrived before her staff.

Lisa made it a point to visit the coroner's office whenever there was a valid excuse. This morning's excuse was to sift through the ashes in the evidence room. Then there would be a monotonous car ride up to Newark, Delaware, with the state trooper, Denny, who'd talk for the entire time about his wife's orthodontia or his power tools. In her next life she'd be a medical examiner like Zera, or a forensic scientist. In her next life she'd be able to do molecular biology and genetics. In this life, she sucked at math and science. She pushed through the glass doors, juggling a box of pastries and her travel mug filled with Monster drink. She chewed her gum excitedly. Visiting Zera Lim was the highlight of her job. It wasn't that she was gay, or had some weird fascination with female coroners, or was a creepy stalker of forensic scientists, or anything. When joining the River Glen PD, she'd expected the medical examiner to be an old curmudgeon like those on TV. Instead the examiner was a mature woman who exuded intelligence and mystery. #zeraoozedcoolness Best of all, Zera, loved solving mysteries as much as she did.

Zera was standing behind her desk, squeezing hand grips, when Lisa dropped the pastries on the desk. The doctor said nothing, but waited expectantly for their ritual game to begin. Lisa thrilled in showing off her astute powers of observation, which was why she'd be the Chief of Police one day. She moved to Zera's bookshelf and wrote the number "2" in a fine sheen of dust.

"The cleaning woman hasn't dusted your office in two days," Lisa said confidently.

"Close," Zera said. "Three."

She lifted Zera's coffee cup and sniffed. "Sumatran with hazelnut creamer."

"That's cheating, Lisa. You know that's all I drink."

She smirked. "Your scrubs. They're brand new."

Zera glanced down at herself. "Correct. You can tell that by the sharp, fresh creases."

"And the plastic bag smell. Let me see the soles of your shoes."

Zera moved in front of her desk and lifted one shoe and then the other.

"The sneakers are between two and three months old," Lisa said. "And they're only for work. There's no grass or dirt on them. They've only been on a waxed floor."

"Correct again."

"You favor your left foot."

"Cheating again, Lisa. You know that because I'm left handed."

She stepped into Zera's personal space and sniffed. Zera didn't pull away, because she was used to being sniffed during the game. "You've switched brands. You're wearing Estee Lauder's Bronze Goddess." Lisa's rainy days off were often spent wandering the perfume counters at the mall. One never knew when a murderer's identity might be revealed through perfume or aftershave. Jay wore Calvin Klein's Obsession. Norman in IT wore Old Spice, and too much of it; Will wore the cheap, generic stuff from Target.

"I thought I'd live dangerously and try a new brand," Zera said humorously. "Estee Lauder was on sale."

Like most single women, herself included, Lisa reflected, Zera watched her pennies. Lisa poked her finger into a potted plant. "Your artillery plant, *Pilea microphylla*, was watered before you left work last night." She and her mother shared a subscription to *Living Green Magazine.* In addition to cars and perfumes, she was an expert on houseplants.

"Genus and species. I'm really impressed," Zera said.

"Hold out your hands."

Zera did as told.

"You applied a layer of clear nail polish last night because there are no chips at the edges yet."

"My nails constantly break. It's an occupational hazard."

"You haven't put on your surgical gloves yet today, or your fingers would be wrinkled and pink."

Zera sighed. "With any luck, I won't have to open any bodies today."

"But that's what we live for. For others to die."

"That's the sad truth."

Lisa stared in frustration at Zera's nails. "What's baffling me is the white substance behind your fingernails. There's too much of it to be the powder from your latex gloves. What is it? Baby powder?"

Zera teasingly squeezed the hand grips in front of Lisa's tormented face. "I'll never tell."

"Oh, come on!"

"No." Zera peeked into the pastry box. "You shouldn't bring me these. Let me pay you."

"Don't sweat it. I get them free. My uncle owns a bakery." Lisa opened the box, reached for an apple Danish, and stuck her gum onto the corner of Zera's desk.

"No, Lisa, no way!" Zera lunged for a tissue, grabbed the gum, and tossed the wad into the trashcan.

"Hey, that gum was new!"

"I don't care. Never, ever do that again." Zera sprayed hand sanitizer on the corner of her desk.

Lisa was unfazed by the reprimand. She'd seen Jay do the same thing countless times. "I came to look at the ashes from behind Desmond Whitby's gas station."

"Everything's in the evidence room, but there's no food or drink allowed in there. Eat first."

Lisa dropped into a chair, her breakfast in hand. "Will's been telling me about this centuries-old blood feud between the Whitbys and Allaways, all going back to a pyrate village in River Glen. So many things about the Allaway case don't sit right."

Zera sat down and curled her hands around her coffee mug. "Go on."

"For instance, why would Randall Allaway be listening to music and drinking with his mortal enemy, some Whitby? It just wouldn't happen, right?"

"Right."

"An Allman's Brother CD was playing at Allaway's place. The same CD was in the duck blind. Both had the same fingerprints, right?"

"Right."

"So, what if the killer knew where the duck blind was, and took the beer cans and CD and planted them in Allaway's place? He then replaced the stolen CD with a new but identical one. That way the owner of the duck blind would never know the CD was missing."

"In one of the beer cans from Allaway's place was a dead ant," Zera said. "We looked through his house to see if there was an ant infestation, but there wasn't. If your scenario is true, the ant crawled into the beer can at the duck blind."

"Also, if the killer knew the location of the duck blind, he or she knew about the marine station. The killer could have obtained Frank Whitby's coffee cup from trash at the marine station."

"So you're suggesting that the killer planted the beer cans, CD and Frank Whitby's coffee cup to place their fingerprints and saliva at the crime scene, to frame him?"

"Yes."

"The respective salivas from the beer can and coffee cup were not identical but extremely similar. They very likely belong to siblings."

"Frank Whitby's parents are deceased. He had a sister, Brooke, who currently lives in Los Angeles, and a brother, Clyde, who lives in Newark, Delaware."

"You said had? Did you locate Frank's body?"

"No and we probably never will. Check this out." Lisa pulled her phone from her pocket and held Laura Braden's last mural out for Zera's scrutiny. "Laura Braden whacked Frank Whitby, and the two old guys almost certainly disposed of the body."

Zera stared. "I can't imagine what's going through Jay's mind."

"And Laura's taken off somewhere with Jay's gun!"

Zera exhaled long and loud.

"Frank was never seen again after May 21st," Lisa said. "He could have been killed on that night. But Randall Allaway wasn't killed until June 15. If my theory's true, Frank Whitby was never at the crime scene. He was already long dead."

"So why does our very clever killer, that we now have no prints or DNA for, frame the Whitbys for Randall Allaway's murder?"

"Revenge. For burning Colin and Carole Allaway alive."

At sea

His oppressive cloud of worry lifted when Ben Hancock spotted the *Njörðr's* mast inch over the southern horizon, just at the position Dott had said would be the rendezvous point. Out beyond the jurisdiction of the Coast Guard, and outside the shipping lines. "No electronics, Ben, just charts and compass; that will get us to our love nest."

Love nest ... how incredible to be marrying for the first time at his age! How incredible to have found his soul-mate at the age of seventy-three. Never, ever had he believed that such a thing could be true—as he was not a particularly romantic man—but now he was a believer. Ben had seen wives and girlfriends come and go from Randy's house over the years, as well as his friend's oscillating euphoria and angst, while he'd found serenity and contentment in his quiet cottage, building boat models, solving mathematical problems in math journals, and listening to NPR and CDs of the Rolling Stones.

There was such a thing as love at first sight. The women on the cruise ship had signaled for Randy and Ben to join them at their table. His eyes had leapt to Dott. He'd hoped that his charming friend Randy would not take the available seat next to her. To his relief, Randy had set his sights on the fifty-something brunette at the opposite end of the table. Dott had pulled out the chair next to hers, dictating where Ben was to sit. Though she was seated, it was evident that she was a tall woman, close to his height. She had white-red hair, a tanned face, and brilliant, slate-blue eyes. No more gorgeous woman existed on the planet. At her first words, spoken in a heavy Swedish accent, he'd feared that she lived abroad ... after the meal he might never see her again. But to his delight, she mentioned a condo at a marina in Norfolk, Virginia, just hours away from his home in River Glen.

"You must see my *Njörõr*." She'd reached excitedly for her smartphone.

He'd half expected an image of a cat or dog, possibly a parakeet, but instead it was a magnificent motor sailer, the sails and rigging vast and complex. He was awestruck; he was in the presence of a master sailor. *Njörõr* dwarfed his tiny *Star Gazer*, and he felt a bit inadequate showing her a picture of his nineteen-footer. But she'd patted him on the hand and said, "It's delightful ... just lovely." Photographs of Swedish sjektes that her boat-builder father had built in her home port of Halmstad were followed by those of the Swedish Navy's stealth ships on which she'd served. They bent toward each other's smartphones. The rest of the table, the dining room, vanished. Maybe they ate salmon; who could possibly remember the food? Images of the Viking Ship Museum—the *Oseberg* and *Gokstad* ships, Nansen's *Fram*, Heyerdahl's *Kon Tiki* from Oslo, and the ill-fated, top-heavy warship *Vasa* in Stockholm, passed before his eyes. America's nautical history was significantly younger than Scandinavia's, yet he thrilled in showing her his images of the *USS Constellation* in Baltimore Harbor, Hooper Island draketails, and the *USS Arizona* Memorial in Pearl Harbor. He'd been to Newport News, right near Norfolk, to see the *USS Monitor* at the Maritime Museum. So had she!

"Have you ever been on a British canal boat?" she'd asked.

"No."

"Neither have I. We should rent one and explore the canals near Oxford together."

Dott's enthusiasm was contagious. "Yes!" His confidence swelled. "How about a boat tour through Amsterdam and the tulip-bordered canals of the Netherlands?" he'd proposed.

"Let's do it!"

They departed from their dinner companions early to walk the decks until well after midnight, discussing cruises throughout the Aegean, and voyages as remote and exotic as Polynesia. Both of them had always wanted to ride in an outrigger canoe.

Ben's attention returned to the present when the *Njörðr* came about and Dott in her red survival jacket appeared over the gunwale. The days at sea had tanned her face to the shade of Oklahoma soil. She tossed him a line. "Going my way?" It was an attempt to lighten the mood. Their dreaded task was now imminent. A serious cast appeared on her face. "Are you okay, älskling?"

"Just. It was horrible."

"And it's behind you. Now we move on."

He'd once asked her what she'd done for the Swedish Navy. "Oh ... many assorted things." She'd shrugged dismissively.

On the cruise she'd refused the Russian vodka ... Finnish and Icelandic yes, Russian, absolutely no. And Russian caviar, forget it. Theirs was an unspoken agreement; he'd not talk about Vietnam, she'd not talk about her capture in the Ukraine by the Russians. During the weekend of planning over New Year's Eve at the snow-covered beach house in Bethany, he and Randy had nervously paced and swilled scotch, while she'd drunk hot chocolate and gazed calmly into the fire. Cool Viking blood flowed through her veins. He was certain that Dott had been Naval Intelligence.

"Memento mori. Isn't that the phrase you and Randy taught me?" she said.

"Yes," he said glumly. He lifted his sea bags to her outstretched hand. She disappeared beyond the gunwale, and he heard the rumble of a generator. She passed a heavy-duty extension cord over the side of her boat and he attached the end to his chainsaw. His eyes traveled over the lines, the angles, every nick and ding on his beloved sailboat.

"I don't know if I have the heart to scuttle my beauty," he said. "I learned to sail on her. I have so many memories of wonderful afternoons on this boat."

She watched him procrastinate, hooked a ladder over the side of her vessel, and climbed onto *Star Gazer*. "*Skit! Jag ska göra det själv.*"

He was still learning her nuances. When she spoke in Swedish, she was pissed off. "Skit" was easy to translate. He looked questioningly at her.

"I'll do it myself," she huffed. She bent her head into the cabin and quickly retracted it. "Disgusting! Why didn't you dump this bag of shit before now?"

He grimaced also. "He was a large man. I couldn't move him alone. My back is shot, from lifting crab pots over the years. I slept outside on the deck the whole time."

"I can see why." Dott's face twisted in revulsion. "So what happened?"

"It was late evening. Randy and I were sitting on our beach, having a drink when he stopped by. Randy's puppy ran up to him. He lifted the puppy by the scruff of the neck, then pulled a pistol from the waistband of his shorts. He held the gun to Water Boy's head. He said he was going to blow its brains out, and ours, if we ever mentioned anything about finding the car. The man was a sadist. He *smiled* as the dog was writhing and crying. Randy stood and reached slowly for the dog. Said he only wanted to know what happened to his son and daughter-in-law. How the accident occurred, how the fire started. 'Put the gun away,' he said. 'We can talk about this like rational adults.'"

"What did Frank say?"

"He wasn't just sick; he was insane. He lied to our faces, shouting, 'There was no car, no accident, no fire!' And he kept shaking the puppy."

Dott grimaced. "Only a very bad man is cruel to animals."

"Then *she* appeared out of the darkness, dripping wet. She was enraged by his treatment of the puppy. She looked like a Fury, with that oar in her hands. Randy tried to warn him! 'Behind you Frank,' he said.

"But Frank just snarled, 'That's the oldest trick in the book. Clyde and I will be watching you two. Mark my words.' He cocked the gun and pointed it, first at Frank, then me, then back at the puppy quaking in his hand.

"She swung the oar and caved in his head. He was probably dead before he hit the ground, but she was crazed, and kept whacking and whacking. There was blood all over her, her nightgown, her face, her hair ... we panicked. Randy told me to drag her into the water, to wash the blood away. He got one of Alex's nightshirts from the house and changed her, right there on the beach. For a moment she seemed completely lucid. He told her to dispose of the nightshirt when she got home, that we'd get rid of the body. She nodded as if she understood and swam back to the promontory. We were terrified. Who'd suspect a cop's wife of murder? Who'd believe two old stoners?"

Dott gazed into the cabin for a moment. "You're right. You two would be the scapegoats. Let's get this over with." She turned on the chainsaw and headed for the mast. She halted. "It's too beautiful a boat to carve up and scuttle. We'll take it with us, but it will create drag and slow us down."

He pointed. "Everything's in that plastic bag, the bloody nightgown and gun. We burned the oar."

"Why do you still have that? Put your mushroom anchor in there and get rid of it!"

He undid the aft anchor shackle, stuffed the anchor into the bag and tossed it overboard.

"Help me with this," she said.

They tugged the plastic-shrouded body out of the cabin. "Ahh ... this is beyond vile," she gasped. "Get me the Danforth anchor and the chain." He moved to the bow and detached the fluke anchor. For some minutes they struggled with the ropes and chains around the body, rotten and dripping through the plastic. Finally they dragged it up to the gunwale and rolled it over the side. It hit the water with a resounding splash, then sank in a cloud of bubbles.

"We feed the shark to the sharks," she said coolly.

They tied *Star Gazer* to the stern of *Njörðr* and raised *Njörðr's* sails.

Dott turned the wheel northward. "Now let's start our Amazonian adventure."

The Morgue

Zera Lim's eyes circled the board of known individuals whose fingerprints had been found in Randall Allaway's house. Alice and Harry Hoffman, Alan Johnston and Jacob Horrigan, and Marv and Sue Denniston, who all had solid alibis. Her gaze fixed on the photographs of Alexandra Allaway and Benjamin Hancock, whose fingerprints and hairs were located all over the house. Of course, that was to be expected, considering that those individuals had been in and out of the house for years. Alexandra had been seen on security camera at a mall in suburban Washington DC on the night of Randall's murder. Benjamin Hancock had up and vanished into the Atlantic that same day. To flee a murderer? To dump the body of Frank Whitby for Laura Braden? Both?

If what the gum-smacking millennial cop had said was true, the murderer saw him/herself as an Avenging Angel. If he or she planted misleading evidence in Randall Allaway's house, had they also planted the map of Cooper's Creek and leads to McKibbin's Apartments to further implicate Whitbys in past crimes? After all, both Hancock and Allaway had left their homes open all the time. It would have been easy to sneak in and plant the incriminating evidence. Did that person also plant the bull's-eyed photos of the two Allaways and Hancock at McKibbin's place? How could they tell evidence form subterfuge?

She studied a photo of Randall Allaway from a few years in the past. He had the characteristic build of a waterman: muscular arms, shoulders and chest, and a narrow waist; yet when her team had found him in the recliner he'd been a skeleton of his former self. Stranger yet was the single stab wound. The point of entry was between the left ribs, where there was just muscle, not cartilage or bone. A doctor or a trained killer, an assassin, would have known that path of minimal resistance. The scientific direct strike to the left ventricle had stopped Allaway's heart quickly. It was unlikely that the killer was intoxicated like Allaway; the killer must have been stone-cold sober to have inflicted such an exacting blow.

She turned to the photos of Penelope Bannister and shuddered. She's seen decades of violent murders, but

Bannister's was among the worst. There were no traces of drugs or alcohol in her system. She'd fought back desperately; her hands and forearms had been covered with defensive wounds, but they were little match for a hunting knife or machete. After her death, her chest had been sliced open. Her heart had been cut from her chest, a symbolic gesture seen in warrior cultures.

The two murders were completely different. Allaway's killer was a cold, calculating professional, while Bannister's was a frenzied mad man.

Zera's laptop chimed and she opened Lisa's attachment. It was the accident report from November 1991. She studied the burnt vehicle from all angles. The two charred bodies were wrapped in each other's arms in the front seat. According to the report, what had started the fire were two gasoline canisters in the back seat of Colin and Carole Allaway's car. Doubtful, not from that burn pattern. Her eyes fixed on the signature at the bottom of the report. The final signoff was by the Chief of Police, Stanley Whitby.

Newark

Ugly, ugly, Lisa thought, critically assessing the building. When she became the Chief of Police or a crime consultant for CNN making big bucks, she'd never buy a McMansion like this one. Clyde Whitby was sadly out 600K—all for a multi-gabled house in Newark with tacky plastic siding, separated by ten feet of lawn from his neighbor's house. All of the executive homes were identical, down to the plastic white fences and green plastic mailboxes. Lisa's home was an apartment shared with her mother for over two decades, but one day she'd be buying them a single-floor ranch home, with a ramp for her mother's wheelchair and high speed internet so she could be in touch with Norman day and night. She'd splurge and get them the deluxe cable packet so they could watch any crime show at any hour, even reruns like the original *Hawaii Five-O* and *Mannix.*

Denny stopped the patrol car next to a Lexus in the Whitby's driveway. What wasn't she right about? As predicted, the state trooper had described his wife's transparent braces all the way up Route 896 to Newark, while she'd turned up the volume on her ear buds and listened to Abba. One never knew if some killer might be motivated by cheesy lyrics from bands from the seventies and eighties.

"Denny, you stay here, outside, in case they attempt a run for it."

She hated physical activity of any kind. She'd leave it to Denny to tackle the runner in the driveway.

"No gum chewing during interviews," Jay had said. "It lacks professionalism." Yada-yada ...

She stuck her gum to the dashboard and hopped out of the car. She circled the Lexus a few times before striking the brass door knocker, a pineapple, like all the others on the block. She displayed her badge to a middle-aged woman in a flowered blouse, capri pants, and Crocs. The lady two doors down, who was watering her tiger lilies—species *Lilium tigrinum*—wore almost the exact outfit. #stepfordwives

"Detective Paco, River Glen PD." She spoke in a no-nonsense voice to compensate for her youthful appearance. It sucked to look sixteen at the age of twenty-seven. It doubly sucked to have stopped growing at a height of five three. "May I come in?"

"Sure, yes, of course." The woman's forehead wrinkled in confusion.

"Are you Francine Whitby?"

"Yes."

Francine's body language projected bafflement, not defensiveness or fear. That might work to her advantage, Lisa decided. The house looked like an Ethan Allen showroom, full of bulky, faux-colonial furniture. It was a domicile occupied by females: handbags were draped over the dining room chairs and pink backpacks were dropped carelessly in the foyer. There was no evidence of boys. The dining table had been set up as a workspace to make jewelry.

"The Lexus GX. Nice wheels. Is it yours?" Lisa asked. Her strategy was to first ask questions that she knew the answer to, to see if Francine was disposed toward prevarication.

"Yes."

"What were you doing in River Glen two nights ago?"

"River Glen? You're mistaken. The only time I go to River Glen is for the annual pyrate festival, to sell jewelry. There. See?" Francine pointed to the dining room table.

She nodded; she'd already noticed it. "Has anyone else been driving your car recently?"

Francine's eye dilated slightly, a sympathetic reaction, a jolt of nervousness, uncertainty. Lisa waited. This was Jay's tactic. It never failed. Silence disconcerted. Silence prompted the suspect to fill the awkward void with incriminating words.

"My girls don't drive yet," Francine said.

"Your husband, Clyde?"

Francine shifted slightly and scratched the back of her neck. Bingo! Lisa was making headway.

"Was Clyde driving your car?" Lisa pressed.

"One of his tires is low, so he's been taking my car to work until he can replace it, but he wasn't in River Glen. He just opened a new shop in Maryland. He's been in Maryland for the past few weeks. Forest Hill, Maryland."

"Does he come home every night from Maryland?"

"Yes," she said, a bit indignant at the insinuation. "It's not that long a commute."

"Where's he now?"

"Ohio. He flew out last night to meet with potential business associates."

"Where in Ohio? Which airport did he leave from?"

"I don't know. He received the call last night, and then left suddenly. He usually travels from Philly."

"A call from who?"

"I don't know. I was watching TV with my daughters. He was in his office."

"He has an office here?"

"Yes."

"I'd like to have a look. What does he do for a living?" It was another question she knew the answer to. So far, so good. Francine had answered her truthfully.

"He owns a chain of plumbing supply stores."

Francine led her down a hallway to the kitchen and family room separated by a kitchen island.

"Here." Francine stepped into the room adjacent to the family room.

Clyde's office, a macho man cave, made Lisa's skin crawl. Camo lamps and a central light in the ceiling were constructed of deer antlers. The computer workstation and bar were dark, heavy wood. The photos on the wall were of deep sea fishing excursions, golf tournaments, and deer and bear hunts. Each photo had the same central feature, the towering blond Frank Whitby grinning brashly at the camera, surrounded by a pack of toadies.

Thank you, Laura Braden!

Conspicuously absent were photographs of Clyde's wife and daughters. There was not a single image of a female in the entire room. As far as Clyde Whitby was concerned, the planet had one gender.

"Which is your husband?"

"Him," Francine pointed, her finger shaking.

The robust décor of the man cave suddenly made sense. Clyde Whitby had a Little Man Complex. Compared to his Golden Boy brother, Clyde was scrawny, with squinty eyes and thinning brown hair. #furtiveweasel

"You're investigating the River Glen murders, aren't you?" Francine blurted.

Duh … yes. "Correct. A Lexus like yours was in the area on the night of the Bannister murder. We're hoping to locate that person. They might have seen something that will help us."

"Oh. Sorry that Clyde and I can't help you. I was home with the girls and Clyde, as I said, was in Maryland then, having drinks at the club."

"Which club?"

"We're members at Tidewater Greens. It's a bit of a drive to northern Maryland, but it's very scenic with its location on the bay."

Lisa nearly guffawed. Clyde, like Frank, must have gotten a complimentary membership from the Club's cuckolded president. #betterthanfiction

"Then you won't mind if I take a quick fingerprint scan of this room and yours, just to eliminate you all from further questions?"

"I guess it's okay." Francine held out her hands while Lisa moved the scanner over her fingertips.

"Thanks." Lisa scanned the brandy decanter, glasses, and desk. The laptop was predictably absent. "I see by the photos that your husband's a hunter. Can you show me his gun?"

"They're in the garage."

"He has a few?"

"Yes, two rifles and two pistols."

They passed through the kitchen to a laundry room where a door led to the garage. Francine opened the gun cabinet. It was empty.

"Maybe he's going hunting with the men in Ohio," Francine suggested.

"He wouldn't be allowed to take guns on a plane."

"Then they're probably locked in his car."

"He drives a ...?" Again, Lisa knew the answer to her question.

"A pickup truck. A Toyota."

There was no pickup on the premises.

"Again, just to eliminate your Lexus, I'll need to have a look inside. It's just procedural."

"No problem." Francine disappeared into the kitchen and met her in the driveway, car keys in hand. She pressed her key and the locks popped open.

Lisa pulled the compact luminol scanner from her bag and leaned into the front seat. "I'm the girl with the toys," she said pleasantly. Francine smiled back weakly.

After a few minutes, Lisa headed back to the patrol car. "Thank you, Mrs. Whitby. And good luck with your jewelry business."

"Oh, thank you. Good luck to you, catching that killer," Francine said politely.

Lisa slipped into the front seat, unstuck her gum from the dashboard, and popped it into her mouth. She chewed energetically and read the data on the fingerprint and luminol scanners. "Living the life, Denny. Living the life." She lifted her cell phone and called Jay. "Houston, we have a problem."

River Glen

Clyde swallowed another extra-strength aspirin. "Dismal night's sleep," he complained. During his boyhood, he and Frank had camped out in all types of weather and on all kinds of surfaces, and slept like babies. Though last night had been spent in relative comfort, in the back of a delivery van full of plumbing components, in a soft sleeping bag with his jacket for a pillow, he'd tossed and turned all night. There was no way the back tire of his truck was going to withstand a trip to Maryland, so he'd dropped it off at Store 3 and switched it out for a van. He'd met Desmond the night before at the usual meeting spot, behind Uncle Bobby's barn, where they'd stashed Frank's Saturn years before. Since Bobby was a half-blind, drooling old codger, the van's presence would never be noticed.

Clyde climbed out the back door of the van and stretched his inflamed back. He pissed in the weeds along the side of the barn and checked his watch. No phones, laptops ... no technology at all while hunting. The last thing he needed was

Francine distracting him about dance slippers, leotards and hula skirts for the girls' play.

Clyde's stomach growled. Desmond should be by with his breakfast any time. He climbed back in the van to escape the swarms of gnats in the grass.

Fucking bad luck to be lured to River Glen by Allaway on Thursday night and spotted by the bridge security camera! Worse, on the night of Allaway's murder. Fucking horrible timing! Was Allaway already dead when they knocked on the door? Thankfully they hadn't picked the lock, or broken in as Desmond had suggested. No worries. None of his prints would be found there. He'd rapped on the door with the handle of his pistol.

Desmond's truck finally appeared on the dirt road bordering the farm; a pair of jet skis on a trailer were in tow.

"You're late, Des."

"Hectic morning." Desmond handed him a cupboard tray with a coffee and breakfast sandwich. "I went to stock up the jon boat and it was gone! Had to borrow these from Blanche's brother." He glanced to the personal watercraft.

"The teenagers who left the condoms must have stolen Frank's boat. Fuckers. I'll get them." Clyde examined the PWCs. "There's nowhere to store the guns."

"I thought of everything," Desmond said. "Plastic trash bags will protect them from the water. They fit perfectly in the foot wells. And PWCs are a hell of a lot faster than the pokey old jon boat. And I got us wetsuits so we won't get sunburned."

Clyde eyed the jet skis, unconvinced. "Hmm."

"My pal, Perry at the boatyard, has been watching the tugboat for me. He said it was heading north."

"Back to the Bohemia?"

"Don't know, but let's put these in at the boat ramp north of town. The village is crawling with cops."

"Was anyone in the boat with Allaway?"

"Only some staff person from the Smyth Marina."

"Good. No cops."

"Allaway's a looker. Before we kill her, let's have some fun with her." Desmond laughed and grabbed his crotch.

Clyde chuckled slyly and climbed into the pickup truck. "Let's."

On the water

That Will was in a state of jumbled emotions was an understatement. Jumbled and more jumbled. The primary emotion was extreme gratitude ... gratitude to Jay for enlightening George Bannister as to the true nature of his daughter, and gratitude for the promise of a long, happy future with Carly. Gratitude to his parents for their assistance. Gratitude to his clever partner Lisa, who had linked the fingerprints on the beer cans, jon boat, and Lexus to one Clyde Whitby, who lived in Newark Delaware. An APB was out in Delaware and Maryland, all PDs searching for a black Toyota pickup. Whitby had never boarded a plane to Ohio, and his hunting gear was missing. Gratitude to the charmer, Julia Hale, who made Jay smile, if only for a brief flicker of time. Finally, to Alex Allaway for simply being.

The emotions of longing, desperation, and frustration jostled him, demanding attention. And of course there was lust. There was not one inch of the Allaway property where he'd not envisioned himself making love to her ... the dock, the beach, the river, the porch, even Ben's hammock.

After Jay and Julia had left the tugboat, Alex had ordered him onto a bench seat and appeared with a shoebox of first-aid supplies. She'd knelt next to his knee, which allowed a bird's eye view down her tank top. She'd wiped the blood off his calf and bandaged him up, all the while enumerating her various injuries from her crabbing days with Randy and Ben.

"Here's where the spine of a giant Jimmy went through my glove." She had a scar next to her thumb. "The salt water stung more than the spine. Then I messed up this finger when it got caught between the spring line and a cleat. But the worst was when I got my pinky pinched in the door of the crab pot. It bled all over the place. And I can't tell you how many times I chased escaped crabs around the deck, while Papa and Ben laughed at me."

She chattered on while he fought the impulse to grab her hand and pull it to his lips. She seemed as tense as he was. After all, they'd have a whole day on the boat together. Alone. He'd already checked out her berth. It was neatly made, for once. Bummer, one pillow.

"You're not fatally wounded. You'll probably live." She stood and spilled the first-aid kit all over the floor.

He bent over. "I'll get it. "

"No, no, I'll get it." She knelt again and tossed the bandages back into the shoebox.

They relaxed a bit as the morning went on, largely because she occupied herself by studying the depth sounder; the Chesapeake was remarkably shallow in parts. He distracted himself with calls to Jay.

Their first destination was the Bohemia River. At the Old Gray Mare location they waded ashore, the metal detector held aloft. Starting at the place where the milk canister and skull had been found, they swished the metal detector across the ground for nearly an hour, swatting at mosquitos and hearing nothing but a slow ping from the instrument. Near a circular wire, corroded and covered with leaves, the ringing increased in frequency. They looked cautiously around the green ruin. They were alone.

"Turn down the volume," he whispered.

"Okay," she whispered back.

She inched the instrument a few inches further. Low, fast pings sounded. "Here!" They dropped to their hands and knees and clawed the ground, because they'd forgotten a shovel. A bit of leather appeared. Then more. He reached into the hole and pulled out a leather pouch. He untied the laces. They peered inside. Gold—pieces of eight—dribbled into her cupped hands.

They quickly filled in the hole, covered it with leaves, and returned to the boat with their newfound booty. Awestruck, they set off for Mutter Island, as it was closer than the Sassafras River. He checked in with Jay once again.

"The black pickup truck was located in back of one of Whitby's plumbing supplies stores in southern Delaware. Its rear tire was flat," Jay informed Will. "We're now looking for a white delivery van. Worse, Desmond Whitby has also disappeared. According to Blanche, he decided to take a personal day, and he refused to elaborate. He left the house at the crack of dawn. He was also out the previous night, at some alleged watering hole. More likely, he'd met with Clyde Whitby. Norman in IT is getting nothing from their phones. The last electronic signal of any kind was a text between Desmond and Perry Bennett at the River Glen boatyard. Bennett's been taken in for questioning.

"The Lexus has been towed in by forensics," Jay continued. "It's definitely the same car that passed over the

River Glen bridge. There's a glue residue from duct tape that concealed the license plate. Clyde Whitby attempted to clean blood from the steering wheel and armrest. The smears match Penelope Bannister's blood type. Zera's group is analyzing the blood proteins as we speak.

"Perry Bennett admitted to telling Desmond Whitby that the *Vital Spark* was traveling north. According to Perry, Desmond was following the activities of Alex Allaway. We're sending teams into the marshes north of River Glen. It's possible that they'll try to take a potshot at her from the shoreline. Where are you now?"

"Just approaching Mutter Island," Will answered. "We should be okay out here."

"Are you seeing anything?"

Will scanned the horizon with his binoculars. "A regatta from the sailing school. A few sailboats. A fishing boat. Paul Culp's speed boat. Some teenagers on jet skis. Any word on Laura?"

"No. I'm in the village going door-to-door. I'm hanging up. Be alert, Will."

"I will, sir."

Alex dropped the anchor. "Is everything alright?"

"Yes, they're looking for Desmond and Clyde Whitby for questioning. They have pretty conclusive evidence, so there should be closure to this investigation shortly."

"Finally," she sighed. "I should be planning a funeral, and Mr. Ward from Annapolis is coming to the lab at the end of the week. I need to be able to show him that I've accomplished something." She lifted Water Boy over the stern and he paddled through the shallows. He barked happily and disappeared into the woods.

They waded through the water, the metal detector over Alex's shoulder. She zigzagged the approximate area where she'd found the Gimpy Gill gasoline canister. For a while only low crackling electrical noise was heard, but then, near a rotten slat of wood, the bell pinged. They pawed through the muddy sand. It was another leather pouch. This one contained a heavy gold chain with a crucifix and a handful of gold coins.

"I wonder how much this is worth if we had to cash it in. I hate to sound greedy, but I was expecting something larger, like a treasure chest," she said. "I've watched too many pyrates movies."

"I guess it's all that's left after three hundred years."

"Ask your father. He should know."

"I tried the other night. He acted as though he had no idea what I was talking about."

They returned the metal detector and pouch of gold to the boat.

She checked the position of the sun. If Randy had taught her anything, it was how to tell time by its location over the bay. "It's too late to make it to the Sassafras and back before dark."

He scanned the bay once again with his binoculars. Only the fishing boat and sailboats were on the water. "How about we take a swim before heading back?"

"Last one in ..." She rushed to the ladder.

"Alex ..." he called after her, "... that night at the Point. I just need to get it off my chest. It was wonderful."

His words arrested her steps. "I don't remember."

What! How could she not remember that amazing evening? True, he was younger than she by two years, and certainly less experienced, but she'd seemed to enjoy it. They'd seemed to connect. Shit ... had she been faking it?

She smiled kiddingly. "Remind me."

River Glen

Jay bent over the railing of the River Glen Bridge. There was no way that Laura could have drowned. Absolutely impossible. She was too strong a swimmer. Still, if she couldn't be located by evening, he'd have to ask his dithering police chief to have divers search the river. He started toward home. G & Ts were out of the question at this time of the day, but a cigarette would settle his nerves. With any luck he'd be able to get down a sandwich. His search that morning had been fueled only by Harry Hoffman's coffee. He, Luna, Julia Hale and Alice Hoffman had gone to every shop, business and restaurant on the pier, and to every house up and down Main Street, Horseshoe Crab Road, and Seagull Cove Drive. No one had seen Laura. For the moment there was nothing else to do but wait to hear from Zera about the bloodstains in the Lexus, and from Lisa and Norman, who were monitoring the e-traffic. At least at home he could get into the AC for a few minutes, and take a piss. He crossed the Denniston's waterfront yard.

His minister father's mantra, "Good behavior is rewarded, bad behavior is punished," pushed into the foreground of his thoughts. It was the stark, over-simplified tenet of the Braden household. Being of a rebellious mind, he'd thought the whole idea ludicrous and articulated his objections countless times, mostly to rattle his old man. Perhaps, in light of recent events, his father's words held a glimmer of truth. This was his punishment. Punishment for lusting after Zera and Julia, ignoring his gym membership, smoking once again ... drinking himself into a comatose state so that his ill wife could slip from the house unheard.

He started across the Culps' lawn and spotted Paul Jr. sitting on a bench at the dock. The teenager was hard to miss. At the moment his spiky hair was dyed purple and orange. He was the wiry, athletic boy who worked at the rock climbing gym and lived with his father. The mother had taken off long ago to "find herself".

"Hey, Mr. Braden," Paul Jr. said vapidly.

The boy's tone was uncharacteristic. "Is something wrong, Paul?"

"My father's going to kill me! He told me no friends over, no parties while he was away on business."

"So what happened?"

"It was only a few people. We weren't loud. We didn't drink that much. No one was drunk, I promise. We stayed in the house. I didn't want anyone outside to make noise and piss off Mr. Denniston."

"So what's the issue?"

"Someone stole my father's boat! I saw it last night when I took the beer cans out to the trash. I just came outside and noticed. It's gone!"

"Show me!" Will had mentioned a regatta, jet skis, a fishing boat, and Paul Culp's speedboat out near Mutter Island.

They hurried to the arched canopy that covered the slip. "Dad always keeps the keys here." Paul opened a plastic box full of flotation vests. "They're gone. So is the red flotation coat. My friends are awesome. I thought so, anyway. I don't know who would do this. I'm dead. I'll be grounded for an eternity!"

"You say you saw it last night?"

"Definitely."

"Don't sweat this yet. I'll tell my men and see if we can locate it."

"Thank you!"

Jay rushed from the Culps' property and crossed the Larsens and Wynskis' yards. Could Laura have stolen the speedboat? These days anything was possible. She knew all about the operation of small boats; her family had a summer house in Maine. If it wasn't Laura who had stolen the boat .... His stomach constricted. Just then his phone vibrated; it was Lisa.

"Cruiser 2 located Desmond Whitby's pickup at the boat ramp north of town. Those assholes are out on the water on two jet skis!"

"Roger that." He picked up his pace. "I'm on my way to Mutter Island. Get police boats out there ASAP!"

He rung off and pressed Will's number. No answer. "Will?" Still no response. "Will, please call me. The Whitbys are on jet skis! Call me, Will! Call me!"

Mutter Island

"This is better than a porn movie," Desmond whispered. He peered through his rifle sight. "I say we kill him now and take over while she's all heated up. What a body! Can she ever fuck!"

"They found something with the metal detector," Clyde said. "I wanna know what. Do not do anything until I give the order. Des, do you understand?"

"Yeah."

"You stay here and keep a lookout. I'm going to circle around and climb onto their boat. Do not do anything yet! Just watch until I get back."

"Gladly." Desmond's eye was glued to the sight.

"If the dog appears, silence it." Clyde made a slashing gesture across his throat.

"This is so good!"

"Are you even listening?"

"Yeah, yeah, kill the dog."

Clyde lifted himself off the ground and pressed his spotting scope to his eye. Alex Allaway and the Smyth Marina employee were thoroughly captivated by one another. First they were in the throes of passion in the water, her legs circling his waist. In round two they rolled around on the beach behind the fallen tree. Then, as luck would have it, the couple took off into the woods and tangled themselves under the shady nook of a tree. Both had impressive stamina, but they were tiring. The languid fuck would give him just enough time to climb onto the tugboat undetected.

Though he'd never admit it aloud to Desmond, the jet skis had been a brilliant idea, allowing them to meander along the coast, hide in inlets in the marsh and watch from behind the tall grass. Fortunately, Desmond had been too busy swatting at mosquitos and studying the intricacies of Alex Allaway's leopard-patterned bikini to notice the glint of gold in her cupped hands. Some treasure map must have directed her to Neville Whitby's portion of the treasure from the *Espiritu de la Virgen* ... that the thieving Allaways and Hales had stolen! Allaway had found at least two portions. Perhaps the third share was at the Sassafras River? He'd check later, alone, without Des. Conall Whitby's memoir, scribed by Brother Guillermo, alluded to astonishing riches ... pearls, rubies, emeralds, and gold. Clyde crouched forward through the underbrush. So far, so good. No sign of the lovers. By day's end he'd have the treasure, and River Glen would be free of the last remaining Allaway!

The marina employee would have to be eliminated, too. No loose ends, Frank used to say. The firearms could be dumped in the middle of the bay; bullets extracted from the bodies by the medical examiner would never be traced to him. Frank had acquired the guns in an under-the-table deal eons ago, from a vendor at a gun show. Clyde looked back and forth down the beach and quickly waded out to the boat. The tug was only in a few feet of water. He glanced back to the forest. The lovers were still going at it. Ah, to be young again. Perhaps they'd move on to round four in the discarded rowboat on the other side of the island where the jet skis floated. If so, Desmond probably had enough initiative to kill the guy, which was fine with him, so long as he left the Allaway bitch for him to deal with.

He climbed up the boat ladder, passed the crab pots, and bent into the hatchway. Two leather pouches were on the galley table, next to two cell phones. Both pouches had substantial weight. He glanced inside one of them, and his eyes widened. Pyrate gold! He zipped them into his wetsuit, tossed the cell phones into the bay, and dropped down the ladder. He was jogging across the beach when ...

YIP!

BANG!

He dove behind a tree and cowered. Had the lovers, or the dog, discovered Desmond? Had Des started the slaughter without him?

Silence.

He looked frantically around, only to see green forest and filtering rays of sunlight. He prayed that Desmond had only taken down the man. It was *his* bullet—the bullet of Clyde Whitby—that must rub out the Allaway woman! That lusty Allaway would breed no more. No more Allaways would infest River Glen, like the colony of roaches that they were. He'd make sure of that.

A salty breeze whistled through the branches, disrupting the silence. Desmond surely had him covered. It was safe to rise, he figured. His one, singular purpose was to locate his rifle. It was he who was the greatest Great White Hunter of the Whitby clan. His bullet would be the one. It was destiny.

"YIP!"

BANG!

"Shit!" Will rolled off. "That shot was close!"

Alex groped mentally to regain her wits. She had been seconds from coming for the nth time that afternoon.

He yanked on his swim trunks.

"Where's my bathing suit?" she whispered.

"Here." He grabbed the bottoms from the twigs.

She whipped the bottoms up her legs. "My top?"

"I have no clue! There's no time to look now!"

"I have to run across the beach topless?"

"You've just been all over this island butt naked, and now you're having modesty issues? I've got to get to the boat and get my gun! We're sitting ducks here! We need to make a run for the boat. Climb in at the bow. If we climb up the ladder in the stern, we're too exposed."

"Water Boy—I heard a bark!"

"I'll come back for him, but I need to get my gun first! Let's go!"

"Promise?"

"Yes!"

They scrambled to their feet, dashed through the forest and across the beach, swam underwater to the bow, and climbed up the tire fenders. They spilled over the gunwale and crawled to the cabin.

"You stay here, at all times, stay inside until I know what's happening," Will insisted.

"Someone was here! The bags of gold—they're gone!" She pulled on a t-shirt at the berth.

He found his gun and binoculars and crouched between the crab pots. He peered over the transom. "Maybe it's just a hunter?"

"You're just saying that to keep me calm. Hunting season's in the fall. Someone was on this boat and stole our gold! For all I know, he also has Water Boy!"

"Can you slide me my cell phone? It's on the table, I think."

She crawled across the galley floor and glanced over the edge of the table. "The thief also took our phones!"

"I'm screwed! Jay's gonna kill me for letting down my guard." The reason for his lapse stole him from the present. "But it was so worth it."

She smiled briefly also. What was the adjective for exceeding the unsurpassable? There was a word for everything in the English language. Julia would know. She had an amazing vocabulary. Hyper-unsurpassable? Uber-unsurpassable?

He regained his focus. "Start the boat! Let's get out of here!"

"But Water Boy ..."

"I promise I'll come back for him. But with manpower."

She reluctantly turned on the engine and hit the switch that raised the anchor.

BANG!

"Get down, Alex!"

BANG!

"Where the fuck is Desmond?" Clyde slogged through the woods. The heavy bags of gold in his wetsuit made for slow going through the underbrush. "Nowhere to be seen! No doubt jerking off somewhere after watching Alex Allaway. Which probably caused his gun to misfire. The stooge can't do anything right!"

Clyde stepped from the woods near the jet skis. A tall, slender woman in a nightgown was pulling a hunting knife from the haunch of Allaway's black dog. The knife was definitely Desmond's. He'd seen it carve through flesh a thousand times.

The woman viewed him with disinterest. There was an otherworldliness to her, like an apparition or a hallucination. She was fearless and indifferent to his presence, unnerving qualities in a woman. She flung the knife onto the sand.

"Go home now," she said to the dog.

The dog limped into the forest and she wandered nonchalantly down the beach, her nightgown luffing in the breeze. A speedboat—hers?—was beached by the bend in the shoreline.

"Cl- Clyde ..." Desmond lay in the shallows, his wetsuit unzipped, blood streaming from his chest.

"What the fuck?"

"I threw my knife at the dog and this crazy bitch appeared out of nowhere. The bitch shot me! Call 911!"

A handgun, a Beretta, lay in the sand near Desmond. His cousin was useless to him now. He'd have to do the job himself. Besides, he still seethed that the dolt had told the cops that he was in the tow truck the night they were lured to Randy's Allaway's place. Big fucking mouth!

And no way was he sharing the gold with his cousin. The news of the pyrate treasure would be all over River Glen in seconds. He was the sole keeper of the Whitby diary; he was now the keeper of the Whitby gold.

"Please, Clyde, call 911, before I bleed to death!"

Focus on the task at hand. Focus, focus. Clyde grabbed the leather hunting gloves from his bag and slipped them on. He lifted the Beretta. He stood over his cousin. "You couldn't even handle a puny dog and a woman."

BANG!

He grabbed Desmond's rifle from the foot well of a jet ski.

"You!" He fixed the woman in the rifle sight. "You, stop!"

What? She chose to ignore him, him—the Great White Hunter! The aloof bitch continued her leisurely stroll down the beach. She'd pay for her arrogance.

"Bang," he said, and pulled the trigger. She collapsed in a cloud of white lace. He dropped the rifle next to Desmond, ran through the water, leaving no footprints, and tossed the Beretta into the sand next to her. To the mindless cops it would appear as if Desmond and the ghostly woman had shot each other. Mutual homicide.

Clyde Whitby was never at Mutter Island. Yes, yes, he'd started off the day with Desmond, but they'd split up early in the morning, he'd tell the bungling police during the inevitable interview. Yes, yes, Desmond seemed very agitated, but about what, he didn't know, he'd say in a pensive, helpful tone. He'd wear his new tailored suit to the interview. That never ceased to impress. Once or twice, he'd casually allude to his successful business, prestigious golf club, and membership in the local business leaders' association. Maybe he should mention that he walked with his daughters and wife at the junior high breast cancer walk? A miserable experience all in all. Giant blisters had formed on each heel. Droning babble with a bunch of women.

Focus!

The two bodies on the beach were already attracting flies. His business was done on this side of Mutter Island. He hopped onto his PWC and fired up the jet engine.

It was time to hunt Allaways.

BANG!

"Get down, Alex!"

BANG!

JINGLE. Alex recognized the sound immediately. Water Boy emerged from the forest, his collar tags jingling. His hind leg drooped. He limped across the beach, panting and struggling.

"Come, boy!" Will poked his head over the transom.

She pushed through the hatchway. "Water Boy, good boy, swim!"

"Alex, get back in the cabin! Stay there. I'll get him."

"He's hurt!"

"Alex, please!" Will turned toward the water. "C'mon boy, c'mon."

Water Boy paddled to the dive platform. Will had no choice. It would only be a second that he'd be vulnerable. He climbed over the transom and reached down for the dog, pausing momentarily when he saw blood streaming from Water Boy's back leg. The fur gaped open, a red slice in the wet black fur. He heaved, then gently placed the dog on the deck.

"Come boy, come on, sweetheart!" she urged.

Will whipped his long leg over the transom.

BANG!

The bullet propelled Will into the boat. He spun and crashed amidst the crab pots and Clorox bottles.

Alex peered through the porthole. The shooter was on a yellow and black jet ski, a rifle poised on his shoulder, his eye behind the sight. It was Will's order that she stay inside, but she scrambled across the deck. He was sprawled face down.

"Will?" She nudged frantically and pressed her ear to his back. "Will?" The side of her face was wet with blood.

There was no answer, but he was still breathing, and his heart thumped. What do to? What do to? She wiped tears from her eyes. She had no medical training whatsoever. During her college health class, she'd failed the CPR segment of the course because she'd overslept. What next? She crawled back inside and pulled a t-shirt from her duffel bag, and crawled back out. She stuffed the t-shirt against his wound. "Will?" Still no response.

A bullet plinked against the metal gunwale. Another thudded against a rubber tire. Water Boy, who'd curled himself in a shaking ball under the galley table, whimpered. The jet ski engine revved and approached.

"Alex Allaway, come out, come out, wherever you are," a voice taunted.

Jay Braden was right! The psycho knew who she was! The psycho was killing Allaways! He circled the boat like a furious bee, flashing black and yellow.

"Today the last Allaway dies!" He laughed fiendishly.

Bullets plinked off the metal gunwales. If she could just get to the middle of the bay ... he wouldn't dare shoot at her if others were around. Someone would certainly call the police. She crawled back into the cabin, to the helm. The marine radio had long since been removed, with the advent of cell phones; all that remained were bolts where it had once been affixed. She pulled down the throttle. The old tug lumbered forward. A bullet shattered the windshield by the captain's seat and glass rained down on her. Water Boy yowled. Another shot hit a porthole, showering the galley table with glass. That insane Whitby had deadly good aim!

"Come out, come out," he goaded again.

She steered the boat toward him, but the jet ski fleetly veered away.

"Trying to run me over with that old slug?" He laughed again and blasted away another window.

Suddenly a gun was fired from her boat. She spun toward the aft deck. Will had inched himself up against a gunwale and lifted himself on a crab pot. A strained grimace was on his face. He fired off another shot, and ducked with a moan of pain. His bullet splashed into the water, and another Whitby bullet plinked against the gunwale.

Whitby howled in laughter. "Is that the best you can do?"

Will dragged himself and a streak of blood across the deck. He lifted himself again, and fired. This bullet hit Whitby in the chest and knocked him backwards on the seat. Briefly stunned, Whitby righted himself and sped off.

"How did that not kill him?" Will coughed.

"Lucky bastard! He must have the bags of gold in his wetsuit. Please don't move! You're bleeding badly!"

Whitby floated in the haze and fixed another clip. He put them in his sights once again. They ducked. Bullets whizzed over their heads.

"I am immortal! Bullets won't kill me!" Whitby motored forward for another assault.

With all the effort he could muster, Will lifted himself and shot again. This bullet hit Whitby in the leg. The exertion was too much. Color drained from Will's face and he collapsed.

"Fucker!" Whitby's face twisted in indignant disbelief. Blood seeped from his leg.

"Will? Will!" There was no response.

She lifted the gun, her hand twitchy. She'd just be wasting bullets. She'd never even held a gun before. She pressed the t-shirt against Will's wound, while the PWC buzzed around her.

"Got rid of Mommy and Daddy! You're next! River Glen will finally be rid of Allaway vermin."

Her parents? Is that what he said? Her parents! Everything was instantly clear. Rage infused her blood. She rushed to the helm and slowed the boat.

"Giving up, you cowardly Allaway?"

She clawed her way to the fore deck. How long had it been since the water cannon had been turned on? Would the motor even work? She pressed the *on* switch and heard the motor hum. Yes, one thing was going right!

"Never ever remove the duct tape from that impeller speed nob," Papa had warned her time and again. "Always keep it at the lowest setting, so it spurts like a gentle rain shower. At the highest setting, you could blow an object clear across the bay to Annapolis."

She peeled off the duct tape and turned the impeller nob to its highest setting. For the moment she couldn't make out Whitby's whereabouts. Then she located him. He was at the stern of the boat, determining if he could board with his wounded leg.

"I'm up here, asshole!"

"You're a dead, fucking Googan!" He pulled down the throttle and buzzed toward the bow.

She knelt behind the water cannon, listening, swiveling the nozzle in the direction of his engine. Her hand on the trigger, a deathgrip, quivered. "Please work, please work." She lifted her head to check on him. His gun was at his shoulder. She ducked; a bullet whizzed by her earlobe. But she had seen just enough and moved the nozzle a few degrees to the right.

"Do your worst!" she screamed savagely.

She squeezed the handgrip ... *a cannonball splintered planks ... a man flailed among sharks ... a severed head jammed onto a pike* ... a jet of water ripped from the cannon, the tug shuddered ... *a spark flickered in the piney dark* ... molten blood coursed through her pyrate veins. A subterranean rage of twenty-six years, transferred from her elders to her, erupted with ferocious vengeance.

She squeezed harder.

It was a direct hit. Time paused. Bone and cartilage bowed and snapped—the crack raised goose bumps on her skin—as his chest imploded. A guttural wail filled the air, a last breath from crushed lungs. He was launched through the air before he hit the water. He floated briefly, before disappearing in a mist of bubbles, pulled to the bottom by the weight of pyrate gold.

In northern seas

The spit of land in the distance was Nova Scotia, the southernmost point of Canada, Ben reckoned. Their destination was not far now. They'd soon pass St. John's, cross the Labrador Sea, cruise up the eastern coast of Greenland, and then sail directly east. They'd be at the cabin just in time for the peak colors of the aurora borealis, Dott had promised. Snow wisped around *Njörõr* and Ben pulled on his hood. Snow flurries in the summer, a peculiar concept to get one's mind around after so many hot, humid summers on the Chesapeake.

Snow had been falling for two days and had shown no signs of stopping when Ben, Randy and Dott had finalized their plan over New Year's weekend in Bethany Beach. Beyond the sliding glass door and the deck at the beach house, the dunes had appeared like snowy mountains. The tips of sea grass were like barren trees on alpine ridges. Ben would never get used to snow on sand. Sand was meant to be tan and warm, kicked with bare feet. Despite the growing drifts and high winds, Dott had insisted that he take her for beach walks. Snow-covered beaches were nothing unusual to a Swede. They'd trudged for miles while the furious, frothy ocean cast freezing spray against their coats and wool hats. He was always glad to be back inside and looking outward. The screen of the sliding door had trapped the snowflakes and he'd studied each one; their crystalline spokes were as unique as fingerprints.

Fingerprints were at the center of their plan. For twenty-six years, while pulling up the crab pots in some isolated inlet of the bay, never elsewhere, Randy and he had discussed the pros and cons of countless scenarios of revenge. And always when Alex was absent, at school.

"Make them pay later. For now, there's a child to raise," Luna had said on the night of the accident. On the night of the deadly fire. Every so often, flighty Luna dropped a pearl of wisdom. That was one of them.

After twenty-six years of waiting, of planning ... *later* had finally come. Later was now, Ben realized as he watched a snowflake melt into the screen. Not one of the snowflakes deviated from the hexagonal, six-pointed pattern. Theirs, too, was a six-part plan. Timing was essential. He'd turned inside and dropped into a recliner next to the fireplace.

Dott was stretched across a sofa. She'd found the channel with soccer, Denmark versus Italy, and was rooting for her fellow Vikings, the Danes. She was also passionate about the NHL, but American baseball and football bored her to tears.

In front of the fireplace, Randy had been grinding a bud of weed onto a saucer. Then he'd sifted it between his fingers, the flakes filling the length of a rolling paper. Next had come the unique Allaway joint-sealing technique that Ben had first observed in Nam: Randy pulled a flask of whiskey from his down vest, dotted his finger with scotch, and ran it down the length of the joint.

"Royal Lochnagar, Ben. You'll notice a hint of oak, lemon and toffee."

Ben had reached for the joint and inhaled gratefully.

"How you two have a single functioning neuron in your heads is beyond me," Dott had quipped, her eyes fixed on the soccer game.

"It dulls the pain," Randy said.

"Take the OxyContin I brought you," she said.

"I need to save that for later. Royal Lochnagar was Julia's favorite." Randy smiled distantly.

"Don't forget to contact her," Ben said. "Alex will need her during the funeral. Alex will be devastated, feel abandoned."

"Yes, but we must carry this out," Randy said adamantly. "Alex is a grownup and has found herself a young man, Richard, and a life in Washington. Her life is far, far from River Glen now." Sadness tinged his voice. "Julia will have to tell her of the treasury, but I suppose John Wilkins' boy will have to oversee it, since he's settled back in River Glen and Alex is away in the city."

"What treasury?" Dott asked.

"A pyrate treasury for the citizens of River Glen," Randy said earnestly.

Dott had laughed out loud. "What's in that weed? There are no such things as pyrates."

"In River Glen there are," Randy said, undeterred. "It's a community treasure to pay for various incidentals. Last year it paid for a hip replacement, braces, and student loan debt. It's always been administered by two families, the Wilkinses and the Allaways."

"Whatever you say." She chuckled. "It will be a miracle if we pull off this plan, with your heads in the smoke. But just remember, after this weekend, all communications are in letters, snail mail only. No phone calls, texts, or email. The cops will be all over our cyber-correspondence."

The severity of her warning had silenced Ben and Randy. Inexorable sacrifices would be made, and the lives of all players drastically and irreversibly changed. The six-part plan had put Ben on edge. After all, his was the pivotal role. The original plan had been admittedly harebrained. Dott, whose IQ exceeded both Ben and Randy's combined, had pointed out all of its flaws. She was a master of detail. A new plan had been devised over numerous meals and bottles of wine, while snow blanketed the dunes of Bethany Beach.

Step 1: Preparation of the crime scene. Remove beer cans with Clyde Whitby's saliva and fingerprints from the duck blind and plant items at Randall Allaway's crime scene. Remove coffee cups from trashcan at marine station with Frank Whitby's saliva and fingerprints and place at crime scene. Steal Clyde's Allman Brothers CD, also covered with fingerprints, and put in CD player at crime scene. Replace with new CD at duck blind so Clyde wouldn't miss it. Leave condoms and junk food wrappers, garnered from parks and trash cans, at duck blind to make it appear as if the site was visited by teenagers, thus deflect suspicion from two old men.

Step 2: Expose the Whitbys' past crimes. Plant amidst Randy's belongings a map to a sunken car at Cooper's Creek, linking Frank Whitby to Colin and Carole Allaway's hit-and-run. Plant business cards to McKibbin's Apartments to expose the blackmailing operation.

Randy and Ben knew every backwater marsh and channel for setting crab pots. They'd been curious about a duck blind being constructed by the Whitby brothers in the State marshlands, not coincidently across from Frank's marine station, some years before.

Step 3. Lure the Whitbys to the crime scene. Send a letter to Frank Whitby requesting that he and Clyde come to the house to discuss the hit-and-run, thereby capturing them on the security camera on the River Glen bridge on the night of the murder.

Step 4: Commit a murder.

Step 5: A fool-proof escape plan. Ben would be witness to a horrible killing and need to flee the Whitbys. Both he and Dott needed to buy time while they set out to sea. Dott's dearest friend, Libby Hinchcliff, a resident at the Hampton Haven senior center, would be Dott Garski's voice, fielding calls from the River Glen police and sending chirpy, affectionate emails about Bahamian cruises and the like to Ben. Libby would be thoroughly briefed, given a script. She had nothing to lose and everything to gain. Where Dott was going, there'd be no need for Donald Garski's federal medical benefits. On the other hand, Libby's sister, Tammy, in the last stages of Alzheimer's, could badly use full-time care, but had neither the insurance nor the funds to join her sister at the nursing home. It would take some weeks to doctor the forms, but it could be done. Then Tammy Hinchcliff would become the physical presence of Dotthea Garski, and join her sister at Hampton Haven to live out their final days together. Should the police check Tammy's fingerprints or DNA, which they would, they'd realize that the identities had been switched, but by then Dott and Ben would be well on their way to ... Amazonia.

Step 5. Connect Alex with the Scottish branch of the family. Contact Julia to assist with funeral arrangements, wills, and property transfers, and inform Alex of Giles Hale's treasure.

Step 6: Retribution. Watch from afar the murder trials of Frank and Clyde Whitby in River Glen, Maryland, from a safe house in Árneshreppur, Iceland.

Chapter 9

October, 2017

It was time, Jay decided. He had put enough distance between himself and that horrible day on Mutter Island. He could probably do it now—box up Laura's things. He trudged upstairs, sipping from a water bottle—he was on a G & T moratorium—recalling the singular day that had led him to this task.

That terrible afternoon, he reached the island at the same time as a police boat, but the damage was already done. A police helicopter swooped in low over the island. The *Vital Spark*, a wreck of shattered glass, was adrift. Jay climbed aboard. Alex Allaway was collapsed against a crab pot, the forlorn dog's chin on her knee. Will's blood had dried along the side of her face like war paint. A single pillow was under Will's head, and he appeared to be asleep under a beach towel that shielded him from the sun. She was murmuring to him, recalling pleasant events from their interwoven childhoods.

"He's been shot, but he's still breathing." As she spoke, a mist clouded Alex's eyes.

Jay grabbed his phone. "Medevac! Man down! We need help down here!"

"There are two down on the beach over here," a voice had crackled from the helicopter hovering over the opposite side of the island. "Both dead. A man and a woman. Both shot in the head."

A woman. The words felt like a lightning strike. The need to gag overwhelmed him. "Is there a speedboat over there?" he'd choked. He'd known the answer to that as well.

"Yes," the navigator had said through the static.

Jay's muscles went limp. He grabbed the gunwale for support. What had drawn her to this island, of all the countless miles of islands and coastlines of the Chesapeake? Why here?

"The second man, Alex?"

"There was only one. I killed him," she said from her trance.

"Where is he?"

She pointed to nothing in particular. "Out there." In the distance, a pilotless PWC bobbed in the swells.

Now, months later, the body of Clyde Whitby, like his brother Frank, had never been located. According to Alex, Clyde had allegedly been dragged to the sandy bottom by bags of pyrate gold. People imagine all sorts of cockamamie things during extreme duress.

Jay entered the master bedroom and stood in front of Laura's dresser. Where to even begin? After the funeral, his mother-in-law had offered to perform the dreaded task for him, but he wasn't keen on her rummaging around in his personal life. He had no idea where Laura had kept his letters to her, from the time when one actually wrote handwritten letters, before computers, email, and texts. The ones from their college days—they'd attended schools in different parts of Vermont—were the typical romantic confessions of a lovesick twenty-year-old. Laura had loved the sexy, explicit ones the best. She'd had a wonderfully dirty mind. It was impossible to imagine that she'd gotten rid of those. They had to be somewhere.

He opened her top dresser drawer. Bras and panties. He searched underneath them. No letters. He smiled upon spotting the black and pink garters and fishnet stockings ... that had been a most excellent date. He was glad, touched, she'd saved those.

The shirts from a middle drawer could go to the women's shelter, so he placed those in a box on the bed. So could the jeans, workout pants, and slacks, and the hoodies and sweaters from the bottom drawer. He had second thoughts about the hoodie bought during their vacation to Bermuda, so he placed it back in the drawer. That was a keeper. Nothing was lovelier than Laura in a soft hoodie with a bikini underneath on a beach at dusk. No letters in those drawers, either. All of the socks could go, unless Mrs. Pulacki wanted them for dust rags.

So far he had no regrets about remaining in River Glen after Laura's death, despite a tempting job offer from his former captain in Baltimore. The quietude of the river and the village of oddballs and assorted misfits had a healing effect. Every day after work, he talked to Laura at the River Glen cemetery. The house was excessive for a single man, but giving up the Boston Whaler and leaving Laura was out of the question. And it was excessive to have a housekeeper, but he'd become spoiled by waking up to the scent of fresh coffee —black, what else?—and bacon, eggs and grits. And there was solace in returning home every evening to a warm meal, usually some unpronounceable Eastern European dish, and chitchat with an opinionated old immigrant about antique clocks or price gouging at the organic supermarket. All of it drew his thoughts away from sharp edges, entry wounds, blood spatters, and misdirected semen.

Best to wait on placing the socks in the donation box. He'd be relentlessly scolded if Mrs. Pulacki needed more dust rags. In the walk-in closet he loaded one box with shoes, then another. Shit, what was it with women and shoes? He'd loaded five goddam boxes by the time he was done. The dresses, blazers and skirts were easier to deal with. He hefted those in clothes-hangered-stacks down to the living room, where a fortune had been spent on wallpaper removal and new paint. He dashed back upstairs. He could move freely again, since he'd quit smoking and lost ten pounds. He returned to the walk-in closet, where there was a door to the attic. The attic was never used for storage, as it was easier to dump excess gear in the garage, but it was possible that Laura had put his letters there. The door opened with surprising ease.

The first things he spotted after climbing the short stairs were stacks of Laura's favorite novels; she had double-majored in Art and English literature. Moving forward, he located a box of letters ... his love letters to her. She *had* kept them! And the pressed flowers and other mementos he'd given her over the years. He'd always wondered if, in her madness, her rage, she'd discarded them. But all of it was there! His mood lightened.

"There you are." He crossed the creaky plywood floor to his telescope. He'd been looking all over for it. His guess had been that Laura had broken it, perhaps in a fit of anger, and thrown the pieces away. He'd not dared broach the subject, fearing another outburst.

Laura had positioned the telescope at the window. He looked through it. Strange. It was directed at the Allaway's beach and porch. An inexplicable shudder moved through him. On a fold-up cocktail table was a sketchbook and colored pencils. He opened to the first page. It was a drawing of an unknown woman handing a tiny puppy to Randy Allaway. The picture was dated in the spring and was titled "Baby WB arrives." The next picture was of Water Boy chewing on a bone. Title, "WB cuts his first teeth." The sketch after that showed Randy and Ben with the puppy on a leash, entitled "WB's first walk." He thumbed through pages, all of which had dates and titles. "WB's first swim," "WB dancing," "WB at a porch party," "… at the pyrate festival," and so on. The realization struck at once. His wife had envisioned the dog as a child, as the child she could never have. The last sketch was dated the week of the River Glen murders. Alex and Will were on the dock next to the *Vital Spark*. The black dog, now months old and leggy, was eagerly looking up at them. It was entitled "WB loves boat rides."

What had drawn Laura to Mutter Island, of all the countless miles of islands and coastlines of the Chesapeake, was answered by this sketchbook.

For some time, Jay's arms straddled the attic window. Red and orange leaves speckled the river and flowed out to the bay. Amidst the neurochemical imbalance and misfiring neurons, Laura had envisioned herself as the champion of a little black dog.

The northern lights

Ben hurried through dinner for a second night in a row. Nothing was wrong with herring; it was fine and fresh, pulled from the fjord that morning, even if it lacked the satisfying zing and burn of spicy Maryland crabs. He hurried his meal because what was outside could not be missed.

"Don't forget your hat," Dott reminded him. "We want no more ear infections."

"Join me."

"In a sec."

Dott was set in her ways. The dishes would be soaked in hot soapy water before she'd be out with the neighbors. Ulfur the fisherman was already on his front step, watching the sky as his people had done for a thousand years. He said something in Icelandic and laughed. Ben nodded, as if he had a clue what the fisherman said.

Be careful what you wish for, he thought to himself. Long ago he'd longed to travel to far and exotic places. In the past few weeks alone, he'd climbed a glacier, submerged himself stark naked in a hot spring, watched orange lava bubble from black crevices, and smelled a seeping volcano. But nothing would surpass this. His eyes were glued to the sky. The door creaked and Dott's gloved hand slipped into his and squeezed. All was well.

"*Listaverk af Týr,*" Dott called to Ulfur.

"*Falleg,*" Ulfur answered.

"What did you say?" he asked.

"The sky is Týr's artwork. Ulfur said 'Beautiful.'" She studied his puzzled face. "Týr is the god of the sky, and of war. He has one hand. The other was bitten off by the wolf, Fenris."

His wife, Ben realized, was a woman guided by the gods of her ancients, the same gods as those of the Icelanders. What she said was true. The sky was artwork, on that night, exquisite purple and pink watercolors streaming across a deep blue canvas.

His next action would embarrass him, yet he still pulled out his cellphone and took a picture of the sky. He sent the image to Alex Allaway with the message: "You're here with me." With the difference in time zones, it was the middle of the afternoon in River Glen. The Chesapeake would still be warm in early October. She was either in the lab or out on her boat, he guessed.

"*Fánýtar*," Ulfur called with a chuckle.

"Futile," Dott said, translating.

"True," he admitted. "One can only see this with one's own eyes."

His phone vibrated. "*Já!*" Alex's message read. He held it out for Dott. "Alex knows more Icelandic than I do."

Dott nodded.

He breathed in the crisp, clean air. "Gratitude," he said on the exhalation.

"Yes." She squeezed his hand once again.

Their carefully designed plan had almost unraveled at Step 3. The letter sent to Frank Whitby's home had said to meet at Randy's house on May 22nd, and to bring Clyde along to discuss the accident and the fire. That way both brothers would be captured on the security cameras. But instead, Frank showed up on May 21st, and alone. Ben and Randy had been on the beach, spending one last evening together. By late May the pain in Randy's abdomen was nearly incapacitating. He could no longer keep food down. He'd lost nearly forty pounds since the diagnosis in late December. Chemo and radiation might give him a year, the VA doctor had said. Without, six months at best. Randy chose the six months. He was sustaining himself on scotch, weed and the occasional OxyContin left over from Donald Garski's illness.

An infuriated Frank strode from his car and grabbed Water Boy. Randy struggled out of his chair, the slightest movement of his abdomen now excruciating. Frank was a bully and a lecher, but not entirely stupid. He would not shoot two old men on a beach. They knew his cowardly, devious mind; after all, they'd been watching him for twenty-six years.

For twenty-six years they'd patiently waited for an opportunity. It came with Randy's diagnosis, a death sentence. A dying man would be murdered, Randy had decided. But then their plan had careened off the rails. Lauren Braden had risen from behind the dock, boat oar in hand. With the crack of oar to skull, the well-laid plan was foiled. They had a dead body on the beach!

After they'd changed Laura and she'd swum off to the promontory, John Wilkins had wandered down the river road, smoking a joint on his way to the Point, like he did on most nights. Ben had turned over the canoe that hid Whitby's body, exposing Laura's handiwork. He and John, a gentle giant, had sealed the body up in heavy plastic and duct tape, and stuffed it into *Star Gazer*'s cabin. Randy had watched from the porch, too weak to assist. What to do? What to do? Dott was cool-headed; she'd know.

Ben rushed off a letter, express mail, to a post office box in Bermuda where the *Njörðr* was moored. He'd awaited her letter. May had turned into June. Randy barely hung on.

Finally her letter had arrived. "The plan does not change. It's only delayed," Dott had written calmly. "Only now you write a letter to Clyde. We meet at the same coordinates around June 22nd. Remember where I showed you and Randy. Between ribs 4 and 5."

On the evening of June 12th, the Allman's Brother sang "Sweet Melissa" when beer cans and a spent coffee cups were placed in the kitchen trash. Some of Frank Whitby's hairs were dropped casually on the floor by the recliner. Ben had let himself into the McKibbin's apartment late one night with Frank's key.; he'd collected strands from a comb, and tacked Xeroxed photos of Randy, Alex and himself to the wall of the apartment.

"Let's do this," Randy had whispered, his voice dry. Ben had lifted his old comrade from his bed and assisted him into the recliner. With gloved hands, Ben had poured Randy a huge volume of Royal Lochnagar. Randy had swallowed a lethal amount of OxyContin and the scotch, grateful for the cessation of pain. They'd talked about Nam, about Colin and Alex, Atlantic blue crabs, Giles Blood-hand parties, and lovely women, until Randy fell asleep. Ben listened with a stethoscope as Randy's heart slowed. When it was barely perceptible, he took a carving knife from the wood block in the kitchen and, with a hammer, drove it with one swift blow into Randy's fourth intercostal space. Blood oozed into his friend's Pink Floyd t-shirt. The suffering was over.

Ben had shut off the lights in Randy's house and his own, and fled to the grow house in the woods. Around ten o'clock, Desmond's tow truck had pulled into the driveway. Water Boy, who'd been locked up in his cottage, began to bark. Two silhouettes had climbed out. He'd heard a strident rap of metal on wood and curses from the porch. Finally the truck had disappeared down the blackness of the river road. Ben's phone had vibrated in his pocket. He'd pulled his shaking hands from his armpits. The screen had glowed in the darkness of the old shed. Dott had ordered no more e-communications; who could it be from? *Oh, no. Oh, God!*

Hi Ben, I have a big surprise for Papa. I have a second interview tomorrow in Annapolis. 99%

sure I'm going to get the job in River Glen. Keep him around town tomorrow evening, will ya? Party! ox

Alex was coming home? At this time, of all times! Randy hadn't even told her that he was sick when she'd come home for Christmas. "She can't see me this way, Ben! She must remember me like I was," he'd said.

Randy had sent Alex the map with the locations of the treasure to her apartment in DC, hadn't he? Ben felt woozy and unsure. What if Randy hadn't? He needed to check. He hurried to his cottage for a flashlight and crept back to Randy's. He'd opened the door and crossed the living room, refusing to look at his dearest friend. He'd opened the desk drawer. "No!"

Just as suspected. The old road map with the three numbers was still in Randy's top drawer. The piece of eight had shimmered in the beam of the flashlight. His old pal had forgotten; he'd been sleeping most of the time the last few weeks. Nor had Randy finished the second part of the map with the specifics, 1OMG 2CC 3GG.

In the off-chance that someone entered Randy's house before Alex, they could not find both parts of the map together and steal the River Glen treasure. In that moment he decided to leave the second page in his house, with his will.

In large handwriting, he'd quickly scrawled *"ALEX ... open my hand,"* on an envelope, and stuffed Randy's roadmap inside. He'd placed the envelope on the table next to the recliner. He'd tucked the piece of eight into Randy's cold fingers and placed his hands in his lap.

It would be a long time before he'd be in Randy's house again, a very long time. He'd rushed back to his cottage and wrote on a piece of paper, "*Alex ... 1OGM 2CC 3GG Love you honey, Old Ben*", and placed it in an envelope on which he wrote, "*Whoever finds this, must deliver this message to Alexandra Allaway immediately. URGENT. Please deliver immediately.*"

Ben was exhausted. He dropped into his reading chair and lifted the black dog into his lap. The dog had been living with him for the last month, because Randy was unable to walk him. Ben felt himself beginning to doze. But sleep would have to wait. He pulled himself out of his chair and circled his cottage once again. What to do with Water Boy? There was no room for an energetic young dog on *Star Gazer*. The dog needed space to run. He tied a long rope around the dog's neck and attached him to a front tree. He sliced open an entire bag of dog food and filled a bucket of water. Alex would need a dog to comfort her.

There was one thing left to do. It would be the last text for a very long time. To Julia.

Blue crabs are moving to deeper waters

All of the loose ends were finally tied up, he supposed. If not, it was too late now. He grabbed his sea bag and thermos of coffee and set off across Randy's backyard with his flashlight. He passed the abandoned grow house, and wound through the forest until he found the marsh. All day *Star Gazer* had been hidden in the tall grass, awaiting her long journey to northern seas.

Memento mori, he'd said to himself as he'd pulled up the anchor. Death is part of life. It would be the worst of homecomings for Alex, but at least she'd find the map and the piece of eight before anyone else. "Once upon a time ... once upon a time there was a boat named ..." Randy had told her infinite times. From the three clues "1OMG 2CC 3GG," she'd figure out the location of the fourth site. The mother lode.

Chapter 10

Giles Blood-hand Day
June, 2018

Mungo Jerry's "Summertime" was playing from the bandstand when Alex left the crowd of dancers. For over an hour she had danced wildly, spinning, leaping, holding nothing back ... unrestrained and orgiastic, primal dancing fueled by rum and the Pitchers Family wine. She'd danced with Will, Alan and Jacob, Gary Smyth, Jim Pitcher, James Collins, and a tipsy Captain Hook with a long black wig and eye patch ... God only knows who he was. She headed toward the table occupied by the Wilkins family and an available chair next to John, who was slipping Water Boy bits of a Philly cheese steak. Carly climbed into Alex's lap and stroked the feathers of the green parrot on her shoulder.

"Blind Pew's never missed a pyrate festival," Gillian White had said to Alex the previous night. The parrot was thusly named because, long ago, when Gillian had been dancing on the pier, one of its plastic eyes had fallen through the slats. "It's tradition, Alex. Pew must go to the festival and you must wear him!" Gillian's water had broken the night before. Earlier ultrasounds had revealed twins. En route to the hospital, Gillian had dropped the parrot off at Alex's place.

"Anything from Gillian?" Will leaned across a table.

Alex glanced at her smartwatch. "Nothing yet."

Despite the festive atmosphere, the music and dancing, the pyrate flags and Giles banners snapping in the breeze, Carly was uncharacteristically quiet.

"Are you all right, sweetheart?" Will asked her.

"My belly hurts," she whimpered.

"Because you two let her eat junk food all afternoon," Belle Wilkins said, admonishing her husband and son.

"Do you want me to tell you a story?" Alex asked. "Sometimes when I didn't feel well my grandfather would tell me stories. They were always about four tugboats named—"

"I have to poop!" Carly leapt off her lap.

Belle stood abruptly. "I will not permit this child to go into one of those horrible porta-potties. The germs! And look at the line. It's quicker to walk home. Do you want Grandmom to take you home?"

"Yes!" Carly grabbed her grandmother's hand.

"I'll give her a nap," Belle said to Will and John. "You two kept her up way too late last night watching Ravens highlights. She's exhausted."

At a nearby bollard, Julia rolled her eyes, twisted a cigarette butt from her cigarette holder and stubbed it out with her black boot. She returned to the table and settled herself with a rustle of black skirts and petticoats.

Without a doubt, Alex and her grandmother had the coolest costumes going. Julia was an expert at applying make-up. They'd gone heavy with the eyeliner and mascara, red lipstick and rouge, and looked vaguely like pyrate Goths. People had been photographing them all day; they'd be all over Facebook and Instagram by the end of the festival, and probably on the front page of the *River Glen Gazette*. The dresses had been obtained from a theater friend of Julia's in Philly, where they'd just finished a production of *The Pirates of Penzance*. On the drive to the city to pick up the costumes, Julia had sung the praises of Gilbert and Sullivan—they were British, after all—but those talentless Americans, Rodgers and Hammerstein .... Regardless, her grandmother showed no signs of leaving the States. Instead had planted a vegetable garden—corn, soy, and tobacco—and she, Alan and Jacob raised free range chickens back by the old grow house.

Jay Braden emerged from the crowd of dancers. At the cop's appearance, John Wilkins stood. "Honey, wait!" he called to Belle. "I'm coming with you." He dashed through the crowd.

"May I?" Jay asked Julia, looking at John's vacated seat.

Julia gestured to the chair, her large sleeve billowing in the wind. "Charmed."

He placed a bottle of Royal Lochnagar on the table alongside some plastic cups.

"I was wondering when you were going to pay up," Julia said.

He looked approvingly at her vampish gown with the low neckline. "Miles Harlow's had to order it special."

"It's good to see you out, sir," Will said.

Jay nodded thoughtfully. This was his first social outing since last summer. He seemed to have something on his mind.

"Will, I'm a little concerned about the company you keep." He poured scotch into four cups. "These be murdering pyrates." A hard, accusatory gaze fell on Julia.

She shrugged innocently.

"We know what you all did," Jay said.

"Who's 'you all'?" Julia asked.

"Randy, Ben, Dott, and you. The blue crabs that moved to deeper waters."

An uncertain silence hung over the table, while dancers spun in kaleidoscopic colors behind them to the croon of "My Maria".

"Sometimes it's not about the law, but justice." Jay held up his cup. "To justice."

"Cheers." Julia knocked her cup against his. An expression of relief passed across her face.

Water Boy raised his head and barked excitedly. His leash tugged at Alex's chair.

"I knew I'd find you here!" a voice screeched. "These mutts are yours! Your fucking dog was obviously *not* neutered!" The shrew with the black roots wrapped a handful of leashes around the arm of Alex's chair and fled into the crowd. Alex sprang to her feet. Beyond the blockade of orange traffic cones, the woman jumped into a waiting car and sped off.

"You horny bastard!" Alex said.

Water Boy took no notice, as he was happily sniffing his pups.

Julia laughed. "Those are the ugliest mutts I've ever seen."

"What the hell am I going to do with ... four dogs?"

"I'll take one." Jay pointed. "That one."

"That's the ugliest of the ugly," Julia said.

"I need a fishing partner. That one's for me."

Alex looked expectantly at Will. "For Carly?"

He nodded with dread. "My mother will kill me."

"Luna's dog, Aquarius, died last month," Julia said. "Ask her."

"That leaves one for you, Julia," Alex said.

Julia sipped her whiskey and carefully studied the litter. "That one, the little girl."

The dogs had tangled themselves under the chair at the next table. "Sorry, sorry." Alex knelt under the chair of the grimacing woman. "I better get these guys home."

Jay added more scotch to Julia's cup, so she settled contentedly into her chair. "Alex, I'll pick up my pup later, after I buy some dog supplies."

"Okay." She struggled with the mess of leashes.

Will stood, sensing an opportunity. "I'll walk you home."

She and Will dragged the dogs through the crowd, across the bridge flapping with pyrate flags and banners, and down the river road lined with the cars. Her wad of ten-dollar bills from the parked cars would pay for new bowls, dog food and chew toys. She glanced again at Will's pyrate costume. Way hot. But too many tourists were roaming about outdoors to satisfy that particular itch.

She circled behind Ben's cottage and put the dogs in the screened porch. She'd been living in his cottage for some time now, since she'd received an email and a photograph from him. The photo was from the Aegean. He was on a weatherworn, sturdy motor sailor, a vessel of spectacular beauty. His likewise weatherworn, sturdy bride was at his side. "Watch my place for me while I'm gone, will you?" A gut feeling told her that she'd be watching his place for a very long time. His message ended with the usual sign-off from his various ports-of-call. "You're here with me."

Alex had found an English to Greek translator link. "*Vaí!*" she'd typed back. An affectionate "yes!" was her usual response to his messages.

The water bowls filled and the dogs settled, she found herself alone with Will. They'd shagged—Julia was expanding her vocabulary—in the hammock. And the flower bed, herb garden, and on the table in the grow house amidst the potted plants and trowels. Ben had a single bed; they'd done it there one rainy afternoon, but it was too narrow and too uncomfortable. They'd ended up in the recliner. Wide, open spaces were always best. A horn honked down the river road, reminding her that people were about.

"Relax in the tug?" It wasn't outdoors, but it would suffice. And rocking boats always enhanced the rhythm.

He grinned. "A pyrate fantasy. Perfect."

Will was always agreeable. That was his best feature, second best, and third best ... She grabbed his hand and hurried him along the dock. They hopped over the crab pots and Clorox bottles and ducked into the hatchway, under the figurehead with the voluptuous breasts. Comparatively, Alex was lacking, but she had other assets. She opened the portholes and the hatch door. A warm summer breeze swished through the cabin. There was no time to waste; she slid the black vest down Will's shoulders. His chest heaved in anticipation. They grabbed each other for a ravenous kiss. Finally she pushed herself away and dropped onto the bench seat, her eyes level with his glistening belt buckle. She undid the black belt slowly, tension escalating. His heavy belt clanked to the wooden floor. Next she unknotted the wide red sash. At that moment the sun shifted and struck the eye of the figurehead.

A stream of green light hit the sash and belt on the floor. They both froze, then their eyes followed the beam of light back to the glowing green eye. She stood unsteadily and pulled a knife from a drawer.

"Hold me." She dragged the bench toward the figurehead and climbed up, while he held her firmly by her hips. She pried loose the green eye and handed it down to him.

He turned it over in his hand. "I don't think this is glass."

"Nope." She lifted the lei of necklaces from around the figurehead's neck, jumped down, and spread them across the galley table. "The plastic ones are from Mardi Gras. But those ... feel the weight. Those babies are real!" She laughed incredulously.

From the plastic baubles, he untwisted a heavy chain with a gold crucifix embedded with red stones. "That one's real also. Twelve huge rubies!"

"Hiding in plain sight!"

A memory hit like a rogue wave. She grabbed the table for support, as if the earth faltered beneath her feet. "Remember what I said to Carly today? Every story my grandfather ever told me started the same exact way. 'Once upon a time there was a tugboat.' Then he'd stop and make me squirm. 'Named ...,' he'd say. I'd beg him to tell me more. He had these bushy eyebrows that would dance up and down his forehead. His gull's nests." She was briefly lost in the past.

Entranced, Will dropped onto the barrel seat by the ship's wheel. "Then what?"

"The tugboats always had the same names, every single time. The *Old Gray Mare*, the *Crabby Crab* and the *Gimpy Gull*. The same as clues 1, 2 and 3 on Papa's map. But most often he named the tug the ..."

"The *Vital Spark*," they said in unison.

"That old dog!" She laughed. "For my entire childhood Papa was telling me the locations of the treasury in his stories!"

"And the clues also revealed your family history, dark as parts of it may be."

"I feel dizzy. I've completely lost equilibrium."

For a moment they sat silently.

"Alex," he said with an air of mystery, "what was the common thing found at each site?"

"I'm not sure what you mean."

"A wire loop, a barrel slat, and a circular lid." He jumped to his feet and stared down at the barrel.

"No way!" She laughed again.

"Do you have a screwdriver or crowbar?"

She opened the cabinet where Papa had kept his tools, batteries, extra line, and bungee cords. "Here!"

He shoved screwdriver under the lid and pushed down with all his weight. The wooden lid groaned and squealed, and finally gave way. They peered inside.

Her face went warm. "The other one, Will," she whispered.

He heaved against the second lid. It flipped off the barrel, spun across the floor and cluttered to rest. She reached in and sifted through the tangled metal objects: necklaces, bracelets, crucifixes, gilded knives and goblets. The only sounds were the pull of the ropes on the cleats outside, and a clink of metal as she ran her hands through the treasure. The contents of the barrel glistened in the afternoon sun, glints of green, red, white, gold and silver.

"Emeralds from Colombia, rubies from Brazil, pearls from Margarita Island," she whispered, recalling the ship's manifest.

In a trance, they moved back to the first barrel. It was filled to the brim with silver and gold bars and pieces of eight. "Peruvian gold and silver."

She glanced nervously out a porthole. "Now what?"

"Who knows? I guess we seal it back up."

"Right." She lifted the circular lids off the floor and grabbed a hammer from the cabinet.

"Quietly, Alex."

She gently tapped the lids back into place, while he stood guard at a porthole. "Is anyone watching us?"

"No, but that drunken Captain Hook is passed out in his car," he said. "I wouldn't want to be on the road when he drives home tonight."

She placed the tool back in the cabinet.

"Now what?" he asked.

"I have no clue. I guess we draw from it when it's needed. I guess one day Carly will be ..."

"Yes. So now?"

"We give the figurehead back her jewelry and eye." She stepped up on the bench. He handed her up the bundle of necklaces, then she pushed the emerald back into its wooden orbit. He lifted her down and she closed the hatch door and locked it behind her.

"Now what?" He eyed her provocative wench gown.

"Now the pyrates relax." She pulled him toward the berth with two pillows.

Professor Levon Bakanian squinted from under the brim of his black Captain Hook hat with the skull and cross bones. "What are those two up to on that old tug ... Alex Allaway and her boyfriend?"

More than once she and the boyfriend had peered anxiously through a porthole. Had they found a treasure map to the hoard from *El Espiritu de la Virgen*? What was making them so cagey in that old tug? She had asked him during their brief phone conversation last summer, "What happened to the alleged Incan gold from the Spanish galleon?"

"Who knows?" he'd said. "They were pyrates. I'm guessing that they drank and whored it away long before they reached the Chesapeake."

He knew better. But did she?

Amazing luck that Francine Whitby, when going through her deceased husband's belongings in the attic, had had the wherewithal to contact him, the country's leading pyrate scholar. Conall Whitby's memoir, scribed by Brother Guillermo, had described a treasure of incredible riches— pearls, rubies, emeralds and gold.

"This valuable resource should be in a university archive, in a climate-controlled vault, so that it's available to historians of the colonial Chesapeake for years to come," he'd explained to Francine in his most pompously erudite tone. The bimbo fell for it. She'd FedExed the memoir to him the next day, certainly before reading its entire contents. University archive, right. It was sitting in his briefcase, where it would remain, at least until the treasure was his.

Conall Whitby's memoir was astonishingly detailed in accounting the pyrates' pathway north after burning *El Espiritu de la Virgen* to the waterline near modern Tampa Bay. The *Raven* had bypassed the usual pyrate haunts of Tortuga and Port Royal, where fortunes were quickly squandered on whores, liar's dice and rot-gut. The crew of the *Raven* had had no place to spend their riches! The treasure, according to Conall, was kept intact in a tavern treasury in the nascent village of River Glen. Rumors of pieces of eight poking from the sandy shoreline had been circulating amidst the tourists at Giles Blood-hand Day for years. He'd been attending the event since he was a boy.

"Keep your ear to the ground, son," his father had urged him. "Keep your ear to the ground."

The eye patch, captain's hat and long black wig, hot as it was in June, were ideal for concealing his identity year after year. And weaving about with a rum bottle, stumbling on occasion, laughing too boisterously, allowed him to simply blend in with the other happy, intoxicated pyrates. Every once in a while, in the presence of one of the villagers, he'd mumble about Giles' treasure. The locals always took the bait. Who didn't love dreaming aloud about pyrate treasure? Then came the impossible task of sifting through their speculations. What was pure fabrication? Which words held a glimmer of truth?

Now the days of speculation were over! The treasure of *El Espiritu de la Virgen* had made it to River Glen! Conall Whitby had said that the treasure was vast. It was possible that some treasure had survived to this day.

The stars were aligning in his favor. An ad in *the Chronicle of Higher Education* read that the nearby Tolchester College was hiring a sociologist, psychologist, mathematician and ... yes, a historian. He'd read the ad repeatedly to make sure his eyes weren't deceiving him. Yes, it was correct ... they wanted an assistant professor of American history. Of course Tolchester was many steps down from UVA in both prestige and reputation, really not much more than a community college, but the move would permit a full-time search for pyrate treasure in River Glen.

During the interview, he'd dazzled the history search committee with his knowledge of the Chesapeake during the colonial era and his thoughtfully constructed list of projects that would involve the undergraduates. Yes, he'd be delighted to teach sections of Intro to American History, the Colonial Period to the Reconstruction, and the Senior Seminar. Sure, no problem, he'd be happy to serve as the faculty mentor for the History Club. The job offer came through in less than a week. He had the dark, brooding looks of Edward Teach, sans the long black beard. Any woman that he pursued fell dizzily into his arms. His appearance no doubt impressed the women professors on the search committee, who'd taken him to the restaurant Nauticus to wine and dine him the evening before the interview with the administrators.

And his dashing good looks would certainly catch the eye of Alex Allaway. She had an interest in her family's genealogy. Perhaps she had contacted Clyde Whitby or Ben Hancock and knew something of the treasure.

He glanced once again at the *Vital Spark*. The tug was rocking quietly on the water. Yes, that comely pyrate wench, Alex Allaway, was going to help him find Giles Blood-hand's treasure.

THE END

EXCERPT

From *Spider,*
the next Chesapeake Tugboat Mystery, coming soon:

"Goddamn spiders!" Alex Allaway leapt off the barrel seat and grabbed a broom. One swift swish vanquished the web dangling in the corner of the galley. "That's all I do, Nina, every morning, clean spider webs off this boat. I hate spiders almost as much as ticks." Her accompanying frown was directed at the black dog sleeping under the table. "Water Boy's a tick magnet. They're impossible to find in his black coat." She eyed the other corners of the *Vital Spark's* cabin, her broom poised for attack.

"You work in a marsh all day. You, of all people, should be used to creepy crawlies," Nina Vega said from a bench at the table.

"Yeah, I guess." Alex relaxed her threatening stance. "I don't mind snakes, eels, or snapping turtles, because they hurry away at the sight of humans, but spiders are defiant and territorial. I sweep them away every morning, and they return every single night just to torment me."

Nina couldn't help but grin. Nothing had changed. Alex was the same insectophobe she had been their senior year at the University of Maryland (UM), when she, Alex and Courtney Raney had shared an apartment on Paint Branch Parkway. At the time, it wasn't spiders that were the bane of Alex's existence, but cockroaches.

"The goddamn computer geeks next door never do their frickin dishes! That's why *their* cockroaches come into *our* apartment." Alex's nightly tirade was punctuated by a biology or chemistry textbook flattening a scurrying roach against the kitchen counter, ruining Nina's appetite for dinner. Alex's crusade wasn't always against cockroaches. Once it was a squirrel, like the deranged one that chewed through their cable line and impelled Alex to camp out between the bicycles on their puny balcony and shoot rubber darts at it with a plastic gun from the Dollar Store.

Yes, nothing about Alex had changed, and that was a good thing. Their friendship would resume just where they'd left off, when they'd packed up their apartment after graduation and departed to their various graduate programs. Alex had headed to a UM fisheries lab, Courtney to medical school at Georgetown University, and she northward to the University of Rhode Island's Department of Sociology.

Nina's dissertation at URI had focused on the socioeconomics of the fishermen of southern Rhode Island, but it was time for a change, time to expand her research horizons beyond the Ocean State. If she were ever to earn tenure and eventually achieve the rank of Full Professor, her research and publications needed to encompass many types of maritime fishing communities. This would earn her an international reputation for her scholarship. Her first idea was to move northward to study the Maine lobstermen, but she was from New Mexico, and the Maine's winters would be more brutal than Rhode Island's. Then Alex's Facebook post displayed photos of a pyrate festival in the village of River Glen on the Chesapeake. Alex's companions at the event were an attractive grandmother, a brawny boyfriend and his daughter, and a pack of black dogs in skull and cross bone bandanas. Alex, she remembered, was from a family of crabbers. This prompted her to give Alex a long-over due call.

"Of course," Alex had said, "I know them all ... the crabbers, oystermen, herring fishermen, middlemen, distributors, and pickers. I can introduce you to anyone you need to talk to." With Alex's connections to the fisheries network in the Chesapeake, Nina would have access to countless people to conduct oral histories and interviews.

A move to Maryland's eastern shore sounded better and better. Even Ricardo liked the idea. A study of the socioeconomics of the Chesapeake watermen seemed just the ticket. Two tenure track jobs were available in the area, one at the University of Maryland Eastern Shore (UMES) and one at Tolchester College. She didn't make the short list at UMES, but she did get an interview at Tolchester.

Tolchester College was a pretty, undergraduate institution on a cliff overlooking the bay. The views of white-capped water were stunning, and the immaculately groomed grounds burst with flowers in lovely arrangements. Her interview was during the week of MayFest, so white and blue balloons, the school's colors, had been tied to the Victorian lampposts that lined the walkways. The college was in solid financial shape, the president and academic dean had explained to her. Enrollments were on an upswing, so much so that the college was expanding their faculty numbers. In addition to two new sociologists, also joining the faculty in the fall would be a new psychologist, a mathematician, and a historian. A fresh new tier of faculty would be her cohort. The college pulsed with energy and promise.

The job offer came through so quickly she realized she must have made a very good impression. Tenure at Tolchester College was in the bag. Plus, the River Glen area with its expansive farms, quiet rivers, fresh organic food, and clean air would be the ideal place for Ricardo and her to start a family.

Nina gazed out a porthole to take in the unfamiliar terrain, while Alex navigated the *Vital Spark* through a narrow channel. On Narragansett Bay in Rhode Island, where she'd shared a house with other sociology grad students, the rocky shoreline was battered by waves. It was a wind-lashed landscape of greys and blues. But here, orange cliffs crowned with lush green forests loomed over the old tugboat. Green water lapped against muddy beaches, and the August air was heavy, hot and still. This was her new world.

"This looks like a good place to anchor," said Alex at the pilot's wheel. "For its size, the Chesapeake's an amazingly shallow bay." She shut off the motor. A grinding clank of a rusty anchor chain sounded from the bow, then a splash. "But the water's just deep enough here so we won't scrape the keel." Spiders and ticks no longer a distraction, Alex said, "Now we initiate you to Chesapeake life! Steamed crabs in Old Bay spices. No one can live on the bay without knowing how to eat crabs." Alex removed a plastic thermos from a small fridge and filled two plastic mugs. "Here Nina. Cheers! To your move and new job!"

Nina took a sip from her mug. "Delicious. What is it?"

"A Hurricane. Two shots of light rum, two shots of dark rum, one shot each of vodka, grenadine, grapefruit juice and pineapple. All shaken, not stirred." Alex pulled nutcrackers and picks from a drawer and headed to the aft deck with a roll of paper towels under her arm. She unfurled newspapers across a wooden crate, onto which she dumped a pile of steamy red crabs. "This is how we do it here. No plates, no silverware. Just newspapers, nutcrackers and crabs. Just toss the exoskeletons overboard, since they're biodegradable."

Leave it to Alex to improvise. There were no chairs in sight. Their seats would be the hard planks of the deck. Nina felt ridiculously overdressed. When Alex had invited her to dine, she'd expected that they'd be seated at a table in her cottage, so she'd brought a bouquet of flowers and a bottle of wine. And inappropriately, she'd put on her new summer dress that she'd bought to wear to the Welcome Meeting of the Tolchester faculty. Alex had greeted her in her green camo cargo shorts and a bright purple t-shirt that read "Ravens Country"; Nina had forgotten that Alex was the queen of quirky casual. They'd be taking a river cruise up the Glen River and eating on the water, Alex had explained, leading Nina down the dock.

Nina glanced at the hard planks once again. Oh, what the hell; she was a Chesapeake girl now. She hiked up her dress and dropped amidst the crab pots, Clorox bottles, and mooring lines. Besides, after a few more sips of the potent cocktail, her butt would be numb to the hard boards underneath.

"So, you open the crab like this." Alex pried off the carapace. "And don't eat anything in the central cavity, or you'll be eating assorted guts, the heart, and parts of the vas deferens."

"Waay too much information," Nina laughed. The August heat and alcohol were already taking effect.

The drink was also affecting Alex. "That's the downside of being a biologist, knowing all of the anatomical parts of the things you're eating. Oh, definitely don't eat that." She giggled. "The testes and the gills. Only eat the white meat in those lateral chitin compartments and the meat in the legs. There's not really much meat in those rear swimming legs." She flung them over the gunwale.

"Okay. I see."

Alex watched her break open the crab, like a teacher supervising a pupil on an important task. "The ring's really beautiful."

Nina stretched out her left hand, her fingers wet and covered with brown spices. It was the nth time that she'd admired the engagement ring. "It was Ricardo's Abuelita's ring, and then Mamacita's."

"Mamacita? That's what he calls his mother? A mamacita's usually a sexy woman. Is she hot?"

"No, she's hideous and five hundred pounds!"

"Really?"

"No, only three hundred. Ricardo's the only boy in the family. He's spoiled rotten by all the women. The wedding's sometime next year in New Mexico. I'd love it if you'd be a bridesmaid."

Alex's eyes widened, probably in the realization that she'd have to wear some frippery and footwear other than sneakers or flip-flops. "Yeah, okay," she said unconvincingly.

Nina pointed up at the cliff's edge. "What's that place?" Her changing of the subject was deliberate. At the moment the wedding was a testy topic with Ricardo's family. Her ideal wedding was small and intimate, but Abuelita wanted to invite the relatives from Mexico, all four hundred of them.

An abandoned cottage perched precariously on the edge. Sometime before, its porch had plummeted to the beach, evident by its rotting planks in the sand below.

Alex squinted into the sun. "That's Henry Herssen's place. People build too close to the cliffs. It's a big problem around here. Then the cliffs erode away during storms and hurricanes. A lot of people have lost their homes that way. Herssen was an insane man, allegedly. We wouldn't go near that place when we were kids. He up and disappeared years ago, a decade or more. I don't know for sure. Some people report seeing lights in the place at night. Others say the place is haunted. They're probably just tall tales to keep children away from there and from getting hurt near the cliff."

"There's a lot of tall tales surrounding this region. Like the legend of Giles Blood-hand. I just read a history of Kent County. I always like to know the local history before I move to an area."

"That's why you're the professor. Giles Blood-hand Day is the best day of the year. You're going to need a pyrate costume for the celebration, now that you're a local. Giles actually did exist. I'm related to him."

"No way!"

"Yeah, I am. Distantly, on my father's side of the family. And there's a pyrate graveyard here in River Glen. I can show it to you sometime, if you're game."

"Sure, that sounds interesting. Does anyone know what happened to Giles' treasure?"

Alex shrugged. "Who knows? The pyrates probably pissed it away in the Caribbean."

A roaring sound caused Alex to stretch her head up over the gunwale. She jumped to her feet.

"Nina, wrap up the crabs and grab your drink! I need to move the boat or that idiot's going to swamp us!" Alex dashed to the helm, switched on the engine, and raised the anchor. Water Boy yowled. "This idiot from Miami thinks she owns the river! Shit! If I can't turn this boat ..."

"What!"

"Every summer this asshole in a big yacht moors at the Smyth's Marina," Alex shouted from the pilot's wheel. "She has no idea that there's something called a no-wake-zone!"

Nina rolled the crabs in newspaper, hurried to the helm, then pushed her face next to Alex's scowling one at the windshield. A glistening white yacht raced toward them.

"Brace yourself, Nina!" Alex wrestled with the wheel, turning the bow toward the channel.

The yacht flew by as a white streak. An ominous row of waves approached.

"Hold on!"

The bow reared upward and slammed on the backside of the first wave. Water splashed over the bow, around the water cannon, and collided with the windshield, temporary blinding them. The bow reared upward again ... up-slap, up-slap ... frothy rapids cascaded over the deck. Water Boy yowled.

"Shut-up, goofball!" Alex yelled. "You're only making matters worse!"

He howled in reply.

The waves finally dissipated and water trickled off the deck. Henry Herssen's broken porch floated in the swells.

Then they noticed something else ... the surge of waves had carved away the base of the cliff.

"We're getting out of here!" Alex jammed the throttle forward.

But she was too late. The dirt wall crumbled and burst into an orange-brown cloud, followed by a groan and creak as the old foundations of Herssen's house faltered. The house teetered, shook, and plunged from the cliff, hitting the water in a thousand brittle shards. It was as though a glacier had calved into the water. There was no time to turn the bow into the approaching wave. It crashed against the stern, lifting the *Vital Spark* skyward. Water rushed across the deck and smashed the crab pots into the gunwales. For long minutes, everything aboard swayed and creaked in the afternoon heat.

Eventually it grew quiet. Planks, dry wall, and window frames floated in the shallows surrounding the tugboat.

"Do you see that?" Nina whispered, as if unsettled phantoms might hear.

"Yeah," Alex whispered back.

They gazed upward. Poking from the cliff were grey bones —countless bones—bones from bodies buried under Henry Herssen's floorboards.

About The Author

Leah Devlin

Leah Devlin is a mystery writer and marine biologist who grew up in the Washington, DC area. *Vital Spark* is the first novel in Leah's new Chesapeake Tugboat Murders. These stories are set in the fictional village of River Glen on the upper Chesapeake, a site of a 1680s pyrate massacre that lures modern day treasure hunters and various unsavory characters to the village in search of the elusive treasure of Giles Blood-hand. *Spider*, the second novel in the series, will be published in 2017. Leah is presently writing the third in the series, *The Death of a Chrome Diva* (working title).

Leah's first novels, *The Bottom Dwellers, Ægir's Curse* and *The Bends* centered on the scientific village of Woods Hole, Massachusetts, where Leah was a marine biologist at the Marine Biological Laboratory for over ten summers. At the epicenter of the action is the brilliant yet disturbed Nobel laureate, Lindsey Nolan, her colleagues and family.

Leah enjoys outdoor adventures of all kinds: motorcycle journeys along winding back roads, boating, diving, rock-climbing, skiing, and long-distance trekking. When not traveling, she divides her time between Philadelphia and her tugboat on the Chesapeake.

Visit Leah at www.leahdevlin.com, and Leah Devlin's Mystery-Thrillers on Facebook for her essays on the characters and landscapes that appear in her novels, and her own nautical adventures aboard her boat ... named ... what else ... the *Vital Spark.*

THE BOTTOM DWELLERS

BY

LEAH DEVLIN

Bioengineer and Party Girl...

Lindsey Nolan has it all: inventions paying large dividends, a dream job in the scientific village of Woods Hole, Massachusetts, and a stable of eager playmates. But when Lindsey wakes up in rehab with no memory of how she got there, her world is turned upside down. Her roommate, an HIV-positive teenage prostitute named Maggie, is the most volatile patient on the ward. The facility is plagued by disturbing thefts. And another theft unfolds when her competitor, an engineer named Karen Battersby, discovers and steals Lindsey's astonishing new invention from her Woods Hole lab. Lindsey and Maggie must face the consequences of past transgressions if they hope to deal with present perils and ascend from the desolate world of the Bottom Dwellers.

PENMORE PRESS
www.penmorepress.com

ÆGIR'S CURSE

BY
LEAH DEVLIN

A thousand years ago, the Viking colony of Vinland was ravaged by a swift-moving plague ... a curse inflicted by the sea god Ægir. The last surviving Norseman set the encampment and his longboat ablaze to ensure that the disease would die with him and his brethren.

In present-day Norway, a distinguished professor is found murdered, his priceless map of Vinland missing. The ensuing investigation leads to the reclusive world of Lindsey Nolan, a scientist and recovering alcoholic who has been sober for five years. Lindsey reluctantly agrees to help the detective who's hunting the murderer, but she has a bigger problem on her hands: a mysterious disease that's spreading like wildfire through the population of Woods Hole. As she races against a rising body count to discover the source of the plague, disturbing events threaten her hard-won sobriety—and her life. Will Lindsey be the next victim of Ægir's curse?

PENMORE PRESS
www.penmorepress.com

THE BENDS
BY
LEAH DEVLIN

Maggie May has only weeks until graduation when Edward Gripp, a wealthy benefactor and the architect of Maggie's art college, goes missing from a campus Halloween party. Bill Bleach, the gawkish young detective assigned to the case, discovers a mysterious labyrinth within the walls of the art college where it appears Gripp spied on the activities of the faculty and students. When Gripp's mutilated body is found and a gorgeous art professor is also slain, panic spreads through art college. No one escapes Bleach's scrutiny, from the party's most distinguished guests to the terrified art students. But his investigation is complicated when he finds himself attracted to Maggie, whose dark and troubled past makes her a prime suspect. Bleach fights to stay focused, determined to untangle the web of lies and stop a devious serial killer from striking again.

Leah Devlin is rapidly establishing herself as a writer of modern day mystery-thrillers. This story is as tight as a piano wire. Life at a seaside town in New England is full of treacherous undercurrents and peril, as residents are threatened by a menace from a thousand years ago. Murder, romance and deceit are a potent mix in this gripping novel, which I didn't want to put down.—James Boschert, author of the Talon Series and *Force 12 in German Bight*

PENMORE PRESS
www.penmorepress.com

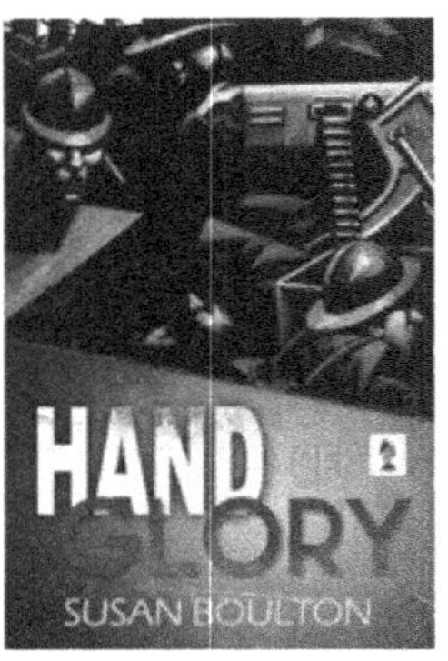

Hand of Glory
by
Susan Boulton

"And all that awake now be as the dead, for the dead man's sake . . ."
In Passchendaele near the end of the Great War, Captain Giles Hardy is trapped on barbed wire, wounded in mind and body, convinced he should be dead. But Giles's true battle begins after he's rescued and sent home. In the small town of Stafford, he struggles with terrifying visions of the atrocities he's witnessed—and a recruit he served with.

The visions lead Giles to a man who exploits the grief of the bereaved with the help of a Hand of Glory, a mythical tool of thieves. A new friend, Agnes Reed, and the ghost of an old one, Corporal George Adams, aid Hardy in his investigation. Now he must catch the thief, destroy the hand, and lay to rest the men who will otherwise never leave the fields of Flanders.

PENMORE PRESS
www.penmorepress.com

A Gathering of Vultures

Donald Michael Platt

Murder, mutilation, and carrion... in paradise?

"There shall the vultures also be gathered, every one with her mate." - ISAIAH 34:15

Professional ballroom dancers Terri and Rick Hamilton aspire to be world champions. Unfortunately, Terri's recurring back and health problems place that goal well out of reach. They travel to Terri's birthplace, Florianópolis, on the scenic island of Santa Catarina off the coast of Brazil to vacation and visit their best friends and mentors.

Along the picturesque beaches, dead penguins and eviscerated bodies wash up on the shores of paradise, and Antarctic blasts play counterpoint to the tropical storms that rock the island. The scenic wonder is home not only to urubús, a unique sub-species of the black vulture, but also to a clique of mysterious women who offer Terri perfect health and the promise of fame—at a terrible price.

PENMORE PRESS
www.penmorepress.com

Penmore Press
Challenging, Intriguing, Adventurous, Historical and Imaginative
www.penmorepress.com